Jill,
I hope you enjoy
this! Best wishes!
Tonya Royston

Only a few weeks ago, my town had felt so safe. No one even locked their doors, until now...

"Dakota!" I called as I scrambled to my feet. I stood right where I was, watching and listening, but only silence and darkness loomed.

The back door opened, and I spun around as Noah approached with my gray fleece in his hands, his denim jacket already covering his maroon shirt. "Sorry that took so long. I made a quick visit to your bathroom." He abruptly stopped half-way across the patio when he noticed the fear on my face. Concern swept across his eyes. "Where's Dakota? What happened? I was only gone for a minute."

"There." I turned around and raised my arm to point at the woods. "I saw something, no, I mean someone. Someone was out there."

I didn't hear Noah approach, but I felt him behind me when he stopped. "What are you talking about?"

"I saw a shadow, and it wasn't a moose or a deer or a bear. It was human," I told him, my eyes glued to the dark, sinister woods.

A loud snarl pierced the silence. Another one ripped at it, and the image of the golden-eyed wolf sinking its teeth into Dakota flashed through my mind. The snarls and growls of what could only be two wolves out for each other's blood grew louder in the distance. They continued for a minute, and then a sharp, pain-filled yelp cut through the air like a knife, followed by an eerie silence.

"Dakota!" I screamed, my heart racing with panic. I took off, running for the woods. I had to find him, no matter how far I had to go.

She never thought her ability to communicate with wild animals was anything more than a unique gift. But this gift is tied to a long history of secrets that threaten to shatter her one chance at true love...

Laken Sumner isn't your average teenager. Ever since she realized that wild animals could hear her thoughts, she's spent more time in the woods with them than with other children. Even her wolf is a better friend to her than most people. She trusts him—so much so that she follows him out into the wilderness in the middle of the night to find a lost little boy. But the boy's disappearance is only the beginning.

The one bright spot in her life is Noah Lawson, the handsome new town deputy. Charming and mature, he almost seems too good to be true. Then she meets Xander Payne, the new boy at school, who seems to know something about her. But how could that be possible?

As strange things begin to happen in her sleepy New England town, Laken wonders if Xander has something to do with it. Or is it just a coincidence that danger targets her soon after he arrives?

~

Twenty-five cents for every print and ebook copy sold will be donated to the Ian Somerhalder Foundation.

KUDOS for *Shadows at Sunset*

In *Shadows at Sunset* by Tonya Royston, Laken Sumner is a high school senior who talks to animals. They trust and protect her and she spends more time with them than she does with her human friends. Laken falls for Noah, the new deputy in her small New England town. But when a new boy moves into town and starts at the local high school, trouble begins following Laken everywhere. Royston does a good job of character development, both for her human and animal characters. This is a coming of age story with a twist—one both YA and NA should love. ~ *Taylor Jones, Reviewer*

Shadows at Sunset is a paranormal coming of age story about a young woman who can talk to animals. She lives in a sleepy New Hampshire village in the mountains and, until a new boy moves into the neighborhood, Laken's town feels safe and secure. But with the arrival of Xander Payne, things begin to change. Now little boys disappear from their backyards, bodies are found in the woods, and someone seems to be stalking Laken. *Shadows at Sunset* is well written and portrays the problems that come with not only growing up and turning from a child into a woman, but also suddenly finding yourself in danger. It's a well-written story of courage and innocence—one that anyone who loves animals or who has ever been a teenager should thoroughly enjoy. ~ *Regan Murphy, Reviewer*

Shadows at Sunset

Book One of the Sunset Trilogy

Tonya Royston

A Black Opal Books Publication

GENRE: PARANORMAL THRILLER/YA/PARANORMAL ROMANCE

This is a work of fiction. Names, places, characters and incidents are either the product of the author's imagination or are used fictitiously, and any resemblance to any actual persons, living or dead, businesses, organizations, events or locales is entirely coincidental. All trademarks, service marks, registered trademarks, and registered service marks are the property of their respective owners and are used herein for identification purposes only. The publisher does not have any control over or assume any responsibility for author or third-party websites or their contents.

SHADOWS AT SUNSET ~ Book One of the Sunset Trilogy
Copyright © 2015 by Tonya Royston
Cover Design by Jennifer Gibson
All cover art copyright © 2015
All Rights Reserved
Print ISBN: 978-1-626943-17-9

First Publication: AUGUST 2015

Published by Black Opal Books **http://www.blackopalbooks.com**

DEDICATION

For Macie McDonald

Never give up. Never stop dreaming.

Prologue

Six-year-old Laken Sumner climbed up her backyard swing set ladder until she reached the top of the slide. Her wispy blonde hair hung in a tangled mess behind her shoulders and her green eyes reflected the clear blue sky. She was alone, except for a squirrel that scampered across a branch in the woods surrounding the yard. Within seconds, the squirrel disappeared, the leaves swaying in its wake. The air was warm, not hot or humid, typical for northern New England in July.

Laken hummed as she pushed herself down the slide, lifting her legs so that they wouldn't stick to the yellow plastic. At the bottom, she jumped to her feet and ran around to the swings hanging behind the slide. She settled onto the supple rubber seat, grabbed a hold of the chains, and pumped with her feet. A brilliant smile was plastered on her face as she soared high into the air. The only sounds were that of the creaking chains as she rocked back and forth and a breeze whispering through the leaves overhead.

After a few minutes, Laken grew bored and let herself slow. Just before the swing stopped, she launched into the air, bending her knees as she landed. Then she ran across the yard to her mother's garden. The red roses climbing up the white trellis never failed to distract Laken from her swing set, if only for a moment. As she admired them, breathing in their familiar sweet scent, she noticed a shadow moving through the dense trees out of the corner of her eye. A twig snapped and leaves rustled from somewhere within the woods.

Laken stood still, staring in the direction of the movement and shuffling leaves. She wasn't scared, just curious. She knew it was an animal. The forest behind her house extended for miles into the mountains of New Hampshire. Deer, moose, and even black bears were a common sight from her bedroom window.

She didn't have to wonder what it was for long. A spotted fawn emerged from the cover of the trees, stepping cautiously into the yard. Its nervous eyes darted in each direction until they settled on Laken. Then, suddenly, the apprehension in the fawn's expression disappeared. As if feeling safe, it dove its muzzle into the lush grass and started grazing.

Laken watched the fawn for a few moments, surprised by how comfortable it seemed in her presence. She remained still, not wanting to scare it. As she waited, the fawn moved closer to her without raising its nose from the ground.

Laken had seen countless deer in her life, but never had she been so close to one. She took a step toward the fawn, and it jerked its head up.

"I'm not going to hurt you," Laken said softly. "I just wanted to say hi."

The fawn stared at her, its body frozen for a few seconds. Finally, it took a breath. A trusting look came into its eyes. The fawn began walking toward Laken and only stopped when it was close enough to nuzzle her hands with its black nose.

Laken giggled, a big smile crossing her face. "Can you understand me?"

The fawn glanced at her, its eyes relaxed and calm. It nudged her hands again.

"You can understand me. You know I won't hurt you." Laken slowly raised her hand to pet the fawn's soft neck. Her eyes widened in amazement. She couldn't believe that it trusted her enough to let her touch it.

Her awe was cut short as a doe appeared at the edge of the yard. It trotted over to the fawn, its wild eyes and stubby upright tail telling Laken right away that it wasn't comfortable with the close contact between her and its baby.

Laken froze in fear at the sight of the larger animal rushing toward her. She remained silent, but thought, '*I won't hurt your baby. We just want to be friends.*'

The doe stopped beside the fawn, the worry in its eyes disappearing as if it suddenly approved. Laken resumed stroking the fawn, her eyes never leaving the doe in case it changed its mind and charged at her. Instead, the doe stretched down to nibble the grass as if Laken wasn't standing there.

The silence was broken when the back door to the house abruptly slammed shut. The doe and fawn jerked their heads up in alarm. Before Laken could calm them, they ran back into the woods on their spindly legs. Within seconds, their shadows disappeared and the leaves and underbrush that rustled from their movements could no longer be heard.

Laken's mother rushed across the yard, her brown eyes distraught with fear. "Laken! What in the world were you doing with those animals?"

"Mommy! Did you see that? They weren't afraid of me. They understood me."

"Laken, don't be silly. The deer can't understand you. And you should never get that close to wild animals. It's dangerous."

At that moment, Laken realized how alarmed her mother was. Laken's delight faded into regret. Regret that her mother had seen her, not regret that she had touched the deer. "I'm sorry, Mommy."

"Laken, wild animals are very dangerous. They could hurt you, even a baby deer. It could bite you or kick you." Her mother's voice was calmer now, but still deeply concerned. "I need you to promise me that you'll never get that close to a wild animal again. Can you promise me that?"

Laken caught her mother's imploring stare. For a moment, she wondered how to respond so that she wouldn't have to lie. She studied the ground while she snaked her right arm behind her back and crossed her fingers. Then, as a twinge of guilt poked at her, she uncrossed her fingers and lifted her gaze to meet her mother's eyes once again.

"I promise," she said, silently adding, *Unless they want me to*.

Chapter 1

Not much had changed since I was six years old. I still lived with my parents in the same white farmhouse on the outskirts of a small northern New Hampshire ski town. My father was still a local police officer, although he was promoted to sheriff a few years ago. My mother still taught fifth grade at the local elementary school. I still spent as much time outside as possible, even in the dead of winter, wandering for hours through the mountains bordering our backyard. And I still talked to wild animals.

A few things had changed, naturally. Ever since I realized I could talk to animals, I thought I would never have a human friend. The animals became my friends. I could tell them anything and they listened endlessly. Even though they couldn't speak, the look in their eyes told me they understood.

It started with deer and, by the time I was nine, my circle of friends included black bears, moose, all kinds of birds—from woodpeckers and cardinals to hawks and owls—foxes, squirrels, and sometimes even snakes and turtles. I could feed songbirds and squirrels out of my hands. Hawks and owls often swooped in close to me, and the black bears loved a good scratch between the ears.

I never felt comfortable with the other children at school. I knew I was different. I wanted to fit in, to be more like everyone else, but I knew that would never happen. The animals accepted me unconditionally, something I knew the other children would never do. For years, I kept to myself, counting the minutes each day until I could return home and escape into the wilderness to enjoy the silent company of a bear, moose, or any other animal that happened to cross my path. Except for a dog or cat. My talents had never worked on domestic animals. I never knew why it worked on some animals and not others. But I had to admit, the wild animals were much more intriguing and fun. They made me feel special since no one had a bear or a moose for a pet.

When I was ten, a family from Boston moved into the house on the other side of the woods next door. Their son, Ethan, was my age and we immediately struck up a friendship. I often wondered if we would have become such good friends had it not been for the fact that he lived next door. But he accepted me, never asking why I didn't have any other friends or why I disappeared into the woods for hours at a time. He was just there when I needed someone who could talk to me.

We spent our summers in the treehouse his father had built in his backyard. Ethan read his endless pile of comic books while I watched the birds.

They often landed on the ledge, studying us as if wondering why two humans would spend almost as much time in the trees as they did. They weren't afraid of us, either, because of me, of course. I never forgot the day a red-headed woodpecker landed on my shoulder. Ethan's jaw nearly dropped to the floor, but he didn't ask a single question when it took off a moment later.

My parents seemed relieved that I finally had a friend. Until that year, I had spent most of my time away from school alone, at least that's what they thought. But I was never truly alone. I was always surrounded by my furry and feathered friends.

In my freshman year, Brooke Carson moved to town. Quirky, spunky, and free-spirited, Brooke was as extroverted as I was introverted. We weren't instant friends like Ethan and I had been. She actually met him first, and he brought the three of us together. Before I got to know her, I was as distant and withdrawn as I was with other classmates. But she quickly put me at ease, never once judging me for being a loner. Throughout high school, we were as different as two girls could be. I took up wildlife photography—a hobby that pushed me farther and farther away from people. She pursued her love of dancing and joined the drill team. Despite our differences, our friendship flourished. She was like the sister I never had. She challenged me to step outside my comfort zone, forcing me out to an occasional party or dance. She made me feel like I could fit in, and for that, I was grateful.

My only other friend was given to me when I was twelve. My uncle who served as the Boston Chief of Police discovered a wolf pup about three months old chained up in a drug dealer's backyard. He seized the pup when no one was looking and brought him to us. My parents were skeptical at first. I remembered my father asking his brother how he thought we could possibly take care of a wolf. A wolf was entirely different than a dog. A wolf had wild instincts, not to mention that owning one required a permit that we didn't have the money for. But I begged, promising that I could handle it. I was never sure how I did it, but I convinced my parents to let me keep him.

I named him Dakota, and I raised him on my own. He grew up fast, weighing over one hundred pounds by the end of the first year. His fur was smoky black and his eyes bright amber, the color of honey. He had a few white markings—a heart on his chest and a few spots on his paws. Like other wild animals, he understood me. I never used a leash on him, and he came and went as he pleased, often striking out into the mountains for days. But he always made his way home safely. He avoided people, never once hurting anyone. It was a good thing, too, since we had never gotten that permit.

As the town sheriff, my father couldn't let anyone know that his daughter kept a wolf as a pet. Although truthfully, I didn't keep him as a pet. Dakota lived wild and free except for an occasional nap on the bed tucked into the corner of my room. Over the years, as Ethan and Brooke spent more time at my house, I couldn't hide him from them. They thought it was really cool that their loner friend had a wolf and they promised to never tell a soul. They knew he meant the world to me.

Dakota never left my side when I ventured into the woods. Sometimes I took my camera to take pictures of the animals I had come to know, and other days I escaped with a book. This mid-August afternoon was no different. I sat upon a large rock shaded by maple trees, a novel in my hand as Dakota lay by my feet. This was one of my favorite spots because I could hear the stream trickling a few feet away. A moose ambled by, nibbling at branches on its way to the water. Shadows danced around me as clouds darted in front of the sun directly overhead in the bright blue sky.

I loved living in the White Mountains. Summers were mild and pleasant, definitely worth enduring the bitter cold winters. Unfortunately, the summers always flew by way too fast. This summer had gone by even faster than the last few. Now that I had my driver's license, I also had a job at a local pizza shop. So my free time to read and capture wildlife on camera was limited to my days off, like today.

I glanced at my watch. Four o'clock. I had two more hours before I needed to head home. Ethan was coming over for pizza and a movie at six-thirty. Brooke said she might come over too, if she could use the car she shared with her sister. Since school was only a few weeks away, we were trying to hang out together in the evenings we had left.

I turned my attention back to my book, a novel about fallen angels. Ever since paranormal stories had become the rage, I couldn't get enough of them. They made me feel better about my unique gift. I could certainly relate to characters who were different and didn't fit in.

As I turned another page, a black-capped chickadee landed on my shoulder. I smiled at the tickle of its feet, losing my place in the book. I lifted a hand, and it hopped onto my fingers. Holding it in front of me, I studied its beady eyes as it tilted its head, watching me. Then, without warning, it fluttered its wings and flew up into the trees. With a sigh, I looked back down at my book, wanting to finish a few more chapters before I needed to head home.

⁊⊃℮⊃

At six-twenty that evening, I emerged from the forest into the backyard I had known all my life with Dakota in tow. We bounded through the back door that led into our modest country kitchen to find my mother looking for something in the refrigerator. "Hi, Mom."

My mother looked nothing like me. She had brown curls that reached her shoulders and matched her warm eyes. Her skin was an olive tone, now bronzed from the summer sun. She was a few inches shorter than me with more curves. I stood five feet, seven inches tall, and my pale skin burned if I spent too much time in the sun. My blonde hair hung in soft waves, and my green eyes seemed to be something of a miracle considering that both my parents had brown eyes.

My mother closed the refrigerator door and turned to me, her white blouse tucked into her khaki slacks. "There you are. I was just trying to figure out what to do for dinner. What are you in the mood for?"

"Ethan's coming over with a movie and we were going to order a pizza. Where's Dad?"

"He's held up at the station. I'm not sure when he'll be home."

"Really? What's going on?"

"Oh, it's probably some drunken tourists in a scuffle. He said not to wait up for him. So pizza, huh? Mind if I have a piece? I'll buy."

"Mom, if you buy, you can have half the pizza. Is veggie supreme okay with you?" A few years ago, I had given up meat. I had never liked the chewy, greasy texture of it, especially red meat. But I hadn't gone vegan, at least not yet. Cheese and ice cream were still two of my favorites.

"I wouldn't expect anything else. I'll probably just have one piece. I'm not very hungry."

Even though she tried to hide it, I could tell she was worried. She always told my father that the one time she let down her guard, trouble would find him on the job. It didn't matter that nothing remotely dangerous ever happened in our town. She still worried.

I ignored her concern. Whatever was keeping my father couldn't be that serious. "Good, because Ethan will probably eat half of the whole pizza and Brooke might be coming over too."

She grabbed a book off the kitchen desk. "Well, there's cash in my wallet. Go ahead and use that when they get here. I'll be outside."

"You better get a jacket. It's starting to get chilly out there," I told her.

Up in these mountains, the nighttime temperatures ranged from the seventies during the most intense heat waves to as low as the forties, and sometimes even the thirties. Tonight would be one of the latter. It was a sign that fall was not far away.

My mother flashed a brief smile. "Good point. I heard there's a cold front coming through tonight. Summer sure flies by around here." After grabbing a fleece jacket from the coat closet, she disappeared outside.

A few minutes later as I hung up the phone from calling in the pizza order, I heard our front door open. We kept our doors unlocked, as did just about everyone else who lived around here. Our town was as safe as they come. Besides, having a wolf to protect our home meant the chances of someone breaking in and getting away with whatever they intended to do were pretty slim. And everyone in town knew that this was the sheriff's house. Only a stranger to the area would try to break in, and Dakota would take care of that.

Ethan came around the corner, all six feet, three inches of him. At eighteen, he was tall and boyishly handsome, with thick brown hair that flopped across his forehead framing his warm brown eyes. I had noticed lately that he was starting to fill out.

His black T-shirt stretched across his broad shoulders now, when, a year ago, it would have hung loosely on his thin frame. Having known him since he was ten, I still remembered when he was shorter than me and skinny as a stick. I had watched him grow up and witnessed all of his awkward phases. Even though he was turning out really cute, he was like a brother to me.

He greeted me with a smile. "Hey."

"Hey, yourself. I just ordered our pizza. Veggie supreme."

"Why am I not surprised? I had a burger for lunch just because I knew dinner with you would be vegetarian."

"And you're right. But there's ice cream for dessert. So what movie did you bring? It's a romantic comedy this time, right?"

"Keep dreaming," Ethan said with a groan. "Of course not. You know you have to save those for Brooke." As he rambled off the name of an action movie I vaguely recognized, he opened the refrigerator and pulled out a Coke.

"Okay. I'll save the romance for another time."

He nodded, popping open the can. "Do you think you'll actually stay awake tonight?"

I grinned at his teasing. He knew me so well. Rarely did I make it through a movie without dozing off, since hiking in the mountains wore me out. "I don't know. I'll try, but

I'm not making any promises. Can you grab me a Diet Coke? That will help."

Ethan was closer to the refrigerator, so he reached in for another can of soda and tossed it to me. Then we sat down at the kitchen table to wait for the pizza.

"Where's your dad tonight?" Ethan asked.

"Work. Mom said he would be late."

"Really? Wonder what that's all about."

"I don't know. How was work for you today?" I asked, changing the subject from one boring topic to another.

"The usual. Another fun summer day spent manning the deep fryer for hungry tourists. I never thought I'd say this, but I can't wait for school to begin."

"I'm not crazy about working the summer away either, but at least we've got some cash," I reminded him. "And I can definitely wait for school to start." Just the thought of lugging heavy books home and spending hours cooped up in my room working on homework dampened my mood.

"You never want school to start. Personally, I think college is looking better and better every day. Have you thought any more about where you want to go?"

I averted my eyes to the side, not wanting to meet his gaze. College was a sore subject with me. I couldn't imagine leaving Dakota, but I didn't expect Ethan or anyone else to understand that. "No. I'm trying to put off that decision as long as I can."

"You can't run from it forever."

"I know. It's not the college part that upsets me. It's Dakota. I know I can't take him with me."

"You got that right. I don't think he'll be allowed in any dorm. But your parents will keep him and you can visit. They're not going to get rid of him once you leave. He's better behaved than any dog I've ever known."

"I still wish I could take him with me. It just won't be the same."

Dakota knew we were talking about him, and he also knew I was upset. He rose from where he was lying, walked over to me, and rested his big wolf head in my lap. His amber eyes gazed up at me, unblinking.

I scratched at the base of his ears. "See? He agrees with me," I told Ethan.

"Of course he does. He always takes your side," Ethan stated. "Okay, we'll change the subject, for now. But you will have to deal with this soon."

"After Christmas," I promised.

"Halloween. You need to get your applications out by Christmas."

"Thanksgiving then, and that's my final offer."

"I guess I'll have to live with that. I just think it would be cool if we went to the same school and I don't want you to lose your chances by applying late."

"That's very sweet of you." I had already considered applying to several of the same schools as Ethan if I had to apply to any. As long as there was a photography program, I could at least pretend to be interested. "And I agree. It would be nice to know at least one person at college. But we said we were going to change the subject."

"You're right." Ethan sighed, and Dakota, sensing that I felt better, lay down at my feet. "Where's Brooke tonight?"

"She was going to try to come over, but—" I glanced at my watch. It was almost seven o'clock. "If she's not here yet, I don't think she's going to make it."

"You know, one of us really needs to have a car at our disposal this year. We're going to be seniors. How lame will we be if we have no way to get out on a Saturday night?" Ethan asked.

As I tried to cheer him up, my cell phone buzzed. It was a text message from Brooke. Her sister needed the car for her night shift at a bar in another town and didn't have time to give Brooke a ride. Ethan and I would be on our own tonight which happened a lot since Brooke lived across town. I flashed the message at him before we continued talking about what it would be like to be seniors this year.

The pizza arrived a little later, and we shared it with my

mother. We still hadn't heard from my father, and the worry in her expression had deepened. She ate one slice before retreating to her bedroom with a glass of white wine and her book.

Ethan and I polished off the pizza and then scooped Rocky Road ice cream into bowls and smothered it with chocolate sauce. We carried our dessert into the family room where the big flat screen TV beckoned. Dakota followed us, seeming reluctant to leave my side. He usually preferred to be outside on a cool summer night, but he hadn't gone to the back door all evening. Perhaps he didn't want to leave until my father returned home. Whatever it was, it was a nice change to have him around.

As the movie began, I snuggled under a blanket in the recliner while Ethan sprawled out on the couch. With the lights off, we ate our ice cream by the glow of the TV. All that could be heard was the music of the opening credits and our spoons clanking against our bowls. When I finished, I set my bowl on the side table and rested my head back against the chair. As hard as I tried to stay awake, I lasted about ten minutes before my eyelids grew heavy and I drifted off to sleep.

℮ↄ℮ↄ

"Laken, wake up," Ethan whispered, gently shaking my shoulders.

I opened my eyes and smiled at him.

"You fell asleep. I think you missed the entire movie."

"That's nothing new," I said in a sleepy voice. "Was it any good?"

"Yeah, it was. I'll leave it for you and you can watch it tomorrow."

"Thanks." I yawned. "What time is it? Did my dad come home yet?"

"Ten-thirty and, no, he isn't back yet."

Just as he answered, headlights reflected against the sheer window curtains and we heard a car pull into the driveway. I sat up quickly, suddenly wide awake. I could tell by the low rumble of the car that it was my father. That, and the fact that Dakota didn't move a muscle. If it had been anyone else, Dakota would have been on his feet, growling, in an instant. "He's here. Finally. It's pretty late. Now I'm kind of curious to know what's been keeping him."

"Come on, Laken. Nothing ever happens in this town. A tourist probably hit another moose and totaled their car," Ethan mused.

He stood from his kneeling position by my chair as my father appeared around the corner. We both turned our attention to him. His jacket was slung behind his shoulder, his wrinkled light blue shirttails hanging over the waist of his jeans. Worry etched through his usually soft facial features and warm brown eyes. His salt-and-pepper gray hair appeared disheveled, even down through his neatly trimmed beard.

He nodded slightly. "I didn't expect anyone would be up when I got home." His voice sounded exhausted, drained of energy.

"Well, she wasn't until a few minutes ago," Ethan explained.

"Yeah. I fell asleep during the movie, again," I said sheepishly.

A faint smile crept across my father's tired face before he looked at Ethan. "It's getting late. You'd better get home, son."

Usually my father didn't care how long Ethan stayed. He had even allowed Ethan to sleep on our couch a few times. But tonight, Ethan took the hint right away. "Yes, sir. I was just about to head out." He looked over at me. "Talk to you tomorrow?"

"Of course," I replied—like he even had to ask.

As Ethan headed into the entry hall, my father turned to

him. "Ethan. Do you have a jacket? It's pretty cold out there."

"No, I didn't think to bring one. I'll be fine. It's not far."

"I can give you a ride."

"No thanks, Mr. Sumner. You just got home, and I'm sure you don't want to go out again. Besides, I've been making this trek for years now."

"Okay." My father followed him to the front door. "Have a good night, son," he said as he shut the door behind Ethan.

When my father returned to the family room, I watched him curiously. "What happened today?"

He ran his fingers through his hair and sat down on the couch with a strained sigh. "Ryder Thompson disappeared from his backyard this afternoon. He was playing on his swing set when his mother had to run inside. By the time she returned, he was gone. Vanished without a trace. We spent all afternoon and evening combing the area and came up empty."

I sat straight up, my back stiffening. I knew Ryder from babysitting him a few times over the last year. At three years old, he was a quiet little boy who didn't talk much yet. He would be helpless out in the wilderness alone, and tonight the freezing temperatures could be dangerous. "How did he disappear?"

"I'm sure he just wandered off after a butterfly or something. There were about ten of us searching, and he must have gotten pretty far. Unfortunately, he got a good head start on us. His mother tried to find him herself. By the time she called us and we got there, he'd already been gone for a few hours."

I cringed to think of Ryder lost in these mountains, especially in the dark. There had to be something we could do. Tomorrow morning would seem like forever to such a small child. He was probably scared to death right now.

"And to make it even worse, he's only wearing shorts and a T-shirt." My father shook his head. "He's going to freeze out there, probably already is. We called the nearest canine search and rescue team, but they can't get here until the morning."

"Morning? Dad, that could be too late."

He rested his elbows on his knees. "I know. That's the best they could do. I'm just sick over this whole thing. I've been with the Lincoln Police Department for over twenty years and nothing like this has ever happened. We've had car accidents, bar scuffles, and the occasional break-in, but this is a child. We searched really far tonight, but we finally had to give up."

"Have you told Mom?"

He nodded. "I talked to her a few hours ago, and I'm sure she didn't want to interrupt your movie or, in your case, wake you up, to tell you. I think she was hoping we wouldn't have to tell you at all. It brings up bad memories for us."

I raised my eyebrows. "I never ran off when I was three."

"No, try six. That's when you started wandering off, but somehow you always made it home safely before dark."

I avoided his gaze as the memories came back to me. He was right. As soon as I had learned I could talk to animals, I ventured into the forest alone all the time, even when my parents scolded me time after time.

What they hadn't known was that I was never really alone. And if I lost my way, the animals led me home. "I remember."

"I still don't like you out there alone, but at least now I know you're with Dakota."

I glanced over at the black wolf sprawled out across the carpet. "He never leaves my side."

"Speaking of Dakota, I'm surprised he's not out tonight," my father commented.

"He seemed to want to stay in. I think he sensed something was wrong."

"He's a good boy. I remember being a little reluctant to keep him. But I'll tell you what, I've never regretted it. He's been really good for you. I don't know how you do it, but you really get through to him."

"I don't know what I'd do without him." I briefly recalled my conversation with Ethan tonight about going away to college and realized how empty a college dorm would feel without Dakota lying at the foot of my bed.

"Well, listen, I'm going to turn in. I don't know if I'll sleep, but I'd better at least try since the search teams are going to be at the station at six in the morning." He stood up. "How 'bout you? Are you going to head up to bed soon?"

"In a few minutes."

"Okay. Good night, Laken."

"Good night, Dad."

As soon as he disappeared around the corner, I sat still, staring at Dakota. My mind was spinning out of control with thoughts of the lost little boy. *You have to do something. You can't leave him out there alone tonight. Dakota will help. Together, you could find him. He could freeze or animals could get to him. You have to at least try,* I told myself.

Taking a deep breath, I began to piece together the situation. The Thompsons lived about a mile down the road from us. Their house was even on the same side of the street. That meant if Ryder had wandered off from his backyard, he was probably somewhere in the wilderness behind our houses. I knew these mountains better than anyone, and I could organize a search party of animals who had nocturnal abilities that a trained search-and-rescue dog couldn't match. Suddenly, I knew what I had to do.

I stood up abruptly, tossing my blanket aside. Dakota sprang to his feet like a soldier ready for battle. His solid stance told me he knew we needed to find Ryder, and fast.

My eyes met Dakota's knowing stare. "Come on, Dakota," I said confidently, but softly enough that my parents wouldn't hear me. "Let's go find that little boy."

Chapter 2

Adrenaline pumped through me as doubts crept into my mind. Would this really work? I knew I could make the animals understand that a little boy was lost, but how could they tell me where he was? I realized quickly that I couldn't dwell on these doubts. I had to at least give it a shot. I would never forgive myself if I didn't try.

Still dressed in jeans and a short-sleeved shirt, I grabbed my hiking boots and a fleece-lined flannel jacket from the coat closet. Then I headed for the door that led to the garage, slowly opening it and cringing as it squeaked. I stopped for a moment, listening to make sure my parents didn't wander out of their bedroom to see what I was doing. If they knew that I was about to attempt to find Ryder on my own, they would surely stop me. After all, they had no idea that I would have help. No doubt, they would think I was crazy. They would never believe that I could find a little boy lost in the dark when my father couldn't find him in the daylight.

When I was sure that the coast was clear and my parents hadn't heard the squeaky door, I flipped on the light and crept down the two steps into the musty-smelling garage. To my right, utility shelves lined the wall. The flashlights were exactly where I remembered, on the middle shelf closest to the door. I reached for two of them, one for a back-up, and tested them. They came on immediately, their lights beaming circles onto the garage wall. Then I turned them off, put the smaller one in my pocket, and carried the larger one.

I left the garage, tiptoeing back into the house as quietly as I could. Dakota was waiting for me at the back door. He turned his head to watch me, his eyes begging me to hurry up. I could tell he was eager to start the search.

"I'm coming. A little patience, please," I whispered as I crossed the kitchen to the back door. Still expecting one of my parents to emerge and stop me, I inched it open. But no one showed up. This was it. Time to move out.

Dakota leaped through the doorway as soon as there was enough room for him to squeeze by. He bounded across the patio and down the steps before disappearing into the darkness. As soon as I stepped outside and closed the door behind me, I hurried to the edge of the yard, hugging my flannel jacket as I adjusted to the brisk chill in the air. I paused for a moment to glance up at the sky. The full silvery moon, pocketed with craters, had risen above the treetops, muting out the stars. Closing my eyes for a moment, I took a deep breath. *Please let me find the strength to do this,* I thought. *Ryder needs me. I may be his only chance.* My inner voice sent shivers up my spine. There was nothing like a little pressure at a time like this.

I opened my eyes, giving them a moment to adjust to the darkness. The night was particularly quiet for August. The crickets that usually chirped after the sun set were silent due to the cold, making it seem more like late September. An owl hooted in the distance, bringing my attention back to the matter at hand. I turned on the flashlight and set off into the forest.

"Dakota!" I called in a low whisper.

He trotted across the beam of light, his eyes glowing for

a moment. Then he focused his attention on the woods, taking in every scent and sound as if looking for clues.

Another owl hooted, this time sounding much closer. I stopped and looked up straight in front of me. A gray, long-eared owl perched on a low branch of an oak tree. Its yellow eyes focused on me, not blinking. It seemed to know I needed help.

"Hello," I whispered.

I thought I noticed the slightest nod of its head. I maintained eye contact with it as my thoughts did the talking. I had learned over the years that speaking out loud wasn't necessary because the animals could read my thoughts. Once I realized that I could communicate silently, I felt silly speaking to them out loud, as if someone might hear me and think I was talking to myself.

'*A little boy is lost somewhere out here. He's small and alone. He means no harm, and I'm sure he's cold and frightened. I need to find him. Please, if you see him, come back and lead me to him.*'

Understanding registered in the owl's stern expression. After a deep hoot, it stretched out its large, strong wings and launched into the air, darting through the forest trees.

Dakota took off in the direction of the owl and I followed. It was an uphill climb. I aimed the flashlight beam at the ground so that I could maneuver over the rocky terrain. They didn't call New Hampshire the granite state for nothing. Dakota circled back every few minutes to check on me, making sure I was still headed in the right direction.

After about fifteen minutes of hiking up the mountain, I stopped, leaning against a tree to catch my breath. Despite the plummeting temperatures, I was sweating under my jacket. A few owls hooted in the distance, as if talking to each other. Dakota returned to me again before trotting ahead, his black shape a shadow in the moonlight. Then he halted, listening, sniffing the air, concentrating. He stood motionless, focusing on clues that no human could sense.

Instead of continuing up the mountain, he turned and

headed across the side of it. I followed, stumbling a little as I tried to balance on the uneven terrain. It took a few minutes, but I finally got the hang of walking lopsided. I lost sight of Dakota as he disappeared in the distance again, but I continued straight ahead, stepping carefully over the rocks, logs, and tree roots I watched for in the flashlight beam.

As I trudged ahead, still stumbling from time to time, doubts crept back into my head. What in the world had I been thinking? Did I really think I could find Ryder before he succumbed to hypothermia or a hungry wild animal? Although I knew many of the animals that lived here, I certainly didn't know them all. And talking to them occasionally didn't mean that they would know what to do with a little boy unless I specifically told them.

Lost deep in my concerns of all the possible outcomes, most of them less than desirable, I suddenly tripped over a tree root. My foot stuck to the ground and my body lurched forward. As I instinctively reached out to break my fall, the flashlight fell to the ground with a thud. My hands landed on a few rocks, scraping my cold palms. Before I could catch myself, my head struck the jagged corner of a small boulder. Searing pain shot through my skull. I could only imagine the black and blue mark this would leave.

I finally came to a stop on the ground. Breathing deeply, I shivered—not from the cold, but from the fear that I could have really been hurt. As I sat up, trembling, I brushed the dirt off my hands by rubbing them against my jeans. My shaking began to subside and I raised my hand to gingerly touch the throbbing side of my forehead along my hairline. It felt sticky and moist and I knew at once that I was bleeding. *Great,* I thought. *Ryder's in big trouble if I'm the only one who can help him. I have to be more careful out here!* Not only was I worried about Ryder, but now I had to keep myself alive, which apparently was a lot harder than I had bargained for when I set out. I was very familiar with these mountains, but the time I had spent wandering through them had always been during the day. I couldn't remember ever venturing out at night like this. And now I knew why. Under the cloak of darkness, every rock, log, and root posed a threat.

As soon as I composed myself, I scanned the sloping forest floor for my flashlight. Fortunately, it was still on and I caught sight of it resting against a large tree trunk, the beam of light a dim circle against the bark. It was downhill from me, and I crawled toward it. I didn't trust my own two feet until I could use the flashlight to make out the tree roots and rocks. I grabbed it and spun the light around until I saw the boulder I had slammed into. My legs were still a little shaky as I stood and trudged up the hill. Reaching the rock, I sat on it to take a quick rest.

All this time, while I was nearly killing myself, Dakota had disappeared and I suddenly wasn't sure where I was. I heard an owl in the distance and wondered if it was the same one I had seen when I had first set out. Then, without any warning, a tree branch behind me snapped under the weight of someone or something, and I jumped. Spinning around, I moved the flashlight beam into the eyes of a large black bear. It winced from the bright light as it let out a low growl.

I immediately angled the beam at the ground to avoid blinding the bear another second. I recognized it as a female I had encountered last summer. I remembered her by the distinct, jagged scar that ran along her brown muzzle. She had two cubs the last time I had seen her, and she had watched protectively as I played tug of war with them using a broken tree branch. She had trusted me like she would have no other human, but I remembered being cautious. One false move with those cubs, and she could have turned on me. It had been a humbling experience, testing my powers like that. But it had also been exhilarating and just plain fun.

She was alone tonight. Her growl faded, and I thought I saw recognition in her eyes. Good. If she remembered me from before, perhaps she'd be more receptive to my plea for help. I smiled. *'You're probably wondering what I'm doing. There's a little boy lost out here and I need help to find him. He's alone and might not survive if I don't find him soon. Can you please help?'*

The bear's eyes met mine and I knew at once she understood. With a subtle nod of her head, she turned and lumbered off into the forest. The search party was growing, as was my hope that I could find Ryder and bring him home.

Still sitting on the boulder, I waved the flashlight beam around me, trying to remember which direction I had come from and which direction I had been heading when I fell. Exhaustion and fatigue were starting to set in as my adrenaline began to fade. The thought of giving up and turning back crossed my mind. My bed would feel wonderful right now. It was all I could do to stop those thoughts and persevere. I would not give up. Tomorrow could be too late for Ryder and I knew that these animals, the ones I had grown up with and come to love for years, wouldn't let me down. I had to trust them like never before.

A black shadow darted toward me and I recognized Dakota's amber eyes glowing in the moonlight. Just seeing him comforted me. I needed him, as I knew I couldn't do this without him. He trotted up to me and nuzzled my hand. His nose took several quick tiny breaths as he picked up the scent of the blood on my forehead. *'I'm fine,'* I thought. *'It's just a little scratch. We have to keep moving. Please show me which way to go.'*

Despite the concern in his eyes, he turned back to the task at hand. He spun around and took off across the mountain. With a deep breath, I hauled myself to my feet and followed him. Only, this time, I was more careful to watch my step. I couldn't afford to trip again, especially as the terrain became steeper. I couldn't risk falling to the ground and tumbling down the mountain. Dakota didn't get too far ahead this time. As soon as I lost sight of him, within a minute or two, he reappeared to keep me on the right track.

We started heading up the mountain again. My legs burned from the exertion, and I stopped frequently to catch my breath. On one of those stops, an owl landed on a branch in the tree I leaned against. It hooted again before taking off through the trees, the leaves rustling in its wake. Dakota shot off in the direction it went, and I ran after them.

Hours seemed to pass as I followed Dakota straight up the mountain. My eyelids became heavy with fatigue and my legs grew weaker with every step. I stopped to check my watch at one point. Ten minutes past midnight. It had been nearly two hours since I had left the house. I was beginning to wonder how a three-year-old had covered this much ground since the afternoon.

When we finally reached the peak, the terrain leveled out and we continued across the top. We had gone too far to be near the areas that I visited frequently. I generally went straight behind my house to where the stream ran in between the mountains. I hoped Ryder wasn't much farther away. We still had to get home, but at least that would be downhill.

I followed Dakota through a patch of pine trees. The needles brushed against my arms as I slipped between the branches. Fallen logs crossed our path, and Dakota leaped over them, stopping for a few seconds on the other side to wait while I carefully stepped over them. The underbrush was much thicker here. I crept through bushes and pushed low-lying branches, from my waist to my head, out of the way. Then, suddenly, the underbrush and forest gave way to a clearing. The moon glowed brightly overhead, now visible from the opening in the trees. As I shined the flashlight across the open space, Dakota halted and an owl hooted from a nearby tree. Dakota's attention was focused on a black shape at the center of the clearing.

He turned back to look at me, his expression satisfied now that he had accomplished his mission. I hurried past him to the big black shadow straight ahead. As I got closer, it moved and I realized it was the black bear I had seen earlier. She rose from where she had been laying and stepped to the side, revealing the still body of a little boy curled in a fetal position. As my father had mentioned earlier, he wore shorts and a T-shirt. One of his toddler shoes was missing.

"Oh my God!" I rushed over to him and knelt beside him. Holding my hand next to his nose, I felt the faint blow of air and tears brimmed my eyes. He was alive! He was also warm to the touch, thanks to the bear, who had snuggled next to him until I could get there. I turned to her, my eyes meeting hers. "Thank you," I said.

She nodded her head once, the motion very subtle. Then she approached me and I reached out my hand for her to sniff. I gently rubbed the thick fur on her cheek. "I don't know if he would have survived without you."

She leaned into my touch for just a moment before turning on her heels and taking off. I watched her disappear into the night, wishing I could understand her thoughts the way she understood mine. Then I turned back to Ryder.

He was lying in the grass. I scanned the surrounding area with my flashlight and gasped at what I found. A fire pit had been carved out of the ground about fifteen feet away. Large rocks formed a circle around a pile of charred logs. My first thought was that someone had been here, but the idea that someone had taken Ryder made me sick to my stomach. My heart heavy with worry, I approached the fire pit and knelt down to inspect the remains. When I touched the logs, I sighed with relief. They were cold and dry, putting my suspicions to rest.

Rushing back over to Ryder, I scooped him up and pressed his chest against mine, the flashlight still in my hand. He stirred for a minute, opening his sleepy eyes and looking at me, before resting his head against my shoulder. I fumbled with my open jacket, pulling it around his back to keep him warm. He was heavy, and I worried that I wouldn't be able to keep my balance as I carried him down the mountain. I would just have to be extremely careful.

"Okay, Dakota, lead the way home," I said. "And can

you please find a way around the underbrush and big logs? I barely got through them on the way here. With my luck, I'll kill us both if we go back that way."

Dakota sighed as he rolled his eyes at me. Sometimes, I couldn't believe how human he seemed. I still wished I could understand his thoughts, but he was pretty good at letting me know how he felt through his body language. He trotted to the edge of the clearing where he followed the tree line rather than disappearing into the woods. When he stopped, he stared into the trees and then looked back at me as if to say, "This way."

As I headed toward him, he waited until I was near enough to touch him. Then he walked slowly into the woods, constantly glancing back over his shoulder to make sure I was right behind him. He found a much easier path than the one that had brought us into the clearing. There were no branches scraping my arms and face to push away, no logs to step over. It was a good thing, too. Ryder was awkward in my arms and my hands were no longer free to catch myself if I tripped.

Dakota wandered around the trees and I followed, keeping him in sight. As we trekked deeper into the forest under the cover of the leafy branches, the moonlight faded and I watched for rocks and tree roots in the flashlight's beam.

Dakota kept a steady pace this time, not getting too far ahead. He occasionally stopped to let me catch up when I fell behind. Owls hooted in the distance, breaking through the silent night. I welcomed their calls, thinking of how one of them had helped tonight. I continued slowly, stepping cautiously, as we started our descent down the mountain. Ryder sighed, shifting against me and I hugged him tighter to me.

"It's okay. You're safe now. I'm taking you home."

He lifted his head slightly and his tired eyes fluttered open for a moment. Then he yawned and dropped his cheek back against my shoulder. His soft blond hair tickled my neck and I smiled. I had made the right decision to come out here tonight. Feeling this little boy in my arms and knowing he was safe made all the risks of the night worth it.

Dakota led me down the mountain at an angle so that I didn't have to descend straight down the steep slope. The adrenaline that had helped keep me going before finding Ryder had disappeared. Instead, all I felt now was fatigue. Once I started yawning, it was all I could do to keep moving forward. I wanted so badly to take a break, but I knew if I did, I wouldn't be able to start up again.

My legs grew more tired with every step. Even though I held my gaze to the flashlight beam on the ground, I missed seeing an exposed tree root and suddenly stumbled. As panic raced through me, I threw my weight backward to prevent the two of us from catapulting down the mountain. Somehow, I managed to catch my balance before smacking my backside into the ground, or something worse. But the misstep at least woke me up for a while. I forced myself to hold my eyes open as I concentrated on each step. I would be home soon enough where I could hand Ryder to my parents and collapse into my bed for an eternity of sleep.

After I had dodged countless rocks and tree branches, the terrain finally leveled out. I started to recognize the area and knew we were close to home. Dakota ran farther ahead, another sign that we were almost there. Relief overwhelmed me as I realized that I had managed to get home safely.

"We're almost there," I whispered to the little boy in my arms, even though I knew he wouldn't hear me in his sleep.

Dakota trotted back to me just as my flashlight died. Darkness settled around me and my eyes adjusted to the moonlight, but all I could make out were dark shadowy trees. The other flashlight was buried in my pocket, and I didn't want to risk dropping Ryder to get it. We were almost home, anyway.

"Dakota, help, please."

I didn't need to say anything more to him. He approached me and leaned against my leg so that I could feel him.

From that point, he led me through the trees to my back-yard, never leaving my side.

I had never been so happy to return home as I was at that moment. The minute Dakota led me into our yard, he broke loose from my side. I felt the ground change from dirt, twigs, and leaves to the softness of grass. Moonlight filtered into the backyard and I could see the white clapboard siding of our house. My leg muscles burned and my feet became heavier with each step. The sudden exhaustion was over-whelming, and I wasn't sure that I would make it to the back door.

"Dakota," I whispered. "Get Dad. Hurry!"

He took off around to the side of the house. My parents' bedroom was on the first level and Dakota knew exactly which window to go to. He would alert my father. He wouldn't let me down.

Dizziness suddenly struck me and the world started spinning around me. Or was I spinning? I couldn't tell. My eyelids fell and every ounce of strength I had used to keep them open all night vanished. *No, you're not going to fall now,* I thought. *You can do this. Just a few more steps and you're there. You're home. You did it*! But I couldn't move another step. My feet felt as though bricks had been tied to them. In a split second, the world turned pitch black and I collapsed into the grass with Ryder still in my arms.

Chapter 3

Beep, beep, beep…
I heard the continuous monitor and I knew I wasn't tucked safely in the comfort of my own bed. My eyes fluttered open to see the sterile white walls of a hospital room. It was dimly lit and smelled of toxic ammonia cleaner. A needle had been taped into place in my arm for the IV and I wore a hospital gown. My empty stomach rumbled, but I was too weak to really care. All I wanted was to see a familiar face. My mom, my dad, Ethan. And I wanted to know that Ryder was okay.

"You're awake," my father said from the doorway, holding a Styrofoam cup of steaming coffee. He looked tired, but relieved, as he entered the room. When he reached my bedside, he stroked my hair. "How are you feeling?"

"Just tired. How is Ryder?"

My father smiled brightly. "He's going to be fine, thanks to you. You're a hero, you know."

"No, I'm not. Anyone in my shoes would have done what I did."

"And what exactly is that? How did you find him?"

I shrugged as I looked away from his questioning eyes.

"I followed Dakota. He's the real hero." I paused, desperately wanting to change the subject. I couldn't tell my father that I had been communicating with wild animals for years and they helped us find Ryder. "What am I doing here?"

"I found you unconscious in the backyard. I wasn't leaving anything to chance."

"I was just so tired, I couldn't make it to the house. But I'm fine," I insisted. "And I want to go home."

"I'm sure you'll get out of here soon. The doctor said you probably had a little low blood sugar, but that your labs looked fine once they got some fluids into you. Are you sore?"

I shifted in the bed and tried to sit up. Yes, I was definitely sore. And I could feel the bruise along the side of my face where I had hit the rock. I reached up to touch the wound and felt a gauze bandage taped in place. "Oh, no. I didn't have to get stitches, did I?"

"No. They just cleaned it up so it wouldn't get infected. It was quite a scrape."

"That's good. Where's Mom?"

"She stayed behind to get some of your things after the ambulance left the house. She should be here soon. But back to Dakota. How did he find Ryder?"

"Dad, I don't know. He just did and I don't think it matters how he did it. Let's just be thankful that things turned out okay."

My father ran his hands through his disheveled graying hair. "We're going to have to come up with a cover story. People will want to know how you found Ryder all on your own. They're already asking me about it. We can't exactly tell them that a wolf led you to him."

"So we tell them it was a stray dog I've been feeding for a few months. When they ask to meet him, we just tell them he's shy and doesn't like strangers."

"You already have this figured out, don't you?" my father asked, shaking his head. "I guess that's all we can do."

I could tell my father didn't like the idea of lying, but

what else could we do? Dakota might be a hero, but he was still a wolf. We couldn't jeopardize his well-being or my father's position as the town sheriff.

"Knock, knock," came a soft, unfamiliar female voice at the door to the room.

My father and I simultaneously turned our attention to see a pretty blonde nurse holding a vase of pink, purple, and white flowers.

"These are for Ms. Sumner," she explained.

My father stood and took the flowers from the nurse. "Thank you," he said. "Can you tell me if they will be bringing anything for her to eat soon?"

The nurse nodded. "Yes. Lunch should be coming around in the next hour." With that, she turned and disappeared out the door.

My father placed the flowers on the table next to my bed and handed me the card.

As I took it from him, I asked, "Lunch? What time is it?"

"Almost noon."

I shot up from the pillows I had been leaning against. "Oh, no! I was supposed to work the lunch shift today."

There were still a few weeks of summer before school started and I didn't want to lose my job for not showing up.

"Don't worry. Your mother called Mike to let him know you couldn't make it in today. He was very understanding." He looked down at my hand. "Open the card."

"What does that mean? Did Mom tell him what happened?" I asked as I opened the small envelope.

"She didn't have to. You were brought to the hospital at four this morning. By eight, most everyone in town knew you'd found Ryder in the middle of the night all by yourself."

"Great," I muttered sarcastically. I hadn't considered the aftermath of my actions from last night. As uneasy as I felt knowing that I would probably be the center of attention for a while, I wouldn't have done anything differently. "Dad, I don't want anyone making a big deal out of this. Please."

"I knew you wouldn't, but it is a big deal. You're seven-teen and you found a lost child in the middle of the night all by yourself," he repeated. "The media is going to have a field day with this."

"Media?" Alarm rang out in my voice. The town's atten-tion was bad enough, but the news media was a whole dif-ferent story. I pulled the small card out of the envelope, but it got stuck in my hands, forgotten. "As in the local news-paper?"

"As in the major networks. Laken, honey, this is big. It's gone to the national news." My father took the card out of my hands while I processed what he had just told me.

I sat frozen as I imagined being stalked by reporters and losing every semblance of privacy.

"Don't worry. This will blow over soon. Some other big story will come along and you'll be forgotten. Besides, I won't let them get near you if that's what you want," my father assured me.

"Dakota wouldn't let that happen, either."

"Except that now we have to be extra careful to make sure no one sees him."

"I know." I fell silent as I continued to realize all that had happened. I suddenly longed for the familiar surround-ings of home.

My father shifted his gaze down to the card in his hands. "'Our many thanks. You are truly a hero in every sense.' The flowers are from Ryder's parents." He slid the card back into the plastic stake pointing out of the flower ar-rangement and smiled at me. "The Thompson's are very grateful for what you did. They want to stop by the house later tonight after Ryder's released to personally thank you."

I managed to smile. While I didn't want anyone to make a big deal out of this, I had no choice but to accept some of the attention. "I guess that will be okay."

Another soft knock sounded on the door. A gray-haired doctor in a white lab coat, a stethoscope looped around his neck and a clipboard in his hand, stepped into the room. He approached my bedside as he flipped through his papers. "Hello. I'm glad to see you're awake. How are you feeling?"

"Tired, sore, hungry. But otherwise, I feel fine."

"Well, that was an amazing thing you did, finding that little boy. We're all just relieved that both of you are fine," he said.

I had a feeling that I would be hearing this from a lot of people for several days, if not longer. I would have to get used to changing the subject. "So can I go home today?" I asked.

"Yes, I'm actually here to do a final check-up and fill out your discharge papers." The doctor set his clipboard down next to the flower arrangement on the bedside table and pulled a penlight out of his pocket. He shined the light in my eyes, one at a time, and checked the monitor next to the bed. After a few minutes, he said, "Everything looks good. I don't see any reason to keep you here any longer. I'll have the nurse paged to remove your IV and get you ready to go." He turned to my father. "I just need you to sign here, Mr. Sumner."

My father took the pen and quickly scribbled his signature on the form. "Thank you, Doctor."

"My pleasure, Mr. Sumner." With one last parting smile, the doctor left the room.

My father turned to me. "That's it. I guess we're free to go soon."

"But I'm hungry. Looks like I'll miss lunch. Do you think I can grab something from the cafeteria before we leave?"

"I'm sure we can arrange something."

My mother suddenly appeared in the doorway. My overnight bag hung from her shoulder and she carried a small white paper bag. She greeted me with a warm smile. "How's my baby?" She held out the bag. "Guess what I brought."

"Mom!" I felt a huge smile break out across my face as I recognized the white bag from my favorite deli in town. "Is that what I think it is?"

"Yep. Egg salad on whole wheat, a bag of Cheetos, and a pickle." She handed the bag to me. "And—" She reached into her purse. "—a cold raspberry tea."

I took the bottle from her. "You're the best." I put it on the table and reached into the bag for the sandwich. As I bit into it, she dropped the overnight bag onto the corner chair.

"You just missed the doctor," my father told her. "Laken's been given a clean bill of health and she's being discharged. We're waiting for the nurse to remove her IV."

"Then I'm just in time. I brought you some clean clothes and your toothbrush." She scanned the room, her gaze stopping when she noticed the flowers. "Those are nice."

"They're from the Thompsons," my father explained. "Speaking of which, now that you're here, I should probably check in on Ryder one last time before getting back to the station. Pete's been on his own all day with the new recruit."

"Okay, but try not to stay too long. You've been up since four this morning," my mother said with concern. "And after last night, you'll need some rest today."

"My thoughts exactly. I'll be home as soon as I check in and make sure everything's under control." He kissed her and blew me a kiss. "I'll see you both at home in a few hours."

He left the room, and I found myself alone with my mother while I devoured the sandwich and Cheetos. My conversation with her was pretty much a repeat of what I had discussed with my father. She asked how I felt and how I had found Ryder. Then she reiterated what my father had explained about the media. I had a sinking feeling that I wouldn't escape them for several days, at least.

A nurse arrived as I polished off the last Cheeto and sip of tea. After she removed the IV, I changed out of the hospital gown into the jeans and gray sweatshirt my mother had brought. While I brushed my teeth, my mother gathered my clothes from last night that had been stored on the shelf under the hospital bed. When I finished in the bathroom, I stuffed my toiletries into my overnight bag, hoisted the strap over my shoulder, and then grabbed the vase of flowers. Eager to escape the hospital, I followed my mother out the door.

Before we got very far, the nurse returned with a wheelchair. She gestured for me to sit. When I made a face, she explained, "Hospital protocol. Get in. I'll take you down the employee elevator to the back door. I called the front desk and there are reporters swarming in the lobby and outside the entrance."

"Lovely," I muttered as I handed my bag to my mother with one hand while balancing the flowers in my arms. Sitting down, I asked, "Are you sure they haven't found the back door yet?"

"I only know what the front desk told me," the nurse replied.

She wheeled me down a sterile, white-walled hallway to a big silver elevator door. Once inside, we rode down in silence, except for the tone that sounded when we reached the ground floor. Each second seemed to last forever. I couldn't wait to get to the car.

When the door opened, the nurse picked up the pace. We passed through the maze of nondescript hallways for what seemed like forever until I saw a red exit sign next to a heavy door. My mother held it open as the nurse wheeled me outside. The bright sunlight nearly blinded me as I scanned the parking lot beyond the tree-lined sidewalk. "Can I please walk from here? I'm fine."

"I'm supposed to put you into your car from the wheelchair," the nurse said. "But I'll let you up here. Just be careful, okay?"

"I will," I promised as I stood up and followed my mother across the parking lot.

We almost made it to our black SUV when a reporter in

a suit ambushed us from between two cars. He was tailed by a cameraman who easily kept up, even as he carried a towering TV camera.

The reporter flashed a bright, movie-star smile. "Ms. Sumner, can I get a statement? I'm with the local news and we'd like to get your story. You're quite a hero."

I quickened my pace. "No comment. Please leave me alone," I whispered loudly as I reached the SUV and climbed in while my mother tossed my overnight bag in the back and slid into the driver's seat. I held the flowers in my lap as she sped away. Turning, I saw a swarm of reporters rushing away from the red-brick hospital into the parking lot. But the scene disappeared from sight when we merged onto the street.

I looked over at my mother as she focused intently on the road ahead. "Thanks, Mom. Good driving. What would Dad think if he knew you could drive like that?"

She chuckled and relaxed, easing off the accelerator to settle into the right lane at the speed of traffic. "I just did what I had to do. That was close, but we probably haven't seen the last of them. They may show up at home."

"Can Dad issue a restraining order?" I asked.

"I'm sure he can if he really needs to. It might be better if you give them a statement. If they get what they're after, then maybe they'll leave us alone."

"I'll think about it," I muttered with a deep sigh, not at all happy about the prospect of being on the evening news.

How would I answer their questions about last night? The only option would be to lie. The less the world knew about the truth and Dakota, the faster my life could return to normal.

I really hoped this would blow over soon. Closing my eyes, I rested my head against the seat and pushed my thoughts of the media out of my mind for the rest of the way home.

❧❧❧

My afternoon was a whirlwind of activity. As expected, the reporters showed up on our doorstep soon after we arrived home. My mother convinced me to give them a short statement. Hoping they would leave if I gave them what they came for, I slipped outside and faced the cameras. Questions were fired at me and microphones were shoved under my nose. I spoke in a shy, quiet voice, mesmerized by the crowd in the front yard and scared that I would say the wrong thing. But I calmly relayed my stray dog story before my mother told the reporters they'd had enough time with me and shooed them away.

I also spoke to Ethan, but only for a minute between his shifts. He rarely worked a double shift, but when someone wanted to give one up, he never turned down the opportunity to add few more hours to his timecard. I was relieved that he didn't have time to give me the third degree. Brooke called a few times, and I felt badly letting her calls dump into my voicemail. After dealing with the reporters, I didn't have the energy to talk about last night again.

That evening, I stepped out of my bedroom freshly showered wearing skinny jeans and a purple sweater. My hair fell out of a loose ponytail at the base of my neck, a stray blonde lock tickling the side of my face. A dry bandage covered the scrape along my hairline.

Before I reached the stairwell at the end of the hall, my mouth watered from the smell of lasagna. After a long day and hot shower, I was definitely hungry. When I turned at the bottom of the stairs, I saw my mother cutting a tomato for the salad. "Shall I set the table?" I offered.

"That would be wonderful."

As I pulled three dinner plates out of the cabinet, our doorbell rang. My mother and I looked at each other and then stared at the kitchen entrance that led to the front door.

"Oh, no, not more reporters," I groaned. "Where's Dad?"

My father's police car and badge had been enough to discourage the straggling reporters that had shown up after the first group I had spoken to.

"He's working on something in the garage. I'll handle this."

My mother wiped her hands on a dish towel before heading toward the front door with a look of determination on her face.

"Thanks, Mom." I resumed setting the table, first with the plates and then the silverware. When my mother didn't return immediately, I crept along the wall to the corner beside the entrance to the kitchen. Listening carefully, I heard a familiar soft voice.

"I'm sorry to just drop by, but we only got home with Ryder about an hour ago. I wanted to personally thank Laken for what she did."

"It's not a problem. I'm sure she'd love to see you. Laken!" my mother called softly.

I immediately stepped around the corner and stopped when I saw Mrs. Thompson in the doorway. Her long, ash-blonde curls reminded me of Ryder's almost white halo of hair. Her belly swollen with her unborn child, she wore maternity jeans and a white blouse rimmed with lace around the neckline and sleeves.

She smiled as I slowly walked toward the open door where she stood. It was still light outside, but shadows extended across the sidewalk and yard from the descending sun.

"Hi," I said when I stopped at the doorway.

"Hello, Laken. It's wonderful to see you." Mrs. Thompson's blue eyes brimmed with tears as she embraced me in a warm hug. I responded, gently placing my arms around her shoulders. Then she pulled back quickly, as if embarrassed. "I'm sorry to be so emotional, but I'm eternally grateful for what you did."

An awkward silence hovered between us as I didn't quite know what to say. My mother noted it and jumped in. "I need to get back to making dinner. I'll leave you two alone to talk." She squeezed my shoulder reassuringly before returning to the kitchen.

"How are you feeling today?" Mrs. Thompson asked.

"Fine. I was just a little sore and tired when I woke up at the hospital earlier, but that's all."

She touched my bandage for a quick moment. "What happened here?"

"I fell last night. I can be pretty clumsy sometimes."

"But you were very brave to do what you did. I can't begin to imagine where Ryder would be right now if it hadn't been for you."

I felt a blush heating up my cheeks. "It was nothing, really."

"Laken, it's anything but nothing. I want to explain what happened. Ryder was outside in the backyard playing on his swing set when I had to go to the bathroom." She rubbed her swollen belly. "Frequent trips to the bathroom are one of the many joys of pregnancy. I could have sworn the fence gate was secured. He can't open it, you know that. But when I returned, the gate was open and he was gone. I tried finding him myself at first, but it was hard to get through the woods carrying this extra weight."

"You don't need to explain. I'm sure you did everything you could to keep him safe. These things happen sometimes."

As I smiled at her, something nagged at the back of my thoughts. If the gate really had been secured, then how had he gotten out? My smile faded as I remembered how far away he had been when I'd found him. Mrs. Thompson noticed my frown immediately and was about to say something when I asked, "How is Ryder? Has he said anything about last night?" I tried to smile again, not only to distract her from my worried expression but also to wipe out my concerns. Our town was safe. The thought that someone could have taken Ryder out of his yard sent shivers up my spine. Children weren't kidnapped around here. Surely there was another explanation.

"He's doing just fine. The doctors were really impressed that he only had a few scrapes and bruises. He even seemed to stay warm enough. And you know, he still doesn't talk much. But he keeps talking about a bear. He keeps saying, 'The bear hug me.' Does that make any sense to you?"

Of course it did, but how could I possibly tell this woman that a full-grown black bear had helped find her son and kept him warm? "No. Does he have a teddy bear that he wanted to hug when he got home? He didn't have one with him when he left the yard, did he?"

"No. Oh well, it's probably just him babbling. He doesn't make much sense, yet." She shrugged, accepting that there was no logical explanation for his words other than the rambling of a three-year-old. "Did you get the flowers?" she asked, changing the subject.

"Yes. They're beautiful. Thank you. I put them up in my bedroom and they smell like heaven."

"I'm glad you like them. It's a small token of our appreciation. We'd love to do more for you, give you a reward, but our finances are pretty tight with one young child and another one on the way."

"That's completely unnecessary. My reward is knowing that he's safe."

"Can I ask you something? How did you find him? Your dad told us a stray dog led you to him. That's really amazing."

"Yeah. He's an amazing dog. Just showed up one day and I've been feeding him ever since." I looked away from her for a moment as I lied.

"Is he here? I'd love to meet him."

"No. A couple reporters came by earlier and they scared him off. He's very shy. But I'll leave some food out for him tonight in case he comes back."

"Please tell him how wonderful and special he is for me. Oh, wait a minute. Is he big and black like a bear? Maybe that's where Ryder got this idea of a bear."

"Sort of. That must be it." It was too easy to just agree with her so that she had an explanation for her son's babbling.

She glanced at her watch. "I need to get home to help Wes put Ryder to bed. Thank you again, even though a simple thank you doesn't come close to expressing how I feel right now."

"You're welcome," was all I could think of to say. I could tell by the look in her eyes how grateful she was.

"Why don't you and your parents stop by for dinner sometime? I make a killer pot roast."

"That—would be great," I said, forcing myself to smile. I didn't have the heart to tell her I was a vegetarian.

"Okay. Good night, then." She hesitantly turned to walk away, but after two steps, spun on her heels and gave me another hug. "You're an angel," she whispered in my ear.

After a quick squeeze, she let go and started to leave again. Only this time she kept going to her car and waved out the window as she backed out of our driveway.

I smiled and waved back before retreating into the house and closing the front door once her car had disappeared down the winding road.

After dinner that evening, I slipped out back to sit on the patio steps. The sun had dipped behind the mountains and the darkening sky had faded to purple. A chill had crept into the air, but I was warm in my fleece jacket. It wasn't nearly as cold as last night.

I whistled softly, calling out Dakota's name. I hadn't seen him all day and I missed him. I was relieved that he'd had the sense to stay away today, but it felt strange not to have his company. His presence comforted me in a way I couldn't put into words.

The back door opened and my father approached behind me as it fell shut with a bang. He sat down beside me, a steaming coffee mug in his hand. The bittersweet scent of coffee mixed with a nutty-flavored creamer filled the air. "Let him go," my father said. "He'll be fine, and he needs to stay away for a while until this blows over."

"I know. I miss him, that's all."

My father acknowledged my sentiment with a brief nod.

"The mayor called. He's holding a town gathering on Saturday in your honor."

"What?" I gasped. "Dad, please tell him not to. I don't want that. I just want to go back to working at the pizza shop and being the girl that no one pays attention to. This is crazy. The reporters were enough and I answered their questions. I don't want this being turned into a circus. Please."

"I agree with you that it is a little crazy. But I know Mayor Hobbs, and when he decides to hold a town gathering, there's no changing his mind. Unlike you, he loves the attention and will use any excuse to bring everyone together."

"Do I have to go?" I knew it was a dumb question, but I had to ask anyway.

"Of course. You're the sheriff's daughter and the guest of honor. If you don't show up, both of us will be in trouble."

"I was really hoping that by the weekend, this whole thing would be forgotten. I'm not even sure I want to go back to work because I don't want people asking me questions."

"Unfortunately, that's just human nature. People are curious. Didn't you think about the fall-out of becoming a hero when you decided to traipse out into the wilderness all on your own to find Ryder?" he joked.

"No, actually, the thought never crossed my mind," I replied honestly. "Although, even if it had, I still would have done what I did."

"Of course you would have. Most people would enjoy the attention, you know."

"I guess I'm not most people."

"You never have been and you never will be," he said lovingly. He paused, gazing up at the milky sky that was quickly giving way to blackness. "Okay, I have an idea. You know Pete McKay who's been the town deputy practically all his life is finally retiring, right?" I nodded. "We have a new recruit in training to take his place when he leaves at the end of the summer," he continued. "Let me use Saturday to formally announce the transition and introduce Noah to the town. That will help draw some of the attention away from you."

"I still wish I didn't have to go. Can you promise me no reporters?"

"I'll do my best, but this is the kind of thing they love."

I sighed. I knew I would have to go to the ceremony and get through it no matter how uncomfortable it made me. "Okay, but I'm not going to like it. I don't have to give a speech or anything, do I?"

"The mayor will probably want you to say a few words," he admitted slowly.

"No. No, no, no. I can't do that."

"Yes, you can. You'll come up with something great, I'm sure of it. But you're going to have to deal with this. It'll eventually be forgotten, it's just going to take some time." He wrapped his arm around my shoulder and squeezed gently. "I'm proud of you, honey."

"Thanks, Dad."

"You're welcome." He paused then said, "It's almost dark out here. I'm going in. Don't stay out too late."

"I won't. I just want to wait a little longer for Dakota." I glanced at him before he rose to his feet and retreated back into the house. As soon as the door shut behind him, the outside light turned on, casting shadows across the yard.

I leaned my elbows on my knees and looked up at the sky. It was another silent night in the chilly mountain air. No crickets chirping, no wind whispering through the leaves, just a dead calm like last night. Suddenly, a shadow moved, catching my attention out of the corner of my eye. I jumped for a moment before realizing it was Dakota. He trotted over to me, his movements as silent as the night. He was quite good at sneaking up on me. I hadn't heard a sound before seeing him. Not a single leaf rustled beneath his paws and not a single twig snapped. He could make his way through the forest as quietly as a ghost.

When he reached me, Dakota nuzzled my neck with a greeting.

"Hi, there," I said, rubbing the fur between his ears. "I missed you today."

He nodded and I noticed the familiar understanding in his honey-colored eyes. Then he turned and sat next to me, his fur brushing against my legs. We both stared into the darkness, lost deep in our thoughts.

I wasn't sure how long we sat there before I heard a low rumble coming from Dakota. He watched the trees hidden by the black cloak of night, his growl deepening.

"What is it, boy?" I asked quietly, even though I knew he couldn't answer me.

He curled his upper lip, baring sharp fangs, as his growl grew more intense. I shivered, wishing he could tell me what he heard or sensed.

A stick snapped somewhere out in the not-too-distant forest. It was loud enough that whatever had stepped on it must have been fairly heavy. Dakota jumped to his feet, his posture tall, straight, and ready to strike. The coarse smoky black fur on his back stood straight up along his spine. He continued growling, and I knew that whatever was out there was no bear, moose, or other harmless animal. Dakota spent as much time around them as I did, and he knew none of the animals who lived here were a threat. Whatever it was, I was sure Dakota had picked up its scent. He knew exactly what was out there. He just couldn't tell me.

I had the distinct feeling that we were being watched and my spine tingled with fear. I stood up cautiously, my eyes darting from Dakota to the woods in the direction the sound had come from.

Before I could turn back to the house, Dakota launched into a stealthy run. He crossed the yard in a few long strides before disappearing into the darkness, his shadowy figure a blur. A deathly silence hung in the night air. I shivered and hugged my arms around me, not from the cold, but from the strange feeling of being watched. After one more glance at the woods, I hurried into the safety of the house. As I shut the door behind me, I instinctively raised my hand to the light switch. But I hesitated, staring at the dim light outside the window panes.

With a deep sigh, I lowered my hand without flipping the switch. Leaving the light on made me feel safer. And for the first time in my life, I locked the door. Then I turned and headed upstairs to my room for bed, hoping that I could forget all about what had just happened.

Chapter 4

Paralyzed with fear, I watched from the front passenger seat of our SUV as the town citizens gathered on the lawn in front of a white gazebo. Young families lounged on blankets with their picnic baskets. Children kicked soccer balls and threw footballs, and adults sat in folding chairs. It was quite the crowd, and it looked like the entire town had shown up.

At least it was a beautiful day, so typical of our summers in the mountains, with bright green maple and oak trees reaching up to the blue sky. I tried to tell myself that these people had come out to enjoy the weather rather than to see me, but it wasn't a convincing argument. The story of my rescue of Ryder had not only aired on TV, but it had also been written up in the local newspaper, *The Boston Herald*, *The Concord Monitor*, and countless others over the last few days. The people had gathered here because of me, not the gorgeous weather.

I leaned back against the head rest and closed my eyes for a quick moment before a knock on my half-open window jolted me back to reality. I turned to see Ethan leaning toward the window with a smile.

"There you are. You can't stay in there all day."

I pushed my sunglasses up onto the bridge of my nose as if I could hide behind them. "Why not?" I asked sarcastically.

"You're the guest of honor. Everyone's asking about you."

"Great. Until this week, no one in this town knew I existed unless I was serving them pizza. I'd rather keep it that way."

A pretty red-haired girl suddenly appeared next to Ethan, and I smiled. I wouldn't be able to get through this day without my two best friends.

Brooke stood nearly eight inches shorter than Ethan, but that didn't stop her from cutting in front of him. She wore her red hair cropped to her shoulders. Her fair skin was as pale as mine, and her blue eyes were nearly transparent in the bright sun.

"Hey there, hero girl," she quipped.

"Don't call me that," I muttered.

She ignored my request. "You're going to have to stop sulking and suck it up. Get out here."

Ethan stepped aside as Brooke opened the door. Like me, she was dressed up, at least what we considered dressed up in our small town. Her floral peasant skirt and billowy white top mimicked the blue sky and puffy clouds. A silver cross hung around her neck, glinting in a ray of sunlight.

I reluctantly slid out of the SUV, tugging my light purple sundress down toward my knees as I stepped on the uneven gravel in my wedge-heeled strappy sandals. "Okay, I'm out, but I'm not happy about it."

Brooke met my frown with a teasing smile before hugging me. "Oh, stop. It's your big day." As she pulled away, she sucked in a deep breath, gently brushing the faint red mark from where I had scraped my head on the rock. "That must have hurt."

I immediately wished I hadn't pulled my hair back into a loose side braid. Even though that kept it from blowing in the breeze, it made what was left of my bruise that much more visible. "A little," I said with a shrug.

"You're so nonchalant about this. If it were me, I'd be eating up all the attention. Now, you need to lose the sunglasses. It's like you're hiding behind them."

I am hiding behind them, I thought. *I don't want to be here, but no one seems to care about my opinion.* "Not until later. It's sunny out here." I wished I could keep them on through the ceremony, but Brooke was right. They would have to come off.

"Are you hungry? We have a picnic basket and a cooler over there." Brooke pointed to a Navajo-patterned blanket spread out under a maple tree along the edge of the lawn.

"Not at all." The truth was, my stomach was tied up in knots over this whole event and just the thought of food made me nauseated.

"I am." Ethan grinned. Of course he was. Like every other teenage boy, he was always ready to eat. "Let's go."

I followed them to the blanket, and the three of us sat down. Scanning the crowd, I saw Brooke's and Ethan's parents in the center. My father was wandering around somewhere to find his new recruit, and my mother had disappeared since arriving to catch up with some friends.

As Brooke opened a bag of chips and Ethan dove into the cooler for a sandwich, I continued watching the lawn for familiar faces. I recognized a lot of kids from school and groaned to myself. The last thing I wanted was this attention so close to the start of a new school year. I had managed to stay practically invisible during my high school career, and I wasn't about to stop now. Unfortunately, I didn't seem to have much of a choice.

My gaze came to rest on a group of four girls milling about across the lawn, and I frowned. Until I had seen them, I hadn't been too worried about the aftermath of this circus. "Oh, no. Marlena and her friends are here," I said.

Brooke's eyes followed my gaze, and she, too, frowned. "What did you expect? She's the mayor's daughter. Of course she's here. And she never goes anywhere without her friends. Don't worry. I'm sure she doesn't want to be here any more than you do." I glanced at Brooke who quickly explained, "After all, she won't be the center of attention today."

"I'd gladly switch places with her," I muttered, returning my gaze to the four girls across the lawn. Marlena was the tall one with long, platinum-blonde hair. She was the head cheerleader and the most sought after girl in our class. All of the boys were in love with her, but she treated them like toys. Her friends, also cheerleaders, followed her like puppies. A part of me envied them. Not just because they were pretty and popular, but because they were normal and they fit in, something I couldn't relate to. As I continued watching them, a guy I didn't recognize approached them. From a distance, I could only tell that he was tall and lean with dark hair. "Who's that?"

"Who?" Brooke asked.

"That guy over there talking to Marlena."

Marlena beamed at him, flipping her hair back over her shoulder. I could tell even from across the crowded lawn that she was trying to impress him.

"Oh, him. That's Noah Lawson, your dad's new recruit. I saw him a few days ago in town from a distance. He's really hot. I told you about him, remember?" Brooke rolled her eyes. "Looks like Marlena has staked her claim on him."

"Isn't he a little old for her?"

"She's eighteen. Remember her huge birthday party that we weren't invited to? Although, if he has any sense at all, he'll stay away from her. Because, if he doesn't, he'll have to be very careful where he puts his hands, not to mention other things." Brooke looked back at me with a sparkle in her eyes, and we both laughed. Then she asked, "So, are you ready to start your senior year as the local hero?"

"You're giving me too much credit. Dakota's the real hero." I stopped short as her parents approached us and asked about the night I found Ryder. I answered them politely, only this time referring to Dakota as a stray dog. As I spoke, my attention reverted back to the scene across the lawn. Marlena had moved closer to Noah, and he had turned slightly so that I could see the side of his face. He was wearing the town police uniform of blue jeans and a light blue button down shirt, a silver badge pinned to the front pocket. From a distance, I could tell that Brooke was right. He was gorgeous.

As I watched him, his gaze wandered across the lawn until it settled on me. Even hiding behind my sunglasses, I felt like I'd been caught staring and I snapped my attention back to Brooke's parents. They looked at me expectantly, as if they were waiting for me to speak. "I'm sorry. Did you ask me something?" I asked sheepishly.

Brooke's mother smiled with understanding. "I'm sure this is a lot to handle right now." She motioned to the crowd. "They all came to see you. I was asking if you had prepared a speech."

I nearly choked at her question. "Speech? Um, no. I haven't even thought about that. I have no idea what to say."

"Well, you better think fast," Brooke said. "It looks like the mayor is about to begin."

I looked over at the gazebo. Mayor Hobbs, dressed in khaki slacks and a white polo shirt, his short gray hair brushed perfectly into place, stood at the front and center. He held a microphone in his hand. "May I have everyone's attention?"

A hush fell over the audience as his voice echoed from the loudspeakers. A baby cried and the voice of a young child broke through the silence every few seconds.

Once all eyes were focused on him, the mayor began. "Good afternoon. Thank you all for coming. We couldn't have asked for a more beautiful day to gather here to pay our respects to one very special girl."

As he rambled on about Ryder's rescue as if no one knew yet, I tuned him out and looked at Brooke. She took a deep breath and mouthed, "Sorry."

I turned my attention back to the mayor just in time to hear him say, "Please give a warm welcome to Laken Sumner." He held his free hand up over his eyes to shield them from the sun as he scanned the crowd for me. "Laken, please join me up here."

I slowly rose to my feet and handed my sunglasses to Brooke. Everyone watched me as I walked along the outer edge of the lawn. Nerves fluttered in my empty stomach and I tried to ignore them. I glimpsed my father behind the gazebo with Pete McKay, the deputy who would be retiring at the end of the summer. Deputy McKay's hair was frosted white and his face weathered from years of outside exposure. My father smiled, nodding at me as I approached the gazebo.

I was especially careful as I climbed the wooden stairs. The last thing I needed was to trip and fall flat on my face with everyone watching. At the top, I hesitated before walking across the platform. All eyes were focused on me, making my heart race. The mayor tossed a kind smile my way as I stopped beside him. I took a deep breath, trying to relax.

"Hello, Mayor Hobbs," I said quietly.

"Laken." He extended his hand, but when I reached out for it, he pulled me into a quick hug. As he let go, I noticed the slightest glaze of tears in his blue eyes. But he composed himself at once before speaking into the microphone. "I think I speak for the entire town when I say thank you. You did an amazing thing by rescuing Ryder and we are all grateful. It's people like you that make living in this town very special." He paused, reaching into his pocket for an envelope. "The business owners in town have come together to give you this." He handed it to me. "It's not much compared to what you did, but it's the least we could do. These are some gift certificates to restaurants and stores. We hope you enjoy them."

I graciously took the envelope from him. "Thank you," I said softly, but I knew no one except for him could hear me.

He noticed right away and handed the microphone to me. Holding it up hesitantly, I repeated, "Thank you." The loud words echoed as I peered out across the sea of faces watching me, waiting for me to say something more. I took a deep breath and prayed for courage. "I just want to say that this is completely unnecessary. I only did what any one of you would have done if given the chance. I was in the right place at the right time, that's all." I turned to face the mayor and held up the envelope. "This was very thoughtful. I will enjoy these."

"It's a small token of our appreciation for what you did."

I nodded in understanding as I scanned the crowd, honing in on Ryder who sat on his mother's lap, his father beside them. Tears of happiness streamed down her face as she kissed the top of Ryder's head. I sighed and looked over at the mayor. Covering the microphone with my free hand, I leaned toward him. "I don't have anything else. Can I go now?"

"Sure." He took the microphone from me and held it up to his mouth. "Thank you, Laken. That was wonderful."

Then he tucked it under his arm to clap his hands. Applause roared out from the audience. I smiled shyly at him before hurrying back to the steps. Flustered, I couldn't wait to get as far away from the gazebo as possible.

My thoughts lingered on the applauding crowd as I started to rush down the stairs. Unfortunately, I wasn't nearly as careful as I had been going up the same steps minutes ago. I misjudged the second one and tripped on my own two feet. As I felt myself falling forward, I reached for the only thing I saw in front of me, two strong arms. I grabbed a hold of the stranger as his hands clasped around my waist to steady me back onto my feet.

Neither one of us let go as I stepped down off the last wooden stair and stood firmly in the grass. It wasn't until that moment that I looked up at the handsome stranger who had come to my rescue. And I knew exactly who he was by his light blue shirt.

"Whoa. Careful," he said quietly, his warm brown eyes studying me. "Are you okay?"

"Um, yes, I think so. I—uh—just wanted to get out of the spotlight up there. It's really not my thing," I rambled on nervously.

His hands hadn't moved from my waist and I was suddenly very aware of his touch. When I looked up at him, our eyes met.

"Even so, you don't need to break your neck getting away. I'm Noah, by the way."

After what seemed like forever, he dropped his hands away from me. I let go of his arms, but as I did, a fleeting moment of disappointment washed over me. That was the most exciting guy moment that had ever happened to me.

"I know. I saw you from across the lawn earlier. I'm Laken, but everyone pretty much knows that now."

"Yes. It's very nice to meet you. I was wondering when I was going to get to meet the sheriff's daughter, even before you found Ryder. I saw your picture on your dad's desk at the station," he admitted with a grin.

I felt a blush creeping over my cheeks. "I bet you didn't expect I would fall into you like that," I joked.

"No, I certainly didn't." He flashed another smile and I thought I saw a subtle blush on his face for just a moment. "I guess I was in the right place at the right time."

I caught his gaze and, for a split second, noticed a flirtatious spark. Or was it my imagination?

"I mean, we can't have the girl who rescued a three-year-old boy breaking her legs during a ceremony to thank her," he explained.

"Unfortunately, that would be just my luck. Then I'd never get rid of the reporters. Speaking of which, you haven't seen any here today, have you?"

Noah turned and pointed across the lawn. "They showed up just as the mayor started. Don't worry, your dad already asked me to keep them away from you."

"Good," I said, relieved.

"So, you really meant what you said a few minutes ago?"

"What's that?" I suddenly had no idea what he was talking about as I looked up at him again. I was having a hard time focusing on this conversation.

"That you don't enjoy the spotlight."

"Oh, that. Yes, I meant it."

"Well, I don't think you got that from your father." Noah nodded toward the gazebo where my father had taken the microphone from the mayor as I was falling down the stairs. He had been up there this whole time talking about Deputy McKay's retirement. I turned to see him out of the corner of my eye as he mentioned Noah.

Noah rolled his eyes. "That's my cue. My turn for the spotlight."

"You'd better get up there, then. You can't keep everyone waiting."

"I know." He started to head up the steps, but hesitated, gently touching my shoulder. "I'll see you soon?"

I met his questioning gaze. "It's a small town. We'll see each other again. Now go. Everyone's waiting for you."

He flashed a smile before turning back to the gazebo and racing up the steps to the platform.

I tried to keep my cool as I crossed the lawn. Brooke met me halfway back to the blanket. "If he had caught me in his arms like that, I'd be smiling too," she chided.

I felt a blush race across my face. "Is it that obvious?"

"Yes, but only because I know you too well."

"Okay, guilty as charged. You were right, he is hot. But he works for my dad, so it's not like anything can happen."

We walked together across the lawn in a direct path to the blanket where Ethan waited. "Why not? He's probably only a year or two older than us," Brooke countered. "Besides, you can go out with anyone you want after you turn eighteen next month."

"Maybe, but I doubt my dad would allow it."

"Are you kidding? Who do you think he'll trust more, his deputy or some punk from school? But you know your dad would be the least of your problems. I think Marlena would have your head on a platter."

"Why? What do you mean? Where is she, anyway?" I stopped and scanned the crowd, but I didn't see Marlena before turning my attention back to the direction we were headed.

"Right now? Not sure. But she saw you and Noah together. And if looks could kill, we'd be picking out your casket right now."

I stopped again. "Really?" I asked. "Why would she care who I talk to? She's gorgeous. No guy can resist her."

"Oh, please," Brooke groaned. "She may be gorgeous, but so are you. And you are something she is not. Nice. Someday, guys are going to see that her beauty is only skin deep."

"You really think I can compete with her?"

"You obviously haven't looked in the mirror lately." Brooke grabbed my hand, turning and pulling me with her toward Ethan. "Now, come on. You guys are coming over tonight for pizza and movies."

We had gotten close enough to Ethan who heard her. "Pizza?" he asked, his attention suddenly focused on us.

Brooke laughed. "You just ate like three sandwiches and all you can think about is pizza?"

"I'm a growing boy. I can eat around the clock," Ethan responded matter-of-factly.

I smiled at them. They always knew how to take my mind off my worries. Ethan stood as he and Brooke started packing up the picnic items. "Think fast, blondie," Brooke said, tossing my sunglasses to me as soon as I looked her way.

I caught them and slipped them on. "Thanks."

Ethan stood up, holding the basket in one hand and the cooler in the other like they weighed nothing, while Brooke folded up the blanket.

"Let's go," Brooke said, taking the lead.

I suddenly remembered the reporters. "Can we take the

long way around? I saw some TV cameras over there at the entrance to the parking lot."

"Sure." She changed direction to lead us through the trees surrounding the lawn.

I followed behind them, reminding myself to call my mother and let her know I was going home with Brooke so she wouldn't wonder where I was. I stole one last glance off to the side to catch a glimpse of Noah beyond the trees. He stood in front of the gazebo next to my father greeting some of our town's citizens. I sighed, wondering if Brooke was right, that I could be competition for Marlena. If she was, life was about to get a lot more interesting. Maybe this town gathering had been worth getting up in front of a crowd after all. With that thought, I smiled to myself as I jogged to catch up with Brooke and Ethan.

❧❧❧

I didn't have long to wait before I saw Noah again. I only wished I had a warning before our next encounter. I spent the next day in the woods with Dakota and the book I had been reading the afternoon Ryder had disappeared. When I returned home that evening, my parents had a surprise dinner guest waiting for me.

At first, it seemed like every other evening. I approached the house from the backyard and came in through the door to the kitchen. My mother was in the midst of tossing a garden salad. "There you are," she said. "I was beginning to wonder when you'd get home."

"You weren't worried, were you?"

"Always," she said seriously. Then she smiled. "But I'm sure you were with Dakota, so no, I wasn't really worried."

Before I could respond, I heard two male voices in our family room. "Mom, do we have company?"

"Yes, actually, Noah is joining us for dinner tonight."

I gasped. "What? Really? Why didn't you tell me?"

"We only just decided to have him over a few hours ago, and you, my dear, were out in the woods. We didn't think you would mind…"

My mother's voice faded as I turned and rushed up the stairs. There wasn't enough time to shower, so I wiped my face and arms with a damp cloth. I exchanged my dusty hiking jeans and T-shirt for clean skinny jeans and a black shirt with three buttons down the front. All I had time for with my hair was to pull it out of my ponytail and run a brush through it. Then I added some eyeliner, slipped on silver hoop earrings, and spritzed a dash of perfume on my wrists before hurrying back downstairs.

"Okay," I told my mom. "I'm ready now."

"That was fast," she said, grinning. She had finished with the salad and was setting glasses next to a pitcher of lemonade on a tray. "Your dad and Noah are out on the patio. Would you take this out to them?"

"Of course."

I picked up the tray, carefully balancing it. My mother held the back door open for me as I slipped outside onto the patio.

Noah and my father stood beside the grill. They looked over at me as I placed the tray on the table. Noah caught my eye and smiled, causing me to nearly lose my balance. It was a good thing I had already set the tray down, or the pitcher and glasses surely would have fallen.

"Laken, I believe you met Noah yesterday. I don't know if Mom told you, but he's going to stay for dinner," my father said.

"Yes, we met yesterday and Mom filled me in a few minutes ago. Hi, Noah."

"Hi, Laken. It's good to see you again," Noah said.

All I could think about was that fateful moment yesterday when he had caught my fall. I could almost feel his strong arms where I had touched him, and I vividly remembered how his hands had felt around my waist.

"Yes, you too," I replied politely, trying to push the

memory of yesterday out of my mind at once. "Would you like some lemonade?"

"I'd love some."

As I poured two glasses, my father turned his attention back to Noah. "I need to get a few things inside. I'll be back in a couple minutes. Noah, can you keep an eye on the grill?"

"No problem." After my father disappeared into the house, Noah smiled at me. "So how is it being a small town sheriff's daughter?" he asked as I handed him his glass of lemonade.

"Considering I don't know anything else, it's fine." I sipped my lemonade as I walked around the table to sit on the steps leading down to the grass. I always preferred to sit there rather than at the table because it was closer to Dakota while he was out in the yard. Even now, when he wasn't around, I sat there without thinking.

Noah joined me, sitting so close that our shoulders almost touched.

"The town seems like a very close-knit community. I like that. I'm from a big city where you can get lost in the crowd," he explained.

"Really? Where's that?"

"Pittsburgh."

"I would welcome a big city right about now. Getting lost in the crowd would be great after yesterday." I looked at him, meeting his steady gaze.

Noah raised his hand, gently brushing his fingers along the side of my face where I had hit my head the other night in the forest. All that remained was a faint bruise, and in a few more days, even that would be gone. "What happened here?"

"I fell the night I found Ryder. I've done a lot of hiking in these mountains, but only during the day. It turns out that it's a much more dangerous place in the dark."

He laughed softly, pulling his hand back. "I'm sure it is."

"And you saw first-hand how coordinated I am during

the day. It's a wonder I got Ryder home safely without killing both of us."

Noah's expression suddenly turned serious. "How did you find him? All I heard was that you have some pet stray dog that led you to him. Is that how it really happened?"

I shrugged and looked away. I hated lying to him, but I had no choice. "Pretty much."

"So where is this hero dog of yours?"

"He's not really mine. He's just a stray I befriended. I leave food out for him and he trusts me, but he's very shy and terrified of everyone else." I gazed straight ahead, focusing on the trees and the setting sun. The crickets were starting to chirp again tonight since it had warmed up. I listened to them for a moment, not knowing what else to say. Finally, I changed the subject. "So you're from Pittsburgh? Is this your first time living in New Hampshire?"

"Yeah. I just moved here this summer."

"Do you have any family or friends here?"

"No. I moved here for the job. And I wanted to get away."

"Well, you're definitely away. There isn't much to do around here."

"That's good. I wanted a change of pace. It seems really peaceful here. Not at all like where I lived in Pittsburgh."

"You do realize you moved to the middle of nowhere, don't you?" I laughed softly. "Sorry. Most of the kids at school can't wait to move away. And you're probably close to our age. I can't imagine anyone wanting to move here." *Except that I don't want to leave,* I added to myself, realizing the irony. All of my classmates couldn't wait to go to college somewhere far away, and I dreaded the day I would have to. But it was only because of Dakota.

"Don't think I've completely lost my mind. I'm writing a novel. I needed a little space and quiet time."

"You'll get lots of that here. What's it about?"

He looked away, scanning the trees at the edge of the yard. "It's kind of hard to explain. It's horror, like a Stephen

King novel. I figured he lives in Maine and all his stories are set there, so when I found this job, I decided to take it right away."

"So you're the next Stephen King. Remind me to get an autograph so I can say I knew you when," I said.

"Nope. No autographs, at least not until I publish my first book. I don't believe in jumping the gun like that."

I nodded. "I guess I can't argue with that. Is your story set around here?"

He had just opened his mouth to respond when I smelled something burning. I glanced over at the grill to see smoke billowing out from under the cover. Noah also noticed it and immediately jumped to his feet. He rushed over and opened it, ducking as smoke burst out at him. Once the air had cleared, he straightened and flipped the burgers. "Looks like they're a little on the well-done side, but I think they can be saved," he said as he glanced at me with a hint of mischief in his eyes. "It's a good thing, too. The last thing I need is to have to tell your dad I ruined our dinner because you were distracting me too much."

I smiled as I rose to my feet and walked over to him. "Then I guess we won't tell him."

"Tell me what?" My father emerged from the back door with a tray of buns and condiments.

"That I never should have been trusted to watch the grill," Noah said smoothly, not missing a beat. "Sorry, sir, but I guess I lost track of time."

My father set his tray on the table and approached the grill. "They don't look too bad. Well-done, maybe." He flipped the burgers as though he had done it hundreds of times. Then he focused on me. "Laken, you'll need to run in and grab a veggie burger or two. It's about time to get those started. I forgot to get them when I was in the kitchen."

"Okay." I cast a shy glance at Noah as I headed toward the back door. He smiled softly, as if we shared a secret that my father was completely unaware of. I smiled back for just a second before I turned and reached for the door handle.

As I stepped inside the house, I heard my father say, "Ever work a grill before? There's nothing better than an outside barbeque around here in the summer."

His voice faded as I shut the door behind me. I took a deep breath as I leaned my back against it. I could only imagine the goofy smile that was plastered on my face. At least my mother was nowhere in sight to see it. *Get a hold of yourself,* I thought. *He's so cute and so nice. How did this happen? Nothing this exciting ever happens around here! But Mom and Dad are having this dinner, so take it easy. It's no big deal.* Even as I told myself that, I knew I would be nervous for the rest of the night. I wasn't sure how, but I needed to pull myself together and act like our dinner guest was nothing more than one of my parents' boring friends who had eaten dinner with us on many occasions.

My thoughts were interrupted when my mother appeared from around the corner, her blue jeans and knit shirt exchanged for khaki capris and a white blouse. She grabbed the wooden salad bowl to carry it outside. "Are we almost ready?"

I nodded. "Dad just sent me in here to get my veggie burger." I passed her as I walked across the kitchen and opened the freezer to look for the package.

"Sounds good. I'll meet you outside."

"I'll be right there." I plucked the box of garden burgers from the middle shelf, shut the door, and turned to head back outside. I was determined to enjoy the evening with Noah, but more importantly, to not let my parents notice that I liked him, probably more than I should.

Chapter 5

Hardly a moment passed after our dinner with Noah that I didn't think about him. I tried to push him out of my thoughts, but it was useless. I spent all my free time daydreaming, including my jaunts into the woods with Dakota. Even though I kept a book with me at all times, I didn't get much reading done. My fantasies of Noah proved to be far more interesting. Unfortunately, Dakota always knew what I was thinking. He kept giving me scolding looks every time I thought of Noah.

"What?" I finally asked him one morning as I sat upon a rock, savoring the late summer sun. "If you don't like it, stop paying attention to my thoughts. I like him, and I think maybe he likes me, too. So get over it."

Without any warning, Dakota leaped toward me and knocked me off the rock, licking my face. "Okay, okay," I laughed. "I love you, too. Now stop." I kept giggling until he eased back and stood over me with a serious look in his eyes. "I get it," I said, sitting up. "You have nothing to worry about. You come first."

He huffed as though he had finally heard what he was waiting for and backed away so that I could stand up. I made a mental note to keep my thoughts far away from Noah when Dakota was around. It simply wasn't worth the battle.

I returned to work at the pizza shop with only one week left before school started. I needed to pick up as many shifts as I could to beef up my savings. My goal this summer had been to buy a car, but I was far from having enough money saved for that. Since my mother was a school teacher and home during the summer, we had shared the Explorer for the last few months. But I had really hoped to have my own car by the time school started so that I wouldn't have to take the bus. Ethan also didn't have a car to drive to school, or I could have ridden with him. The only other option was to ride with my mother which appealed to me even less than riding the bus.

On my first day back to work, the staff greeted me with cheers and applause. The locals thanked me, reminding me that I was the town hero, or something else equally embarrassing. Fortunately, by mid-week, the hype died down and I was able to relax and get through my shifts without fielding questions about how I had found Ryder.

It wasn't until Thursday that I saw Noah again. I was cleaning up from a busy lunch shift when I saw him walk through the front glass door and sit at one of the empty tables. He was hard to miss in his deputy uniform of jeans and a light blue button-down shirt. After removing his sunglasses and placing them on the red and white checked table cloth, he looked around.

Our eyes met as I wound my way through the maze of tables, some clean and some still cluttered with empty glasses, dirty plates, and crumpled napkins from the lunch rush. I suddenly wished I had the chance to run to the bathroom to check my hair, but it was too late for that. Earlier that day, I had braided my hair in two sections that fell loosely down my back. But as the day wore on, I felt the escaped strands tickling the sides of my face. The only uniform the owner insisted on was a white polo shirt with

"Mike's Pizza" embroidered on the upper left corner. Aside from that, jeans, khakis, or shorts were allowed. I preferred blue jeans. Tied around my waist was a burgundy waitress apron with large pockets to hold a notepad, silverware, and anything else that I might need for the customers.

"Hi, Noah," I said as I reached his table. I bit back a huge grin, trying not to show how happy I was to see him.

He smiled. "Hi. I have to apologize. I've been meaning to come by all week to see you, but it's been so busy that I haven't had a chance until today. How's it going since you came back to work?"

"The first few days were a little crazy. Everyone was asking a lot of questions about Ryder, but it seems to have finally calmed down. I think people are actually starting to forget about it."

"I doubt they've forgotten."

"Okay, maybe not. But at least it's starting to be old news. They're moving on to new town gossip, like what it will be like once Deputy McKay leaves and the new deputy takes over," I teased.

He played along. "Yes, that could be scary."

"And it's only what, about two weeks away?"

"A little less than that. He's working through Labor Day weekend and then he'll be gone. I think he said something about taking a month to go fishing up at some lake in Maine."

"That doesn't surprise me. So are you ready to be on your own?"

"I won't be completely on my own. Your dad will be here. But it's not my first law enforcement job, so no one has to worry. The town will still be safe."

"That's good to know," I said with a soft laugh. As an awkward moment of silence came between us, I reached into my apron for a pen and notepad. I couldn't forget that I had a job to do. After all, he probably wasn't here just to talk. "What can I get for you?"

"I'm not sure. What's good?"

"Everything. Most people come for the pizza, but we also have salads, subs, and pasta. What are you in the mood for?"

"Nothing in particular. What's your favorite?"

"The pizza with the hand-tossed crust. I hear it's as good as pizza from New York, but I wouldn't know because I've never been there."

"Then I'll have to go with that. Two slices of pepperoni and a Coke."

I scribbled his order on my notepad as if I could forget it. "Got it. I'll get your order placed and be right back with your Coke."

"Thanks, Laken." He smiled warmly, that same smile he had flashed the other night on the patio, and my heart glowed.

I turned and approached the counter that separated the dining area from the kitchen, wondering if he was watching me. After placing his order, I poured a fountain Coke into a red plastic cup. As I slid a straw into my pocket, I looked across the room at Noah. He was the only customer in the restaurant at the moment, just the way I liked it. I started to make my way back to him with his drink, hoping that we'd have a little more time to talk. But before I reached his table, the glass door opened, signaled by the chiming bell that hung from the handle, and Marlena strutted in.

I stopped dead in my tracks, my smile quickly fading to a frown. She looked like a fashion model in her designer jeans and tall black boots. A tight red sweater outlined her perfect curves, leaving nothing to the imagination. Her platinum blonde hair cascaded down her back in perfect curls, not a hair out of place. Determination was set deep in her blue eyes as she walked directly over to Noah. I had no doubt that he was the only reason she was here.

"Hi, Noah," she said, her red painted lips curling into a flirty smile. She sat down beside him without waiting for an invitation. "You've been a difficult man to find this week. Where have you been hiding?"

Noah rolled his eyes, looking annoyed. "Hello, Marlena. I've been around. Perhaps you weren't looking hard enough." He avoided her gaze, his eyes wandering to me.

Suppressing a big smile, I started walking toward him again. As I reached the table and set his Coke down in front of him, Marlena responded, "Oh, I wasn't looking. I figured I'd run into you sooner or later." A lock of her long hair fell over her shoulder as she leaned in his direction. She casually flipped it behind her.

"Thank you, Laken," Noah said, ignoring Marlena.

"You're welcome. Marlena, can I get you something?" I asked politely.

Without as much as a glance my way, she answered, "Diet Coke, with lemon." Her eyes never left Noah.

"No problem. I'll be right back," I said. Before I turned to head back to the kitchen for her drink, I glanced at Noah. "Sorry," slipped silently from my mouth.

As I left their table, I could only imagine what was happening between them. Marlena knew what she wanted, and when she had her sights set on a guy, he never stood a chance. Hopefully, Noah would hold his own with her.

As I filled another red plastic cup with Diet Coke from the soda machine, Mike, the owner and pizza chef, slid a plate along the chrome counter. "Pizza's up, Laken. Two slices of pepperoni for our new deputy."

"Thanks, Mike."

He flashed a smile beneath his dark mustache. "Make sure you treat him well. I want him to become a regular."

"Me, too." I grabbed the plate in one hand, the Diet Coke now adorned with a lemon slice in the other, and carried them back to Noah and Marlena.

As I approached the table and set the plate and soda down, Noah's phone buzzed. He pulled it out of his shirt pocket and glanced at the screen. Immediately, his expression darkened. He stared at it for a few moments, his eyes somber. After sliding it back into his pocket, he looked at me. "I have to go."

"Really?" I asked. "Do you want me to box up your piz-za?"

"There's no time," he said as he stood up, reaching into his back pocket for his wallet.

Marlena watched incredulously. "Noah, I can bring it by the station for you. It would be no trouble," she offered, her voice so sugary sweet that it made my stomach turn.

Noah pulled a twenty-dollar bill out of his wallet. "Don't bother. I just lost my appetite. Besides, I've got to handle something with the sheriff and there isn't time to eat. Laken, I hope this will cover the pizza and my drink." He dropped the money on the table.

"That's too much," I said. I caught his gaze for a moment, suddenly worried that something was terribly wrong. The pizza and the money seemed to be the farthest things from his mind right now. "Tell you what. I'll box up your pizza and bring it home with your change tonight. You can pick them up later or my dad can take them to the station tomorrow."

He forced a weak smile. "I'll take you up on that for the pizza, but not the money. Keep the change. I'll see you soon." He reached for his sunglasses, putting them on as he hurried toward the door.

Marlena and I watched in silence as he disappeared out the door. We were both shocked. But while I wondered what had happened to change his mood so quickly, Marlena seemed angry more than curious, as if she had been stood up.

"I wonder what that's all about," I mused, not expecting the wrath that was about to be unleashed upon me. Shrugging, I reached for the plate of pizza and the money.

"Well, well," Marlena said sarcastically as she focused her stone cold gaze on me. "I hope you're happy."

"What's that supposed to mean?"

"Oh, come on, Laken. I see what's happening here. You like him. Admit it."

"I don't have to admit anything to you." I started to turn away, but stopped when she continued.

"You may think you're the shit around here now after saving that little boy, but in a few more days, no one will even remember your name. Don't fool yourself, Laken. He's way out of your league," she warned.

I took a deep breath and glared at her. "You must feel threatened, or you wouldn't waste your time talking to me. That's actually a compliment, Marlena." A smile crept onto my face, sparking a raging storm in her eyes as though I had thrown gasoline on a fire.

"Don't underestimate me. If I don't get what I want, I can have your dad fired in a heartbeat. And you know you'll never be able to live with yourself if you let that happen."

"Oh, please. My father's been with the town police department longer than you've been alive. He is respected and trusted by everyone who lives in this town. You don't scare me, Marlena." Wanting to have the last word, I started to turn, intending to return to the kitchen.

Marlena jumped to her feet, her chair scraping the floor. She quickly pushed her way around the table to block my path. We were the same height and stood facing each other eye to eye. "We're not done here."

I raised my eyebrows. "We're not?"

"Stay away from Noah, and there won't be any trouble. Got it?"

"What if he doesn't want to stay away from me?"

She paused. "I'll take care of that. He won't remember you exist once I get a little more time with him."

"Like just now? He seemed to talk to me more than you." I felt a pang of satisfaction and, for a moment, I thought smoke would puff out of her ears by the fury that raced across her face. "You're actually worried that I'm competition. He's not some kind of property you can buy, you know. He's capable of deciding who he wants to spend time with. And you're afraid that he'll pick me over you? Thank you. I'm extremely flattered."

"You bitch," Marlena fumed.

I stepped back, wondering if she was about to take a swing at me.

Mike suddenly appeared behind Marlena. He wasn't very tall, but his bulk made up for it. He was stocky and powerful, and I could tell by his expression that he wasn't amused. "Is there a problem here, ladies?"

Marlena narrowed her eyes at me before turning around to Mike. Her anger instantly folded into feigned innocence. "No, sir," she replied, smiling. "I was just leaving."

She waltzed back to the table, took one last sip of her Diet Coke, and stormed out of the restaurant, not bothering to leave any money for her drink.

"You okay?" Mike asked me.

At that moment, I noticed how fast my heart was pounding. It had probably been beating out of control this whole time, but I had been too busy concentrating on defending myself to notice. "Yeah. I can't believe I just stood up to her."

Mike smiled like a proud father. "Me, neither. We don't need the likes of her in here if she's going to treat my staff like that. Not to mention not pay for her drink. Don't ring up her soda. I don't want that coming out of your tips."

"Thanks, Mike."

"No problem. I'm proud of you for not backing down. You done good, girl." He winked before heading back to the kitchen.

I stood in place for a minute as my heart rate returned to normal. I still couldn't believe what had happened. My confidence surprised me.

I wondered what Marlena was thinking right now. She was probably as shocked as I was that I had the nerve to stand up to her.

"Hey, Laken!" Mike shouted across the restaurant. "Your dad's on the phone."

My attention returned to the pizza I was still holding as I realized I hadn't even heard the phone ring. I hurried over to the kitchen, set the plate on the counter, and rushed over to the phone next to the register. "Dad?"

"Laken, I'm looking for Noah. He left here about an hour ago to visit you and get a late lunch. Have you seen him?"

"Yeah. He was just here. But he got a text from you and then rushed out the door. He should be at the station by now."

"I'm not at the station." Sirens sounded in the distance on the other end of the phone. "Oh, there he is. Never mind. I've got to go."

"Dad, what's going on?"

"I can't talk now, Laken. I'll see you at home tonight and tell you everything. I love you."

A feeling of dread washed over me. I remembered the dark worry in Noah's eyes when he had read my dad's text. Suddenly, I forgot all about my confrontation with Marlena. "I love you, too, Dad."

As I slowly hung up the phone, a sickening feeling settled in my stomach. Something was going on, and I would have to wait to find out what it was.

೧೨೧

The house was empty when I returned from my shift. I took a long hot shower, washing the greasy pizza smell out of my hair and off my skin. After brushing the tangles out of my wet hair, I slipped into a pair of blue pajama pants and a white hoodie.

Silence loomed through the house when I headed back downstairs with a book in my hand. As if a teenage vampire novel could take my mind off whatever it was my father hadn't told me. I set it down on the kitchen table and opened the refrigerator to grab a ginger ale. As I filled a glass with ice, my mother shuffled in through the door from the garage, a few shopping bags in her hands. She pulled her sunglasses off and put them with her purse on the kitchen desk built into the cabinets, her keys clanking against the countertop. "Hi, honey," she said. "How was your day at work?"

I popped open the can of soda and poured it into the glass. "Fine. I saw Noah today. He came by the pizza shop for a late lunch."

"Oh, that was nice." My mother placed her bags on the desk chair before turning back to me.

I was dying to ask if she had talked to my father in the last hour or so, but I refrained. "Did you go shopping?"

"Yes. Nancy and I went over to the outlets. I was thinking about taking you there this weekend for some new school clothes. Are you working on Sunday?"

"Not unless someone asks me to pick up their shift. I'd love to go if I don't end up working." I paused, deciding it was time to just come out with my questions. "Mom, have you talked to Dad this afternoon?"

Her expression grew somber. "Yes, about an hour ago."

"Something happened today. While Noah was at the restaurant, he got an urgent message from Dad and then he bolted without saying a word. Mom, what's going on?"

She took a deep breath. "You better sit down for this."

I sank into a chair at the kitchen table. "Okay, now you're scaring me." Nothing could have prepared me for what she was about to say.

"A couple of hikers decided to explore the back country off the trails today. They found a body."

"What?" I wasn't sure that I had heard her correctly. It sounded like she said a body had been found in the mountains that we called home. As far as I knew, that had never happened here, at least not in my lifetime.

"And that's not all."

I cringed, not sure I wanted to know anything more at this point. "There's more?"

"A little boy's shoe was found near the body."

"Ryder," I whispered.

She nodded. "It looks like Ryder didn't wander off, after all. It looks like he was taken."

It made perfect sense. I knew a little boy, just barely three years old, could never have walked that far up the mountain by himself. Not to mention that his mother was certain she had left him in a secured backyard with a locked gate.

But with those answers came more questions. I frowned, thinking about what this meant. "Why would anyone take a little boy out of his own backyard? Does Dad know who this guy is? Is he from town? It was a guy, right? How did he die?"

My mother shook her head. "Slow down, Laken. You're asking too many questions, and I don't have any answers. Your dad only had a few minutes to let me know what was happening. I don't think he knew much yet."

"He'll know more by the time he gets home, right?"

"I'm sure he'll have some answers, but it may take a while for them to unravel all of the details of what happened."

An unsettled feeling washed over me. "Oh."

"Well, I'm going to put my things away. You're not the only one starting school next week," my mother said. Even though she changed the subject, I could tell she was still thinking about the body that had been found today. She picked up her bags and started to leave the kitchen, but stopped and turned. "What are you in the mood to have for dinner tonight?"

"I'm not sure. I'll just make my own dinner when I get hungry."

Acknowledging my answer with a nod, she disappeared around the corner.

I twirled my glass, clanking the ice against the sides, and sipped the remaining soda. After finishing it, I grabbed my book and headed upstairs to my room to wait for my father to return home, hopefully with answers to at least some of my questions.

⍥⍥⍥

I often spent long hours in the comfort of my bedroom, and this afternoon was no exception. My bedroom and bathroom were the only rooms on our second floor, giving me the privacy most teenagers only dreamed of. I had selected the oak furniture, pale purple comforter set with matching curtains, and the silvery gray paint for the walls. The hardwood floors surrounding the huge white throw rug under my full-sized bed were scuffed enough to give a distressed look. Some people paid good money for that look, but my floors looked like that from years of old-fashioned wear and tear. Over my headboard hung a large white-framed print of a gray wolf standing ankle-deep in the snow as fluffy flakes fell from the Rocky Mountain sky. Framed photographs that I had taken of moose, bears, foxes, and owls lined the other two walls. My desk sat facing the only window in my bedroom so that I could glance out into the backyard as I did my homework. I loved gazing outside as I sat at my desk, but it often backfired. The mesmerizing snowflakes drifting down from a winter sky were enough to cause me to forget whether I was trying to solve Algebra problems or write an essay.

I spent the afternoon in my room trying to read with little success. The text messages coming in on my phone were distracting. One from Ethan and another from Brooke, both asking the same question. Had I heard that a body had been found in the woods today? News like that spread like wildfire in our town. I didn't answer either one of them. I was certain that as soon as I did, they would fire back with the same questions I had asked earlier and still had no answers to. As much as I loved both of them, I needed a little time to process this. It hit too close to home in so many ways. I felt like I was at the center of this since I was the daughter of the town sheriff and I had been the one to find Ryder.

A soft knock sounded on my bedroom door. Tossing my

phone aside, I propped myself up against the purple pillows that matched my comforter. "Come in," I called.

My father stepped into my room, his hair disheveled once again and his eyes worried. He sat down in the wooden chair at my desk, facing the backside and resting his arms on it. He sighed as I met his uneasy brown eyes. "Your mother said she told you what happened today."

"Yes, she did. But she didn't have any details. Do you know who it was?"

"No. He wasn't from around here. He had an ID on him, so we now know he was from a pretty rough part of Boston. We think he took Ryder last week because a little boy's shoe was found about thirty feet away from him. Of course, we can't be sure until we check with the Thompsons, but I can't imagine that it isn't his."

Fear raced through me. I had really hoped that I was wrong and that Ryder had just wandered off like my father originally thought. Knowing Ryder had been taken chilled me to the core. "Why would someone take a child out his backyard?"

"I have no idea. I think that's the worst part of this whole thing. Frankly, it makes me sick. Children should be safe in their own backyards, and in this town, they always have been. At least until now."

My father had addressed all of my questions except for one. "How did the guy die?"

"We can't be sure until the coroner finishes with him, but it looked like he fell down a ravine and hit his head on a rock."

"Wow. Really? He must have been even clumsier than me."

As if it was even possible, my father's frown deepened and his voice grew more serious. "I don't think he just suddenly tripped and fell, Laken. I think he fell because he was chased."

"Chased? By who?"

"You tell me. He had bite marks on his forearms. They

were about the size of a wolf bite. Do you think Dakota did this?"

"What? I don't know. Maybe, if he was trying to protect me or Ryder. But he was with me all night. He ran ahead a few times, but I don't think he had enough time to chase this guy down in the few minutes he was out of sight. Unless it happened after I got home with Ryder."

My father ran his hands through his hair. I could tell that this weighed heavily on his mind. "I have mixed feelings about this. First off, all I can think of is that this guy was out there that night while you were traipsing through the mountains, alone."

"I wasn't alone. Dakota was with me." And an owl, a black bear, and possibly other animals.

"What if this guy had a gun? Dakota wouldn't have been able to protect you."

"Did he?"

"No, at least not as far as we can tell. We searched the area and didn't find any weapons. But that doesn't make me feel any better. Laken, what you did that night was far more dangerous than I first realized."

I nodded in understanding. "I guess I didn't think about anything other than getting Ryder home safely. I didn't see any signs of another person where I found him." Except for the fire pit, but it had been cold and dry to the touch.

"Where did you find him? Could you take me there?"

Pursing my lips in thought, I slid my gaze away from his questioning eyes and stared at one of my photographs on the wall, studying the black bear that stood amongst the green ferns on the forest floor. It immediately reminded me of the bear who had kept Ryder warm until I could get to him. "I don't think so," I said.

"What if I take you to where the body was found? Maybe you'll remember it."

"It was really dark. I don't know that I'll recognize anything." *Unless Dakota comes with us. He would take me back there if I asked him to, but how am I going to tell my father that Dakota understands every word I say?* I just wanted to push the whole thing out of my mind. Pretend it had never happened. But unfortunately, it had and there was no way to erase it.

"Okay. I'm not going to force you. There's not really anything left to solve aside from his motive and I doubt we'll learn anything by dragging you back to the scene of the crime. But we have another problem. A wolf problem. Once the town realizes that an animal bit this guy, and believe me, they will find out once the coroner's report is released, people are going to worry that this animal will attack an innocent person next. I don't know what we're going to do with Dakota once that happens."

I shot up away from the pillows I had been leaning against, not quite sure what he meant. But I knew I didn't like the sound of it. "What does that mean? Dakota's not a threat to anyone. He's lived here for five years. Five years, and he has never caused any trouble. Besides, I really don't think he did this."

My father sighed as he rose to his feet. "Well, let's just hope this blows over fast. Please be extra careful with him for a while. I know how much he means to you and I don't want anything to happen to him. I know he's been keeping his distance lately, so just see to it that he's extra vigilant for now. This would not be a good time for anyone around here to find out we have a wolf."

"Okay. I'll make sure he stays away," I said earnestly.

My father offered a faint smile. "Good. I knew you'd understand. Your mom and I are going out for a walk. Will you be okay here alone for a while?"

"Yes, of course. I'll be fine. While all of this is unsettling, I still feel safe." As I said it, I suddenly remembered my first evening back from the hospital when Dakota had growled at something in the woods. I flashed a smile at my father, hoping that I had convinced him because I hadn't convinced myself.

"Good. Because it doesn't change anything. It was a

freak thing and I don't think it will happen again," my father said before slipping out of my room and leaving me alone. I froze for a moment as I turned my attention to Dakota's extra-large dog bed on the floor next to the wall. It normally bore an impression from his hundred-pound frame, but right now, it was soft and fluffy from not being used. It had been over a week since Dakota had slept on it. I suddenly felt more alone than I had in five years. The silence and emptiness was overwhelming.

I jumped up from the bed, rushed out of my room, down the stairs, and out the back door to the patio. The sun had dropped below the mountains, darkening the sky to a hazy purple. A gentle breeze whispered through the leafy trees. The crickets were hiding from the cool temperatures again, and it was quite possible that we had heard the last of them now that the cool fall nights were right around the corner.

I scanned the shadows buried within the woods, looking for any movement, hoping to find Dakota. "Dakota!" I called. "Here, boy!" But there was no sign of him. I stood on the edge of the patio, not ready to give up. "Please come here, Dakota. I just need to know that you're out there."

A movement deep within the trees caught my eye. As I glimpsed a smoky black shadow and amber eyes, relief washed over me. He was still out there, watching over me. But as quickly as I saw him, he took off, disappearing into the woods without a single sound.

"I thought I would find you out here," a familiar voice said from the edge of the yard.

I gasped as I turned to see Noah walking through the grass from around the side of the house. His sudden appearance explained why Dakota had taken off like he had.

I sighed, managing a weak smile. Forgetting about Dakota, I raised a hand to tuck my loose hair behind my ear, at once feeling self-conscious in my pajama pants. Noah still wore the jeans and light blue shirt he'd had on earlier, but he looked tired from the day's events, so maybe he wouldn't care. "Hi."

"I rang the doorbell, but no one answered. I thought I'd see if anyone was out back. Were you talking to someone?"

I felt a blush creep along my cheeks, but it was getting dark, so hopefully he couldn't see it. "Stray dog."

"Was he here? Did I scare him away?"

"I thought I saw him in the woods, and yes, he bolted just before you walked around the house."

"Sorry about that."

"That's okay. He'll be back."

"Well, I won't stay long." Noah walked up the patio steps and stopped beside me as he held out a large letter-sized envelope. "I was just bringing your dad a report from the Boston PD about our friend from the woods."

"Mom and Dad went out for a walk, but they should be back soon. You can wait or leave it with me and I'll give it to him." I really hoped he would choose to wait. I didn't want to be alone right now.

He must have read my mind. "I'll wait. So how are you handling all of this?"

I looked up at him to meet the concerned look in his eyes. "It's a lot to process right now. I've lived here my whole life and nothing like this has ever happened. I keep wondering, if this guy really did take Ryder, which seems pretty likely, why did he do it? What was his motive?"

"I don't know. I wish I had the answers, Laken."

"The only thing I can think of was that he was going to hold Ryder for ransom, but there's no way he could have thought he'd get a huge payout from it. The Thompson's aren't rich. Anyone can see that. So if it wasn't money, then what did he want? What if he planned to abuse him or kill him? What if he planned to keep him?" I shivered, thinking of all the sickening possibilities, and gazed at Noah, wishing he had the answers.

He reached his free arm out around my shoulders, pulling me against him. With a heavy sigh, I rested my cheek against his chest as he rubbed my back.

"I've always felt safe in this town until now," I admitted.

It felt good to open up to someone. I knew I couldn't tell my parents how nervous I was. They would just worry about me.

"You're still safe. He's dead and, from all we can see, he worked this alone. It was a one in a million freak thing. Like you said, nothing like this has ever happened here before and, more than likely, nothing like this will ever happen here again."

I breathed deeply, feeling a little better from his reassurance. As my fears subsided, I became aware of his hand rubbing my back, moving up my sweatshirt to massage my shoulders. His touch felt nice, but it also made me nervous in a good way.

He seemed to sense my tension. "If there's anything I can do to make you feel better, let me know."

I pulled away from him, a soft smile tugging at my lips. "Thanks. Do you want to come inside while you wait for my dad?"

"Sure."

"Your pizza is in the fridge. I can heat it up for you if you're hungry."

He smiled. "That would be great. I'm starving."

As I met his gaze, my heart skipped a beat. "Follow me." Then I turned and led him across the patio and through the back door to the kitchen, leaving the dark night and my dark thoughts outside.

$\mathcal{C}hapter\ 6$

I rarely saw my father over the next few days as he worked to learn more about the body found in the woods. Most of his initial suspicions were confirmed. As if there had been any doubt, the toddler shoe found near the body was confirmed to be Ryder's missing shoe. The guy had died from blunt trauma to the head, and the bite marks on his arm were blamed on a large dog. My father also visited the Thompsons again to ask if they had noticed any signs of abuse on Ryder. Between what they told him and the hospital records, there was no indication that he'd been hurt that night. It was a relief, although I still couldn't shake the unsettled feeling that our town was no longer safe.

Monday was the first day of school. After showering that morning, I slipped into the new jeans I had picked up at the outlets with my mother on Sunday, tall black boots, and a white tank top. A lightweight matching sweater completed my ensemble. I curled my hair, applied a touch of make-up, and finished with a silver necklace and hoop earrings. Sighing, I paused to gaze at my reflection in the bathroom mirror. I dreaded returning to school after being the center of attention at the town gathering and defending myself from

Marlena at the pizza shop. Hopefully, the ceremony had been long forgotten by my fellow students, but there was no way Marlena would have already forgotten our confrontation.

"Laken!" my mother called down the hallway from the top of the stairs. "Are you ready? We have to go. Ethan's waiting downstairs."

My mother and I had reached a compromise on our daily transportation for the school year. I could drive, but I had to drop her off at the elementary school first. It meant leaving thirty minutes earlier than I really needed to, but the early departure was a small price to pay if it meant I didn't have to ride the bus. And Ethan had jumped at the chance to ride with us, even though he, too, would lose a half hour of sleep.

"Coming!" I rushed into my bedroom to grab my book bag. Then I hurried into the hallway and followed my mother down the stairs. She had spent the summer in casual jeans and capris. It was odd to see her wearing a navy dress with matching high heels, her hair pulled up into a twist.

Ethan was waiting in the kitchen, a denim jacket over his shoulders and his backpack hanging behind him. "Morning," he said, smiling. "Ready to be seniors?"

"Sure. It had to happen sooner or later."

He playfully touched my shoulder. "Don't sound so excited. It's going to be a great year. I can feel it."

"I wish I had your confidence," I said honestly.

My mom waved us toward her with one hand, her keys and a coffee thermos in the other. "Come on, you two. You can talk in the car. Let's go." Then she disappeared through the side door to the garage.

Ethan looked at me knowingly. "After you. We can talk more about the awesome year we're going to have after we drop your mom off."

I rolled my eyes at him before following my mother into the garage. Morning sunlight filled the dark enclave through the open door.

She tossed her keys to me. "You're up, Laken."

After we piled into the Explorer, I drove to town. My mom chatted with Ethan about the upcoming school year during the five minutes it took to reach the elementary school. When I pulled into the parking lot of the one-story brick building, only a few cars and teachers had arrived. The school buses wouldn't pull in until later, and I was grateful I didn't have to dodge them and the young children.

As soon as the SUV stopped, my mother climbed out with her purse, school bag, and coffee. "I'll see you both this afternoon. Have a great day."

"Thanks, Mom. You, too."

Ethan took the front seat and, as soon as he clicked his seatbelt into place, I eased the Explorer out of the parking lot. We passed through rows of two-story buildings that made up the business district of our town. There was a white church, a red-brick bank, and a funeral home, not to mention several bed and breakfast inns and specialty shops. The mountains loomed beyond the buildings in every direction, topped with lush greenery that seemed to scrape the clear blue sky. Despite the beautiful morning, a sense of gloom hung in the air. The recent discovery of Ryder's abduction had cast a dark shadow over the entire town that even the brightest sunshine couldn't cut through.

"Is there any new information on that guy who took Ryder?" Ethan asked.

I glanced at him out of the corner of my eye. "Not since we last talked. I only know what I already told you. He had quite a history of stealing cars, burglary, and domestic abuse, but no kidnapping. Apparently, this was his first."

"Doesn't it seem weird to you that he would show up here out of the blue and snatch a kid?"

"Yes," I groaned, wishing we could find something else to talk about. "But you know what's even harder to believe is that the guy had his own child. I keep wondering what he could possibly have wanted with a little boy from up here." I shook my head, trying to push the thoughts of him out of my mind. "Can we please talk about something else now?"

"Sure, but don't be surprised if you get asked a lot of questions about that today."

"I won't."

"So where's Dakota been hiding out lately? I know you've been worried about him."

"I'm not really worried. I just miss him. I always feel better when he's home at night. But he can't come back for a while. Dad wants him to keep a low profile. Not that anyone would even know if he spent a night up in my room. Man, I can't wait for this whole thing to blow over and life to return to normal."

Ethan grinned at me. "Don't worry. In a few days, we'll both probably be buried in so much homework that we won't even remember it."

"How is it you always know the right way to cheer me up?" I asked sarcastically, but with a smile. The school loomed up ahead between the trees. I slowed just in time to turn into the parking lot and stopped on the far side under a huge maple tree that would provide plenty of shade by the afternoon. "The kidnapper and homework, my two favorite subjects to start the day with."

"You're right. Sorry. We can talk about Noah. I know you like him," he teased, his eyebrows raised over his curious brown eyes.

I shrugged as I shut off the engine. "There's nothing to tell. I haven't seen him since last week."

"Well, that's about to change."

I looked at him curiously. "What do you mean?"

He didn't have a chance to answer. A knock tapped on my window and I jumped, turning away from Ethan to see Noah waving at me. He stepped back as I opened the door and slid out of the Explorer. "Good morning," I said with a smile as I heard Ethan shut the passenger door. "What are you doing here?"

"I thought I would stop by to say hi before your classes begin." Noah lifted his gaze, looking beyond me.

I whipped around to see Ethan's head poking above the truck on the other side. "Noah, this is one of my friends, Ethan. Ethan, Noah."

"Hi," Noah said, sizing up Ethan.

"Morning, Deputy. Be careful with this one. She used to chase me around with snakes she found in her mother's rose garden," Ethan said, his tone half joking and half serious. I shot him a warning look. "Okay, that's my cue. Laken, I'm going to find Brooke. We'll wait for you outside."

As Ethan hoisted his book bag over his shoulder and walked away, I turned back to Noah. Butterflies danced in my stomach as he smiled at me, amused. "Snakes?" he asked, his eyebrows raised.

I felt a blush race across my cheeks. "Mostly garter snakes. And sometimes a frog. But I was like, ten years old." As he laughed, I quickly changed the subject. "Are you always up this early?"

"Yes, it's a curse. I'm a light sleeper and I get up with the sun, sometimes even earlier to work on my book." He paused, his eyes meeting mine for a moment before he continued. "I brought you something." He pulled a hand out from behind his back and held up a white carnation. "This is for you. I know it's kind of cheesy, but I thought you should have something special for today."

"No, it's not. It's very thoughtful. Thank you." As I took the flower from him, my fingers brushed against his.

"It's also a token of my regret."

I quirked my eyebrows, not understanding him. "Regret? What could you possibly regret?"

"That I haven't had a chance to stop by your house or the pizza shop in the last few days to see you. I wanted to, but this whole thing with the dead guy has kept us really busy. And it's not because we're trying to piece together what happened. The phone keeps ringing off the hook. The town residents are chomping at the bit to find out what happened."

"That's okay. I know things get really busy for my dad

around this time of year, and that's not when he's pulling bodies out of the woods."

"So I'm forgiven?"

"Of course."

"Good. I'll try not to be a stranger from now on."

"That would be nice," I replied.

He smiled, the sun reflecting in his brown eyes. "Well, I'd better let you get to class and I should be heading to the station."

I leaned against the SUV as nerves fluttered in the pit of my stomach. "Yeah. We don't want to be late."

"Especially you on your first day." He put his sunglasses on as he backed up a step. "Have a great one. I'll talk to you soon."

"You, too." I watched as he turned and walked across the parking lot to the police car. "It's already a great day," I muttered to myself, staring down at the flower in my hand. A smile lingered on my lips, and I suspected it would be there for a while.

As soon as Noah drove away, I took a deep breath, reminding myself that I would have to concentrate on my classes at some point today. *Good luck with that,* I told myself, knowing it would be a losing battle. Then I retrieved my book bag from the truck and tucked the flower safely in it before setting off to find Brooke and Ethan.

Students were starting to assemble outside the school on the lawn. The hum of chatter rang out across the yard as friends were reunited for another year. I looked around as I approached the sidewalk, searching for Marlena and her friends. I hoped she hadn't seen me talking to Noah. I didn't want this perfect morning to be ruined by her. Fortunately, she was nowhere to be seen.

Brooke and Ethan were waiting for me at a picnic table in a shady spot on the front lawn. Brooke sat on the table, her feet propped up on the bench. Her long skirt fell loosely around her booted ankles and sunglasses hid her pretty blue eyes.

Ethan sat beside her feet on the bench, a half-eaten sandwich in his hand. They both stared at me.

"What?" I asked as I placed my book bag on the table.

"You can stop smiling now. You look way too happy to be back at school." Brooke paused thoughtfully. "Wait a minute, it's not school making you smile like that, it's Noah," she teased.

I pretended to be frustrated, but I could feel my grin poking through. No amount of teasing could sour my mood. "Oh, be quiet. But look at this." I pulled the carnation out of my book bag and held it up. "He brought me a flower for the first day of school. That was so sweet."

Brooke turned to look at Ethan. "How come high school boys aren't romantic? Can you imagine a guy from school doing something like that?"

"No. We're scared to death of you girls," Ethan answered between bites. "He's obviously a little older than us, so he's had time to get over the fear."

"Oh, please, we're not that scary," Brooke retorted before turning her attention back to me. "So, Laken, while you were busy working this weekend, I went to a party at Brian's house. It was really fun. They're having a bonfire up at the old abandoned campground at Matthews Pond Friday night. Ethan has already agreed to come. You in?"

Curious, I looked at Brooke. "Really?"

I wasn't sure if I was ready to jump back into a year of parties, but I knew that Brooke wouldn't take no for an answer. She was always looking for ways to get me out, and I had to admit, I appreciated it. If it wasn't for her, I'd probably spend all my time alone or with animals. But Matthews Pond parties were a little more rowdy than some of the other ones she had taken me to. Rumor had it there was always a keg and a picnic table cluttered with bottles of tequila, whiskey, and any other alcohol the kids could get their hands on.

"Yes, really. I won't forgive you if don't come, so it's settled. You're coming."

"As long as Marlena and her friends aren't there."

Brooke knew all about my confrontation with Marlena at the pizza shop. The only way she'd let me skip the party would be if Marlena was going to be there.

"They won't be. That's not her crowd. She wasn't at last week's party. It's mostly the girls from the drill team. So it looks like you're out of excuses, my dear."

"Well, I'll have to ask my parents. I'm not sure my dad will be okay with it."

"Laken, stop," Brooke said. "We went through this last year and you actually had some fun. You're not going to hide this year. I know if you want to do something, you'll find a way around your parents. Besides, you can't tell your dad about this. He'll bust the party. You'll have to tell them you're coming to my house."

"I don't know. Ethan, are you really going, too?"

"Yes," Ethan replied earnestly. "Brooke's right. It'll be fun, you'll see. Everyone likes you. You just need to give them a chance. Besides, if you can't be brave enough to go to a party like this, what are you going to do if Noah asks you out?"

I frowned, realizing I had been wondering the same thing as he said it. "Okay," I agreed reluctantly. "But if anything goes wrong, I'm blaming both of you." I checked my watch. Five more minutes until the homeroom bell would ring. The crowd outside was thinning as students started filtering into the building to find their assigned lockers and homerooms. I reached for my book bag. "Shall we head inside?"

Brooke hopped down from the table and grabbed her tied-dyed bag. "Yeah. I'm ready."

"Ethan?" I asked. "I'm sure we're in the same homeroom again."

Ethan shoved the last bite of his sandwich into his mouth before standing up. "Yep. Let's go." He stepped into place beside Brooke as I followed behind them, my thoughts returning to Noah's visit this morning. It was a perfect start to the day, and nothing could dampen my mood, not even the idea of a wild party I would be obligated to attend on Friday.

We marched up the steps to the school doorway. As I reached the top, a cool breeze brushed a few strands of hair across my face and a shiver suddenly ran up my spine. I stopped, frozen in my tracks as the students chattering around me became a blur. Then I heard the rumble of an unfamiliar engine.

I turned just in time to see a motorcycle pull into the parking lot. The rider wore black, from his helmet and black leather jacket to his black jeans and boots. He pulled into a parking space between two pick-up trucks and leaned the bike on a kickstand before swinging his leg over the side. He looked at the school, his helmet shielding his face.

"Who—is—that?" Brooke whispered from behind me.

We watched as he pulled his helmet off. From a distance, all I could tell was that his hair was as black as his clothes and he had a gorgeous tan. He was undeniably handsome, and he looked like he didn't belong in a small New England town. As he studied the surroundings, he appeared bored and reluctant to approach the school. Students stopped on the sidewalk to stare at him. In our small town, word usually got around about new students before the first day of school. But no one seemed to know him.

"He's hot," Brooke said, peering out over the top of her sunglasses. "This year is already proving to be quite interesting." She smiled, and I could practically see the fantasies flashing across her eyes.

Ethan laughed at her. "You might want to wipe the drool off your chin."

That got her attention. She slapped him on the shoulder. "Hey! Like we all haven't seen you drooling over Sarah Waters."

"How did you know about that?" Ethan gasped.

"It's hard not to notice." As Brooke teased him, they turned toward the school, the mysterious new student forgotten.

But I found it nearly impossible to pry my gaze away from him. He looked our way, and I couldn't be sure, but it felt like he was staring directly at me. My spine tingled and my blood ran hot. The other students passed me in a blur. The only thing I could see clearly was him. But who was he?

"Laken!"

Brooke's sharp voice finally got through to me and I tore my attention away from the stranger to see her calling me from inside the school doorway.

"Are you just going to stand there, or are you coming?" Brooke asked.

I smiled sheepishly as I jogged to catch up to them. "I'm coming," I said, following them into the building.

After locating our lockers in the crowded hallway, Ethan and I separated from Brooke to find our homeroom. Because homerooms were assigned alphabetically, Brooke always ended up in a different room from us. We claimed two empty seats in the back while other students continued filing through the doorway. Ethan sat on my right, and the seat to my left remained empty.

I glanced over at him and sighed. "So what's going on with Brooke? Is she going to become a party animal this year?"

Ethan shrugged. "Probably no more than last year. You know how she likes to hang out with her friends on the drill team. I wouldn't worry about it."

"I guess you're right."

"But you are coming to the bonfire on Friday, right?"

I took a deep breath. "I don't think I have a choice. She'll never forgive me if I don't."

"She only wants you to come because she wants you to have fun, you know."

I turned away from him and gazed out the window at a church steeple rising up from between the trees in the distance. "As long as Marlena isn't there," I muttered.

As I watched the branches sway in the gentle breeze, I

saw the reflection of a dark figure in the glass. My chills returned, even more intense now. I gasped, spinning around to see the motorcycle guy heading for the empty seat beside me. My heart pounded out of control and I looked over at Ethan, hoping to engage him in an engrossing conversation that no one would dare interrupt. But I couldn't think of anything to say.

"This seat taken?" asked a deep voice to my left.

I glanced at the stranger for a split second. It was enough time to notice his blue eyes and handsome tanned features. "No. You can have it." I looked away quickly, but not before our eyes met for a moment. I swore he could hear my heart pounding.

"Thanks."

I nodded before looking straight ahead at the balding, middle-aged teacher who sat at the front desk, rifling through his papers. Out of the corner of my eye, I saw my new neighbor slip out of his leather jacket, revealing sun-kissed muscular arms below the sleeves of his tight black T-shirt. A tattoo of two daggers crossing to form an X with a diamond floating between the handles marked his upper arm just above his elbow. I tried to focus on the teacher, but all I could think about was the stranger beside me.

Ethan reached over, gently tapping my arm. I slid my eyes his way to see him mouth the words, "You okay?"

I smiled weakly and nodded, appreciating his concern. Then we both turned our attention to the teacher as he read names off the list for homeroom attendance. Before he got to us, he called a name I didn't recognize. "Alexander Payne?"

"Here," the guy sitting next to me replied in a bored voice. "And it's Xander."

The teacher peered curiously at Xander from behind his glasses. "Welcome, Xander. I hope you enjoy your senior year here."

"I'll try," he muttered, seeming relieved when the teacher moved on to the next name on the list.

I sat completely still as the seconds ticked by slowly. I couldn't wait to escape homeroom and the stranger beside me. I wasn't sure why, either. He made me nervous and it scared me. I had never felt anything like it before.

When the bell finally rang after the roll call and announcements from the principal over the intercom, I jumped up from my seat. Turning to Ethan, I explained quickly, "I'm going to find my first class. I'll see you later, okay?"

Before he could answer, I grabbed my book bag and ran out of the room and away from Xander Payne as fast as I could without knocking into the other students.

ↄ⁄ↄↄↄ

I got through the rest of the day without coming face to face with Xander until after my last class. We shared one class, History, and by the time he showed up, the only empty seat was far across the room from where I sat. I also managed to avoid Marlena who shot me dirty looks every chance she got during lunch and between classes. The one thing that made me smile all day was the memory of Noah, which vividly jumped into my thoughts every time I glimpsed the white flower in my book bag. It was already starting to wilt, but no matter how limp the petals became, it still brightened my mood.

After the final bell rang, dismissing the last class, I trudged through the crowded hall to my locker. As I focused on the numbers to find mine, someone slammed into me from behind. I stumbled forward and the books I carried in my arms went flying onto the floor. A dull pain throbbed in my back from the impact as I knelt down to retrieve my things. I frowned when a pair of tall black boots walked by. High-pitched laughter broke out in the hallway as Marlena and her friends passed me. I should have known the day wouldn't end without her finding a way to get to me. I watched as they disappeared down the hallway, several football players wearing green and gold varsity jackets following them. Relieved once they were gone, I focused on gathering my books that were now scattered all over the floor. The other students ignored me while skirting around the mess, but I didn't care. I just wanted to get my things and escape as fast as I could.

As I knelt on the cold, hard floor and reached for a book, a tanned arm extended toward it at the same time. I looked up to see Xander's blue eyes studying me. "Here. Let me help you," he offered.

I shivered nervously. Instead of ignoring him or trying to run away this time, I had no choice but to accept his help. "Thank you." I picked up the book as he turned to reach for another one.

After collecting all of my books, we stood up together. Xander held out the last one, waiting patiently while I organized the rest of them in my arms. My notebooks took up most of the room in my book bag, so I often had to carry my textbooks. Once I had stacked the books in my arms, I took the last one from him. "Thank you," I repeated, glancing shyly at him and noticing how light his blue eyes were.

"You're welcome," he said, smiling.

My breath caught as butterflies raced through me.

"I don't think we've met. I'm Xander Payne. We're in homeroom and History together."

I nodded. "I know."

"You're Laken Sumner, right? I heard about how you saved that little boy. That's pretty awesome."

I groaned inwardly. It was the first time today someone had mentioned Ryder. "Yes, that's me," I acknowledged, finally finding my voice.

"Well, it's nice to meet you. I don't really know anyone here yet."

"Then you might not want to be seen with me. It could be social suicide."

He grinned. "I'm sure that's not true."

I smiled weakly as I suddenly noticed that he seemed

older than the other seniors. A five o'clock shadow of dark hair speckled his chin, but it was his tattoo that captured my interest. I studied the intricate details of the daggers and the diamond, the lines of ink sharp and clear. I didn't know any other students who had tattoos. There was something hauntingly mature about him. "Okay, maybe not entirely. But those books didn't just fall out of my arms."

"I noticed. I wouldn't worry about those girls. You're better than them." He said it like he knew me, and yet we had just met.

Out of the corner of my eye, I saw Ethan at the end of the hallway waving for me to hurry up. I nervously glanced at my watch, noting that it was time to pick up my mother. "Excuse me, I have to go." I brushed past Xander, eager to get away from him.

"I'll see you tomorrow, Laken," he said loud enough for me to hear even as I rushed away from him.

A few seconds later when I stopped to look behind me, he had turned. All I saw was his back as he headed down the hall in the opposite direction, his black hair matching his black T-shirt and jeans.

Chapter 7

Ethan was right. By the end of the week, our teachers had dumped so much homework on us that I almost forgot about the body that had been found. I had Calculus problems to solve, an English essay to write, History chapters to read, and Physics formulas to decipher. Between my classes and homework, there was little time left for anything else.

I didn't see Xander much at school the rest of the week. A few times in homeroom or History class, our eyes met, but I looked away immediately as if his gaze burned me. I don't know why I felt compelled to stay away. Perhaps it was the unknown. He was a complete stranger and, after a stranger had taken Ryder, I wasn't comfortable with the idea of more strangers in town. He kept to himself, often appearing bored. He seemed out of place here. Other students speculated on his story, but I didn't pay much attention to the rumors.

After the final bell rang Friday afternoon, Brooke and Ethan caught up with me at my locker. As I sorted through my books, Brooke chatted excitedly. "So if you two can come over to my place around eight, we'll drive up to Matthews Pond together. I'm not sure how late we'll be at the party so, Ethan, you're spending the night on the couch. I already talked to my parents and they're cool with it." I wasn't surprised. Brooke's parents had been hippies in the seventies and they were usually cool with anything as long as it was legal.

"I suppose I'm driving to the party, too," I said.

Brooke smiled hopefully. "Yeah. My sister needs the car tonight. You're okay with that, aren't you?"

"Sure, why not? If I'm going to lie to my parents, I might as well go all out."

"Laken, stop acting like such a martyr. You're not going to lie. You're just going to leave out a few details, that's all."

I raised my eyebrows at her and Ethan as I shut my locker. "I said I'll do it."

The three of us started to head down the hallway, weaving in between the other students. We had only taken a few steps when I saw Marlena saunter up beside Xander as he shuffled through his books at his locker. Her long blonde hair swayed against her white sweater, both a sharp contrast to Xander's black shirt. I tried to look away, but Brooke also noticed her and stopped beside me. She grabbed my arm, a curious look in her eyes.

Ethan towered behind us. "What are we looking at?" he asked, unaware of the scene unfolding across the hall.

Brooke shushed him by pressing a finger to his lips and tossed a swift nod toward Marlena and Xander.

Marlena leaned against the lockers, smiling coyly at Xander. "Hi, Xander. I hope you had a good first week here."

He gave her a quick bored glance with a raised eyebrow, before looking back at his locker.

"Anyway," she continued, oblivious to his lack of interest. "I'm having a party at my house tonight and I'd love for you to come."

Xander grabbed his motorcycle helmet in one hand and

slammed his locker shut with his other. "Save your energy. I'm not interested."

Marlena's jaw dropped, her eyes flashing nervously around her to see who was watching. Students milled about between them and the three of us, so she didn't notice that she had an audience across the hall. "But it'll be fun. Really, I promise."

"Let me get something straight, Marlena," he said, glaring at her. "I'm not interested in you or your friends, so don't waste your energy on me. I see how you treat people around here. You're so caught up in yourself that you'll walk all over anyone who gets in the way of whatever you want. And that isn't something I value. So let me repeat myself. I'm not interested."

I wasn't sure who's jaw dropped lower, mine or Marlena's. Speechless, Marlena watched him walk away. Hurt and disappointment glazed over her eyes for a moment.

Brooke squeezed my arm. "OMG. I knew there was something I liked about him," she whispered.

I couldn't help smiling at her. Then I returned my gaze to Xander as he hoisted a black backpack over his shoulders. Carrying his helmet in one hand, he headed into the crowd. As he walked by us, I caught his blue eyes watching me. For just a moment, his expression softened into a faint smile. Then, without a word, he continued down the hallway, disappearing out the door with the other students.

Ethan finally brought Brooke and me back to reality. "Okay, if we're done staring here, Laken, you and I need to get going to pick up your mom. Brooke, we'll see you around eight."

With that, he grabbed my hand and pulled me away from Brooke, ushering me down the hall. Marlena still stood beside Xander's locker, a scowl on her face as she glanced at me. Looking away immediately, I felt her angry eyes watching me until Ethan and I escaped around the next corner.

∽∾∽

When I returned home, I dropped my book bag on the kitchen table and walked out onto the patio. As soon as I called for Dakota, he charged out of the woods and up the steps, nearly knocking me over when he jumped up to greet me. After he settled down, I knelt beside him and scratched the smoky black fur between his ears. He responded by licking my neck, and I grimaced, gently pushing him away. Then I smiled at him, studying his honey colored eyes.

"I know," I said. "I miss you, too. I'll talk to Dad about letting you back in the house this weekend. I know you love your freedom, but I'm getting a little lonely." Recognizing the look of understanding in his eyes, I continued. "Well, I have a party to get ready for."

He tilted his head to the side as if he hadn't heard me correctly.

"Yes, a party," I repeated. "It won't hurt me to get out a little again this year." I wasn't sure if I said it to convince Dakota or to convince myself.

With one last scratch between his ears, I stood and headed back into the house. At the door, I turned to catch one more glimpse of Dakota, but he had already disappeared into the woods without a single sound.

I retreated into the house, grabbed my book bag from the kitchen table, and hurried upstairs to my room to get ready for the party. After a hot shower, my wet hair dripped against my purple terrycloth robe as I sifted through my closet. Deciding what to wear for a party I wasn't sure I wanted to attend was harder than I had expected.

My concentration on my wardrobe was broken when my phone buzzed from where I had left it on my desk. Grateful for the interruption, I rushed over to it. When I read the caller ID, a bright smile crossed over my lips. I picked it up and swiped the screen. "Hi, Noah."

I sat down on my bed, far more interested in talking to Noah than picking out clothes for a party that I knew he wouldn't be at.

"Happy Friday afternoon," he said. I imagined a warm

smile on his handsome face. "How was your first week at school?"

"As good as can be expected. After all, it is school, and with that comes homework."

"Yeah. I don't miss that."

"You sure? I'd be happy to give you some of mine."

"Not a chance."

"I guess I'll have to suffer through it alone. How was your week? Is there any new information on the guy who took Ryder? I haven't seen my dad much these last few days, or I'm sure he would have told me."

"Nope. Nothing new. I wish there was, though."

"Me, too. I still wish we knew his motive. Might help give all of us a little closure."

"You know, there's a chance we'll never know what his motive was."

I had considered that. "If that happens, I'm sure we'll all move on in time."

"Of course. Now, about moving on. Are you working this weekend?"

"Yes. I'm scheduled for the lunch shift all three days since Monday is a holiday. It should be pretty busy."

"Great. I'll stop by."

That brought a smile to my face and I felt like exploding off the bed into cartwheels. But I calmly responded, "I'll look forward to it." After all, he was probably only being nice to me because I was the sheriff's daughter. Whether or not anything romantic would happen with him remained to be seen.

As I thought about this, I glanced at my dresser where the wilted carnation flopped on its side. *He loves me, he loves me not,* I thought to myself. *There's still hope. Don't give up yet. You'll be eighteen in one more week and then you'll be free to date anyone you want.*

"So will I," he said softly. "Okay, well, it's Friday night and I'm sure you have plans, so I'll let you go now."

I was thankful that he didn't ask what my plans were.

The last thing I needed was to tell the town deputy about the bonfire tonight. I didn't want to be the one to get the party busted. I simply wanted to make an appearance, thereby making Brooke happy. The party was now just an event I had to get through until I would see Noah again. "I guess I'll see you soon?"

"Yes, soon. Good night, Laken."

"Good night."

A huge smile lingered on my face as I hung up the phone. I fell back onto my bed and stared up at the ceiling. The sudden urge to stay home tonight and dream about him shot through me, but I knew Brooke would never forgive me. With a deep sigh, I reluctantly lifted myself off my bed and returned to my closet.

An hour later, my overnight bag filled with pajamas, a hairbrush, toothbrush, and other necessary toiletries bumped against my jean-clad legs as my boots thudded on the hardwood steps. In spite of my better judgment, I was ready for the party in my black sweater and black jacket. I had even curled my hair and applied some make-up, figuring if I had to go out, I might as well look decent.

Ethan was waiting for me in the kitchen with my mother when I came down the stairs. My father was still at the station expecting a busy Friday night now that school had started.

"Where are you kids off to tonight?" she asked as Ethan smiled at me.

I groaned to myself. I had dreaded this moment all week, knowing that I couldn't be completely honest. Fortunately, Ethan jumped right in. "We're headed over to Brooke's, and from there, we're not sure," he said. "We might head out for pizza or a movie, but we haven't decided yet."

"Sounds like fun. Have a good time. Laken, when will you be home?"

"Not 'til tomorrow," I told her. "We're staying over at Brooke's tonight."

"Okay." She briefly met my gaze with her tired brown

eyes. "Send me a text when you get back to Brooke's for the night, just so I know you're safe."

"Sure thing, Mom." I turned to Ethan. "Ready?"

He nodded and, after saying good-bye to my mother, we hauled our overnight bags out to the Explorer in the garage.

ლოლ

We arrived at the party around nine o'clock, well after the sun had given way to darkness. A full moon hovered above the mountains as I parked behind a row of cars on the dark dead-end road that led to the abandoned campground. I shut off the engine, watching the back of the car in front of us disappear as I turned the headlights off. After hopping out of the SUV, I walked around the front to meet Brooke and Ethan on the other side. I hugged my leather jacket around my chest against the brisk air. It already felt like fall. I smiled, thinking about the things I loved about this time of year—the colors in the leaves, pumpkins, Halloween, and my mother's hot apple cider.

"Ready?" Brooke asked, breaking me out of my thoughts and bringing my attention back to the party. Her black top hid under her black jacket which blended into the darkness behind her. Moonlight glinted off her double-stranded silver necklace and silver hoop earrings with every movement she made. Ethan stood beside her, half hidden in the shadows. He looked no different than always in his black T-shirt and blue denim jacket.

"I guess so. Lead the way."

Brooke nudged me playfully as we walked down the dark road. "Geez, don't make it sound like a funeral," she groaned.

"It will be my funeral if my dad catches me up here."

"He won't," she stated confidently.

We passed between the rows of cars on both sides of the road before approaching a metal bar blocking the campground entrance. Ethan slipped over it and then extended his hand to help Brooke and me hoist our legs over it. Beyond the gate, the road changed from flat pavement to an uphill climb over gravel. Our shoes crunched along the stones as we pressed on to find the party.

"How far are we going?" I asked. As soon as I spoke, we rounded a corner and a huge fire flickered in the distance. The flames reflected on the lake behind them, above which stars glittered like diamonds in the sky. Music and voices heightened as we got closer, and I recognized some of my classmates gathered around the fire.

"See, we made it," Brooke said over her shoulder as her pace quickened.

She hurried away from us toward the party. She knew a lot of the other kids here and would want to make her rounds. Eventually, she'd make her way back to us, but I knew better than to chase after her. If I asked her to hang out with me all night, she'd just scold me by asking what good it was to come to a party if I was going to stick with the only two friends I saw every other weekend.

Ethan hung back with me, draping his arm around my shoulders. "Stop worrying so much and loosen up. You're going to have fun." He smiled at me, and I tried to smile back.

"You know me too well."

"Yes, I do. And I know you're worried about being here and getting into trouble."

I shot him a knowing look. "What are you, a mind reader?"

We wound our way through the crowd of teenagers, many of them sipping drinks from red plastic cups. It wasn't a huge party, at least not yet. Music beat through the air and voices chatted over the crackling fire. A few of the kids glanced our way then looked beyond us as a group of boys arrived from the same direction we had come.

"Laken, hi." A vaguely familiar voice interrupted my thoughts.

I turned around to see Brian Collins as Ethan caught a girl's attention and slipped off into the crowd. Brian was my height with curly sandy-blond hair and light brown eyes. He was one of those students everyone seemed to like for his easy going sense of humor.

I smiled faintly at him. "Hi, Brian."

"Brooke said you were coming. I'm glad you made it. How do you like our fire? It took three of us about an hour to find that much wood."

"Impressive. I think I saw the flames a mile back. What are you going to do when the party's over?"

"Oh, we're going to be out here all night. But just in case, we have a bunch of water buckets to put it out."

"Good. Just make sure not to catch the campground on fire." My words of caution were drowned out as another classmate jumped in between us.

"Brian, dude. You better not leave your girl alone over there. Ben's hitting on her," said a brown-haired boy I recognized from school.

Brian looked at me from around his friend. "Hey, I'd better go. I hope you have a good time tonight, Laken," he said before taking off.

They disappeared, leaving me to stand alone amongst the chatting crowd. I saw Brooke on the other side of the fire talking to a few classmates. Her face was lit up with a bright smile. I took a deep breath, not sure what to do next. I wasn't very good at mingling, but I figured I'd better try. I made it through many parties last year, so I knew I could do it again. As I scanned the crowd for more familiar faces, the eerie feeling of being watched from the woods came over me. Shivering, I folded my arms across my chest and spun around.

I peered into the dark woods of the abandoned campground, my eyes taking a moment to adjust to the shadows after staring into the fire. As soon as I could make out some of the shapes in the distance, I followed the gravel road twisting up the mountain toward the campsites. I walked slowly, cautiously, the dim moonlight overhead the only light that danced around the tall trees. As I left the party behind, the music and voices faded in the background.

Suddenly, an animal darted between the trees in the distance ahead of me. *Dakota?* I wondered. *What in the world? How did he get here so fast?* I shook my head, not sure that he could have trekked around town and over ten miles of mountains to the campground since I had last seen him a few hours ago. Curious, I continued in the direction of the movement, ending up in one of the campsites. An old wooden picnic table held together by rusty metal beams and an overturned black grill thrown haphazardly near the fire pit were all that remained.

'*Dakota,*' I thought. '*If that's you, please come out for a second. I need to know that was you.*' A cool breeze whispered through the leaves, sending a chill through me as I searched the darkness for another movement. '*Please, Dakota,*' I begged silently.

A shadow raced across the far side of the campsite. It was shaped like a wolf. Relief washed over me, but it wasn't long lived. The figure stopped between two trees, and I heard a low rumbling growl.

"Dakota?" I whispered, confused.

Why was he acting like this? He never should have come this close to a party, but that was no reason for him to growl at me.

The wolf stared directly at me, its golden eyes glowing bright in the moonlight. I gasped, my heart skipping a beat. I couldn't tear my eyes away from it. This wasn't Dakota. Panic gripped me, and I could barely breathe. If this wasn't Dakota, who was it and how did it get here?

It growled for a few more seconds, its lip curling up to reveal sharp white fangs that gleamed in the moonlight. I didn't move a muscle. My breaths were short and shallow as my heart pounded. I was so surprised by the unfamiliar wolf and its defensive demeanor that I didn't even try to talk to it. I had the sinking feeling that it wouldn't welcome my words and thoughts. Before I had time to change my mind, the wolf turned and took off, silently disappearing into the black night.

I stared into the darkness for a minute, my feet paralyzed in place. My pulse raced as I watched for more movement and listened for any sounds. But the campsite remained quiet. I wasn't sure how long I stood there, but I knew it was longer than I should have lingered. I couldn't believe what I had just seen. Wolves didn't live in New Hampshire, at least not in today's world. If they did, I would have run into them long ago on one of my many ventures into the woods. This wasn't right. Fear settled over me the longer I thought about what I had just seen.

After a few minutes of staring directly at the spot where the wolf had been, I shook my head. *Enough, Laken,* I told myself. *How long are you going to stand here and wait around for it to come back? Go back to the party.* Longing to be with the kids down by the bonfire, I whipped around. I wasn't expecting to see the dark figure that loomed in front of me, and I nearly crashed into him. Stopping within inches of his tall frame, I clutched at my heart as a new fear raced through me.

"Hello, Laken."

"Xander," I whispered, glancing up at his blue eyes. I wondered how long he had been standing behind me and if he had seen the wolf. "You scared me."

He reached up, gently touching my shoulder. "Sorry. I was just wondering what you were doing up here. The party's down there by the water." He gestured in the direction of the bonfire, its glowing orange flames dancing from the banks of the lake.

A couple of boys hollered as a girl chugged her drink. When she finished, loud cheers erupted.

"I thought I saw something," I explained, desperately wanting to change the subject. "What are you doing here? I didn't know you were hanging out with this crowd."

"Brooke told me about the party and I figured if she was

coming, there would be a pretty good chance you'd be here. Besides, there isn't a whole lot to do in this town."

His comment that he'd come to the party to see me was forgotten as soon as he complained about the town. I didn't like his condescending tone. His last statement sounded like a dig at the only place I had ever lived, and I immediately put up my guard. It didn't help that I was still rattled from seeing the strange wolf.

"If you don't like our town, why don't you go back to where you came from?" My tone was harsher than I had intended it to be, but that was probably from my nerves. Nothing was going right tonight. Nothing. "I heard that you moved here from Los Angeles. Is that true?"

"Yeah. That didn't take long to get around."

"Honestly, no one really cares where you're from. We're just curious when people move to town. It's not like a big city where people move in and out every day."

And after finding a strange body belonging to a guy who kidnapped a little boy in the woods, we really need to know about anyone new around here, I added to myself.

"Well, I didn't have a choice in the matter. My father moved us here."

"Why?"

Xander shifted his gaze away from me for a moment. "I got into a little trouble over the summer. My father thought I needed to move where there would be no temptations for my senior year."

"What kind of trouble?"

"I hot-wired a Porsche."

"You stole a car?" I asked in disbelief.

He shrugged as if it was nothing. "What can I say? I was bored."

"You were bored? Well, please don't start stealing any cars around here. We don't want any trouble in our town." *You mean any more trouble,* I thought. I paused, watching him intently. "How did your father end up picking northern New Hampshire?"

Xander frowned. "I'm not exactly sure. I think he threw darts at a map one night, blindfolded, after a couple shots of whiskey, until he hit the smallest, most remote town he could find," he explained sarcastically.

"Wait a minute. Why are you telling me this? Why would you want anyone to know about the trouble you got in before moving here?"

"You're not just anyone. You need to know the truth about me."

He stared at me, and the unsettling shivers I had felt when he first rode his motorcycle into the school parking lot shot through me. I raised my eyebrows. "What? You don't even know me. So I don't think it matters."

His eyes seemed to bore a hole through me. "Oh, it matters. Speaking of telling the truth, I have a question for you. How did you find that little boy?"

It was my turn to shrug. "I followed a stray dog," I replied, avoiding his gaze.

"Really? That's it? A stray dog?"

"Well, he's not exactly a complete stray. I'd been feeding him for a while, so he trusted me."

"What kind of dog was this? A bloodhound?" he asked suspiciously.

I took a deep breath and stared at him. "What are you insinuating?"

"I just think your story is a little far-fetched, that's all. You may have convinced the town, but I think you're hiding something."

My heart pounded nervously. How dare he question me? He knew nothing about me and he had no right to accuse me of lying, even if he was right. "I don't care what you think, and I don't have to tell you anything. I don't owe you an explanation."

As far as I was concerned, this conversation was over. Brushing past him, I started to make my way back to the party.

Xander rushed after me, loose gravel rolling down the

hill as he caught up to me. He passed me, turned, and stopped in my path. "Hey, Laken, I'm sorry. I didn't mean it like that. It just seems…well, you seem pretty amazing. You did something unbelievable, but I don't understand how a dog with no search and rescue training could find a little boy lost in the wilderness."

"It happens all the time," I said. "And who knows? Maybe he does have some search and rescue training. I don't know anything about him since he just showed up one day. Now if you'll excuse me."

I walked around him, my sights set on the bonfire. I listened carefully for footsteps behind me, wondering if he would try to catch up to me again, but I heard nothing. Without looking back, I marched down the hill toward the party around the fire, determined to forget about the wolf and Xander's intense blue eyes.

Chapter 8

The next morning, I returned to an empty house. My parents had left a note for me on the kitchen table. *Gone shopping. We'll be back later this afternoon.*

I wondered what that was all about. My parents rarely shopped together unless it was for something big like furniture.

Dismissing my curiosity about their outing, I hauled my overnight bag upstairs to my bedroom and kicked off my jeans from last night. I pressed them up to my nose, inhaling the smoky campfire scent, then quickly tossed them and the sweater I had worn to the party into my laundry. I pulled on a gray Boston College sweatshirt and black workout pants as I looked wistfully out the window over my desk. It was another beautiful early fall morning with blue skies and cool temperatures. Perfect for a hike before I needed to get ready for work.

I slipped my hiking boots on and headed downstairs. I contemplated taking my camera, but then decided against it. My thoughts were focused on Dakota this morning. I needed to know that he was safe. Ever since last night, I had wished that the strange wolf at the campground had been a bad dream. But I knew it was real. And if Dakota didn't know about it yet, he was about to find out.

I ran out the back door and across the yard to the woods. The bright sunlight blinded me for a moment until I entered the trail, the trees overhead providing plenty of shade. Sunlight danced on the ground in small random patches where it filtered in through gaps in the leafy forest ceiling. Racing up the familiar trail, I searched for signs of Dakota.

"Dakota!" I called out. "Come here boy!"

I stopped for a moment, scanning the sloping forest for any sign of him. A woodpecker drilled like a jackhammer into a nearby tree and I heard a rustling in the brush. I turned to see a moose lumbering toward me. Her dull brown coat blended into the surrounding dense woods as she approached the trail, her ears flopping off to the sides. I gazed at her soft brown eyes when she stopped beside me. As I reached up to stroke her furry neck, the oil from her skin greased my hand.

The moose shook her head in annoyance at a fly and then continued across the path, disappearing into the forest. I resumed hiking up the trail, still focused on finding Dakota. "Dakota!" I yelled, cupping my hands around my mouth.

He suddenly leaped out of the woods about thirty feet ahead of me. He skidded to a halt and stood perfectly still, his huge paws planted firmly on the ground, his expression solemn.

"There you are," I said with a smile as I quickened my pace to catch up to him.

Instead of the friendly gaze and wagging tail he usually greeted me with, he let out a low growl. I stopped dead in my tracks, wondering if I had mistaken the other wolf for Dakota. But I had no doubt that this was Dakota. His honey colored eyes gave him away.

"Dakota," I whispered, stepping toward him again. "What's going on with you?" The rumbling in his throat grew louder as I came closer to him. Heeding his warning, I stopped. "Dakota?" I asked hesitantly as I backed up a step.

His growl faded. "So that's it? You want me to turn back?" His eyes softened with a subtle nod of his head. "Okay. I'll go. But not until I know why. I saw another wolf at the old campground last night. Is that what this is all about?" I waited for his reaction, wishing once again that he could tell me his thoughts.

He turned his head to look into the woods, his ears flickering at the noises he heard. Then he swept his gaze around to the other side, as if looking for something. When he returned his stare to me, he nodded.

A breeze whispered through the leaves high above and the dappled sunlight moved in waves across the trail. I sighed. "Fine. I'll go home, but you're coming with me. If it's not safe for me, I don't want you out here either."

Dakota remained still, his posture tall and solid. I could tell he had no plans to obey me. "I mean it, Dakota." I started walking toward him, although I didn't know how I planned to make him return to the house with me. If I had learned anything about him over the years, it was that he had a mind of his own. But until now, we had never disagreed. This was a battle of wills that I probably wouldn't win, but I wasn't about to give up without trying.

I had only taken a few steps when Dakota charged toward me, his growling louder than before. He halted inches away, glaring at me. I tripped as I came to a stop, spreading my arms out to catch my balance. My heart thundered in my chest.

I backed up slowly, never breaking my eye contact with him. As I did, his warning growl ceased. "Just promise me one thing. Stay safe. I couldn't handle it if anything happened to you. I don't know what I'd do without you."

With that, I spun on my heels and headed down the trail. When I had almost reached our backyard, I stopped and looked back. As I expected, Dakota had disappeared into the forest without a trace.

ℰↃℰↄ

When I arrived at the pizza shop, the lunch rush had already begun. It was the busiest I had seen it all summer, and time flew by as I waited on customers. I welcomed the distraction, although the strange wolf never completely left my thoughts. I was so focused on my job that I at least stopped worrying about it. There would be plenty of time for that later.

The restaurant never entirely cleared out after lunch. Stragglers wandered in throughout the afternoon for pizza and sandwiches. I still had a few tables going at three o'clock when Noah walked through the front door. My heart jumped when I saw him take a seat. He removed his sunglasses, gently setting them down on the red and white checked tablecloth. Looking around, his eyes stopped when he saw me across the room. I smiled and self-consciously pushed a stray lock of hair behind my ear.

My eyes on him, I approached his table. My other customers were eating, so I had a few minutes to spare. "Hi," I said when I stopped next to him.

"Hey. Looks like you've had a busy day. The last time I came in at this hour, there wasn't a single soul left in here."

"Yeah. It's been great." *But it's even better now that you're here.* "How's your day going?"

"Pretty good. Your dad's got both me and Pete on duty since it's the last official weekend of summer, but it's actually been pretty quiet. And quiet is good after the last few weeks. So what were you up to last night?"

"Not much. I just went to a party with Brooke and Ethan."

"Really? How was that?"

"Boring," I lied as the wolf with the yellow eyes flashed through my thoughts. But the eyes quickly changed to a haunting blue. Xander. It wasn't the first time I had thought of him since last night. And every time I did, a shiver crept up my spine. "Hey, I have a question. Could you run a background check on someone for me?"

"Sure, but why? Doesn't your dad know everything

you'd need to know about anyone in this town?"

"Of course. But this is someone who just moved here. My dad wouldn't know him. His name is Xander Payne."

Recognition crossed over Noah's expression. "He must be Caleb Payne's son."

"Caleb Payne? You know who I'm talking about?"

"I know of them," Noah corrected me. "Apparently, Caleb moved here with his only son from Los Angeles. They have a big house hidden on a mountain somewhere around here."

"Is it just the two of them?"

Noah nodded. "Yeah, at least from what I've heard."

I briefly wondered why my parents hadn't mentioned the father and son newcomers to town, but we all had been so caught up with the recent events that the usual things we talked about had slipped by. "Hmm. That's interesting."

"So why do you want me to run a background check on this guy?"

"I ran into him at the party last night. He told me that the reason his father moved them here was because he stole a car. I'm just wondering what other trouble he may have been in."

Noah raised his eyebrows. "Yeah, good question. Stealing a car is pretty serious." He chuckled softly. "And I thought coming here would end up being the most boring job I could ever take. So far, we've had kidnapping, a dead body, and now grand theft auto."

"I'm glad you're so amused," I said sarcastically, but with a smile. I could have added a golden-eyed wolf to the list, but surely he wouldn't have believed me. I didn't want him to think I was some crazy small-town girl who made up stories for attention. "It may not be a big deal to someone from Los Angeles, but we don't have crime like that around here. At least we didn't up until a few weeks ago, and we don't want any more of it. We like our quiet town, even if it is boring. So I'd really like to know what his story is even if I am being a little nosy."

"Then consider it done. I'll look into it as soon as I get back to the station. It won't hurt to know his background. I'm curious now, too, based on what you just told me."

"Thank you. I really appreciate it. But there's one more thing I need to ask."

"Sure, no problem. What's that?"

"Please don't mention this to my dad. He's got enough to worry about right now. I know he's still really shaken up to know a young child was snatched from his own backyard up here. I don't want him to worry about this, too. And I definitely don't want him to ask how I was at a party with some kid who has already been in serious trouble with the law."

Noah grinned knowingly. "Now the truth is finally out. Is there anything else I should know about the party last night? Was there any drinking?"

"What do you think?" Of course there had been a keg and liquor bottles, but not everyone there had been drinking. I suddenly remembered that another party had been held last night. "I'm sure there was a lot of drinking at Marlena's party last night, though. She was advertising all week that her parents were going out of town for the weekend."

"I'll have to remember that for next time. Let me know when that happens again and your dad and I can bust her party."

I raised my eyebrows at him. He still had a lot to learn about our small town politics. "Not that I wouldn't love that because I really would, but that isn't a good idea because her father is the mayor. The unspoken, unwritten rule is that Marlena can have her friends over to do whatever they want as long as they stay at her house and no one drives."

"Thanks for the tip. I'll remember that."

"Be sure you do. I'd hate to see you fired only a month or two after you got here."

"Me, too." He shot another smile at me as our eyes locked for a moment of silence.

Worried that I had lingered a little too long, I pulled a notepad and pen out of my apron.

"Are you hungry? Can I get you something?"

"I thought you'd never ask. Two slices of pepperoni pizza and a Coke. And, hopefully, I'll get to eat them here this time."

I nodded. "I hope so, too."

Turning around, I headed to the kitchen to put in his order and get his soda. For the rest of the afternoon, a smile lingered on my face.

℘℘℘

The sliver of a crescent moon was surrounded by glittering stars in the black night sky. I ran through the woods, my heart racing in fear. Panic gripped me as I dodged the trees and prayed that I wouldn't trip on roots hidden by several inches of thick, heavy snow. I wore a white nightgown that reached my knees, leaving my lower legs bare and exposed to the frigid wintry air. But I couldn't feel the cold in my frenzy to escape.

As I ran, animals darted past me, as if also afraid. To my right, a lynx charged ahead with long, stealthy strides. To my left, several deer leaped through the air, clearing logs in their path, their upright white tails a blur against the wintry landscape. A speckled snow owl flew past me and, while I pushed my legs to move as fast as they could, I couldn't keep up with any of the animals. They disappeared into the distance, leaving me to run alone.

I heard the heavy breathing of something chasing me, but I didn't dare turn my head to look behind for fear of losing speed. Whatever it was, I didn't need to see it to know that I needed to keep running. I pressed on up a hill, gasping for air. My legs burned from exertion and I began to tire. Just when I thought I couldn't run any longer, my bare feet stumbled against a tree root and I pitched forward, slamming against the snow-covered ground. I broke my fall with my hands and, as I caught my breath, a deep growl rumbled behind me. I turned to see the yellow-eyed black wolf standing over me, its dark leathery nose inches away from my face. Its breath billowed out in a hazy fog. I scooted back as quickly as I could until I hit a tree behind me. The wolf crouched down low and slowly stalked toward me.

"What do you want?" I whispered.

In the next instant, Dakota leaped out from the trees beside it. His front legs were stretched out in front of him and his teeth were bared, ready to rip into the wolf that stood above me. On impact, the two wolves became one big ball of black fur. Snarling growls and loud angry yelps cut through the silent wintry night. The wolves tumbled into the snow, their sharp fangs snapping at one another.

"Dakota, no!" I screamed and suddenly shot upright in my bed.

My pulse raced and the sheen of my sweat stuck to the sheets. It was all just a bad dream. My heavy breathing and pounding heart slowly returned to normal as my eyes adjusted to the dark shadows in my room. I pulled the covers up against my chest as I eased back down onto my pillow, trying to shut out the image of the strange black wolf.

As I desperately tried to think of something other than the wolf that haunted my dreams, I heard a faint howl in the distant night. My eyes flew wide open and I scrambled out of my bed. After racing across the room, I leaned over my desk to raise the window. Cool, crisp midnight air blasted into my room, sending shivers through me as I peered into the darkness. Not even the slightest breeze could be heard in the silence. I remained at the window for a few minutes, waiting for another howl. An owl hooted from a tall tree in the distance, but that was all I heard. I couldn't help wondering if I had imagined the howl. It must have been an aftershock from my nightmare.

With a sigh, I slid the window down into place. After locking it, I returned to the cozy warmth of my bed, hoping to forget my nightmare and fall back to sleep.

e/ɔe/ɔ

I didn't have any more nightmares that night. A misty gray sky loomed outside the window when I awoke the next morning. Raindrops tapped lightly on the roof. I sighed as I pulled the comforter against my chin, my nightmare vividly replaying over and over again in my head.

Stop! I finally ordered myself, flipping onto my side. *Can't you think about something else*? *Like Noah.* I smiled at the memory of our first meeting and what his hands had felt like on my waist. I really wanted to go out with him. I wondered what we would do, where we would go, if he would kiss me on our first date. My eyes fell shut as I imagined him pressing his lips against mine.

When I opened my eyes in my mind, I saw Xander's intense blue eyes staring at me. I bolted upright in bed. Where had that come from? It would be one thing to dream about him as I slept, but I was awake in full control of my fantasy. Or so I thought.

I ran my fingers through my hair as I slipped out from under the covers. My bare feet padding softly against the floor, I left my bedroom and wandered down the stairs. When I reached the empty kitchen, a scratching sound scraped at the back door.

"Dakota?" I wondered out loud as I ran to the door and flung it open.

He stood on the patio, his head hung low and his fur soaking wet. Water dripped from him in tiny beads, pooling underneath him.

"Dakota, come in here. You look miserable." I held the door open until he crept into the kitchen and then shut it behind him. He seemed to be limping, favoring his right front paw, but he took so few steps that I couldn't be sure. I knelt down beside him to stroke his damp fur. "What happened to you?"

Dakota looked up at me, his amber eyes tired. He whimpered softly and, once again, I wished he could tell me what was going on. He stood perfectly still beside the door. "Wait here," I told him. "I'll get a towel to dry you off."

I ran upstairs and grabbed a clean towel from my bathroom closet. Then I hurried back down to the kitchen where he waited. He hadn't moved an inch since I had left. "Here," I said, kneeling on the hard floor beside him again. "Let's get you dried off."

I rubbed the towel over his wet fur, starting with his neck. As I rubbed it across his side, I glanced down at the floor and gasped. The water pooling on the white tile was tinted pink.

I looked at the towel in my hands, afraid to turn it over. Slowly, I moved it until I could see the other side. My heart raced as I swallowed the lump in my throat. The white towel was streaked with bright red blood.

Chapter 9

Panic consumed me and tears welled up in the corners of my eyes. I started shaking as I sifted my fingers through Dakota's thick matted black fur to find the source of his bleeding.

"Dakota," I said, fighting for every ounce of composure. "What in the world happened to you?"

He gazed at me soberly, and I now recognized that what I had mistaken earlier for concern in his eyes was actually pain. He nudged my arm as if to reassure me that he would be okay, but I couldn't believe it until I found where he was bleeding from. If it was bad enough to need stitches, I didn't know what I'd do. I couldn't exactly take him to a vet. My hands trembling, I pressed the towel against his neck.

As more blood continued to soak the towel, I yelled, "Mom! Dad! I need help, please!"

Within seconds, their bedroom door opened and they rushed into the kitchen. My mother tied the rope around her navy robe as she hurried toward me and Dakota. Fear shone in her brown eyes, and I felt a little guilty for jolting them up so suddenly on a Sunday morning. My father followed closely behind her in plaid pajama pants and a white T-shirt.

Kneeling beside me, she assessed the situation. Her wide-eyed fear quickly faded when she saw that Dakota was the one injured, not me. "Here," she said, gently taking the towel from me. "Let me do this." She rubbed Dakota's neck with a clean section that wasn't soaked in blood yet. "Laken, get me the kitchen scissors from the utility drawer. We're going to have to cut his fur to find where he's bleeding from. Tom, I need your clippers and the hydrogen peroxide from our bathroom."

My father hesitated. "My clippers?"

"Yes. Once I find where he's bleeding from, I'll need to shave his fur closer to his skin around the wound." She paused, noting my father's curious expression. "We'll buy you a new pair if they get ruined," she said sharply before returning her attention to Dakota's neck. Dakota continued to stand still, fully aware that we were trying to help him.

I scrambled to my feet, rushed across the kitchen to our utility drawer, and retrieved the scissors from their place among the knives, skewers, and other sharp utensils. My fingers closed around the black handles, my hand still a little shaky. Then I returned to my mother's side and carefully handed them to her.

"Thanks. I think I found a puncture wound." She started cutting his fur. Thick black clumps cut straight across fell to the tile floor. "Can you get a few more towels, Laken?"

"Got it." I raced upstairs to grab two more towels. When I returned, my father stood over my mother as she gently ran the buzzing clippers against Dakota's neck. She concentrated intently, like a surgeon focusing on a patient. "How bad is it?" I asked, looking over her shoulder.

"It looks like a bite. There are two punctures." She continued shaving, exposing about three square inches of skin. Two deep round openings seeped with blood.

My mother handed me the clippers when she finished. "Towel, please." I gave her one of the clean towels. She dabbed at the wounds, first soaking up the blood that pooled on his neck and then holding a towel firmly in place, applying pressure to his wound. "Put some cold water on the other towel. It'll help stop the bleeding."

I did exactly as she instructed and handed her the wet towel after taking the bloody one. "Is it getting any better?"

"Yeah, I think it's almost stopped. Can I get the hydrogen peroxide, please?" She held her hand up and my father placed a brown medicine bottle in it. "Tom, can you check our bathroom for gauze pads and an ace bandage?"

"Sure," was all he said before disappearing down the hallway to look for the supplies.

"Laken, now I need you to hold his head. This might sting a little and I don't want him to bite me."

I smiled. "Mom, Dakota would never bite you. He knows you're just trying to help." I knelt beside his head on the other side and looked into his eyes. *'Hold still,'* I told him silently. *'This might burn for a minute.'*

My mother tipped the bottle at a slight angle, pouring the clear liquid onto his open wounds. Upon contact, it foamed and Dakota winced. I stroked the fur between his ears, reassuring him it would be over soon.

My father returned with a box of gauze pads and an ace bandage. After he handed the gauze to my mother, she ripped one of the individually wrapped pads open and blotted the wounds as the hydrogen peroxide foam dissolved. Then she gave it to me and reached for a new one.

"There," she said. "The bleeding has stopped. I think he'll be fine. It looks superficial enough. I'll just cover it up to keep it clean." My father handed her the ace bandage, and she wrapped it around his neck to keep the gauze in place over his wounds.

When she finished securing it in place with a tiny metal clip, I glanced at my father. "Dad, you're not going to send him back outside in this miserable rain, are you?"

"I suppose not. Go ahead and take him upstairs. Things are blowing over around here, so we can try to go back to the way things were before Ryder went missing."

A bright smile lit up my face. "Thank you."

As my parents headed back to their bedroom, I helped Dakota up the stairs to his big fluffy bed in my room. My earlier suspicion that he was favoring his right front paw had been dead on. He winced, jerking his head up every time he stepped down on it.

After hobbling up the stairs and into my room, he plunked down on his bed with a big sigh. His eyes fell shut immediately. Confident that his wounds would heal in time, I left him to rest and returned to the kitchen to clean up the blood-soaked towels.

෨෨෨

Before leaving for work that day, I placed a bowl of water next to Dakota's bed. He slept soundly, not even cracking an eye open as I moved about getting ready for another day of serving pizza. He growled a few times in his sleep, and I watched curiously as his lip curled up while his eyelids fluttered. Perhaps the golden-eyed wolf haunted him, too. There was no doubt in my mind that the wolf I had seen in the woods at the party had bitten him. I was grateful that my parents hadn't asked me what I thought had hurt him. They seemed to accept that it must have been a bear or a lynx or another animal indigenous to these mountains.

The pizza shop wasn't quite as busy as the day before. The gray rainy weather seemed to keep the tourists away. The lunch rush passed quickly, and Mike dismissed me as soon as the last customer left. I returned home to find Dakota exactly where I had left him, sleeping comfortably on his bed.

Still wearing my smelly jeans and white polo shirt stained red near my waist from pizza sauce, I knelt beside his bed and gently stroked him. He flickered his eyes open with a sleepy sigh, stretching out his paws. Then rolling up onto his belly, he rested his big black chin on my knees as I continued rubbing between his ears.

"Hey, boy," I whispered. "How are you feeling? Did you sleep well?"

A soft knock suddenly tapped at my bedroom doorway and I turned to see my mother. "I don't think he moved since I left for work," I told her.

"I think you're right. I've been home the whole time and I haven't seen or heard him. He must have been exhausted, but he looks more alert now. I wonder what did that to him. Whatever it was, hopefully he'll have the sense to stay away next time."

I nodded, acting as though I agreed with her when I was really wondering if he had a choice to stay away from the other wolf. "I hope he at least got up for a drink." I glanced at the water bowl I had left for him, noticing that it was still quite full.

"I put some frozen chicken legs out to thaw," she said. "They might be ready by now. I figured he'd be hungry soon."

"Thanks, Mom."

When we fed Dakota, which wasn't often since he preferred the local game of squirrels, rabbits, and deer, we gave him the closest thing to his natural diet we could get, raw meat.

I had offered him dog food when he first came to live with us, but even as a pup he had turned his nose up at it. When he had climbed up on a kitchen chair to steal a hamburger off the table, we realized a wild animal like him needed a wild diet. Fortunately, except for the winter when food became scarce for him to find on his own, we rarely needed to supplement his diet.

"We've been invited to the Wilson's for a barbeque tonight. Your dad and I are going. Would you like to come?"

"No, thanks," I replied quickly. I didn't even consider the invitation. There was no way I wanted to leave Dakota tonight. "I just want to take a hot shower and stay with him." I nodded toward Dakota. "But you guys go and have a good time. I'll be fine here tonight."

"Okay. Your dad went grocery shopping today, so there's plenty to eat in the refrigerator."

"Sounds good. Thanks, Mom." I looked over at her, meeting her gaze before continuing. "I mean for this morning. You were so calm. How did you know exactly what to do?"

She chuckled, her brown curls swaying next to her face. "I'm a mom. I used to clean up your scrapes and cuts all the time. Of course, I didn't have to find them buried under thick fur, but it's the same protocol. Clean, disinfect, and cover."

"Well, I really appreciate it." I looked down at Dakota's neck. "Do you think we need to change his bandage?"

"I would wait until tomorrow."

"Okay. Well, have fun tonight."

"We will. Call me or send me a text if you need anything while we're gone."

"I'm sure I'll be fine, Mom." I watched as she disappeared down the hallway, leaving me with Dakota. When I gazed back down at him, his honey-colored eyes were alert and bright from his day of rest. "Listen, now that you're better, I have a bone to pick with you. All I wanted was for you to stay safe yesterday when you chased me back to the house. You didn't keep your end of the bargain."

Of course, he hadn't really agreed to the promise since our communication only went one way, from me to him.

He sighed, his tongue swiping my hands as if to apologize.

I grinned. "Okay, you're forgiven. As long as it doesn't happen again. Now let me get cleaned up. Then I'll take you out and get you some dinner." That earned me several more big licks on my hands before I stood and headed for the shower to wash the greasy pizza smell off my skin and out of my hair.

Thirty minutes later, after a hot shower and dressing in clean jeans and a black hoodie, I helped Dakota limp down the stairs to the kitchen. Once he was on level ground, he still limped, but he managed on his own without being lifted around his chest to help take the weight off his injured leg. I opened the back door and followed him outside, my tennis shoes squishing in the small puddles on the patio. The gentle rain from earlier in the day had subsided, but a cool, damp mist lingered. Low clouds hovered, hiding the tops of the tallest trees in their gray foggy cloak.

I pulled the black hood up over my head, my damp hair spilling out over the front collar. Tucking my hands into the front pockets, I stood on the patio since everything was too wet to sit on. Dakota wandered through the yard, his nose buried in the grass as he sniffed along the tree line. He would need a few minutes to go to the bathroom, and I didn't want to lose sight of him in his condition. I paced slowly along the edge of the patio as he limped around the backyard.

Suddenly, he raised his muzzle from the grass and growled. I stopped instantly, my spine stiffening as my pulse quickened. I followed his stare to the side of the house only to see Noah walking through the wet grass. Dressed in jeans, a black T-shirt, and a denim jacket, he froze in place as soon as he saw Dakota's stare locked on him. Dakota continued to growl, the hair on his back ruffling upward.

I relaxed for a moment, relieved to see it was only Noah. However, his timing couldn't have been any worse. Dakota would have run off before being seen if he hadn't been injured. Now I had to explain Dakota to Noah. I wondered how Noah would react to the fact that the sheriff allowed his daughter to keep a wolf.

I turned to Dakota, his lip still curled up, his sharp fangs gleaming in the mist. "Dakota, it's okay. Easy boy." Then my eyes locked with his. '*It's only Noah. He's not a threat,*' I told him silently as I held his gaze. After a few seconds, he stopped growling and the fur settled back into place along his spine. He reluctantly resumed sniffing the ground, watching Noah out of the corner of his eye as he dropped his nose.

I turned back to Noah and grinned sheepishly. "Hi."

The apprehension on Noah's face faded although it didn't completely disappear. He started walking toward me again. He glanced nervously at Dakota as he approached me, amazement and fear shining in his eyes. "Hi. He's not going to attack me, is he?"

"No," I said with a reassuring smile. "You're safe, as long as you don't hurt me."

Noah stopped about three feet away from the patio. "I'll still keep my distance, just in case." His gaze darted from me to Dakota and back to me.

"I guess introductions are in order here. That's Dakota, my stray dog."

Noah raised his eyebrows. "Dog?"

"Okay, he's not exactly a dog. You have incredible timing, you know. How is it you always show up when I'm out back?"

Had he come by when Dakota and I were inside, Dakota would have stayed upstairs, unnoticed.

"What can I say? You're outside a lot."

I couldn't disagree with him on that. I was outside a lot.

"So you have a wolf?" Noah asked slowly, almost as if he didn't believe it.

"Yes. And right now, he's an injured wolf."

"I see the bandage. What happened?"

"Animal attack. He was bitten on his neck, and I think he sprained his right front leg. He's got a pretty bad limp."

"I'm sorry to hear that. I hope he'll be okay."

"I think he'll be fine." I watched Dakota hobble across the backyard and patio. He stopped at the door, waiting patiently for me to let him back inside. As he stood, he turned his head, studying Noah. "Come on," I said, gesturing to Noah. "He's ready to go in, and I don't know about you, but I'm not in the mood to stay out in this dreary weather."

Nodding, Noah jogged over to the steps and up to the patio where I stood. We had only taken a couple steps toward the door when Noah stopped and grabbed my arm.

"Why is he staring at me like that?"

"Don't worry. He's just getting to know you."

"Who else has he gotten to know? Do your friends know him? What about the town?"

"Only Ethan, Brooke, and my parents know about him. It's really important that we keep him a secret." I paused, my eyes silently begging him to understand that no one else could find out about Dakota. "And it would probably be best if you didn't let my dad know you know. He's been really worried about anyone finding out we have a wolf after recent events." We resumed walking across the patio.

Noah's gentle brown eyes met mine. "Consider it done."

"Thank you," I replied quietly as we approached the door. I reached out for the handle and opened it to let Dakota limp back into the house. After Noah and I followed him inside, I shut the door and pulled my hood down to rest behind my neck. "Have a seat," I offered, waving my hand at the kitchen table. "My parents went to a barbeque, but I'm not sure how much fun that'll be in this weather. Do you want to stay for dinner? I was going to make a salad, but we have lunch meat and I can make you a sandwich."

"That would be great." Noah slipped into a chair at the table, his worried eyes still studying Dakota who stood in the middle of the kitchen. "What about him?"

Dakota stared expectantly at the package of raw chicken drumsticks on the counter, hunger in his eyes. Drool hung from the corners of his mouth. I crossed the kitchen and held up the package for Noah to see. "He's ready for dinner, too."

"Raw chicken? No dog food?" Noah asked as I pulled a plastic bowl out of the cabinet.

I grabbed a knife from the silverware drawer and poked a hole in the wrapper. "I think he'd rather starve than eat dog food," I explained as I peeled off the plastic and dumped the drumsticks into the bowl. "I tried feeding him dog food when we first got him, but he refused it. The only thing he would eat was meat. But it has to be raw because cooked bones can splinter." I handed one of the drumsticks to Dakota who snatched it from me quickly, but carefully, avoiding my fingers. Then he hobbled over to the stairs where he stopped and looked at me. "I'm just going to help him up to my room where his bed is. Then I can make our dinner," I told Noah as I carried the bowl with the remaining drumsticks to where Dakota waited.

Holding the bowl under my left arm, I leaned down to help Dakota up the stairs. But I had barely been able to help him with two free arms when I didn't have something to carry. As I tried to lift him onto the first step, I lost my balance and nearly spilled the chicken all over the floor. I stood up quickly, catching the bowl with two hands. Then I looked over at Noah. "I hate to ask you this, but would you mind helping? He's really heavy."

Noah jumped to his feet and walked around the table to us. "Sure. Is he going to be okay with this?" Worry lurked in his eyes as he studied Dakota.

Dakota watched him, his expression seeming to say, "I don't like this any better than you."

"Just reach under his chest right behind his front legs. Every time he steps down with his right paw, lift him up to help him take his weight off of it."

"Got it," Noah said, but his eyes didn't look so sure. Hesitantly, he leaned down, wrapped his arms around Dakota's chest, and helped him limp up the stairs. He made it look a lot easier than it had been for me.

I followed behind them with the bowl of chicken in my hands. As soon as Dakota reached the top step, Noah let go of him and stood up. Dakota headed into my room and we followed as he made his way to his bed, settling onto it with the drumstick still in his mouth. He slid the bone between his front paws to hold it in place as he started gnawing on the meaty end.

"You're going to let him eat raw chicken in your bedroom?" Noah asked curiously.

I set the bowl down next to Dakota and walked over to

my dresser. "First of all, he won't leave as much as a crumb by the time he's done. And secondly—" I held up a book of matches and struck one against the grainy side. It flared with a hissing sound for a split second before diminishing to a small flame. "I have a scented candle to keep my room from smelling like raw meat. In a few minutes, it'll smell like baked cookies up here."

I lit the wick, blew out the match, and carefully moved the candle jar to the other side of the dresser near the wall. Then I turned to Noah who stood with his back to my closet door. I suddenly noticed my purple lacy bra hanging from the closet door handle, and I felt heat flush through my cheeks. My heart raced as I hoped he hadn't seen it when he had walked into my room a few seconds ago. Needless to say, I wasn't accustomed to bringing guys up to my bedroom, except for Ethan, and he didn't count.

"Okay. I'm done up here. We can go back downstairs now," I announced.

Noah swept his gaze around my room with sincere interest. "I like your room, especially your wolf picture." He nodded toward the picture that hung over my headboard.

"Thank you."

As I tried to think of a way to get him to leave my room, he walked past me between my bed and the wall across from the window, studying my photographs. "Wow. These are really cool. Did you take them?"

"Yes," I admitted. "I got into photography a few years ago when I got a digital camera for my birthday. And not some little matchbox camera, either. A real good one, see?" I pointed at my desk where my Nikon D3200 sat beside my computer keyboard, the thick strap dangling over the edge.

Noah followed my stare, immediately noticing the camera. "Nice. That looks pretty fancy. But how did you get such up close pictures? Do you have a telephoto lens, too?"

I shook my head with a shrug. "No. This camera has a zoom that's pretty good." *Please don't ask any more questions. Please,* I begged silently. It had been hard enough to get my parents to understand how I'd gotten most of those shots. I didn't want him asking, too. As we both paused, Dakota's teeth crunching on the raw bone the only sound in the room, I inched toward the doorway. "Come on. You're hungry, right?" I hoped I could get Noah out of there before he noticed my bra. It almost worked.

Noah started to follow me, but stopped and turned back to look at Dakota one last time. When he glanced into the room, I noticed his eyes stop to rest on my closet door. I was absolutely mortified, and I held my breath as my heart raced.

Dakota must have sensed my apprehension because he started growling. Noah jumped back, gently knocking into me. "I think I've overstayed my welcome," he said nervous-ly.

I laughed at the wide-eyed fear in his eyes, realizing how silly I was to worry about him seeing my underwear when he probably just wanted to make it out of my bedroom alive. "You're fine. I think he just wants us to let him eat in peace."

I instinctively grabbed Noah's hand, but dropped it when our eyes met. My heart fluttered as I turned to head down-stairs, his footsteps echoing close behind me on the hard-wood floor.

Once we had returned to the kitchen, Noah shed his jacket and hung it on the back of a chair. His black T-shirt stretched tightly along his broad shoulders, revealing his strong muscular arms. I wondered what it would feel like to have him sweep me into those arms, but I forced myself to look away and focus on making dinner.

We both went straight to the sink to wash our hands. My shoulder gently bumped his, and I quickly moved away as heat rushed through my arm. After we took turns drying our hands with a kitchen towel, Noah asked, "Can I help with anything?"

"Nope. I've got it. Have a seat." I gestured at the table, and he walked across the kitchen to sit down. Then I side-stepped over to the refrigerator and opened it. The cool air felt refreshing against my hot, flushed skin. "What can I get you to drink? We have Coke, ginger ale, Sprite, juice, milk, iced tea, and water," I said, taking inventory of everything on the shelves.

"I'll have a Sprite."

I grabbed a can of Sprite and filled a glass with ice. As I approached the table with them in my hands, Noah asked, "So how did you end up with a wolf?"

Placing his drink in front of him, I shook my head. "It's really not a very exciting story. My uncle who's a cop in Boston found him chained up in a backyard during a drug raid. He took him and brought him up here to us. The only other options probably would have been a zoo or a wolf sanctuary."

"And your parents let you keep him?"

"Only after days of begging. And I had to take an oath that I would get good grades and basically stay out of trouble forever."

"Did you?"

I laughed. "Ha, ha. Seriously though, I don't think my parents can complain." I leaned against the table. "You're still hungry, right? What would you like? We have ham and turkey for sandwiches. And there's some Swiss and cheddar cheese."

"Ham and cheddar would be great."

I returned to the refrigerator and pulled out sandwich and salad ingredients. Ham and cheese for him, lettuce, hard boiled eggs, and cottage cheese for me.

"I still can't believe you have a wolf. And he seems so tame, at least with you. I can tell you're really in control with him."

I briefly thought of yesterday morning when Dakota chased me back to the house. I wasn't in control then. "It's not as much control as it is a bond. I've done a lot of research on wolves and they are very social animals. Basically, I'm his pack."

I finished preparing his sandwich and carried it over to him.

His eyes met mine as he took the plate out of my hands. "Whatever it is, it's pretty cool. You're a fascinating girl who only gets more interesting the longer I know you."

I spun around and returned to the counter to fix my salad. "It's no big deal."

"Maybe not to you, but to the rest of us, it's pretty amazing. And it's how you found Ryder, so you can hardly say it's no big deal."

"Dakota found Ryder, not me," I said with my back to him. I focused on my salad, heaping cottage cheese, eggs, and pre-sliced carrots on a bed of lettuce. I topped it off with creamy Ranch dressing, then grabbed a ginger ale from the refrigerator and joined Noah at the table.

"You know what I mean. Not just anyone can take care of a wolf."

I smiled shyly, suddenly wanting to change the subject. "Why are you here? We've been talking about Dakota ever since you got here and I haven't had a chance to ask you that."

"I ran that background check you asked me to do," he told me between bites of his sandwich.

I froze, holding my fork with a bite of lettuce and egg on it suspended in mid-air. "Oh. What did you find out?"

"Absolutely nothing. There are no police reports on Alexander Payne."

"Did you try the name Xander Payne?"

"I tried every name you can imagine. There's nothing out there on him."

"But he told me he stole a car. Do you think he lied about that? Why would anyone make up something like that?" I finally ate the bite of salad I had been holding up on my fork.

Noah took a sip of his Sprite. "He either made it up or he really did steal a car, but it never got reported to the cops. In any case, there's nothing to worry about. No drugs or drinking or anything else. The guy has a clean record."

I continued eating my salad as I digested this information. I had been convinced that Noah was going to find a long troubled history on Xander. Knowing that he wasn't some dangerous criminal would make it much harder to stay away from him, which was what I knew I needed to do. Only I couldn't explain why.

Noah sensed my frustration. "What are you thinking?"

I glanced at him, noting the curious expression in his eyes. "Just that it doesn't make sense."

"But now you know your school and your town are safe. At least from him." He smiled genuinely. "But enough about him. Thanks for the sandwich tonight. This was really nice. I have to give Xander Payne some credit. He gave me an excuse to come over here."

I felt my cheeks blushing again. Looking down at my salad, I speared a few pieces of lettuce. "You don't need an excuse to stop by. You're welcome any time."

"Thanks. But I had one other reason for coming over."

I looked up at him. "What's that?"

"To ask if you'd like to have dinner with me next Saturday."

I nearly choked on my salad. My heart pounded with excitement as I bit back a glowing smile. He might lose interest if I appeared too eager. I took a sip of my ginger ale before answering him. "Um, yeah, that would be great. But I'll need to make sure my parents are okay with it first." As soon as I said it, I wished I could take it back. I sounded like a child who needed parental permission when I was old enough to make my own decisions.

Noah didn't seem to care. "I think they'll be okay with it."

I nodded my head, embarrassed. "You're right. I'm sure they will be, too," I said quickly.

"Are you okay with it?" he asked skeptically.

I tried to relax a little. "What? Yes, of course. I'd love to have dinner with you Saturday."

With a smile, he suddenly changed the subject by asking me about the week ahead. We talked for twenty more minutes while we finished our dinner. Once we were done and I had cleared the dishes away, Noah stood and slipped his denim jacket on over his T-shirt.

"Thank you for the nice dinner and wonderful company tonight," he said as we walked through the entry hall to the front door.

"It's the least I could do after Dakota surprised you. I am sorry about that."

"You don't have to be sorry. I'm glad I know about him now. And you can trust me. Your secret is still safe."

"Thanks. That means a lot to me."

Noah opened the door and stepped outside, but he lingered on the welcome mat. Taking my hand, he met my gaze. "I'm looking forward to next Saturday night."

I looked down at our hands. His soft fingers curled around mine. "Me, too."

When I raised my eyes to him, I smiled shyly. It was almost dark outside and the light from inside the house reflected in his brown eyes. He leaned toward me, and I suddenly wondered if he was going to kiss me.

At the last second, he shifted to the side and whispered in my ear, "I'd love to kiss you right now, but I think it's only appropriate that I wait until our first date."

His breath blew against my ear, causing goose bumps to break out along my neck under my hair. Despite the damp evening chill winding its way around the door and into the house, heat flushed through me. And yet, I shivered from his nearness.

Noah stepped back, never letting go of my hand. Instead he lifted it to his lips and kissed it. "Good night, Laken. I'll see you soon."

After reluctantly releasing my hand, he turned to walk down the sidewalk and disappeared around the front of the house.

"Good night, Noah," I said softly, even though he probably didn't hear me. Then I felt a dreamy smile spread across my lips as I gently closed the door. In spite of Dakota's injury and the gloomy weather, this was the best night I'd had since finding Ryder. The future suddenly looked better than it had in a long time.

Chapter 10

The misty rain lingered for another day, chasing the tourists away. I worked the lunch shift on Monday since school was out for Labor Day, and business practically died. When I returned home from work that afternoon to hit the books, Dakota seemed to be back to his old self. I removed the bandage from his neck, and his puncture wounds looked clean and dry with scabs covering them as they healed. The short stubble of fur prickled my fingers when I grazed them across his skin before my mother helped me reapply the bandage.

Noah wasn't far from my mind all day long. When I pictured his soft, compelling eyes or his contagious sly smile, my lips curled into a grin. Unfortunately, Xander crept into my thoughts every now and then, too. I seemed to have no control over them. There was something about him that had gotten under my skin. I couldn't tell if it was his handsome face and mesmerizing blue eyes or if it was the mysterious, dangerous aura that followed him everywhere he went. After all, he was the first guy I had ever known who had a tattoo, not to mention had stolen a car, assuming that was true. Each time his eyes flashed through my thoughts, I shook my head and forced myself to focus on my schoolwork or whatever else I happened to be doing at the moment. Dakota lifted his head every time I thought of Xander, his expression curious. He had to be wondering where these thoughts were coming from. I couldn't help feeling as though he was scolding me.

As if my unintentional thoughts of Xander weren't bad enough, I didn't even make it to homeroom Tuesday morning before I ran into him. I was at my locker, the hallway buzzing with chattering students, when he appeared from out of nowhere.

Thinking I was alone, I stripped off my denim jacket to hang it on my locker hook, revealing the light purple sweater I wore with jeans. My hair was pulled back into a braid, but a few stray strands grazed my cheeks. I studied the books on my locker shelf, looking for my Calculus textbook when I felt chills race up my spine. Before I could turn around, I felt a breeze blow against my neck.

"Good morning, Laken," Xander whispered softly in my ear.

I whirled around to face him, shocked by how boldly close he was and dizzy from his nearness, his voice, his breath. "What do you want?" I gasped as I pressed my back against my open locker.

It was narrow enough that my shoulders rested along both sides, or I probably would have fallen right in. Despite my trembling, I was able to steady myself. I stared into his blue eyes, demanding an answer.

"For you to say good morning."

I softened my expression, realizing how harsh my reaction must have sounded. "Good morning. Now can I ask what you want?"

"Just to apologize for questioning your story about the night you found the missing boy."

"It's not a story, it's the truth."

As flustered as I was, I kept my gaze locked with his. He stood several inches taller than me. Gone were the black clothes he had worn every day last week. In their place was a gray waffle weave shirt and blue jeans, the lighter colors making him seem less dangerous, if that was even possible. His shirt stretched tightly along his broad shoulders, the long sleeves covering the tattoo that had become permanently etched in my mind.

"I'm trying to say I'm sorry, that's all. The last thing I want is to start off on the wrong foot with you."

"Why? There are plenty of girls around here who would love to get your attention. You don't need to waste it on me."

"It's not a waste. I'm not interested in any of them. They're not special, like you." He stepped closer to me, and I pressed my back against the sides of the locker so hard that it hurt.

I scoffed. "I don't know what you're talking about. But I'm going to save you some time. Nothing you can say will make me change my mind." I glared at him, wishing he would leave me alone.

"Change your mind about what?"

"You."

"Is that so? What do you think about me?"

"Only that you showed up here with a big-city attitude and challenged something you know absolutely nothing about. I don't take kindly to being accused of lying."

"I suppose I deserve that. But sometimes first impressions are deceiving. You hardly know me, Laken. Give me another chance." He leaned toward me, extending his arms out and caging me against the locker.

I couldn't escape from him if I wanted to, and I definitely wanted to. The other students were a complete blur beyond his intense stare. "I'll think about it," I muttered.

He grinned with satisfaction. "That's more like it. There's a lot you don't know about me, but all will be revealed in due time."

"I have no idea what that's supposed to mean, but let's just say I'm not making any promises."

Xander's smile faded. He pushed off the locker, dropping his hands to his sides and releasing the barriers around me. I relaxed ever so slightly now that I didn't feel trapped any longer. "We'll see," he said. "It should be an interesting year. See you in homeroom."

Before I could respond, he turned and disappeared down the hallway into the crowd of students. I wasn't even sure what else I would have said to him if I'd had the time. Things would probably be better if he had never moved to our town. Everything I knew about him so far seemed to indicate trouble. As much as I tried to deny it, he intrigued me, and my own interest scared me.

Brooke suddenly emerged from the swarming students, but all I saw was her shiny cropped red hair as she looked down the hall in the direction Xander had gone. "What was that all about?" she asked as she turned to me.

I shrugged as I spun around to face my locker and find the Calculus book I had been looking for when Xander had shown up. Finding it between two other textbooks on the shelf, I grabbed it before shutting the door. By the time I returned my attention to Brooke, my books heavy in my arms, she was staring at me.

"Nothing," I finally answered. "He was trying to make up for something he said to me at the party, but I'm not buying it."

"What? He was at the party Friday night? I never saw him and you never told me about him."

"Oh yeah, sorry," I said sheepishly.

Brooke was practically drooling to find out what I had neglected to tell her. "So what happened that's got you so upset? And by the way, we'll talk later about the fact that I'm only finding out about this now."

I rolled my eyes at her, but I knew she was only teasing. "He just said some things about the night I found Ryder that were a little weird."

"Weird? Like what?"

I sighed, debating how much to tell her. After a moment,

I explained, "He pretty much accused me of lying about the dog that found Ryder."

Brooke raised her eyebrows. "That is weird. How else on earth could you have found him?"

"That's what I'd like to know," I said, desperately wanting to change the subject and talk about anything other than the night I found Ryder. "He also told me why he moved here. We probably shouldn't talk about this because I'm not sure if it's true, but he told me he stole a car back in California and that's why his dad moved him here. Less distractions and temptations."

Brooke's eyes nearly doubled in size. "He stole a car?" she gasped a little too loudly.

"Who stole a car?" Ethan approached as Brooke spoke.

I glared at both of them then glanced around us to make sure no one was listening. Fortunately, the other students who passed by paid us no attention. "Ssh," I warned them anyway. I looked at Ethan as I continued. "Xander. At least that's what he told me. But Noah ran a background check on him for me and there's no record of it. So don't say anything to anyone."

"Oh," Brooke teased. "Now Noah is at your beck and call? You better keep that quiet or you'll be hiding from Marlena all year."

"Thanks for the reminder," I gritted out with a scowl. "Can we please talk about something else now?"

"Yes," Ethan jumped in. "Your birthday is Friday. What are we doing to celebrate?"

I frowned as I looked at his eager smile. "I already told you both I don't want anything big. You know I hate being the center of attention." Pausing, I noticed a mischievous look creeping onto Brooke's face. "Please tell me you're not planning something I have to talk you out of," I added.

"No," Brooke said. "We wouldn't do that to you. I was wondering if you'll be celebrating with Noah. Now that's something worth turning eighteen for."

"If you must know, he's taking me out Saturday night.

But don't go spreading that around, either."

Brooke clasped her hands together in delight. "Perfect. Then we have Friday night to do something for your birthday."

"You still haven't told me what you're planning."

"We're not sure yet," Brooke said. "But we'll come up with something. Well, I've got to run to homeroom. The bell's about to ring. Later guys." With that, she took off down the hall, her long skirt swirling against her booted ankles.

Side by side, Ethan and I wandered through the maze of students to our homeroom. "I'm almost afraid to ask," I said with a sigh, glancing up at his familiar brown eyes. "What is she planning?"

Ethan grinned knowingly, putting my nerves at ease. "She's only teasing you. We don't have anything planned except boring cake and ice cream. We know anything more would be too much for you."

As we passed through the doorway into homeroom, I immediately spotted Xander in the back row. He sat sideways at his desk as he leaned across the aisle to whisper in a girl's ear. I recognized the pretty brunette as Carrie Sanders, a popular cheerleader and one of Marlena's friends. She smiled brilliantly, her face lighting up and her brown eyes focused on whatever he was saying.

My mood suddenly darkened as I stopped dead in my tracks. I took a deep breath, silently scolding myself. *Get a hold of yourself! You just told him not to waste his time on you and find some other girl to turn his attention to. And now you're jealous? Is this for real? Especially when you have a date with Noah on Saturday night.* My thoughts made perfect sense, yet I couldn't shake the jealousy sparked by Xander's flirting with Carrie.

A hand touched my shoulder, and I heard Ethan's voice behind me. "Laken, you need to keep moving. You're blocking the doorway."

I tore my stare away from Xander to look up at Ethan.

"Yeah, sorry. I just remembered something I forgot to do this morning, that's all."

As I followed Ethan to two empty seats on the opposite side of the room from Xander, I fought the urge to sneak one more glance at him and his new brunette friend. *Who he's friends with is none of your business. You shouldn't care who he hangs out with*, I reminded myself as the roll was called.

Interestingly, I ended up repeating that to myself for the rest of the day.

☙❧

Carrie and Xander seemed to be together everywhere I turned after that morning. I noticed every detail about the way they interacted—how he smiled when she touched his arm or shoulder, and how she beamed from his attention like she couldn't get enough of it. No matter how hard I tried to think about Noah and our upcoming date or the college brochures that were starting to pile up on the kitchen table at home, Xander was never far from my thoughts.

When my eyes fluttered open Friday morning, I smiled sleepily. My birthday. Eighteen was a big year, although not much would change. I would continue living at home, going to school, and avoiding any decisions that involved my future and college. But somehow, it felt like a big milestone.

I rolled over in bed, snuggling against the pillows as I fantasized about my date with Noah Saturday night. For once, my thoughts of him were pure and not tainted with images of Xander.

As I closed my eyes to savor a few more minutes of sleep, I heard Dakota sigh from the floor. As his neck and leg had healed, he'd become restless from staying in the house day and night. I opened my eyes to see him stretch his legs out. They fell off the edge of his bed, his paws lightly scratching the hardwood floor. With a yawn, he rose and walked a few steps to the side of my bed, his nails clicking against the floor in the silent morning. His black nose rested on my comforter inches away from my face and he stared at me, imploring me to get up.

I glanced over at the glowing red numbers on my alarm clock. Five-thirty. No wonder it was so dark and I wasn't ready to jump out of bed yet. The alarm wouldn't ring for thirty more minutes. "It's too early," I groaned at Dakota, reaching out to gently stroke the black fur between his ears. When I pulled my hand back and closed my eyes, drifting into a light sleep, Dakota never moved from his position beside my bed.

A light knock on my door woke me twenty minutes later. I opened my eyes to see the early morning light creeping into my room from around the window curtains. "Come in," I called hoarsely as I shifted up to a sitting position.

Dakota lifted his head and watched the door. My father, ready for another day on the job in jeans and a blue button-down shirt adorned with his sheriff's badge, appeared in the doorway. "I didn't wake you up, did I?" he asked as he crossed the room to my bed. He sat down next to me, scratching Dakota's cheek in a gentle greeting as his soft brown eyes gazed at me.

I reached over to turn off my alarm clock before it rang. "No," I lied. "I was just getting up."

"Well, happy birthday. I wanted to give you something before I left for the station this morning." He held out a tiny black velvet box. "I know it's early, but I've been waiting eighteen years to give this to you and I didn't want to wait another twelve hours."

I took the box from him and raised the lid. Inside on a white satin cushion rested a silver necklace with a pendant of intertwined circles that sparkled with tiny diamonds. "It's beautiful," I gasped.

"I hoped you would like it. It's been in our family for generations. I can't even tell you how old it is. No one knows."

"Are these diamonds?"

"Yes. This is very valuable, so you need to be extra careful with it."

"I will," I promised earnestly. "I'll take good care of it."

"I trust you will. Do you want to try it on?"

"Yes, but after I take my shower." I ran my fingers gently along the circles, admiring the beautiful pendant. "It's so shiny. It looks brand new."

"I assure you, it's not. I've been told it's at least a couple hundred years old."

"Wow," was all I could think of to say.

"And now it's yours, but it should be passed down to your daughter someday. It needs to stay in the family."

"Of course." I closed the black velvet box, thinking how strange it was for my father to talk about me having children. That seemed so far off in the future, it was practically unimaginable. I couldn't even see past my senior year to college, let alone marriage and children. I placed the box on my nightstand and lifted my gaze to meet my father's stare. "Thank you for trusting me with this."

"You're a responsible young woman. I'm proud to be able to trust you with something this valuable."

I smiled as I suddenly realized I hadn't told him about my date with Noah. This was the perfect opportunity. "Responsible enough to go on a date with an older guy not in high school?"

My father raised his eyebrows. "I'm going to need a little more information to answer that. Who are we talking about?"

"It's Noah, Dad," I said quickly to put his concerns to rest.

A sly grin broke out across his face. "I knew that."

"What? Then why did you ask me who it was?"

"I wanted to hear you say it. Yes, it's okay. I'm not exactly thrilled about it, but he's a fine young man. He already asked me if he could take you out."

"He did? What did you say?"

"Only that if he lays a hand on you, I have a gun and I'm not afraid to use it."

"Dad!" I gasped, mortified.

"I'm only kidding. I didn't say that because I didn't have to. He's a decent guy. I trust him." My father's teasing grin faded as a serious look crossed over his face. "I'm not going to tell you I'm particularly excited about you going out with an older guy, but on the other hand, I'm not going to tell you no. You're old enough to make these decisions and I trust you won't do anything you're not comfortable with."

"You're right. I won't," I said. "Thanks for being so cool, Dad."

He stifled a smile. "So when is this big date?" he asked.

"Tomorrow."

A knowing look spread across my father's face. "That explains why Noah wanted to cover tonight and take tomorrow night off. Well, you need to get ready for school and I have to get to the station." He stood and walked to the door where he paused, turning back for a moment. "Have a great day and I'll see you tonight for your birthday dinner."

"Thanks, Dad. For everything—the necklace and being so cool about tomorrow night." I felt like a broken record repeating how cool he was, but I honestly couldn't believe it. *Why not?* I asked myself. *It's not like you've ever given him or Mom any trouble in the past. Except for taking off into the woods for hours at a time. He's probably relieved you're actually going on a real date. How many did you have last year? One?* I shook my head to clear my thoughts. The voice inside my head wasn't being nice this morning.

"You've earned it, Laken." With a slight nod of his head, he shut the door behind him and left me to get ready for school.

e/ɔe/ɔ

I received a cheerful happy birthday greeting from Ethan, Brooke, and a few other students that morning at school. As I walked through the crowded hallway to my locker, I saw a white envelope sticking out from the slat between the door and the edge. Approaching it, I noticed my name scrawled across the front. Before opening my locker, I grabbed it as I glanced around to see if anyone was watching. Students mingled about, talking excitedly about the weekend, but no one paid attention to me.

I tore the envelope open to reveal a gold-rimmed white card with note written on the inside. *Happy Birthday, Laken. I hope you have a memorable year.* It was signed Xander. I sighed, hoping his gesture wouldn't thwart my determination to stay away from him. Just when I had started to get him out of my mind, he had to do something nice. And so unlike what I knew about him so far. In spite of my uneasiness, a small smile slithered across my lips as I dropped the card into my book bag.

Opening my locker, I tried to remember what book I needed for my first class. As I scanned the stack of textbooks on the locker shelf, my phone buzzed from inside my bag. I scrambled to balance the books I held with one hand as I reached into my book bag with my other one.

I felt around at the bottom until I finally touched my phone and pulled it out. A text message from Noah lit up the screen. *Happy birthday. I'll call you tonight. Have a great day!*

It really would be a great day now. I knelt down to place my books on the floor, freeing my other hand so that I could answer his text message. *Thank you! Talk to you tonight*, I typed and then hit send.

After returning my phone to my bag, I picked my books up off the floor. Standing, I resumed sorting through my locker to get organized for the day. I felt the smile on my face lingering as my heart glowed.

There was no doubt in my mind that concentrating on my classes would be hopeless today.

⌘⌘⌘

Xander skipped school that day, and I scolded myself for the disappointment that lurked in my subconscious. After all, why should I care where he was and why he had left me a birthday card? My classes passed slowly, each lecture seeming to drag on as I counted the minutes until the end of the day.

By the time I returned home, I felt like Saturday night would never arrive.

That night, my parents ordered take-out from the only Chinese restaurant in town. Brooke, Ethan, and I were in our family room when they returned home with the white containers of food. Ethan jumped to his feet from where he sat on the couch when we heard the kitchen door to the garage open and shut.

Brooke rolled her eyes, slowly rising to her feet beside him. "Easy boy," she said, placing her hand on his forearm to keep him from bolting for the kitchen. "The birthday girl goes first, then us ladies. Oh, heck, you should just let all of us get our food first, and then you can have everything that's left."

Ethan's boyish face lit up. "Sounds good to me." He broke away from Brooke's grip to head to the kitchen, but I rushed around him to block the doorway.

"Not so fast," I told him as I studied him and Brooke. "Before we eat, I want to know what the plan is for tonight." They still hadn't told me exactly what we were doing.

Brooke shot a teasing glare at Ethan. "Aw, shucks, Ethan, she's on to us." Then she looked at me. "So, after dinner and cake and ice cream and all the usual birthday ritual stuff with your parents, Brian is having an all-night bonfire party up at Matthews Pond in honor of your birthday. Everyone from school will be there. It'll be great." Pure fear must have shone on my face because Brooke broke out into laughter. "Gotcha! I'm only kidding. The only action you're going to get this weekend is tomorrow night and I'm going to see that you're well rested for it."

Heat flushed through my cheeks. "I don't know what you're talking about," I said innocently.

"Oh, please, if you don't get any action tomorrow night, you don't deserve a guy as hot as Noah. So after the birthday stuff tonight, I'm going to help you pick out an outfit for your big date. Then we can stay up late talking about who I should go to Homecoming with. After all, it's going to be coming up soon and you pretty much already have a date."

"Ooh, sounds fun," Ethan quipped. "Can I stay for the girl talk, too?"

Brooke glared at him and gently slapped his shoulder. "No."

"Thank God," he said with a deep breath. "Now can we please eat? I'm starving and whatever your parents brought home smells really good."

"I can't think of a better idea," I said, turning and leading them into the kitchen where my mother was busy setting out all the food with serving spoons, plates, and silverware.

"There you kids are," she said as she looked up. "Hungry?"

"Yes, ma'am," Ethan responded as he eyed the open white containers of rice, noodle, vegetable, and chicken dishes. The spicy scent of soy sauce and teriyaki filled the kitchen.

"Well, Ethan and Brooke, why don't the two of you get started serving yourselves. Laken's father is waiting for her in the garage with a birthday surprise." My mother glanced over at me. "I need you to come with me."

I raised my eyebrows curiously as I followed her through the kitchen door that led to the garage. I shut the door behind me before stepping down to the cement floor. The garage was open, and we passed between the Explorer and the utility shelves on our way outside. My father stood in the driveway admiring a shiny new maroon Jeep Grand Cherokee as the evening light faded.

"What's this?" The words slowly rolled off my tongue as

I glanced from my mother to my father, trying to read their expressions. I couldn't believe they had bought me a new car for my birthday, and it turned out I was right.

My mother stood by my side, smiling at me. "Your father and I decided that it was getting a little hard for the two of us to keep sharing the Explorer. So, this is for me." She gestured at the Jeep. "And, you my dear, now have exclusive use of the Explorer. We no longer have to coordinate schedules and carpool during the week. What do you think?" Both she and my father watched me, waiting for my reaction.

I smiled from ear to ear. I was happy about my mother's shiny new Jeep, but I was overjoyed to have the Explorer all to myself. "This is awesome! Thank you!" I hugged my parents.

"That old truck still has a lot of life left," my father explained. "You should be able to take it to college next year."

The thought of college dampened my mood, but only for a minute. "Mom, I love your new Jeep. But I am kind of hungry, so can we head back in for dinner before Ethan has time for seconds?"

"Of course," my mother said, leading the way back through the garage to the kitchen door.

My birthday dinner that night was all I could have ever wanted with good food and even better company. We polished off the Chinese food, with a lot of help from Ethan, and ended the evening with cake and ice cream. Ethan and Brooke gave me a beautiful wooden jewelry box with a wolf carved on the lid. It was the perfect place to keep the necklace my father had given me.

After dinner, Ethan escaped a long night of girl talk by taking off for home just after dark. Brooke and I spent hours sorting through my clothes for my date tomorrow night. Noah called around nine, but with Brooke lurking on the edge of my bed, I kept the call short with a quick hello and how was your day? He asked about my birthday and then told me he would pick me up at six-thirty the next evening.

After I hung up with Noah, Brooke and I stayed up late talking about boys. She mentioned Xander once, and I briefly remembered the birthday card he had left for me. I had deliberately not told Brooke or Ethan about it. Before she could say anything more about Xander, I quickly changed the subject to a boy she liked. Then late, long after the sun dipped below the mountains giving way to a dark night speckled with stars, we fell asleep dreaming about the boys we hoped would make our senior year memorable.

Chapter 11

I woke up before the sun peeked over the horizon. All I could think about was my date with Noah that evening. Butterflies danced around in my stomach as I lay awake in bed, waiting for the sun to rise and for Brooke to wake up. Dakota slept soundly on his bed, his breathing slow and rhythmic. I stared up at the dark ceiling, counting the minutes until the day began.

After Brooke finally got up, she left before breakfast since it was the only time her mother could come to get her. I ate a few bites of the blueberry pancakes that my mother made before bouncing up to head outside with Dakota. I missed our long hikes. I couldn't remember ever going more than a few days without escaping into the woods. The last week had felt like forever.

As soon as I stepped out into the bright sunlight, I shivered despite the heavy gray sweatshirt I had thrown on that morning. Dakota trotted through the dewy lawn, sniffing everywhere. I followed him out into the yard, the wet grass sprinkling my hiking boots with a damp mist.

"So what do you say? Is it safe to go for a hike today?"

Dakota snapped his head up from the ground and looked

at the trees. The fur on his neck was still growing back, but now covered the bare skin and scabs. His limp was gone, and I sensed his growing frustration from staying on house arrest for a week. He craved the freedom of the forest and a fresh deer or rabbit meal just as much as I craved a hike in the mountains I had grown to love.

A branch cracked somewhere deep in the woods. Dakota launched into a stealthy run, his stride opening up beneath his bunched muscles. In an instant, he disappeared into the shadows without a sound. Silence loomed as I suddenly found myself alone.

I sighed, realizing that no matter how strong my bond with Dakota was, it would never break the wild instincts within his soul.

I waited for a few moments, hoping he would return. But I quickly realized he wasn't coming back, and I had no desire to venture into the woods alone. I hoped he wouldn't get hurt again, but I had to let him go. He couldn't stay cooped up in the house indefinitely.

"Fine," I said out loud even though he was probably too far away to hear me by now. "Have it your way. But be home before dark and no bleeding this time."

I retreated back into the kitchen where my parents still sat at the kitchen table, both of them sipping nutty-smelling coffee and browsing the newspaper. My mother looked up at me when I reappeared. "That was fast," she commented. "Back so soon?"

"I never left. Dakota took off and I don't know where he went."

"Hopefully to catch himself a deer," my father muttered between sips of coffee. "It was getting expensive to have to feed him."

"Tom!" my mother scolded. "That's a little insensitive. He was injured. Besides, I'm sure he didn't like eating chicken every day any more than you liked paying for it."

"Good. Then hopefully he'll find something else to snack on," my father said before turning the page of his newspaper. "He's probably restless from being cooped up all week. He'll be fine."

"I just don't want him to get hurt again."

"He's smart," my mother stated matter-of-factly. "I'm sure he learned his lesson with whatever did that to him."

"I hope you're right." I still wasn't convinced. "Mom, will you be home all day today?"

"Yes. I have to work on lesson plans for next week."

"Then can you let Dakota in if he comes back?"

"Of course."

"Thanks. Well, I'd better get ready for work."

She nodded and turned her attention back to the newspaper as I headed up to my bedroom. My stomach was suddenly tied up in knots. Not only was I anxious about my date with Noah, but now I would worry about Dakota all day. I wasn't sure which was worse.

ᘓᘓᘓ

Work was slow that day since summer was officially over and the tourists were gone. The few locals who wandered in didn't amount to more than a handful of tables to wait on. Mike canceled my shift for the next day before sending me home early. "Sorry, Laken," he had apologized. "But I can't afford the help when it's this slow. I'll need you in a few weeks when the foliage peaks, though."

When six o'clock finally arrived, I scurried about my room to get ready for my date while listening to a new Pink song on my phone. I dressed in the short black skirt and pale blue sweater that Brooke had blessed last night. My new necklace sparkled above the sweater's plunging neckline. I curled my hair in soft waves and applied a dab of makeup to my green eyes. The ensemble wasn't complete until I added silver dangling earrings, a dash of perfume, and a pair of black high heels.

As I stole one last glance in the mirror, the doorbell rang

and my heart nearly leaped out of my chest. I dashed out of my bedroom and tiptoed down the stairs, my heels barely tapping against each step. With a small black purse in one hand and my black leather jacket in the other, I hoped that I would beat my parents to the front door. Unfortunately, I wasn't so lucky.

When I approached, three pairs of eyes stared at me and I felt a blush creep across my face. I glanced at Noah who stood outside the front door in the fading sunlight. The vision of him in dark blue jeans, a black button-down shirt, and black leather jacket sent my heart into a flutter.

Even with my parents at the doorway, I couldn't peel my eyes away from him. I had dreamed of this moment all week.

I stopped a few feet away from the doorway. "Hi," I said, smiling at him as I slipped into my jacket.

"Hey. Are you ready to go?" He seemed just as anxious as I did to escape.

"Yeah." I glared at each of my parents, hoping they could read my expression. *What are you doing?*

My mother seemed to get the message. "Well, don't stay out too late you two," she said, breaking the awkward silence. When she turned to me, I prayed she wouldn't say something embarrassing. "Have a nice time, honey."

"Thanks, Mom. Good night, Dad. I hope you don't get too many calls tonight."

"Me, too, since I'm letting this guy off and I won't have any back-up," my father teased. "But seriously, Noah, enjoy the night off."

"Thanks, Tom." Noah looked at me and held out his hand. "Shall we go?"

I nodded, never taking my eyes away from his as I walked between my parents and through the doorway to take his hand. "Yes."

His fingers curled around mine, his skin warm and his touch sending goose bumps up my arm.

As we started down the sidewalk, my father's voice rang

out behind us. "Be home by midnight so I don't have to send out a search party."

Noah turned to glance back at my parents. "Midnight it is. And don't worry, sir, she's safe with me."

Whispers sounded behind us, mostly my mother who was probably scolding my father for being overprotective. Then the door finally shut, leaving Noah and I alone at last. I breathed a sigh of relief. "That was embarrassing," I admitted.

Noah shrugged. "They obviously care a lot about you. A lot of parents these days just want their kids out of their hair and don't take the time to know who they're with."

We reached the end of the sidewalk at the driveway and stopped. I looked up at him curiously. "You sound like you're speaking from experience."

"I am. Back in Pittsburgh, I always got sent to handle the kids since I was closer to their ages than most of the other officers. So many times, the parents had no clue what their kids were getting in to. And the kids...well, let's just say it was obvious that they knew their parents didn't care."

I stared at him for a moment, realizing how much I still didn't know about him. He had real world experiences to share, and I suddenly felt very young and sheltered. "Wow. I can't imagine my parents letting me run all over town without knowing where I was, who I was with, and when I would be home."

"Just as long as you see that as a good thing." He smiled down at me apologetically. "I'm sorry. I don't know where all of that came from. Can we start over here?" He paused, his eyes sparkling. "You look beautiful tonight." He dropped my hand and gently touched the pendant hanging around my neck. "That's a gorgeous necklace."

"Thank you. It was a gift from my dad for my birthday. Apparently, it's an old family heirloom."

Noah raised his eyebrows. "Really? It looks brand new."

"I know. That's what I said." Out of the corner of my eye, I saw the sheer curtains behind our family room window flutter. "Oh no," I groaned. "I think we're being watched. Maybe we should go now."

"Good idea."

Noah led me around to the passenger side of his silver sedan and opened the door. I slid into the front seat as gracefully as I could in my skirt and heels. As he circled around the front of the car and took his seat behind the wheel, I tugged my short skirt down. It had ridden halfway up my thighs and I couldn't help wondering if Noah noticed. I glanced shyly at him, smiling as I caught his eye. He noticed.

We snapped our seatbelts into place and Noah started the car.

"Where are we going?" I asked as he backed out of the driveway. I glanced back at the house, but I didn't see any more movement behind the curtains.

"I was thinking we could try Fireside, but I'm also open to ideas if there's some other place you'd rather go."

"Fireside would be great. It sounds perfect."

After the five minute drive through town, Noah pulled into a gravel parking lot in front of a two-story log building. Darkness had fallen, but the restaurant beckoned from its hiding spot away from the road with soft light that glowed from within and candles that had been carefully centered in each window sill.

Noah parked between two SUV's a few spaces from the front door of the restaurant. I started to get out of the car, but he darted around to my side to offer his hand before I could stand. I couldn't have been more grateful for his steady support. My heels wobbled on the uneven gravel, and I grabbed his arm a few times to keep from falling as we walked to the entrance.

Noah held the door open, gesturing for me to go ahead of him.

"Thank you," I said with a smile as I felt like pinching myself. Ten minutes into this date and it already felt like a dream come true.

The restaurant was warm and cozy. The hostess area opened up into a dining area on one side of the building. Above it, a second-level dining area could be glimpsed beyond the balcony railing. To the other side, log beams stretched across a tall cathedral ceiling. A bar bordered the back wall and a two-story stone fireplace extended to the ceiling's highest point at the far end. A pile of wood sat upon the raised hearth as a fire crackled behind a decorative screen. A huge plaid couch and coffee table had been centered in front of the fireplace, and small dining tables were scattered around the perimeter of the room.

The soft hum of voices lofted through the half-empty restaurant and bar. Mouth-watering aromas of savory meats and sweet desserts hung in the air as we approached the pretty brunette behind the hostess stand. Aside from her elegant black dress, bright red lipstick was the only other color she wore. "Good evening. Two for dinner?" she asked, smiling a little too brightly at Noah. I was surprised she even noticed that he had a date.

"Yes, please," Noah responded.

A pang of jealously whipped through me when he smiled back at her. But he quickly redeemed himself by turning to me and asking, "Do you want to sit over by the fireplace?"

"I'd love to." I stepped a little closer to him until my shoulder grazed his arm as the hostess took two menus from the stack on the stand.

She instructed us to follow her and led us to a private table on the far side of the room that gave us a view of the fireplace. I barely noticed the few guests seated at the bar with their backs to us as the hostess placed our menus on the table. "Someone will be right with you," she said before returning to her post at the front door.

Noah stepped behind me to slide my jacket off and hang it on the back of my chair. I shivered, not from being cold, but from his nearness and soft touch on my shoulders. He pulled out the chair, pushing it in as I sat down.

Then he quickly circled to the other side of the table and

hung his jacket on the back of his chair. As he sat down, his eyes scanned the restaurant. "This is really nice. I've never been here before. It has that wilderness lodge feel. Very rugged." He paused. "I mean rustic. That's the word I was looking for."

"You do realize you've moved to the end of the earth, right? Everything about our town and these mountains is rugged and rustic. Just wait until winter gets here. It can feel pretty remote up here when we get a snowstorm."

He noticed the excitement in my eyes. "You really love it here, don't you?"

"Yes. But I've lived here my whole life. I can't imagine living in a city or someplace in the south where the seasons never change." I opened my menu as I talked.

Noah followed suit. "So what's good here?"

"Everything, from what I hear. I've only eaten here a few times."

Before either one of us could say anything more, a waiter in a crisp white shirt and black dress slacks arrived at our table. He quickly took our drink order, a Diet Coke for me and an iced tea for Noah, and then headed back to the kitchen.

Silence came between us as we studied the entrée selections. Food was the farthest thing from my mind, but I decided on a meatless pasta, hoping my nerves wouldn't prevent me from eating most of it. When the waiter returned with our drinks, we placed our orders and handed him our menus. As soon as he left, I quietly sipped my Diet Coke. Looking across the table at Noah, I couldn't help wondering how I had captured his attention when he could have any girl in town, and not just the ones still in high school.

Finally, he broke the silence. "How's Dakota?"

"Much better. His neck is healed, and he was up and about this morning like nothing happened. But he took off today and hasn't come home yet. For all I know, he's been hurt again." I let out a worried sigh, almost wishing Noah hadn't reminded me about him. And yet I was glad he did because it meant he remembered last weekend and cared.

"Why do you think it could happen again? Do you know what attacked him last week?"

"I'm not really sure. Dakota has roamed these mountains his whole life and nothing like this has ever happened." I paused, debating on how much to tell him. "But I think whatever bit him is what bit the guy who took Ryder."

"What? I mean I just figured Dakota had bitten him."

"So does my dad. And I'll admit I wondered about that too, at least until last Friday night."

"What happened Friday night?"

"I saw another wolf in the woods at the party. It actually looked a lot like Dakota except for the eyes. They were gold."

Noah frowned as concern came over his expression. "Have you told your father about this?"

I shook my head. "No, and you can't either. If he knows, he'll just worry about it."

"Where was the party?"

"Up at the old abandoned campground at Matthews Pond."

"Oh," Noah said, smiling. "I've heard that's a favorite party spot."

"Okay, yes, I've heard that, too. But I'd never been there until last week. I only went because Brooke dragged me there. I wanted to be a good friend and give her some moral support, and a ride."

"You don't have to explain to me. You're in high school and you're supposed to go out to a party or two. As long as you're safe, that's all that matters."

"Well, I don't drink if that's what you mean. But if you mean straying away from the party to come face to face with a strange wolf that doesn't belong here, we might have a problem."

"Yes, we might. How far away from the party did you go?"

I looked at him, trying to figure out what he was thinking. "Not very. I could still see and hear the other kids. You're not going to tell my dad, are you?"

"About what?"

"All of it. Any of it. The party, the wolf. He can't know. He has enough on his mind right now."

Noah smiled warmly. "Of course not. But thank you for telling me. It means a lot that you trust me. Just promise me you'll stay out of the woods for a while."

"No problem. The last two times I tried to take a hike, Dakota wasn't cooperative. Last weekend he chased me home. And this morning he took off without me. I'm not even sure I want to go out there anymore. At least not alone." I remembered my nightmare and shivered. Taking a deep breath, I flashed him a smile. "Okay, enough about Dakota and wolves. You now know a secret about me, so it's time for me to learn a little more about you."

Noah leaned his elbows on the table and rested his chin on his hands. "What would you like to know?"

"Well, you said you're from Pittsburgh. Did you grow up there?"

"Born and raised."

"Was your dad a police officer, too?"

Noah's enchanting smile instantly faded as he looked down at the table. "I never knew my father. My mom raised me all on her own."

"Oh. I'm sorry to hear that."

He raised his eyes to meet my gaze. "It's okay, don't be sorry. My mom and I got by just fine."

"But do you know who he was? Did she ever talk about him?"

"I learned long ago that subject was off limits with her. I asked her about him when I was eight years old, and I'll never forget the way she told me there was nothing to tell. She said she barely knew him, but I've always thought there was more to the story."

"Have you tried asking her about him since then?"

"Never." He paused, as if searching for the right words

to say. "I think he hurt her and the memories were just too painful. She did a lot for me over the years, made a lot of sacrifices. She doesn't deserve to have painful memories dredged up from the past."

"That's really nice of you to protect her. Is she still in Pittsburgh?"

"Yeah, but we keep in touch. My move up here was a little hard on her."

"Then she should come to visit. Fall is just around the corner and you wouldn't believe how beautiful the leaves will be. People come here from all over the world for the fall colors. It would be a great time for her to visit."

"Maybe next year. I'm still settling in and I want to know the area a little bit better first."

I shrugged. "Okay. But at least send her some pictures."

Noah grinned. "You know, the leaves change colors in Pittsburgh, too. But maybe I should send her some pictures of things we don't have in Pittsburgh, like you."

I gasped. It seemed awfully soon for that. "You wouldn't!"

He laughed. "I'm only teasing. I wanted to see your reaction."

I smiled with relief, gazing at him and savoring the moment. But my focus on Noah was suddenly interrupted when two loud rowdy boys stumbled in through the entry way and headed straight for the half-empty bar. I recognized them from my class. They both played on the football team, their green and gold letterman jackets evidence of their school spirit.

My smile quickly faded as the unruly scene unfolded before us.

The boys approached the bar, the rhythm of their footsteps uneven and their movements wobbly. As they settled onto the bar stools, they whistled, hailing the bartender's attention.

"Hey, gorgeous," Eric, the dark-haired boy slurred to the blonde, white-shirted bartender. "How 'bout a couple shots o' tequila for me an' my friend?" His voice rang out loudly against the hushed voices in the room.

"Do you boys have some ID?" the bartender asked in a steady voice, remaining calm and stoic.

The sandy-blond-haired boy, Mark, sputtered out a laugh. "Do you know who we are?" He turned to Eric. "I don't think she realizes that our families practically own this town." Then he leaned over the bar, grabbing her wrist and clamping her arm down against the surface. "My father runs the ski resort and his dad is president of the town bank. We get what we want when we want unless you, darlin', want to be unemployed. So I suggest you pour us those shots."

I sucked in a quick breath as I looked at Noah. He couldn't sit by and let some spoiled rich kids bully the bartender into serving them alcohol, especially when they were obviously already drunk. He caught my gaze, shaking his head apologetically before jumping up.

He rushed over to the empty stool beside Mark. "I suggest you let go of the lady. She's only doing her job." His confident posture and authoritative tone reminded me of my father.

Mark slowly uncurled his fingers around the bartender's wrist as his gaze shifted to Noah in disbelief. "Who the hell are you?"

Noah was ready and waiting with his badge pulled out of his pocket. "Noah Lawson, town deputy. And quite frankly, I don't care who either one of you are. It's very simple, no ID, no tequila."

Mark slapped his friend on the back. "Did you hear that? He wants to lose his job, too!" When he spun around to face Noah, anger sparked from his green eyes. "This is none of your business, so why don't you get lost?"

"It is my business. I won't let you harass the bartender. She's not going to serve you, so I think it's time you both leave."

He stared at Mark, his eyes bold and unwavering. He

wasn't backing down, and even though I hoped this would end quickly so that we could get back to our date, I enjoyed seeing someone stand up to Mark and Eric.

Mark looked at his friend. "You ready to leave, Eric?"

The dark-haired boy shook his head slowly. He was obviously much drunker than Mark. "Naw. We jus' got here. I wanna drink."

"I'm with you." Mark turned back to Noah. "We're not leaving until we get what we ordered."

Noah sighed, realizing it was going to take more than simple reasoning to get the boys to leave. "Then I'll have to take you out of here." He grabbed Mark's upper arm to lead him away, but the younger boy wiggled out of his grasp. Curling his hand into a fist, he swung it at Noah.

With lightning reflexes, Noah blocked the punch and caught Mark's arm with one hand. He spun the boy around, wrapping his arms around Mark's frame and locking the boy's arms against his sides. "That's assaulting a police officer," Noah gritted out in his ear.

While Noah kept a hold on Mark, Eric jumped out of his seat. I gasped, watching in horror as Eric lifted his fist and aimed it at Noah's jaw. "Noah!" I cried as I brought a hand up to my mouth in shock.

Before Eric could swing his arm, a man at the end of the bar launched out of his seat and grabbed Eric from behind, pulling the boy back a few steps and out of reach of Noah. I didn't recognize the stranger who had been quietly sitting at the bar with an amber colored drink since we had arrived. He appeared to be in his late forties. His jet black hair had been pulled back into a ponytail, and he wore a brown blazer with a pair of jeans. His black eyes narrowed as he held Eric back. "Easy there, son. It's not worth it. You need to get out of here and sleep it off."

Noah smiled in appreciation at the stranger. "Thanks, man."

Both boys seemed to realize their defeat. Their struggling against Noah and the man ceased. Noah shifted his hold on Mark to one arm while he pulled his phone out of his back pocket. After swiping the screen, he held it up to his ear. "Hi, sheriff." He grinned, listening to my father. "Oh, no, sir, sorry to worry you. Yes, Laken is fine. But we've had some trouble down here at Fireside. A couple of drunk kids tried to get served and then took a swing at me." He paused. "Everything's fine now, but I can't let them drive home." As he paused again, his eyes moved across the restaurant to settle on me.

I met his gaze and suddenly got a sinking feeling that whatever my father was telling him, it wasn't good. I raised my eyebrows as I took a sip of my Diet Coke, waiting for the drama to end.

"Okay, sir. I'll see you there soon." Noah returned his phone to his back pocket. "You both are coming down to the station with me. The sheriff is out on another call right now, and he'll meet us there later."

As my heart sank, Noah mouthed, "I'm sorry" across the room to me. His eyes shone with sincere disappointment, and I smiled weakly in understanding.

"Need some help getting these kids out of here?" the man still holding Eric asked.

Noah's attention shifted from me to the man. "Yes, thanks. I'm not sure how this would have ended if you hadn't stepped in." He nodded toward the door. "Let's go."

Noah gripped Mark's upper arm and led him out of sight. The other man followed closely behind with a firm hold on Eric's arm as the boy stumbled along beside him.

Just before they disappeared around the corner, the stranger holding Eric glanced my way. His black eyes sent a chill down my spine. I had no idea why since he had saved Noah from a punch, but something in their depths unnerved me. In a split second, I averted my eyes as they walked out of the restaurant.

As silence filled the room again, I stared down at the clean white tablecloth with utter disappointment. I didn't know what to do, but I couldn't just sit here, stranded. I had no way of knowing if Noah was coming back. And if he wasn't, I would have to find a ride home. The thought of calling anyone for a ride made me feel like crying. Just as I was about to jump up and run outside to find him, he emerged in the entryway. He hurried around the couch on his way back to the table.

"Hey," he said softly when he reached the table. I rose to my feet beside him as he gently touched my hand. "I'm so sorry about this, but I have to go. That guy who helped is waiting with the kids out there so that I could come back in to talk to you for a minute."

I nodded as I choked back tears. Ironically, had he just ignored the drunk boys, I would have been disappointed in him. I knew this was his job, but it didn't make it any less heartbreaking to have to end our date early. I had looked forward to this night all week, and now it was ruined. Despite feeling sorry for myself, I mustered up a smile. "I know. You have to do what you have to do."

"I don't know how long this is going to take. You should probably get a ride home. Do you think you'll be able to find one?"

"Yeah. I'll call my mom. I'm sure she can come get me."

"Okay. I'm going to make it up to you, I promise."

Hope filled my heart. "That would be nice," I said with a faint smile.

He nodded as he let go of my hand. "I have to run. I'll call you as soon as this is over. Bye." With that, he grabbed his jacket before turning and hurrying out of the restaurant.

I sank back into my seat and reached into my purse for my phone. As I browsed my contacts, I decided not to call my mother. I didn't know what I would tell her and I didn't want her pity. Instead, I called Brooke and relayed the night's events to her.

"Wow," she finally said after a long pause. "What a letdown."

"You're telling me. So do you have a car available tonight to come get me?"

"No. My sister had to work and my parents are out. But you sit tight. I'll find you a ride," she promised earnestly.

I was too tired to ask her what that meant. "Thanks, Brooke." She hung up so quickly, I wasn't sure that she heard me. Before I could put my phone down, she was probably on another call to find someone who had nothing better to do on a Saturday night than to give a girl a ride home.

The next few minutes seemed to pass like hours. The stranger who had helped Noah returned to his drink at the bar. Thankfully, he didn't look my way. The last thing I wanted right now was the pity of a stranger. I drummed my fingers against the white table cloth as five minutes passed, and then another ten. I called Brooke again, but she didn't answer. Then I sent her a text message, hoping she would tell me if someone, anyone, was on their way.

Just when I thought I would be stuck at the restaurant all night, I noticed a movement at the front entryway. A tall dark figure entered the room and I found myself staring into the hauntingly familiar blue eyes I had tried to forget all week. I groaned inwardly, cursing Brooke. Xander Payne was the last person I wanted to come to my rescue, but it appeared as though I didn't have a choice.

Chapter 12

Xander scanned the restaurant, a sympathetic smile crossing his handsome face when our eyes met. He shoved his hands into his jeans pockets under his dark green shirttails as he walked across the room. His eyes never left mine.

"Hey," he said softly when he reached my table. "Brooke called. Sorry to hear about your night."

"Thanks. But Noah couldn't let those boys drive home."

"He did the right thing." Xander sat down in the chair Noah had been sitting in before he had to leave. "Did you at least get to eat your dinner?"

"Oh, no," I gasped, rubbing my hands against my forehead as I stared at the white tablecloth. "I completely forgot about the food. It's going to be here any minute. What am I going to do with all of it? I'm not even hungry now."

"No problem. I'll take care of it."

By the time I lifted my head, Xander was halfway across the room. I watched curiously as he disappeared around the corner for a minute and then returned to the table. "It's all set," he informed me as he sat back down.

"What is?"

"The food. They're going to bring it in to-go boxes and I already paid."

I wanted to object, but the last thing I wanted to worry about right now was paying the bill. "Thanks."

He grinned slyly. "Oh, I'm not as generous as you must think. I haven't eaten yet, so I'll take whatever he ordered."

"What if you don't like it?"

"If his taste in food is half as good as his taste in women, then I'm sure I'll love it."

I felt a blush creep over my face as a moment of silence swept between us. I looked away, not quite sure what to say.

Xander finally broke the awkward silence. "They said the food should be right out and then we can go."

"Okay. I hope this didn't interrupt your night."

"Not a chance. I was just kicking around the house when Brooke called. It gave me an excuse to get out."

"That's right. There's nothing to do in this town." As soon as I said it, I was sorry. Here he was trying to help me and all I could remember was one remark he had made about our town. "I mean, don't you have a date with Carrie Sanders?" I asked quickly, softening my tone.

"Wouldn't you like to know?" he quipped with a devilish smile.

"Not really. I was just making conversation." I shrugged, looking away from him and wondering where the food was.

"If you say so."

I rolled my eyes at him, struggling to think of the perfect comeback when the waiter arrived with two large white Styrofoam boxes. Relieved that we could go now, I stood up and reached for my jacket on the back of my chair. Xander rose from his chair, taking the boxes from the waiter and thanking him. Once I had my jacket on, Xander nodded for me to follow him across the restaurant. Out of the corner of my eye, I noticed that the stranger who had helped Noah was still at the bar. Thankfully, he kept his back to us, his attention focused on his drink.

At the entrance, Xander held the front door open. I

breezed through it out into the darkness, stopping for him to catch up after the door fell shut behind him. The cold air ripped through my panty hose, biting at my legs. Anxious to get warm, I scanned the cars and trucks barely visible in the parking lot from the surrounding streetlamps. "Please tell me you didn't bring your motorcycle tonight," I said as he reached into the front pocket of his jeans for his keys.

"No, but that would have been fun."

"It most certainly would not be fun, especially in this skirt."

"Maybe not for you." Xander's subtle, sly smile sent shivers up my spine. His eyes moved up and down the length of me. "You look nice tonight, by the way. I don't think I've seen you in a skirt before."

"I don't wear skirts to school very often. But thank you." Now if only he would stop staring. "So do you have a car out here somewhere?"

"Not exactly. Right this way."

I raised my eyebrows, wondering what that meant as he turned and headed across the gravel parking lot. I followed, struggling to keep up with him in my wobbly heels. The uneven gravel just made things worse.

After a minute, he circled back to me, gently grabbing my arm for support. "Here, let me help you."

"Thanks." He led me to a huge black pick-up with a four-door cab. Stopping beside it, I gaped at the enormous truck that towered above me. "Is this yours?"

"Yep. And it's ready for winter with four wheel drive and snow tires." Xander unlocked the doors with the remote before opening the passenger door for me. "Just step on the running board. It's not as high as it looks."

I grabbed the interior door handle as I started to lift my foot onto the running board. Before I could pull myself up, Xander wrapped his fingers around my free hand. A fire shot up my arm, nearly causing me to lose my balance. My heart raced as I gripped his hand for support, finally managing to get into the seat.

I swallowed nervously as he shut the door. Xander quickly came around the front of the truck. After dropping the to-go boxes in the back, he jumped into the driver's seat. He turned on the engine and flipped the headlights on.

"You're going to have to give me directions," he said. "I've never been to your house."

As he guided the truck toward the parking lot entrance, I told him to turn right. Once we were headed through the dark town lit up only by a few streetlamps, he said, "I understand you've lived here your whole life."

"Yes. What's that supposed to mean?" I asked defensively.

"It means you must know the area pretty well," he explained, ignoring my snappy tone. "I'd like to get some hiking in before winter gets here, but I have no idea where to go. I could use a guide. Do you know some good trails around here?"

I suddenly felt a little guilty for reacting so abruptly to his question and softened my tone. "I know just about all the trails around here. Some better than others."

"So what do you say?"

"About what?"

"Well, if you're not busy tomorrow, how about showing me one of them? I'll bet there are some great views."

I stared out the front window, searching for an excuse to turn him down. But the truth was I hadn't been out for a hike in over a week. I missed the woods, and if I went with him, I would be safe from the wolf. Maybe I could even take my camera and get a few shots now that the leaves were starting to turn. Not to mention that my day was wide open since my shift at the pizza shop had been canceled. *No, it won't be a good day to get any pictures,* I told myself. *I won't be able to get any wildlife shots with Xander and still life just bores me.* However, I had a feeling I would be anything but bored if I was with him.

"Well?" he asked again.

"I'm thinking about it." As we reached the edge of town,

I directed him to turn onto another road. The town lights disappeared behind us as we drove through the dark forest. I stared out at the black night, still trying to find a good reason to decline his offer. Coming up empty, I finally answered him. "Okay."

He glanced over at me as if he couldn't believe I had agreed. "Really?"

"Yes."

Without another word, Xander eased the truck to a stop as we approached an intersection.

"Turn right. My house is a few miles down this road." We rode in silence as he carefully navigated the dark twisting road, passing an occasional driveway and mailbox. After a few minutes, house lights flickered beyond the scattered trees. We passed the Thompson's white cottage, barely visible from the road with only a single light on downstairs. I thought of Ryder and the baby they were expecting and wondered if someday that would be me in a cozy little house around here. But my thoughts of the distant future didn't last long. We soon approached my driveway, and I warned Xander to slow down just in time for him to make the turn. As soon as the truck stopped in the driveway, he shifted into park and shut off the rumbling engine.

I turned to him, studying his dark hair and blue eyes in the dim light. "Thank you for bringing me home."

"No problem. So what about tomorrow?"

"Pick me up at nine o'clock. The trail I have in mind is about fifteen minutes from here and it'll take about two hours to reach the top of the mountain. Wear loose fitting layers. It'll be cold in the morning, but you'll get hot fast. And I hope you have some comfortable, worn-in hiking boots."

"I do. You know, we have mountains bigger than these in California."

"I know. I just want to make sure you're prepared. I don't want you getting any blisters. Once we head out, we're not turning back." I met his gaze, looking for any sign of hesitation. But he stared back at me with nothing but confidence.

"I wouldn't dream of it. You've met your match."

"We'll see," I replied slowly, my eyebrows raised. Then I turned to open the side door.

"Hey, wait a minute. I'll get that for you." Xander opened his door and jumped down from his seat. Then he rushed around the front of the truck to meet me on the other side.

I reached for the hand he held up to me. With his support, I carefully climbed out of the truck. Another fire from his touch raced through me, and I whipped my hand away from him as soon as both of my feet were planted on the pavement. "Thanks. I can barely walk in these shoes," I muttered, darting a smile at him before I started walking toward the house.

"Laken, wait."

I stopped and turned, wondering what he wanted now.

"You forgot your dinner. Which one was yours?"

"Oh, yeah, I did forget. I ordered the pasta."

"I'll get it for you." Xander disappeared around the front of the truck. After few seconds, he returned with one of the white Styrofoam boxes. "Here you go." He handed it to me.

"Thanks." I chuckled softly. "I seem to be saying that a lot tonight."

"Yeah, well, I bet this isn't exactly how you thought your night would end."

"Not in a million years."

"Maybe now you can see I'm not such a bad guy after all. Can I walk you to the door?"

I looked at him, debating my answer. His dark hair and blue eyes shone in the moonlight, and as tempted as I was to accept his offer, I decided against it. "That won't be necessary. I think I can actually manage the sidewalk in these heels on my own."

"Okay. Good night, then. I'll see you in the morning."

"Nine o'clock," I reminded him. "Don't be late."

He responded with a silent mocking salute and a satisfied grin. I nodded before turning away to head toward the house. As I let myself in the front door, I heard Xander's truck pull out of the driveway. My thoughts quickly shifted back to Noah and my disappointment returned as the rumbling motor faded in the distance. But I held my head up high, hopeful that I would see him again soon. I would just have to be patient.

ॐॐॐ

Sometime later that night, as I leaned against the pillows on my bed and read a book by the soft glow of the lamp on my nightstand, my phone buzzed. I reached for it beside me on the comforter, wondering who could be trying to reach me at this hour. My heart skipped a beat when I saw Noah's name next to a text message on the screen. *R U still up?*

With a smile, I eagerly typed a one-word response. *Yes.*

Within seconds, my phone rang. I answered it after one ring. "Hi, Noah."

"Hey. Did you make it home okay?"

"Yeah. I got a ride. How did it go at the station?"

"As well as can be expected. The boys' parents weren't too happy, but they picked them up. I'm just glad those boys didn't drive home. They really could have hurt someone, including themselves."

"I know." A moment of silence hung between us, and I nervously twisted a lock of hair around my finger.

"The real reason I'm calling you is that I need you to come outside."

"What, now?"

"Yes, now."

"Okay," I replied slowly. "Can I ask why?"

"You'll see."

"I'm kind of in my pajamas."

"I don't care. Throw on some shoes and a jacket and I'll

meet you out front. I'm pulling into your driveway right
now."

With that, he hung up and I jumped off my bed onto the
cold hard floor. I rushed over to my mirror, pulling the ponytail holder out of my hair. After smoothing out the messy
locks and wiping away the mascara smudges under my
eyes, I stared at my navy blue shirt and plaid pajama pants.
Sighing, I realized they would just have to do.

As soon as I slipped my feet into a pair of sneakers, I ran
down the stairs, through the house, and out the front door
without bothering to get a jacket. The door fell shut behind
me as I walked along the sidewalk, my eyes adjusting to the
darkness. Sure enough, Noah leaned against the side of his
car in the driveway, his hair and clothes a bit disheveled. A
smile lit up his handsome face when he saw me.

I stopped halfway down the sidewalk as he walked toward me with confident, determined strides. A cool breeze
blew right through my pajamas, sending a shiver over me.
"What are you doing here?" I asked, confused.

"There's something I have to do before I can go home."
He stopped inches away from me, cupping my chin in his
hands and kissing me.

The world came to a screeching halt as I felt his lips
touch mine. I closed my eyes, shutting out the moonlight
and savoring his touch. He trailed his fingers along my jaw
to the back of my neck, leaving tingling sensations in their
wake. His lips parted, gently moving against mine. I responded to his lead, opening my lips slightly and kissing
him back.

My arms reached up around his broad shoulders, not only to keep my balance but to draw him closer. His other
hand slid down my shoulder blades to the small of my back,
touching me just above my waist. I suddenly felt as though
we were one beneath the stars and moon, and I wished this
moment would never end.

When a cold wind whipped through my hair, I trembled.
Noah suddenly pulled away and my eyes flew open to meet

his intense gaze. I smiled softly, silently studying him for several moments.

"I'm so sorry about what happened tonight," he whispered.

"Ssh." I pressed a finger up to his lips. "It's not your fault, so stop apologizing. Besides, you just turned this into one of the best nights of my life."

He swept his hands up along my shoulders and neck before pressing his lips to mine for one last kiss. When he raised his head, he explained, "I'd better go before your dad gets home and sees us making out in your front yard."

I laughed, knowing he was right. As much as I didn't want his kisses to end, I would be mortified if my father arrived home to see us kissing in front of the house. "Yeah. That would be just a little embarrassing."

Noah picked up one of my hands, holding it as he backed up. He only dropped it when he got too far away. "Good night, Laken. I'll talk to you soon."

"Good night," I whispered as I watched him hop into the driver's seat of his car. The lights flipped on as the engine came to life and he backed out of the driveway.

Only once the red tail lights disappeared from sight and I felt the cold air nipping at my hands and face did I turn back to the house, a love-struck smile plastered on my face.

cscs

The next morning, I put on my black work-out pants as soon as I got up. Then I slipped into a short gray tank top that cut across my abdomen nearly an inch above my waist. It would probably be chilly this morning, but I was bound to break into a sweat hiking up the mountain. Just as I had told Xander to wear layers, I was prepared to do the same. As I pulled my hair up into a ponytail, my phone rang. I grabbed it from my dresser, reading the name that flashed across the screen. Brooke. Good. I was dying to know how Xander had ended up coming to my rescue last night.

"You're in big trouble," I said as soon as I picked up the call and sat down on the edge of my bed.

Brooke laughed. "I trust Xander got you home okay last night."

"Thanks a lot. You could have at least sent me a text to let me know who you roped into coming to get me. I didn't even know you two were friends."

"And ruin the surprise? He's in my Physics class and he asked about you a few days ago. Did I forget to tell you that? Oops, sorry." I could practically hear the laughter in her teasing voice. "Seriously, though. You left for the night with a hot guy, so I thought it was only fitting for you to come home with one."

"Well, you know, he's not my favorite person."

Brooke groaned. "Maybe you just need to get to know him a little better. Remember how he slammed Marlena a week ago?"

It was my turn to groan. "Whose side are you on, any-way?"

Brooke ignored my question. "Enough about Xander. How did it go with Noah? At least up until he had to leave."

A smile crept over my face as I remembered Noah's kiss last night outside under the moon and stars. "Actually, he stopped by here late last night after he finished at the sta-tion. So in spite of what happened, it was a perfect ending to the evening."

"Ooh, I want details."

"I'm afraid you're going to have to wait. I'm on my way out the door to go hiking."

"Hiking? You can't postpone a hike with Dakota for ten minutes to share the details of last night with your poor friend who spent her night watching *Twilight* for the hun-dredth time?"

My smile broadened as I imagined her imploring stare. "I'm not heading out with Dakota. In fact, he took off yes-terday morning and hasn't come home since. I agreed to take Xander out on the trails today. He needed a guide because he doesn't know the area. Since my lunch shift got canceled at work because it's too slow, I figured what the hell."

"I really don't like you right now," Brooke muttered.

I suddenly heard the rumble of an engine and looked down at my watch. Eight forty-five. He was early. "I think he's here. I've got to go. I'll call you later."

"Okay. But you need to start sharing! It's not fair that you have two hot guys eating out of your hands and I have none."

"Then don't send one of them to my rescue. I have to go," I repeated. "I'll call you later."

"Okay. Have fun, but not too much fun."

"Bye, Brooke," I said, finally hanging up the phone and jumping up to my feet to steal a quick glance in the mirror.

I still wore the necklace my father had given me for my birthday. It didn't exactly match my work-out clothes, but I wasn't ready to take it off. It sparkled against my chest above the neckline of my gray shirt. Mesmerized by the intricate circles and tiny diamonds, I traced the silver circles with my fingertip for a quick moment. Then I tore my eyes away from it as I grabbed the small black backpack off my dresser and tossed my phone into it. Without another look in the mirror, I ran out of my room and down the stairs, the rubber soles of my hiking boots thundering against the hardwood steps.

My mother sat at the kitchen table with a bowl of cereal and steaming cup of coffee. Her robe was wrapped over her pajamas as she thumbed through a college brochure. "Good morning, Laken. Care to join me in going through these brochures?"

I glanced at her as I rushed across the kitchen to pour coffee into a silver travel thermos. After adding a healthy dose of hazelnut creamer to it, I twisted the lid into place. "Can't. I'm going hiking with a guy from school. He's waiting out in the driveway." I rushed about the kitchen, grabbing a water bottle from the refrigerator and a few granola bars from the pantry. After piling the loot into my backpack, I retrieved my gray fleece jacket from the coat closet.

"A guy? What happened to Noah?"

I emerged from around the corner, pulling my ponytail out from under the jacket collar. "It's not like that. He's new and doesn't know any of the trails," I explained as I returned to the counter to grab my coffee thermos.

"Does this boy have a name?" she asked.

"Xander Payne."

"And how much do you know about him?"

I sighed, rolling my eyes. "Enough." As much as his mysterious past intrigued me, after last night, something told me I would be safe with him. And that was all I needed to know. At least I tried to convince myself of that. After all, I was using him as an excuse to get out into the woods for a day.

"Okay, but when you get home, we need to go through these college brochures and narrow down your choices. If you don't get started with your applications soon, you're going to miss the deadlines."

"Fine. But I also have to do my homework."

"I understand that. But, Laken, you can't avoid the college decision forever. You're going to have to face it sooner or later."

"I know. I'm just not ready to think about it yet. If Dakota comes home, can you let him in?"

"Of course. Have a good time and don't be out too long."

"I won't." I left out the front door, escaping the mention of college again. I knew I couldn't run from it forever, but at least I got away for today.

The crisp mountain air sent goose bumps racing up from my ankles to where my work-out pants ended just below my knees as I jogged down the sidewalk to the huge black pick-up truck. The windows were rolled up, and loud music thumped inside the cab. Xander sat patiently in the driver's seat, his eyes hidden by dark sunglasses. As soon as he noticed me, he turned the music off and the doors unlocked with a click. He remained seated as I hurried around to the passenger side.

I opened the door, pausing as I studied the running board. The tall truck was a lot less intimidating in broad daylight when I was wearing hiking boots than it had been last night in the dark. I easily climbed into the roomy leather seat and yanked the heavy door shut. Then I turned to him. "You're early."

"You told me not to be late. I wasn't taking any chances that you'd change your mind. Ready?"

I pulled the seatbelt over my shoulder and fastened it in place. "Yes. Let's go." As I retrieved my sunglasses out of my backpack and slid them on, he backed out of the driveway and drove away from the house.

Chapter 13

I sipped my coffee as Xander guided the truck through the mountains. The road wound through forests sprinkled with white birch trees. Towering maple and oak trees hid the rising sun, casting dappled shadows on the pavement. We entered the White Mountain National Forest, and the terrain became steeper as we drove deep into the mountains and away from any semblance of civilization. Splashes of red, orange, and yellow hinted that autumn was on its way. The sky, what little of it could be seen peeking through the dense ceiling of leaves, was a deep blue.

As we turned around a sharp bend, a gravel driveway next to a visitor's center sign came into view. A log building loomed beyond the trees and empty parking lot. Xander slowed, looking to the side. "Should I turn in here?"

"No. That's where the tourists go. I know a better place about two miles up ahead."

He sped up as we passed the entrance. "Really? I didn't see a single car."

"It's still early. If there are any tourists around today, that's where they'll go. I prefer the trails off the beaten path. There's a good chance we won't see any people where we're going. Besides, the visitor center trails are short and boring with no good views. You seem like the kind of guy who would want to go straight to the top."

Xander stole a glance my way from behind his sunglasses. A slight grin formed on his face. "So you've thought about the kind of guy I am?"

"I—well, what I mean is—you just look adventurous," I stammered, staring out the front windshield.

"Hm. I wonder what gave me away."

I took a deep breath, ignoring his comment. "We also have a better chance of seeing some wildlife."

"Really? Like what?"

"Oh, you know, lions and tigers and bears," I teased. He started to slow the truck and I laughed. "I'm only kidding, although we may see a black bear. They're pretty harmless though. They generally keep their distance from people." I suddenly spotted the hidden entrance to a small dirt parking lot. Just as I expected, it was empty. "Slow down. The turn off is just ahead. It's right there," I said, pointing.

He slowed almost to a stop before cutting the tight right-hand turn. As the truck bounced over the deep ruts, he said, "Now back to what you said about bears. Are you serious? Have you ever seen one while out hiking?"

"Yeah. Lots of times."

"Great," he muttered as he eased the truck to a stop inches in front of a huge tree.

"What's the big deal? Don't tell me you're scared of a harmless black bear," I said with a grin.

He scoffed as he shut off the engine. "We had plenty of reports of black bears getting into garbage cans and breaking into houses up in the mountains back in California. I don't think I'd want to mess with one."

I pulled off my sunglasses and turned to look at him. "It's not too late to change your mind."

"No way. We're here, so let's go." He smiled confidently before opening his door.

I pushed the heavy passenger door open and climbed out

of the truck, leaving my coffee thermos in one of the cup holders and my sunglasses on the seat. I hoisted my backpack over my shoulder as I raised my hand up to the door. Before I could give it a push, Xander approached behind me. He was so close that I felt the heat from his body. His fingers gently grazed mine as he lifted his hand to the door. Familiar yet unsettling shivers raced through me, and I whirled around to face him.

"Here, let me." He slowly pushed the door shut behind me. "Looks like we both had the same idea." He held up a backpack. "Let me guess. Water bottle and granola bars?"

I nodded, finally glancing up at him to see that his sunglasses were gone. His blue eyes seemed to look right through me, and I breathed deeply, trying to relax. An unbuttoned, untucked black shirt hung loosely over his tight black tank top and army green cargo pants. His light brown hiking boots were scuffed, evidence that they were worn in. A black rope necklace with a single white tooth pendant rested against his smooth tanned skin, gleaming in the patchy sunlight.

"Want me to put your stuff in mine? It doesn't make sense to take two half-empty backpacks," he offered.

"Sure. That would be great," I replied.

I peeled my eyes off of him, chasing my thoughts away from his broad shoulders. Opening my backpack, I grabbed the water bottle and granola bars and handed them to him. Then I stuffed my phone into the inside pocket of my jacket.

Xander dropped the items into his backpack before sliding his arms through the straps to secure it onto his back. As soon as he tossed my empty backpack in the truck and locked the doors, he stepped back with a gentlemanly gesture. "Lead the way."

I walked past him, heading for the trail entrance between a metal garbage can and a sign reading *Summit 3.5 miles*. As I started up the path, I glanced over my shoulder to see Xander following closely behind. The trail cut narrowly between the dense trees that rose up from the floor of green ferns and thick underbrush. I paced myself, conserving the energy needed to make the three-and-a-half-mile uphill hike to the top. Memories of my fall the night I set out to find Ryder filled my mind, and I kept my eyes glued to the ground, watching for tree roots that snaked across the dirt path.

"So three and a half miles?" Xander asked.

"That's right. And it's all uphill."

"You still sound like you don't believe I can make it."

"I never believe anyone can handle this hike until I see them do it," I replied over my shoulder.

"Thanks for the vote of confidence."

I turned and flashed a reassuring smile at him. "If it's any consolation, I wouldn't have come if I wasn't pretty sure you could." Our eyes met briefly, but I quickly looked back in the direction I was walking to focus on the footing. "So what's with your necklace? Is that a shark tooth?"

"Yeah. It's one of the few things I have right now that reminds me of the ocean," he said wistfully.

"Do you miss it?"

"Like you wouldn't believe. I must have spent every day for the last ten years out in the surf, until a few weeks ago that is. Sometimes, I only got out for an hour or so after school, but on weekends and during the summers, surfing was my life."

"Now I know why you're so tan. I hate to tell you this, but there's no ocean up here."

"I figured that out. At least once the slopes open, I'll be able to snowboard."

"Ah, you're on the dark side," I mused. As I waited for him to answer, the trail angled upward steeply. I scanned the woods on both sides, watching for suspicious shadowy movements. Even with Xander close behind, I hadn't forgotten that the golden-eyed wolf could be lurking behind any tree.

"Always have been," Xander responded boastfully. Then he laughed. "I take it you don't snowboard."

"Nope."

"Do you ski?"

"I know how, but I don't get out on the slopes very often." The truth was between my school schedule, the cost of a lift ticket, ski rentals, my time, and budget, I couldn't afford such a luxury.

"Maybe we can hit the slopes together this winter."

"Maybe," I said softly.

I couldn't agree to any future activities with him. Today was an exception because I had missed the outdoors since the other wolf had shown up and because Xander had been really nice last night. But other than that, I had no intentions of making long-term future plans with him.

We hiked in silence for about fifteen minutes. Our footsteps thudded on the dirt path as an occasional breeze rustled through the canopy of leaves overhead. The birds kept up a noisy chirping chatter, and every now and then a woodpecker pounded into a nearby tree. I savored these familiar forest sounds, realizing how much I had missed them, even if it had only been for a week.

As we continued on our way up the mountain, the cool temperatures steadily climbed. When I began to feel hot, I stopped in the middle of the trail, turning back to Xander. He skidded to a halt just before he would have slammed into me, sweat glistening on his tanned skin. After taking my jacket off, I tied the arms around my waist.

"Good idea. It's starting to get really warm." Xander slipped the backpack off his shoulders and stripped off his black shirt, revealing his broad shoulders and muscular arms. As he knelt to stuff his shirt into the backpack, I studied the intricate details of his tattoo. The dagger blades were rough and dangerous, but the diamond floating in between the handles added a sense of grace and beauty, as if that was even possible.

"So I'm curious," I said, desperately trying to distract my thoughts away from his gorgeous arms. "What did your parents think about your tattoo? My parents would probably ground me for life if I came home with a tattoo."

As he stood up, he stretched his arms through the backpack straps. "First of all, it's just my dad, and secondly, a tattoo is pretty tame compared to all the other trouble I could get into, believe me." He finished securing the backpack into place, but neither one of us was eager to continue hiking up the mountain right away.

"Like stealing a car?" I asked as we stood on the trail.

"I was afraid you'd remember that."

"It's kind of hard to forget. That's not exactly something you hear every day." I wondered how much I could get him to tell me about that. I was still curious to find out why there was no record of it. "Why did you do it?" I blurted out, meeting his gaze.

He shrugged flippantly. "I was bored. So I hot-wired a neighbor's Porsche and took it for a spin. It was really fun to drive." He smiled wistfully at the memory.

"But was it worth the risk?"

"Probably not. It wasn't one of my better judgment calls."

"What happened when you got caught?"

He looked away with a sigh. "I returned it without a single scratch, so the owner decided not to press charges. But my dad was pretty pissed. It wasn't exactly a neighborly thing to do. Not that we were great friends with our neighbors to begin with."

"And then he moved you here. Guess that was a pretty hard lesson to learn. No more surfing." At least now I had an explanation for the missing police record.

Xander's eyes whipped back to me, meeting my stare. "It's not that bad here."

"It's not?" I asked incredulously.

He smiled coyly. "No, not as long as I'm with you."

I blushed, nervously averting my eyes away from his. "Oh, please. Your California charms aren't going to work on me," I stated.

"So you think I'm charming?" he teased.

I rolled my eyes. Eager to end this conversation, I gestured up the hill. "We need to keep going. We'll never make it to the top if we just stand here."

"Yeah, sure."

I took the lead as we resumed hiking up the mountain. Xander followed closely, at least I was pretty sure I felt him less than a foot away.

"What happened to your mom?" I asked between deep breaths.

A few seconds passed before I heard his quiet voice. "My mom died in a car accident shortly after I was born."

I stopped dead in my tracks and spun around. "Xander, I'm sorry. I had no idea."

"Of course, you didn't. It's okay, really. People ask me about her a lot when I first meet them. I'm used to having to explain."

"How did it happen?"

"Drunk driver. But it was a long time ago and I never knew her. It was a lot harder on my dad than it was on me."

I nodded, not sure what to say. Xander set off again, passing me as he took the lead. I watched him walk away for a minute, still shocked by his heartbreaking past before realizing I couldn't let him get too far ahead. I launched into a jog to catch up.

"Your father never remarried?" I asked when I reached him and slowed to a walk.

"No. He dated some, but he always blew it because he spends too much time working."

"Really? What does he do?"

"He makes jewelry."

"He makes it? You mean, like, by hand?"

"Exactly."

"Wow. I didn't know people do that."

"Most don't. But this craft has been in our family for generations. It's in our blood."

"What kind of jewelry does he make?"

"Mostly diamond necklaces."

"That must be lucrative. How does he sell them?"

"Through a broker in LA. They usually end up being sold to movie stars, music executives, athletes, and the like."

My jaw dropped as I imagined Xander mingling with gorgeous movie stars. No wonder our town seemed so boring to him. "Have you ever met anyone famous?"

"Naw. That never interested me. There's only one thing in California I ever cared about."

"The ocean."

"That's right. You catch on fast."

Silence suddenly fell between us as we focused on our ascent up the mountain. After a few minutes, Xander stopped and spun around. He watched me intently as I closed the distance between us. "What?" I asked.

"I would feel better following you. That way I don't have to worry that I've lost you somewhere behind."

"That's not going to happen," I scoffed. "But I'll still take the lead." As I passed him, I felt his stare on me. I got the distinct feeling that he wanted me in front of him so that he could keep his eye on me, *all* of me. At least my jacket covered my backside below my waist, limiting what he could see. "But don't you get lost back there," I said over my shoulder as I marched ahead at a brisk pace.

"You couldn't lose me if you tried," he retorted.

I glanced back to see him keeping a close distance. When I returned my attention to the trail ahead, my thoughts wandered to the first day of school when Xander had ridden into the parking lot on his motorcycle. If anyone had told me I'd be hiking with him barely two weeks later, I never would have believed it.

We continued up the mountain without stopping for the next hour. Few words passed between us as the terrain grew steeper and rockier. I couldn't afford to keep up a conversation when I needed to pay attention to each step I took, making sure to keep my balance. The rocks were tricky as some were loose and shifted under my weight. We crossed a stream about halfway up, carefully jumping from rock to rock to stay above the flowing water, before climbing a steep incline right after it.

When we finally reached the summit, we emerged from a cluster of pine trees onto a small rocky clearing. We stopped short of a steep drop-off, admiring the scenery. Beyond the cliff spanned the vast blue sky dotted with white fluffy clouds. Rugged mountains stretched out before us, abundant with thick trees and patches of red, orange, and yellow.

"Wow," Xander gasped beside me. "This is really beautiful."

"You should see it in about three weeks. The only green will be the pine trees. The mountains will be lit up with color," I told him, breathless from the final climb. My leg muscles burned as I sat down on the flat expansive rock, my fleece jacket providing a thin cushion against the hard surface.

Xander eased down beside me. "Does that mean we can do this hike again in a few weeks?"

I smiled at him. "You can come here any time you want now that you know where to go. You don't need me to come with you."

He returned my smile. "But it wouldn't be as much fun alone."

Our eyes met, and I quickly looked straight ahead at the panoramic view. "You could always bring Carrie."

"Somehow, I don't think she's the type to enjoy this sort of thing."

"Yeah, you're right. She might break a nail."

Another moment of silence passed as I savored the sunshine. I cherished these last few warm days of summer as they were numbered. The snow and ice of winter would be here before we knew it. I leaned back, resting my hands on the smooth rock and tilting my head up toward the sky with my eyes closed.

I heard Xander rustling beside me and opened my eyes

to see him sliding the backpack off his shoulders. "Thirsty?" he asked as he unzipped the bag, pulling out two water bottles.

"Yes. And hungry too." I took one from him, noticing the water condensation that slicked its sides. As I opened the bottle and drank from it, Xander reached back into the bag for the granola bars. He handed one to me.

We ate and drank in silence, both of us admiring the mountains from our perch upon the rock. Surprisingly, in spite of my earlier apprehension about today, it was a comfortable silence.

Once we finished our water and snacks, Xander stuffed the empty bottles and wrappers into his backpack. "So who do you usually go hiking with?" he asked.

I shrugged. "No one. I go alone most of the time." Except when I was with Dakota, but I couldn't exactly tell him I had a wolf.

And I often took my camera to get pictures of moose or bears, but I didn't want to tell him anything more about myself. He already knew too much.

"Isn't that kind of dangerous?"

"No," I said with a smile that quickly faded. "At least I never thought of the mountains as dangerous until…"

"Until they found the body of the guy who took that little boy?"

I nodded as darkness swept over me, despite the blazing sun. "Yeah."

"Sorry. I didn't mean to bring that up."

"It's okay." I glanced at him. "I bet that kind of thing happens a lot in California."

"There's more crime if that's what you mean. But that doesn't mean you get used to it." He paused. "Do they know why that guy took the boy?"

"No, at least not yet." I frowned, desperately wanting to change the subject.

Xander must have read my mind. He slid the straps back onto his shoulders and looked over at me, his blue eyes nearly transparent in the bright sunshine. "Ready to head back?"

Not really, I thought with a sigh, remembering the college brochures on the kitchen table at home. But I couldn't stay out here all day. I still had homework to finish. "Sure." I scrambled to my feet and brushed off my jacket.

As Xander rose to his feet, I felt a faint flush race through me at the sight of his tall muscular frame. His tanned arms glistened in the sun, and the tiny piece of metal that fastened the shark tooth to the rope of his necklace glinted from a blinding spark of sunlight.

"Your turn to lead," I told him, thinking that it was my turn to admire his backside. *Where did that come from?* I thought, immediately scolding myself for having such thoughts, especially after kissing Noah last night.

I was about to change my mind and offer to lead when he agreed. "No problem. I don't have to worry about you keeping up when we're going downhill." He flashed me one last smile before setting off through the small trail opening between the pine trees.

I followed, welcoming the shade from the canopy of trees overhead. I fell into step behind him, returning my attention to the steep rocky terrain as I carefully calculated each step. I had to work hard to keep my balance. The last thing I wanted was to fall down the slope and crash into him. We hiked down the steepest part of the mountain in silence. The scenery of all pine trees slowly transitioned to a variety of leafy trees as we descended. The forest sounds of chirping birds and drilling woodpeckers resumed the farther down we went.

When we approached the stream we had crossed on our way up the mountain, a black shape darted through the trees deep in the woods. I stopped, staring at it, my heart racing with fear. My first thought was of the wolf, but the shape was too large and round. It had to be a bear. It moved through the trees, coming a little closer before it halted and watched us.

Xander didn't notice that I had fallen behind. He was about fifteen feet ahead when I called out to him. "Xander!" I said in a loud whisper.

He heard me and stopped quickly, turning around.

"Over there in the woods." I nodded in the direction of the bear. It stood still, studying us curiously. "A bear."

His eyes followed my gaze and widened as soon as he saw it staring at us. "Oh great. Now what do we do?"

"Nothing. Just don't move." I focused on the bear and suddenly noticed a line across its snout. A scar. This was the same bear that had found Ryder and kept him warm. A smiled worked its way across my lips as an idea formed in my mind. I glanced at Xander who was completely unsuspecting of what was about to happen.

'*Hi,*' I thought as I looked back at the bear, meeting the gaze of her soft brown eyes. '*I don't think I thanked you for helping with the little boy, so thank you.*' She watched me as understanding registered in her eyes. '*This is my friend. He won't hurt you. But I need a favor. Can you come closer?*'

The bear lumbered through the trees, nearing the trail. Xander glanced at me. "What's happening?" he whispered nervously.

"Ssh. Don't make any noise. You don't want to provoke it."

He glared at me. "I thought you said black bears were harmless," he said in a low voice, his teeth clenched.

I bit back a mischievous grin, returning my attention to the bear who had reached the edge of the trail halfway between us. When her gaze met mine, I envisioned her approaching Xander, nuzzling his hand with her nose. She seemed to understand exactly what to do. She looked at him as she ambled down the trail in his direction, closing the distance between them. His eyes grew bigger with every step she took.

He looked at me, the panic on his face shooting a pang of guilt through me. But it was too late to call it off. I would just have to send the bear away quickly after it was over.

"What in the world?" he whispered so softly that I barely heard him over the leaves rustling in the breeze.

"Ssh." I pressed a finger to my lips and watched in disbelief as the bear approached him. She gently sniffed his hand like a big dog greeting him. When she looked my way, I released her with a quick thought. She spun around and loped off into the woods. Within seconds, the black ball of fur disappeared from sight. The smile I had been suppressing finally broke out, and I bit my lip to keep from laughing.

Xander breathed a huge sigh of relief as he glared at me. "What the hell was that?"

I started marching toward him. "You must have forgotten to put on your bear repellent today," I said with a stifled giggle. I felt his hot eyes following me as I walked by, but I ignored them.

I focused on the stream ahead, but I didn't get very far. As I passed him, he reached out, grabbing my wrist. He yanked me to a stop in front of him, pulling me toward him until we were inches apart. As I stared up at his mesmerizing blue eyes, he placed my fingertips on his sternum above the neckline of his black tank top. His heart was racing.

"Feel that?" he asked, his eyes shooting sparks out at me.

My devious smile and the urge to burst out in laughter vanished immediately, replaced by the electricity between us. Our eyes locked, like magnets stuck to metal.

"How did you do that? That was one hell of a trick."

Despite the warmth in the air and the heat rising off his skin, goose bumps prickled my arms. I shivered inwardly. "I—I don't know what you're talking about," I stuttered.

"I think you do," he stated with an overwhelming confidence.

For a moment, I wondered if he knew about me, that I could talk to wild animals. But the moment passed quickly when I realized how absurd it was. How could he possibly know anything about me, much less the one thing I had hidden from people I had known all my life? "Are you crazy? I don't know how that happened any more than you do. Maybe it smelled the granola bar wrappers in your backpack."

Xander's wild eyes softened as he mulled over my weak explanation. "Maybe."

"You're lucky it didn't try to get them."

"Don't remind me. I'd like to forget what just happened. I don't want being flustered like this to tarnish my image as the cool new guy."

My lips curved slightly. "Your secret is safe with me."

I was relieved he had a reason not to tell anyone else about this. I didn't want to suddenly be branded a crazy bear girl by some of the superstitious town people who actually believed in witches. And who knew? Maybe I really was a witch.

As Xander's heart rate slowed, his gaze left my eyes, traveling down to my chest. "That's quite a nice necklace you have. I noticed it last night, but I forgot to say something."

He finally released my wrist and I instinctively moved my fingers up to trace the pendant circles. "Thank you. My dad gave it to me for my birthday. Apparently, it's some old family heirloom."

"It looks valuable. If you have time, we could run by my place before I take you home. I could show it to my dad. He loves to examine jewelry to see what it's worth and where it came from."

"I don't care what it's worth. I have no intentions of selling it." As I spoke, I remembered my mother's insistence that I start looking through the college brochures piled on the kitchen table when I got home. I wanted to put that off as long as I could. "But I wouldn't mind finding out the history behind it. My dad said it's very old," I said quickly.

"Great. When we get back to the truck, I'll text my dad to let him know we're on our way. He'll probably make us some sandwiches for lunch." Xander smiled casually, seeming to have forgotten all about the bear. "What do you say?"

"Sure. That sounds nice."

"Cool. I'm starting to get really hungry." He nodded down the trail. "Come on. Let's go." He turned away, marching toward the stream.

Great, I thought, rolling my eyes as I watched him walk away. *More time with Xander. That's all I need right now. Why did he have to turn out to be nice, after all? What am I getting myself into?*

I shook my head as another voice echoed in my thoughts. *Stop worrying about this so much. You can just be friends with him like you are with Ethan. Nothing has to happen.* Unfortunately, I wasn't convinced. The electricity between us was unmistakable. No good would come from time spent with him if I expected to continue seeing Noah.

"Are you coming?" Xander called from across the stream.

With a quick shake of my head, I pushed the voices out of my head. Then I nodded at him because I couldn't think of a good excuse for standing there as I silently argued with myself. I broke into a jog to catch up with him, thankful for the solid footing on this section of the trail. As soon as I hopped across the rocks to get to the other side of the stream, he continued down the mountain.

Looking down at my feet to avoid watching his backside, I followed him at a brisk walk. The chirping birds, pounding woodpeckers, and whispering leaves were all that we heard as we hiked back to the parking lot without another word passing between us.

Chapter 14

A huge log mansion loomed through the trees up ahead as Xander guided the truck around a tight hairpin turn on the private road. I glimpsed the house in the distance between the dense leafy trees as he pulled to a stop in front of a black metal gate. After rolling down his window, he punched a code on a number pad. The single panel gate swung inward, opening wide enough for the pick-up truck to clear the stone pillars on each side. I couldn't help wondering why it was needed. Security systems weren't used in our town, at least they hadn't been until Ryder had been snatched from his backyard.

As Xander continued along the driveway, I turned to see the black gate close automatically behind us. When I twisted around to face forward, we drove around another turn and the trees suddenly parted.

The log mansion directly ahead appeared even larger up close. Cedar logs lined its high walls and framed each window.

A porch spanned across the front of the house with two Adirondack chairs centered between the wooden railing and the log wall. Double doors with ornate stained glass windows were positioned behind the two steps leading up from the slate sidewalk.

Xander eased the truck to a stop in front of the garage. "Here we are," he announced, shutting off the engine and lifting his sunglasses off his face. "Home sweet home."

"Nice place," I said, my eyebrows raised.

I didn't know what else to say, but calling the enormous log mansion nice didn't do it justice. I was certainly impressed, but I was also grateful that he had explained what his father did for a living. I had been expecting something grand and completely unlike the modest homes we had in town. Needless to say, I was not surprised.

"It'll do," he said flippantly.

As he jumped down and walked around the front of the truck, I remained in my seat, captivated by the house. I suddenly wondered if I was completely underdressed for lunch with Xander's father. *Stop worrying so much. It's not like you're here as Xander's dinner date. It's a casual unplanned drop-in visit so that he can look at your necklace,* I reminded myself.

When Xander opened the passenger door, he curiously looked up at me. "Are you just going to sit there? Come on. I'm starving."

My lips twitched into a pensive smile. After unfastening my seatbelt, I climbed down from my seat with my fleece jacket in one hand. As soon as I stepped onto the pavement, I started to slide my arms back into my jacket sleeves.

"What are you doing? You can't possibly be cold."

"I'm feeling a little self-conscious meeting your dad when I'm half dressed in these work-out clothes," I whispered, glancing about the driveway to make sure his father hadn't come outside to greet us.

"Don't worry about him. The only thing he will notice is what's hanging around your neck. I, on the other hand, will thoroughly enjoy the view of your cute ass in those pants," he said smugly, much to my chagrin.

My face flushed with embarrassment as I looked up at his teasing blue eyes. "Then I really need to wear this. I would never forgive myself for flaunting something you can never have."

I smiled knowingly, pulling my jacket up over my shoulders, thankful that the bottom of it reached below my hips. As I stepped away from the truck, I tugged my ponytail out from underneath the collar.

"We'll see," he said, not willing to let me have the last word. He shut the truck door and then turned to me, a smile gleaming on his face. "This way."

I followed him to the sidewalk of slate rock. As we walked toward the front porch, I noticed the meticulously pruned bright green shrubs planted in the mulch beds surrounding the house. We marched up the steps to the porch and Xander slid his key into the lock. After a soft click, he opened the door. I entered the house, gaping in awe at the two-story entry hall, a wrought iron chandelier hanging overhead. The hardwood floor was shiny and polished, the log walls rustic and campy. As I looked around, Xander stopped and punched a code into a key pad on the inside wall next to the door.

"I thought your dad was home," I mused as I wandered past him.

At first glance, the home resembled a ski lodge. The foyer opened up into a living room with a gray stone fireplace that crawled up the two-story cedar log wall. A dark brown couch and two matching chairs with ottomans surrounded a wooden coffee table that sat upon a red oriental rug covering a large section of the hardwood floor. As I studied the room, I quickly noticed that Xander's love for the ocean hadn't been left behind in California. A bright yellow surfboard had been mounted above a row of windows. Below it, mountains of pastel green rolled out in waves below the powder blue sky outside the glass.

"He keeps the alarm system on even when he's home," Xander explained.

I barely heard him as I noticed a gold-framed photograph hanging at eye level on the wall. In it, Xander stood on his surf board, riding a wave as the white foam crest behind him splashed his black wetsuit. The clarity of the photograph was remarkable. Each drop of the wave's spray was dotted, as if frozen in time. Xander's clear blue eyes were several shades lighter than the sapphire ocean surrounding him as he focused straight ahead. His broad frame and toned muscles rippled beneath the shimmering wetsuit. His knees were slightly bent, his arms raised out to his sides. I pointed at the picture, careful not to touch the glass. "Where is this? California?"

Xander approached behind me. I didn't need to turn around to know that he was only inches away. My heart caught in my chest as I heard him sigh wistfully. "Nope. Hawaii. We go there a couple times a year for a few surfing competitions."

"Really? So you're pretty good, huh?"

He didn't answer me right away. After a moment of silence, I turned to see him staring thoughtfully at the photograph. When he finally moved his gaze to me, he smiled. "Sorry, I was just remembering the day that was taken."

"Boy, your dad must have been really mad to take you this far away from the ocean. I can tell this is your passion. You must be crushed to be here."

"I told you earlier, it's not that bad."

"Are you planning to go back to California for college?"

He shook his head. "No. I won't be going to college."

"Really? Why not?"

"I'm going to work with my dad. I already help him out on weekends and in the evenings after school."

"Lucky," I muttered under my breath.

"It's not as glamorous as it sounds."

"Let's see, making diamond necklaces for movie stars to wear on the red carpet or hitting the books for a career that might pay for a tiny house after making a huge student loan payment every month? Sorry, but I have to disagree."

Xander looked at me, his smile gone and his eyes sober. "I don't have a choice, Laken. This is what I'm destined to do. Lock myself away in an old wine cellar that's been converted into a workshop day and night like my father."

As he spoke, a door opened and closed, followed by the sound of soft footsteps on the hardwood floor. "Oh, I don't know, Xander, it doesn't sound all bad," came a deep voice laced with jovial sarcasm.

A man about Xander's height came into view behind him. He wore a white T-shirt under an open white button-down shirt, both smudged with black soot and wrinkled. His dusty jeans were torn and frayed at the knees. His disheveled salty-gray hair desperately needed combing and a haircut, and a shadow of gray stubble dotted his chin. He smiled at me, his brown eyes warm and welcoming. For a moment, something seemed awfully familiar about him, but I couldn't put my finger on what. I noticed the hint of a resemblance between him and Xander, but that wasn't it.

The man clamped a hand over Xander's shoulder. "Don't mind my son. He sometimes forgets how fortunate we've been over the years."

Xander rolled his eyes. His solemn expression softened as he spoke. "Hi, Dad. I want you to meet Laken Sumner. Laken, this is my dad, Caleb."

"It's nice to meet you, Mr. Payne."

Caleb grinned at me. "Nonsense, my dear. The pleasure is all mine." He extended his hand to me. I reached out to take it, expecting a friendly handshake. But he lifted my hand to his lips for a quick gentle kiss. "Xander has told me a lot about you. You're even more beautiful than he described."

I raised my eyebrows at Xander, noticing a faint blush in his tanned cheeks.

"Okay, Dad, thanks a lot," he said softly.

As I watched the awkward moment between them, I thought that Xander's father couldn't be farther from the truth. I was a mess after our hike. Loose strands of hair had escaped my ponytail, tickling my ears and face, and I hadn't put on any make-up before leaving this morning.

"Thank you," I said before quickly changing the subject. "Mr. Payne, you have a beautiful home. When did you move in?"

"Please call me Caleb. We only moved in, what…" He glanced at Xander. "…a week before school started?"

"Yes, Dad." Xander paused, looking at me before he continued. "We barely had our boxes unpacked by the first day of school. But seriously, Dad, Laken didn't come here to stand in the entry hall and hear about our move. I promised her you would look at her necklace, and I'm starving. Can we please move this conversation to the kitchen?"

"Yes, of course." Caleb stepped aside as Xander led the way through the living room and around a corner. He gestured for me to follow him.

Their kitchen was immaculate with oak cabinets the same color as the log walls, speckled black granite countertops, and wrought iron pendant lights that hung above the center island. The appliances were stainless steel, and a six-burner stove stretched out under a stainless steel hood along the wall. A round table sat in an enclave surrounded by floor to ceiling windows that looked out over the mountains.

"Have a seat, Laken," Xander said as he circled the island on his way to the refrigerator. "What happened to lunch, Dad?"

"You know me. Always working," Caleb answered with a grin.

Xander flashed me a knowing smile before pulling deli meats, cheese, and condiments out of the refrigerator.

I eased onto a bar stool at the island as Caleb approached me. "Now let me see this necklace of yours." He stood beside me, studying it. He was quiet for a moment, his eyes focused on the pendant. "Oh, yes, that's quite lovely."

He shot a knowing glance at Xander, and their eyes met as if they knew something I didn't.

"What?" I asked as I reached up to touch the pendant.

Caleb looked at me. "You wanted to know what it's worth, isn't that right, dear?"

"Yes, but only out of curiosity. I don't plan to sell it."

"Very well, then. I'd like to take it downstairs to my shop where I can get a good look at it under my microscope. Do you mind?"

"Not at all." I reached up behind my neck and unfastened it. As soon as I handed it to him, he left the room without a word.

As Xander set the food out, silence hung between us until I heard a door shut down the hall.

"What would you like on your sandwich?" Xander asked, leaning his hands on the edge of the island.

"Lettuce, tomato, and cheese." I chose everything he had, aside from the meat. "And mayo, please."

"No ham or turkey?"

"No, thank you. I don't eat meat." I watched as he spread mayonnaise on two slices of wheat bread. "I like your dad. He's nice."

"He's eccentric. I've always thought of him as an acquired taste. It could be why he's been alone since my mom died."

"Is that what you're going to be like in twenty years?" I joked.

Xander didn't answer me immediately. Instead, he loaded up my sandwich exactly as I had requested while silence came between us. As he looked down, he shook his head. Even with his head at an angle, sadness could be seen lurking in his eyes. "No way. I don't want to be alone. He's kind of a hermit."

"It's probably not hard to be one in his line of work. He's reminds me of an artist."

Xander patted the top piece of bread into place on my sandwich. Ignoring my comment, he said, "We have potato chips, and what would you like to drink?"

"Water is fine, unless you have some sparkling water."

"We do." Xander dumped a handful of potato chips out

of a big bag onto the side of the plate and slid it in front of me. "Do you want ice?"

"Yes, please." He grabbed a bottle from the refrigerator and filled a glass with ice. After handing them to me, he started preparing his own sandwich.

"So other than working alone, why don't you want to make jewelry like your dad?" I asked quietly.

"It's not that I'm not interested in it or I don't like it, because I actually do. And I realize it has afforded us a particularly nice lifestyle. But it's about choice. I might want to go to college like a normal guy my age, but it's not in the cards for me."

"I'd trade places with you any day," I admitted. "There's a huge stack of college brochures waiting for me at home on our kitchen table."

I bit into a potato chip as I pictured them. I couldn't help thinking how ironic this was. Here I was avoiding the subject of college, and Xander was telling me he'd like to go when he knew he never would. "Have you sent in any applications yet?" Xander looked up from the sandwich he was stacking with turkey, ham, and cheese.

"No." I shook my head. "I've been putting it off, but my parents are starting to bug me about it."

"Aren't you behind schedule?"

"Yeah. Brooke and Ethan have already started sending their applications in."

"What's stopping you?"

I shrugged. "I don't know." I sighed, catching his eye as he finished making his sandwich and added a pile of chips to his plate.

"You don't know? Sounds like you do." He took a bite of his sandwich.

"Well, it's kind of childish, but this is the only place I've ever lived. I don't want to leave," I admitted slowly. Without telling him about Dakota who was really what I didn't want to leave, I was sure I sounded like a sheltered little girl scared to move out on her own.

"So take a year off," Xander said after he swallowed the bite in his mouth.

"You mean don't go to college?" I bit into my sandwich, chewing thoughtfully.

"I mean just don't go right away. It's not like you can't start classes a year later. Get a job and see what it's like to work. I knew a lot of kids back home who did that. They were pretty burned out by graduation."

"Really?" I asked. "That's not a bad idea. I wonder if my parents would agree to that."

As I took another bite of my sandwich, I heard the basement door open and close. Caleb's footsteps shuffled along the hallway floor to the kitchen. Xander and I turned our attention to the entrance as he appeared with my necklace in his hand. He nodded his head at Xander like they had some kind of unspoken language.

"Laken, this is quite a remarkable piece. It is very old, possibly dating back to biblical times." He approached the island, holding it out to me.

I nearly choked on my sip of sparkling water. "What?" I gasped in disbelief. "How can you tell?" I reached for it and fastened it around my neck.

"There's a tiny hallmark on the back. I sketched it on a piece of paper so that I can look it up on the internet, but I'm pretty sure I've seen that symbol before."

"But what's it worth, Dad?" Xander asked abruptly between bites of his sandwich.

"That's hard to tell. The diamonds are very small, and that can take away from the value. But if it is a rare artifact with some historical significance, it could be extremely valuable. I need to do some research on it." He looked at me. "I hope you don't mind dear, but I also took some pictures of it."

"No, of course not. I want to know what you find out about it."

Caleb smiled warmly. "Good. That will give Xander an excuse to bring you back here again. Now, if you'll excuse me, I must be getting back to my work. It was truly a pleasure to meet you, Laken." Without another word, he disappeared out of the kitchen to return to his cellar workshop.

I looked down at the silver pendant hanging against my chest. It sparkled in the light. "I don't understand how it could be that old and still be so shiny. Wouldn't it be tarnished by now?"

Xander gazed across the island at me. "I don't know."

Before I realized what he was doing, he reached his hand out to touch the pendant. As he lifted it, his fingers grazed my skin and my breath caught in my throat for a quick second. He looked up from the necklace to meet my gaze as he touched me.

Suddenly, he smiled with a twinkle in his eyes. "Maybe it's a magic necklace with special powers," he joked. "You better hold on to it. You never know. Maybe it will keep anyone who wears it young forever." He eased the necklace back against my chest without touching me this time.

"Yeah, right," I scoffed, blowing off his remark and taking another bite of my half-eaten sandwich.

As we ate in silence for a few minutes, I stared blankly at the cabinets across the kitchen.

What if he was right? Not about staying young, but about the magic. After all, I could talk to animals with my mind, communicate with them in ways that only existed in fairy tales. Could this necklace somehow be connected to my unusual talents?

"What are you thinking?" Xander's question broke through the silence and my thoughts.

"Just that we should probably hurry up and finish our lunch. I really should get home soon."

"Yeah. I guess our little outing this morning went longer than expected. I'll take you home as soon as you're done."

"Thanks." As I finished my sandwich, a skeptical thought crossed my mind. "Are you sure your dad is right about my necklace? I mean, for it to be one, maybe two hundred years old wouldn't seem so unreasonable. But biblical times? That's like two thousand years ago. Maybe he's got it wrong."

"No way," Xander shot out quickly. "No one knows jewelry, especially jewelry with a history, like my dad. He's been doing this his whole life. The craft goes way back in our ancestry. It's been passed down for generations." Conviction dripped from his voice.

"Then I'll be very curious to learn what he finds out when he researches the hallmark. But for now, I just like wearing it."

"You should. It looks nice on you."

As he smiled at me, I remembered the touch of his fingers on my skin when he had lifted the pendant a few minutes ago.

I felt my cheeks blush at the memory and instantly looked down at the potato chips left on my plate.

"Thank you," I replied quietly as I lifted a chip to my lips.

After we finished our lunch, Xander cleared away the dishes and put the leftover food back in the refrigerator. Then he drove me home. When he pulled into my driveway, I reached for my coffee thermos and backpack from the floor of the truck.

"Thanks for lunch," I told him. "I really enjoyed meeting your dad."

"And thank you for the hike today. Aside from the bear, it was great. Someday, you're going to have to tell me what that was all about."

I had been hoping he'd forgotten about the bear. This was the first time he had mentioned it since we'd left the trail. "There's nothing to tell," I stated quickly in a curt tone. "I'll see you at school tomorrow. Bye."

After tossing him a quick smile, I climbed down out of the truck using the running board that I was now accustomed to. As I raised my hand to the heavy door, I glimpsed Xander one last time. His sunglasses hid his gorgeous blue eyes, something I was thankful for. I had seen enough of those haunting eyes today to last a lifetime.

"See you, Laken," he said before I shut the door.

As I turned away from the truck and approached the sidewalk, I heard him back out of the driveway. I fought the urge to turn and wave, and instead headed up the sidewalk to the front door. The house that I had grown up in suddenly seemed tiny and dull compared to Xander's massive log home with its shiny new hardwood floors, high ceilings, and granite countertops. I wondered what he thought of our meager existence in this small town. *Stop!* I scolded myself. *Why do you even care what he thinks?* But no matter how hard I tried to convince myself of anything different, the truth was, I did care.

Putting my thoughts of Xander aside, I fished my keys out of my backpack when I reached the front door. To my pleasant surprise, Dakota greeted me on the other side. I immediately knelt down with a relieved smile, ruffling my hands through his thick, black fur.

"Dakota! You're back!" I carefully inspected him for new wounds. Finding none, I wrapped my arms around his neck as he rested his big head on my shoulder for a moment. When I released him, I gave him a scolding look. "You scared me! I was really worried about you since you ran off. Please stay home for a few days. I don't want to worry about you this week."

He looked at me knowingly, his honey colored eyes shaming me for not trusting him to stay out of trouble.

I shook my head at him as I rose to my feet. "I know you can handle yourself, but you can't blame me for worrying just a little, since the last time you came home, you were bleeding."

Turning away from him, I headed through the quiet house, grateful that my mother wasn't waiting to pounce on me with the college brochures in the kitchen.

Dakota followed me upstairs, plunking down on his big fluffy bed with a deep sigh as I entered my room. I, too, let out a big sigh as I sank into the chair at my desk and stared at my textbooks, a long afternoon of solving Calculus problems and writing English essays ahead of me.

Chapter 15

On the way to school Monday morning, intermittent raindrops pelted the windshield as I filled Ethan in on most of the details from my weekend. No matter how hard I tried to tell him about my time with Noah, I kept coming back to Xander. Xander and our hike. Xander and his gorgeous log home and warm, good-natured father. When I finally forced myself to stop talking about Xander, I changed the subject. "How was your weekend?"

"Oh, no, you're not getting off that easy," Ethan replied with a wicked grin. "You just spent five minutes telling me about yours, and four and a half were about Xander. He surely turned the tables on you fast."

"What's that supposed to mean?"

"You swore you did not and would not like him, and now you're falling for him."

I gasped, nearly jerking the Explorer to a stop in the middle of town. Taking a deep breath, I focused back on the road. "I am not, and I don't appreciate the insinuation."

"I know you, Laken, and it's pretty obvious. But I won't say another word, at least not until you stop lying to yourself."

With a frown, I glanced over at his boyishly handsome face out of the corner of my eye. The one thing I equally loved and hated about him was his brutal honesty. "You should blame Brooke, you know. She's the one who called him to come to my rescue. If he hadn't picked me up at the restaurant Saturday night, none of this ever would have happened."

"But it did. So now you have to decide, Noah or Xander."

"Noah," I responded a little too quickly. My mouth curled into a smile as I remembered his kiss, a detail from my weekend that I had spared Ethan. Then my smile faded as I realized I hadn't heard from him yesterday. Not a single phone call or text. Maybe it was too soon after our first date and amazing first kiss. "How long should I wait to hear from him before I call him?" I asked Ethan, wishing I had more dating experience.

Ethan laughed. "Are you nervous he won't call?"

I rolled my eyes. "Yes, okay. I really don't know what to do here."

"Laken, he'll call or he'll show up on your doorstep one night. Stop worrying about it. Your bigger problem's going to be Xander."

I narrowed my eyes. "You always know how to make me feel so much better," I told him sarcastically.

The school came into view behind a line of maple trees with red sprinkled in their leaves. I turned into the parking lot and pulled the SUV to a stop under a tall oak tree.

Ethan and I hopped out of the Explorer, our doors shutting one right after the other.

As I locked the SUV with the remote, I caught a glimpse of the sparkling pendant hanging above my black sweater in the window. Every time I saw the necklace, whether in a reflection while I wore it or as it lay on my dresser, I wondered what Xander's father would find out about it in the coming weeks.

"Hey, Laken, we're getting wet! Hurry up!" Ethan called

as he jogged backward across the parking lot, breaking me out of my thoughts.

"Coming!"

He turned around once he had my attention, and I ran after him. Random raindrops spit out of the sky at us in our mad dash to the school. We sprinted up the outside steps, darting around some of the other students as we rushed to the entrance. As we blasted into the building, our shoes squeaked on the floor now slippery from the water being tracked in.

The halls were crowded with students carrying umbrellas and wearing wet rain slickers. Buzzing chatter and slamming locker doors sounded throughout the school. Ethan and I wound our way through the hall to find Brooke at her locker, swearing as she dropped a book on the floor. She knelt down to grab it, flipping her short red hair back as she rose to her feet. Her blue eyes immediately settled on us.

"Hey, guys," she grumbled, managing a small smile before turning to slide her book onto her locker shelf. Then she stripped off her navy slicker that glistened with rain, revealing a black sweater that matched the tall boots she wore with blue jeans.

"I know why Laken's in a mood today, but what's got you down?" Ethan asked.

After shoving her slicker into the locker, she turned to face us. Without a word, she tilted her head in the direction across the hall. We followed her gaze to a Homecoming sign tacked up on the wall. "Homecoming already?" I asked incredulously.

"Yes," Brooke groaned. "The dance is in three weeks and I'm not even close to getting a date."

"Brooke, they just announced it. Nobody has a date yet," I reassured her.

"You'll probably have a date by the end of the day," she said, her sad tone hinting with envy.

I wished I could be as sure of that as she was. But I didn't feel like speculating on my chances of going to the dance with Noah right now. "Then I guess we'll have to focus on finding you a date," I told her with a warm smile.

"Thanks." Her expression softened. "But it sure would be nice if I didn't need help."

"I have a deal for you," Ethan said. "If you don't have a date by the end of this week, then why don't we go together? You know I'm too terrified to ask anyone else." He smiled at her, and I watched curiously as their eyes met. "So what do you say?"

A wide grin broke out across her face. "That would be great. But are you sure? There's got to be someone else you'd rather go with."

"No, I really mean it. I'd much rather go with a good friend than someone who makes my palms sweat."

"Really?" Suddenly, they began talking as if I wasn't standing right next to them.

I excused myself, slipping away and weaving through the crowded hallway on the way to my locker. I wasn't even sure they noticed I had left. I thought I saw a little spark between the two of them, and I was happy to give them some space.

After a quick stop at my locker to hang up my jacket, I filed into homeroom with the other students who were a couple minutes early. I took a seat in the back of the room alone. As I leaned down to sort through my book bag, a dark figure took the seat next to me. I didn't need to straighten up to know who it was. Shivers rippled through me and my heart raced. Xander had arrived.

I sat up and was greeted by his blue eyes and amused smile.

"Good morning," he said. His black T-shirt stretched tightly across his broad, muscular frame, the blades of his tattoo extending down from under his sleeve.

"Hi," I said shyly.

Voices around us were becoming louder as the classroom filled up.

"How are you feeling after yesterday?"

"Fine. Why?" I saw Ethan enter the room and waved to him. He sauntered down the aisle, dropping into the seat to my right.

"Because I'm actually a little sore. You worked me pretty hard."

I raised my eyebrows at him, noticing a few interested glances from the boys sitting nearby. "I guess you need to get in better shape then."

A devilish grin formed on his face as he stared intently at me. "I'll work on that if it means we can do it again."

Rolling my eyes, I broke away from his gaze, thankful that the ringing bell preempted my response.

The chatter quieted down as the homeroom teacher began listing names for attendance. I focused straight ahead on the bald teacher, his wire-rimmed glasses and blue tie against the white shirt that covered his round figure an all too familiar sight. Suddenly, a hand reached across the aisle from my right side. A folded piece of paper was between Ethan's fingers. Grabbing it, I slumped down in my seat to open it in my lap.

You're going to get quite the reputation if you two keep talking like that, it read. I crumpled up the paper, biting down on my lip to keep from laughing. Glancing over at Ethan, I couldn't mistake the mischievous look in his brown eyes. He smiled, and I nearly choked on my laughter when the teacher called out my name. Somehow, I managed to toss out a quick "Here." As the teacher proceeded with the roll call, Ethan chuckled softly and I struggled to keep my own laughter in check. I reached across the aisle, playfully swatting his upper arm.

"Very funny," I mouthed to him, only to see him proudly nod his head. I glared at him, pretending to be mad as I resisted the urge to throw the crumpled note at him.

After the morning announcements were broadcasted over the loudspeaker system, the bell rang. I jumped to my feet and grabbed my book bag. As I slid the strap over my shoulder and followed Ethan out of the room, I sensed Xander behind me, but it wasn't until he called my name once we were out in the hallway that I turned around. Ethan didn't notice and disappeared into the crowded hallway, leaving me on my own with Xander.

I leaned my shoulder against the wall a few feet beyond the classroom door. Students spilled out of the room and passed us, but they were only a blur. All I could see were Xander's now too familiar blue eyes. He stopped inches away. I tried backing up, but students blocked the space behind me. "You're wearing your necklace."

I smiled at him. "Nothing gets past you, does it?"

"Ha, ha, very funny. It looks nice. I'm glad you're still wearing it after what my dad told you."

"Why would that stop me from wearing it?" I chuckled softly, noticing that, for the first time since he had set foot in our school a few weeks ago, he looked a little nervous.

"You're right. That was a dumb thing to say." He scanned the crowded hallway and then looked back at me. "I really just wanted to ask you to go to the Homecoming dance with me. I hope after yesterday, you don't think I'm such a bad guy anymore." He leaned in closer to me. "Maybe you even like me a little now."

My smile faded as I considered his invitation. I had never been asked to a school dance the same day it was announced. As tempted as I was to accept, I thought of Noah. "Um, okay, yes, I don't think you're such a bad guy, and maybe I like you a little as a friend, but I'm going to pass on Homecoming."

"It's because of the cop, isn't it?" he blurted as the hope in his eyes disappeared.

"That's really none of your business," I replied quietly.

I would neither admit nor deny wanting to go to the dance with Noah. The only thing I knew for sure was that I could only go with one of them, and as I had told Ethan earlier this morning, my choice was Noah.

Xander gazed off to the side at the other students, his expression mixed with disappointment and anger. After a moment, his fiery eyes returned to me. "I thought we were really getting somewhere yesterday. What happened? Was it something I did, something I said?"

"No, don't take it that way. It's not you." I smiled sympathetically. "There are plenty of girls who would love to go with you. What about Carrie? You two sure looked pretty cozy together last week."

"You don't understand," he snapped. "She was just a distraction. I guess this is going to take a little longer than I thought," he mused, looking around like he was talking to himself. "Fine. Go with the cop. See if I care."

Before I could calm him down, he stormed off. I whirled around to watch him disappear into the swarm of students. Sighing, I wondered where his dark words and harsh tone had come from. He seemed to think that yesterday meant a lot more than it really did. But it had only been a hike.

Shrugging my shoulders, I set off through the crowd on my way to my first class, hoping I could forget his bizarre behavior.

സൂസ

After the last bell rang that afternoon, I returned to my locker to stack the books I didn't need to take home and gather the ones I did. I hadn't seen Xander for the rest of the day except in History class. He had chosen a seat on the opposite side of the room from me and avoided my eyes every time I glanced his way. I hated to admit it, but a part of me was disappointed by his sudden coldness. After getting to know him, I was starting to like him, at least as a friend. So what if I turned him down for the dance? I didn't understand why it bothered him so much. He could take any other girl in school. Surely no one else would turn him down as I had.

I quickly forgot my problems with Xander when Brooke and Ethan ambushed me as I shut my locker. "Laken!

Thank God!" Brooke gushed with a panic-stricken expression on her face.

She rushed up to hug me as Ethan stood by, watching the crowd of students as if he was standing guard.

"Brooke? What's going on?" Alarm rang out in my voice as I awkwardly hugged her back, her short red hair brushing against my cheek. Confusion and concern shot through me.

When she finally released me, she stepped back as her nervous eyes scanned the busy hall. "It's Marlena."

Fear raced through me as I felt the blood drain from my face. "Uh-oh."

"Yeah. Mark and Eric ratted you out. They told her and the rest of her crowd how you were out with Noah when they got busted Saturday night. And now Marlena is out to get you. I heard her talking to her friends before my last class, and she said she wants to hurt you. She is really, really pissed."

"Why? She can have any other guy she wants. She always has, and she always will."

Brooke nodded in understanding. "I get it. But she wants Noah, probably because she can't have him. Geez, I'd be happy with just one of the guys she can have," Brooke rambled.

"You're not helping, Brooke," Ethan chimed in, listening to our every word as he stood guard and watched each student that passed us.

"We have to get you out of here before she finds you."

I frowned, looking from Brooke to Ethan. "So what if you get me out of here safely today? I can't hide forever. I have to come back tomorrow and the day after that. Maybe we should just let her find me and get this over with."

Brooke's eyes widened. "Are you crazy? Yes, obviously you are. This will probably blow over if you can lay low for a few days. All you have to do is wait until some other guy comes along and she forgets about Noah."

"That could be months," I groaned.

After the crappy day I'd had, I would just as soon get it

over with and confront her. I simply didn't feel like running. I imagined my fist branding Marlena's perfect face with a black and blue shiner and smiled. But when I thought of my parents' reaction to finding out I had been caught fighting the mayor's daughter, my fantasy evaporated.

"Brooke, Laken," Ethan warned, rushing in between us and extending his arms out around both of our shoulders. "Time to go."

He hustled us down the hall, weaving between the other students. As I bumped into a few of them, Brooke asked, "Is she coming?"

"Yep. And she saw Laken, so we have to get out of here," Ethan explained protectively.

"Wait!" I firmly planted my feet and ducked under Ethan's arm. Brooke and Ethan stopped a few feet away from me and turned. "I'm not going to run out of here like a chicken. I didn't do anything wrong except go out on a date. She doesn't own Noah." My eyes searched their faces for understanding and approval.

"Girl, you must have a death wish," Brooke contended.

She looked beyond me, her face ghastly white. I whipped around to see Marlena and two of her friends marching down the hallway toward us. They walked like models on a runway, each step placed evenly with a casual, sexy sway to their hips. Marlena took front and center wearing a purple skirt, tall black boots, and a black sweater that contrasted with her long pale hair. The girls on each side of her were equally pretty and popular, one with long brown curls and the other one with shoulder-length light brown hair. The students in the hallway scattered out of their way. The three of them didn't miss a beat in their expectation that a path would be cleared for them.

My heart pounded nervously as Marlena stared at me, her eyes narrowed and glowering. *What am I doing?* I thought. *Brooke is right. I am crazy. I should have left while I still had the chance to get out of here in one piece.* I cringed and turned away from the approaching entourage, waiting for the shout of cruel words or the impact of a fist. I noticed that the students in the hall had grown particularly quiet as uneasy onlookers watched Marlena.

As I raised my eyebrows at Brooke and Ethan who both stood frozen in place, a dark figure dressed in all black brushed past me. Xander. His shoulder gently touched mine as he walked by. That was the closest he had come to me all day since I had turned down his invitation to the Homecoming dance. I whirled around just in time to see him intercept Marlena. He jumped in front of her, cutting off her direct path to me. She and the other two girls stopped immediately. From where I stood, I could only see his back and I couldn't hear what he said to her. Her expression suddenly softened and her angry eyes moved away from me. She smiled, seeming to forget about me just like that.

The surrounding students resumed their chatter, drowning out any chance I might have to hear Xander and Marlena. Although I was curious to know what he was saying to her, it wasn't that important at this moment. Here was my second chance to escape.

I smiled at Brooke and Ethan. "Okay. I'm ready to go now."

"Finally!" Brooke huffed. "I guess your common sense caught up to you. Let's go before she loses interest in Xander and remembers you."

As Brooke wrapped a protective arm around my shoulders to lead me down the hallway toward the door, I looked behind to catch one last glimpse of Xander and Marlena. Xander's back was still facing me, but I could see that Marlena was captivated by whatever he was saying. With a frown, I turned my attention back in the direction we were going. "What is he doing? Wasn't it just like a week ago that he totally dissed her?" I asked.

"Seriously?" Brooke retorted. "Why do you care? He just saved your ass. I don't think now is the time to question his change of heart."

She continued hustling me through the crowded hallway.

Ethan walked on my other side, blocking my escape route should I suddenly change my mind. But I wasn't about to turn back and ask for the trouble I had just dodged. I only hoped that Marlena would back off for good. I didn't want to return to school tomorrow only to have to run from her like some wide-eyed rabbit taking refuge in the bushes from a fox.

When the three of us emerged outside into the light rain, Brooke finally let go of me. A cool damp mist floated through the air, coating the maple leaves and lawn. The cars and trucks in the parking lot were sprinkled with droplets of water that glistened like beads of sweat. We followed the walkway until we reached the curb and stopped.

"Well, that was fun," Brooke said sarcastically. "I just hope we don't have to do it all over again tomorrow."

"You read my mind," I told her as I reached into my bag and pulled out my keys.

"Until we know for sure that Marlena has forgotten about you, Brooke and I will walk you to your classes this week. But I'm sure this will blow over in time," Ethan said.

"I really hope that's not necessary." I shook my head. "I never thought I'd need bodyguards while I was still in high school. I figured that would be for later, you know, when I become a big movie star," I joked.

Brooke laughed, swatting my shoulder. "You never told me you want to be an actress."

I shrugged my shoulders. "Maybe I just realized it myself."

Xander's stories about California had made me realize there was a big world out there beyond our little New Hampshire town. Even though I didn't really want to be an actress, it was fun to joke about it.

Brooke raised her eyebrows curiously. "Do you?" she asked seriously.

I laughed. "No. I'm only kidding."

"Darn. That could have been fun as long as you took me with you. Well, I see my ride. I've got to run." Brooke embraced me in a quick hug. When she pulled away, she turned to Ethan with a sparkle in her eyes, poking him playfully with her finger. "And you, don't forget our deal from this morning."

Ethan flashed her a bright smile. "I won't." Their eyes locked for a moment, and there it was again—that same connection I had noticed this morning.

With a quick wave to both of us, Brooke turned and rushed off through the drizzling rain to her ride. As Ethan and I walked in silence to the Explorer, I resisted asking him what was going on between him and Brooke. Had it been any other girl, I never would have given him a reprieve. But Ethan and Brooke were the farthest thing from my mind. Nothing could take my thoughts off Xander. I could still see the betrayal in his eyes from this morning and the interest in Marlena's expression as he turned his charms on her this afternoon. Both visions were permanently etched in my memory, both equally disturbing.

As we began the drive home through the dreary rain, I forced the thoughts of Xander out of my mind and wondered when I might hear from Noah again. I hoped it would be soon because he was all I needed to sweep these other troubles away. With that thought, I turned my attention back to Ethan as the windshield wipers rose and fell in a perfect rhythm for the rest of the drive home.

Chapter 16

The drizzling rain persisted for another day. The weather was quite fitting for my dark mood. Between my falling out with Xander, his sudden interest in Marlena, and the fact that Noah hadn't called or texted since he'd left our front yard Saturday night, my foul mood only intensified. Worried that Marlena would stalk me in the halls between every class, I dressed in jeans and sneakers in case I needed to run. A black hoodie completed my ensemble. Black matched my mood, and I could hide under the hood.

Neither the sneakers nor the hood were needed that day. I saw Marlena several times and she barely looked my way. By lunch, Brooke and Ethan reached the conclusion that she had forgotten about me and they stopped chasing me down to escort me to every class. I saw Xander in homeroom, but he ignored me from his seat on the other side of the room. Between classes, I caught glimpses of him flirting with Marlena. I pretended not to notice them, but jealousy whipped through me each time and I pried my eyes away to focus on something else like getting books out of my locker or checking messages on my phone.

Before my last class of the day, I was alone at my locker when I sensed someone behind me. I suddenly wished I had my hood pulled up over my hair as an unfamiliar snicker rose above the chatter in the hall. I spun around to find myself cornered by Mark and Eric, both of them wearing their green and gold letterman jackets.

"Hi, Laken," Mark sneered with an evil smile. "We'd like to have a word with you about Saturday night." His green eyes flashed angrily at me.

"Yeah," Eric chimed in. "What your boyfriend did to us really wasn't cool."

I sucked in a deep breath, meeting Eric's cold dark stare. Without blinking an eye, I said calmly, "He only did what he had to do. You two were drinking. What did you expect?"

"To have some shots and fun with that cute bartender," Mark shot back. "But no, the new deputy in town had to swoop in and be a bigshot."

"Look, he has a job to do. So next time, if you want to get served, look around to make sure there aren't any cops in the room first."

Eric smiled sinisterly, his stare sending hair-raising shivers through me. "She has a good point, Mark." Eric slapped his friend on his shoulder.

"Maybe. But that doesn't change the fact that her boyfriend ruined our weekend."

"That's right. She owes us. How do you think she can make it up to us?"

Mark grazed his eyes up and down the length of me. "I heard you were getting pretty cozy with that new guy, Xander whatever, even after your date with the cop. Sounds like you know how to have a good time."

I didn't like what he was suggesting. "You don't know what you're talking about," I told him.

"No?" Mark looked over at his friend. "She's awfully defensive. You know what that means."

"I don't," I said boldly. "Maybe you should fill me in."

"Sure thing, honey." Mark leaned so close to me that I could feel his hot breath on my face as he spoke. "It means you ruined our night and you owe us. And since we already have just about everything money can buy, we're looking for something a little more basic. Something fun. Maybe Friday night, the three of us can go out."

Eric smiled, his coal black eyes staring hotly at me. "Yeah. You're kind of cute under that prim and proper exterior. What is it with you? Are high school guys not good enough?"

Mark sneered. "How old's the cop? You must be putting out to keep him interested. We just want to share."

He lifted a finger to my lips and I fought back a gag. I whipped my head to the side, nauseated by his repulsive touch.

Before I could respond, a female voice rang out from behind them. "She has plans that don't include you two morons."

Only one person could get away with calling the two star football players morons. Marlena.

Slowly, I turned back to face Mark, my eyes wide and my jaw dropped open. Marlena stood tall and confident behind them, her light blonde hair practically angelic compared to her black pants and black shirt.

She smacked each of them on the back of their heads. "Don't you guys have anything better to do than give Laken a hard time?"

Mark spun around to face her, his expression confused. "Leave it alone, Marlena. This doesn't concern you," he shot at her.

She smiled slowly, her eyes amused. "You're right. But it does concern Lauren and Sophie. I think they'd be quite interested to know what their boyfriends are up to right now."

Eric's dark eyes widened in panic as he turned to Mark. "Hey, man, maybe she's right. I don't want Sophie to know about this." He glanced at me apologetically. "Sorry, Laken.

We were just messing with you. Although it is cool you're not as straight-laced as you've always seemed."

"Gee, thanks," I replied sarcastically.

But Mark didn't give up. He glared at Marlena. "Don't bring Lauren into this. She has nothing to do with this. I'm just trying to even the score. Her boyfriend busted us, so she owes us one."

"She owes you nothing," Marlena stated. "You should be thanking her boyfriend. He did you fools a favor. You could have ended up in the hospital, or worse, six feet under. So drop it."

"When did you start sticking up for the nobodies around here?" Mark demanded.

Marlena let out a bored sigh. "Does it really matter? Leave her alone, or I'll ruin you both, and you know I can."

With a flip of her hair, she turned on her heels and disappeared into the crowd, leaving all of us speechless, including Carrie who had been standing behind her.

After a moment of silence, Mark looked over at Eric. "Fine. I'll give it up." He shot me a disdainful glance. "She's probably not worth the risk, anyway."

Without another word, the two boys turned and walked away into the crowd of passing students.

Relieved, I watched them high-five a few other football players. I hated to admit it, but regardless of her reasons, I was thankful that Marlena had stepped in when she did. As I relaxed, Carrie stepped toward me. She looked the part of the popular cheerleader with her long shiny brown hair, white ruffled blouse and red skirt. A concerned expression settled on her face. "Are you okay?" she asked me.

I smiled appreciatively as I met her warm brown eyes. "Yeah, I'll be fine. Those boys sure like to rattle some chains, don't they?"

She nodded her head in agreement.

"But I'm really confused. Why did Marlena stand up for me? I thought she hated me since I went out with Noah."

Carrie gazed whimsically out at the students before turning her eyes back to me. "She did, yesterday. But that was before Xander asked her to go out with him. He's even already asked her to the Homecoming dance."

"Hmm," I mused, fighting back a sharp pang of jealousy. "Is that so?"

"Unfortunately."

I suddenly recognized a sad disappointment in her voice. "Were you hoping he would ask you to Homecoming?" I gently probed.

"Yes. I don't know what happened. Last week, he seemed genuinely interested in me and then yesterday, poof, it went up in smoke. He just went after Marlena like a moth goes after a flame."

"I'm surprised she said yes. He wasn't very nice to her the first week of school when she invited him to a party at her house."

"She's fickle like that. And he apologized, said something like he didn't know what had gotten into him that day. He blamed it on being so far from home, or something lame like that. So she gave him a second chance. Can't say I wouldn't have either. He's gorgeous. No girl in her right mind would say no to him."

I couldn't help smiling since I had done exactly that just yesterday morning. But I didn't tell Carrie about that. She didn't need to know that he had chosen not one, but two girls over her. Besides, I couldn't trust her not to tell Marlena. There was no telling how Marlena would react if she knew that she had been Xander's second choice.

"Carrie, you're beautiful and everyone likes you. There's still plenty of time before the dance. I'm sure you'll get a date." I couldn't believe that I was trying to cheer up one of the most popular girls in school about her dating life.

"Thanks. I hope so." She smiled weakly. "Well, see you around." With a half-hearted wave, she turned and walked away, leaving me alone at last.

By the time I found the book I needed for my last class, only a few students were left lingering in the hallway. I slammed my locker door shut as the bell rang. Cursing under my breath because I was now late, I took off running down the hall.

છ૭છ૭

After school that day, Noah was waiting for me by the Explorer as Ethan and I headed across the parking lot. The rain had stopped, and sunshine peeked out from behind the thick clouds that were starting to break up.

The cars glistened with beads of water as I jogged across the wet pavement. A smile tugged at my mouth as my heart fluttered.

I swerved around a big puddle right before stopping in front of Noah. "Hi," I said shyly, suddenly self-conscious about my old, boring sweatshirt and lackluster sneakers. They had served their purpose, but now I wished that I'd worn something a little prettier today.

"Hey there," he responded warmly. "Hi, Ethan," he called out over the top of the Explorer.

Ethan nodded. "Hey, Noah. How's it going?" Without waiting for Noah's answer, he added quickly, "Laken, I'll wait for you in the truck."

"Thanks," I replied before returning my attention to Noah. "This is quite the surprise."

"A good one, I hope?" he asked, his brown eyes studying me.

"Of course. I was beginning to wonder when I'd hear from you again."

"Sorry about that. Sometimes I get so carried away with working on my book that I lose track of time. Every time I wanted to call you, it just ended up being too late."

"Oh. I guess that's understandable." *Not really,* I thought. *But it will have to do. I guess he has his thing, and I have mine. Talking to animals.* "What are you doing here?" I asked as I pushed my dismal thoughts aside.

"I just wanted to stop by and say hi because it's been a slow afternoon. Is that okay?"

"I suppose," I answered with a smile. He was so forgiven at this moment. "You can stop by every day if you want to."

"And can I do this every day, too?"

He reached one arm out and curled it around my waist, pulling me against him. His other hand grazed my chin as he dipped his head down to gently press his lips to mine.

As quickly as his kiss began, it ended when he abruptly lifted his mouth away from me. "I hope it's okay to kiss you in the school parking lot."

"Hmmm," I muttered with a deep sigh, trying to find my composure. Finally, I said, "Yes, of course it's okay. I'd be more upset if you didn't. How's that for an answer?"

"Perfect." He slid his arm away from my waist and I shifted my book bag strap as I felt it slide a little. "Well, I know you need to go and I can't stay long either because I need to get back to the station, but I wanted to know if I can see you again this weekend."

"I'd like that, but let's stay away from the local bars."

"Agreed. I hated leaving you like that, and believe me, it was no party at the station when I had to call those boys' parents." He shook his head as if trying to shake the memory out of his mind. "But you'll have to decide what we're going to do because I still don't know the area that well. Is Saturday night okay again?"

After days of wondering why I hadn't heard from him, happiness overwhelmed me. I fought to keep my cool while thinking to myself that Saturday seemed like a lifetime away. Today was only Tuesday! At least I could look forward to it, even if it meant four long restless nights dreaming about him. "Okay. But I have to warn you, I don't have any great ideas of what we could do. Unless..." The only thing I could think of was pizza and a movie.

"Unless what?"

"Unless you'd like to stay in. We could order a pizza."

Noah smiled. "I'd love to." He stepped away from the

Explorer, opening up my access to the door. "I'll see you Saturday, then. But I promise I'll call before the weekend."

I returned his smile as I reached for the door handle. "You better," I teased.

He grinned mischievously, suddenly lunging at me from behind. He wrapped his arm around my abdomen and planted his hand above the front button of my jeans. "Or maybe I'll show up here every day after school to see how your day was," he whispered in my ear. After he kissed my cheek, he released me. "See you, Laken."

I turned in time to see his back as he headed for his police car. I was about to call out a quick good-bye when I noticed Xander leaning against the door of his pick-up truck across the lot. His long black trench coat, black pants, and untucked black shirt nearly blended into the black paint. Despite the overcast sky, dark sunglasses shielded his eyes. A frown flattened his mouth, a five o'clock shadow sprinkling his chin. I felt his intense stare on me even without being able to see his eyes. Shaking my head, I turned to the Explorer as the hair on the back of my neck stood on edge. Facing away from him, I still sensed that he was watching me. And I couldn't wipe the image of his stone-cold expression out of my mind.

Desperate to escape, I tossed my book bag into the back of the Explorer before sliding into the driver's seat. With barely a glance at Ethan, I started the engine and backed out of the parking space. Then I guided the Explorer out of the lot as fast as I safely could, grateful to leave Xander and his unsettling stare behind me.

⌀ↄ⌀ↄ

I almost got through the rest of the week without running into Xander. Almost.

My last class on Friday was History. As I entered the classroom, students chatted eagerly, excited about the upcoming weekend that would begin as soon as class ended. I wandered through the maze of desks to find an empty seat three rows back. Before I sat down, I slid my book bag strap off my shoulder, pushing my light pink sweater back into place as it shifted. I wore jeans again today with tall black boots. My necklace rested against my chest just above the scoop neckline of my shirt. My hair fell behind my shoulders in soft curls and silver hoops dangled from my earlobes. I had dressed much nicer since Tuesday in case I saw Noah again, but unfortunately I hadn't. At least he had called or sent me a text message every night as he'd promised, so I knew he was thinking about me.

I dropped my book bag to rest at my feet and sank into the seat. The classroom had been devoted to American history with a huge United States map marking Civil War battles tacked up on the interior wall. The northern states were colored blue and the southern states blood red. Across the room from the map, large windows extended from a ledge about four feet high to the ceiling. The blinds had been secured at the top, letting sunshine brighten the classroom. Mountains rose up beyond the school lawn, predominantly green with splashes of yellow, orange, and red.

As the noisy students settled into their seats, I gazed longingly at the mountains. I suddenly remembered my hike last Sunday with Xander. I would love to get out there again this weekend, but not with Xander after his strange behavior this week. I shook my head to erase the memory of the nice Xander I had gotten to know last Sunday as I bent down to find my History notebook and a pen in my book bag.

Noah. Think about Noah and his exciting kisses and another Saturday night with him. At least this Saturday night shouldn't be interrupted like last weekend, I thought as I placed my things on the desk. But the image of Noah that swept across my thoughts vanished when Xander filed into the room with a few other students. I shifted my eyes down to the blank page of my open notebook, but not before I glimpsed him in blue jeans and an untucked white button-down shirt. Without his usual black clothing, he seemed less dark, less brooding than he had Tuesday afternoon in the parking lot. Once again, I scolded myself for letting him push my thoughts of Noah away. *Stop thinking about Xander! He doesn't deserve your attention after the way he treated you this week. Besides, he's made his decision to go out with Marlena. You don't even want to be friends with him. She'd probably kill you just for that,* I told myself.

As I stared down at my pen, Xander passed my desk and sat behind me. I turned in my seat, leaning down to sort through my book bag. Only I didn't need anything, except to steal a glance at him. He smiled subtly as our eyes locked in the briefest moment. I whipped my gaze away, unsettled by his blue eyes, and sat back up in my seat. Three days ago, he had glared at me like he wanted to kill me, and now he was smiling again?

The bell rang and those students still standing scrambled to their seats. Our History teacher, Mr. Jacobs, strolled into the room. He was young with dark floppy hair, black-rimmed glasses, and a scruffy shadow of stubble across his face. He wore khaki slacks, a light blue short-sleeved shirt, and a mismatched green tie.

This was his first year at our school and, according to rumor, his first teaching job.

Despite Mr. Jacobs's youthfulness, he commanded the students' attention with ease. Most of us liked his unique teaching style that brought American history to life.

"Good afternoon," he said as he dropped a few books on his desk and leaned against it. "We're going to skip the lecture today."

His announcement was met with loud cheering and clapping. With a patient smile, he gave the class a minute to quiet down.

Once silence and order returned to the room, he continued. "Okay, guys, I know it's Friday afternoon and you're all busting at the seams to get out of here. But we still have to fulfill the class period, so don't get too excited. We're not having a lecture because I have an assignment for all of you to get started on."

A chorus of groans erupted as he reached behind his back to grab a stack of handouts. Then he crossed the room to the front corner desk next to the window, counting heads and enough papers to pass out.

"Here you go. Please pass these back."

As he moved across the front desks, distributing the handouts to each row, the sound of shuffling paper rustled through the room.

When the girl in front of me handed the papers back, I took one and silently passed the remaining copies to Xander. Our eyes met again as he took them from me, but I was careful not to let our hands touch in the transfer. Twisting around to face forward, I read the first few sentences on the handout with dread. "In pairs of two, students shall research a history topic of their choice. Topics shall involve a historical event that occurred in New England."

I lifted my eyes from the paper in time to see Mr. Jacobs return to his desk. As he explained the assignment, I could only focus on one thing—that this project was to be done in pairs. I had no problem with the assignment itself. That was the easy part. But as I scanned the other students in the room, I couldn't find anyone I particularly wanted to team up with.

Frowning, I listened as Mr. Jacobs continued to explain the project. "You'll have about three months for this assignment, but to keep you all on track, I have assigned due dates for various milestones. They are listed on the handout. The final paper and presentation will be due in December, but your first assignment is due next Friday. You'll need to have a partner and a topic by then. You may use the rest of the class today to pair up and start brainstorming on your research topic."

He turned and circled back around to the other side of his desk while the students started chatting. Slowly, everyone began pairing up to discuss the assignment. The room steadily grew louder as my classmates finished reading the handout and turned to their neighbors to find a partner.

"If any of you have questions, don't be afraid to ask," Mr. Jacobs added in a loud voice above the noisy crowd. "And don't worry about not finding a partner. There are an even number of students in this class, so everyone will have someone to work with.

I looked around the room, wishing that Brooke or Ethan was in this class. Without them, I was hard-pressed to find a partner. As the seconds ticked by, I realized that nearly everyone seemed to be paired up already. Desperately searching for anyone who was still alone, I noticed Angela Bradley sitting quietly in the front row. Her shiny black hair hung behind her in a ponytail, her thick bangs skimming the top edge of her blue-rimmed glasses. She sat sideways in her chair, also searching the class for a potential partner. I didn't know her very well, but I knew that she was smart and kept mostly to herself. She would make a perfect partner.

As I stood and began to make my way over to her, a boy walked up her aisle and started chatting with her. Her expression instantly registered relief, and I knew right away that I was too late to ask her to be my partner. I sighed, turning around slowly, scanning the class for another potential partner. My heart sank as everyone was talking to someone else. Everyone, that is, except Xander.

I was about to return to my seat when I felt a light tap on my shoulder from behind. I whirled around to face Xander. His white shirt was unbuttoned at the top, and I noticed the shark tooth necklace he had worn on our hike. I swallowed back my nerves as I raised my eyes to meet his.

"Hi," he said softly.

"Hey," I replied, frowning. I knew what was coming next.

"It looks like we're the only two left without a partner. So what do you say?"

I shrugged as if it didn't matter while my thoughts raged

internally. He was the last person I wanted to team up with. "Looks like I don't have much of a choice."

Where was Marlena or Carrie when I needed them? If one of them was in this class, Xander would have been taken before the teacher started explaining the assignment.

"You don't have to make it sound so dreadful," he said with a soft smile.

"Why not? It's not like you've been that nice to me this week."

His smile faded. "I'm sorry about that. I needed a few days alone after you turned me down. I don't take rejection that well."

I desperately wanted to ask how all his flirting with Marlena constituted being alone, but I bit back my sharp tongue. Mentioning Marlena might make him think that I was jealous. Whether or not I was, I certainly didn't want him to think that I was.

"So what are you saying?" I asked.

"That I'd like to be friends. I had a really nice time hiking with you last Sunday and I think we could do a good job on this project together."

He sounded sincere, but I wasn't ready to believe he actually was. However, I didn't have another option for the History assignment. "Like I said, I don't seem to have a choice." I felt as though I'd been backed into a corner with nowhere else to turn.

"Okay," he said slowly. "I guess we're partners, then. But you don't have to sound like the world is coming to an end."

"It's not?" I gasped, widening my eyes in mock amazement.

"Ha, ha."

We returned to our seats, and I sat facing backward.

"I guess we'd better get down to business," he said. "First things first. We should exchange phone numbers and email addresses."

I reluctantly agreed. *What's the big deal?* I asked myself.

He knows where you live and it would be much better to get a text from him than to have him show up on your doorstep whenever he wants to talk about this project.

We took down each other's phone numbers and email addresses in our notebooks.

Satisfied, he asked, "Do you have any ideas for what we can do this project on? I'm afraid I'm going to have to leave that up to you since you've lived here a little longer than me." He flashed a warm smile, and a slight tingle rushed through me. In spite of his mood swings, he was still very handsome. I couldn't help smiling back at him, suddenly forgetting his question. "Laken?" he asked, breaking me out of my trance.

"Yes?"

"Did you hear me?"

"Um, yes, I heard you," I replied quickly. "But no, I don't have any good ideas right now. Give me until Monday. I'll think of something." With that, I spun around to face forward. I hunched over my desk, leaning my forehead on my folded arms while the other students continued their chatter. A shiver crept up my spine. I was certain of one thing. No good would come from spending more time with Xander, even if it was just for a school project.

Chapter 17

The doorbell rang as I faced the bathroom mirror and applied shiny light pink lip gloss Saturday evening. Nerves fluttered through me, and I smiled. Noah had arrived for an evening that no one could interrupt since we would be staying in. I paused for a quick moment in front of the mirror to make sure that every hair was in place and every dash of make-up was perfect. Except for a few stray strands that framed my face, blonde waves fell over my shoulders. I had chosen a turquoise sweater that buttoned down the front and matched the color of my eyes. Skinny blue jeans hugged my hips, but my outfit wasn't complete until I had fastened my diamond necklace under my hair behind me. The pendant sparkled just above my sweater.

Perfect, I thought as I placed the lip gloss on the counter. *This will make him forget the God-awful sweatshirt and sneakers you were wearing the last time he saw you.* Not wanting to keep him waiting any longer, I hurried out of the bathroom, pausing only slightly to turn off the light.

I rushed down the wooden stairs and to the front door, eternally grateful that my parents were out for the evening. When I opened the door, I smiled brightly at the sight of

Noah in the dusky twilight. His maroon thermal shirt outlined his solid, broad frame under his denim jacket. A large,
flat pizza box was in one hand, a heavy plastic grocery bag
in the other. His warm dark eyes met mine as he returned
my smile. "Hi," he said. "I hope you're hungry."

Although I really wasn't since my stomach insisted on
doing flip-flops in anticipation of a night with him, I pretended to be. "Absolutely. But what's in the bag?" I asked
curiously.

He held it up, and I noticed water condensation glistening on the plastic. "Raw chicken."

I chuckled. "Really? Gee, you shouldn't have."

"It's for Dakota. I figured the way to your heart might be
through his stomach."

"That's very sweet, but I think there are a few other
ways to my heart."

"Good. I look forward to learning what they are."

As he gazed at me, I felt a blush race over my cheeks. I
backed up, giving him room to fit through the doorway with
the pizza box in his hand. "Well, come in. The pizza smells
yummy. What kind did you get?"

"Half cheese, half pepperoni." He glanced around the
house as he entered. "Are your parents here?"

"No," I responded as I shut the door behind him. "We
got lucky. They're having dinner with some friends." My
father was also on call since he'd given Noah a guaranteed
night off, but that never stopped him from going out. Skirting around Noah, I led him back to the kitchen.

Noah set the pizza box on the table as I went to the refrigerator. Then he approached behind me as I scanned the
frosty shelves for drinks. "Can you take this?" he asked,
holding the bag of chicken out to me. "Where is that wolf,
anyway?"

I took the bag from him and placed it on a shelf before
closing the door. When I turned to him, Noah stretched his
arms around me. He slid me over to the counter and leaned
his hands on the edge, locking me between them.

"He's out roaming the woods again," I explained nervously. Dakota was the farthest thing from my thoughts with Noah just inches away.

"Good." He grinned devilishly. "No parents and no wolf. That's just how I like it." He lifted a hand to gently touch my jaw, running his fingertips down along my neck.

My eyes locked with his as his hand slowly moved under my hair. Before I realized what was happening, he leaned down to kiss me. After a few minutes, he abruptly pulled away and took a deep breath. Then he backed up a few inches, releasing me. Disappointment raced through me as our kiss ended. Hopefully, there would be more kisses later.

"So it's just us tonight?" he asked.

"Yes. My parents have a lot of friends, so they usually go out once a week or so. Mostly on weekends." I couldn't help wondering what he thought of being alone with me tonight.

He laughed. "Good to know. I have noticed your dad knows everyone around here." He paused for a moment, taking another step back before changing the subject. "Maybe we should have some pizza before it gets cold."

I nodded in agreement. "Sounds like a plan to me. What would you like to drink?"

"Sprite if you have it."

"We do." I reached into the refrigerator to grab a Sprite for him and a Diet Coke for me. Then I pulled two glasses out of the cabinet and filled them both with ice. Noah carried them over to the table in two trips while I gathered plates and napkins before joining him. His jacket hung on the back of his chair as he waited.

I sat down, deliberately placing the warm pizza box on top of the college brochures that still cluttered the table. Then I reached for a piece of pizza, the cheese stretching in long strings before breaking away. I took a bite as Noah reached for a slice from the pepperoni side.

"You might not want to leave the box on top of those brochures. They could get ruined from the heat," he said as he broke off the cheese from the sides of his pizza.

"Good. I really just want to throw them in the trash. But, unfortunately, everything you see here can also be found online. So I'm sure whatever does get ruined will only be reprinted by my parents." I frowned as I always did when the thought of college crossed my mind before taking another bite.

Noah recognized my frustration as I had explained to him a few nights ago that I was having trouble picking a college. "Oh yes, the dreaded subject of college."

I swallowed as my eyes met his. "That's right. So let's not ruin tonight by talking about it, okay? Tell me about your week. Anything exciting? Did you pull any more bodies out of the woods?" I really didn't mean to make light of the body that had been found before school started, but it just slipped out.

He smiled faintly. "No, thank goodness. If we had, you'd already know about it."

I nodded. "Yeah, you're right."

"But I did rescue a cat."

"A cat? Wow, that's definitely newsworthy," I teased.

"Yeah. We got a call from a little old lady on Evergreen Road. She was frantic because her cat was up in a tree."

"Oh, that must be Mrs. Parks."

I pictured her old colonial house that I had passed by often. It had once been painted bright white, but now had patches of gray aging planks where the paint flaked off like pieces of paper. Cobwebs stretched across the corners under the eaves and could be seen in the windows, and tall weeds had taken over the lawn. Mrs. Parks hadn't been able to properly care for the home since her husband had died. But even as it fell apart around her, she had continued to live there alone for years.

"You know her?"

"I know of her," I corrected. "What was she like when you went over there?"

"A little odd, but nice enough."

"Did she invite you in for tea and cookies after you rescued her cat?"

Noah chuckled. "Hardly. She thanked me and then carried her cat back into the house." He wrinkled his nose at the thought of the dilapidated house. "I'm actually glad. I don't think I'd want to go into that house if it looks as bad on the inside as it does on the outside."

"I would," I said quickly, grinning at his astonishment.

"What? Are you nuts?"

"No. It's rumored that her house was part of the Underground Railroad. Supposedly, it has secret compartments and passageways where they hid escaped slaves who were trying to make it up to Canada."

"Really? That's pretty cool. Now if I had known that, I might have tried a little harder to get an invitation from her to come in."

"Rumor also has it that she rarely lets anyone in. It's really a shame because the house is pretty much a historical landmark." Suddenly, an idea popped into my head. "That's it," I mused, thinking out loud.

Noah gazed at me, confused. "What?" he asked, tilting his head as he took another bite of pizza.

"Sorry. I was thinking about a History assignment from yesterday. We have to do a research project on a topic of our choice as long as it has something to do with New England. The Underground Railroad is perfect. Our topic is due next week, so you just helped me. As long as my partner agrees to it, that is. But I don't know how he could turn it down."

"Partner?"

I took a deep breath. "Yes. It's a group project. Actually, we were paired off in teams of two. I hate group projects, even if it's only with one other person."

"I'm sure it'll be fine. Maybe you can convince Mrs. Parks to give you a tour of her house for your project."

"I doubt it, especially if she knows we're doing a project that has to be presented to the whole class. But it's a great topic. Maybe I'll find some other houses around here or in neighboring towns that were part of it."

"Or your partner could do that."

Why did he have to mention my partner? I bit into my half-eaten piece of pizza, delaying my answer for a few moments while I chewed and swallowed my food. "No. That will probably be all me. He's not from the area," I replied hesitantly, avoiding Noah's gaze as I mentioned that last part. When I finally looked back at him, I noticed the curiosity in his eyes. "I ended up stuck with Xander Payne. I'm not too happy about it."

"Well, maybe now you can ask him if he really did steal a car."

I glanced away from Noah, staring across the kitchen with my eyebrows wrinkled. "I don't need to. I already did. He told me he returned it without a scratch and the owner didn't press charges." I shifted my gaze back to Noah, hoping he wouldn't ask me how I knew this.

"Well, there you go. He didn't lie after all. And maybe he learned his lesson."

"I hope so. I don't want my History partner getting in trouble with the law since the law around here is my father and my—um, my friend." I started to say boyfriend, but I stopped, afraid that he might get spooked if he knew I wanted to call him that.

Disappointment registered on Noah's face. "That's all I am to you? A friend?"

"No—I mean yes—I don't know," I said nervously, grasping for the right answer. I just didn't know what that was. "What am I to you?" I asked, turning his question back on him.

"If I didn't think it would scare you off, I'd say maybe my girlfriend." His eyes studied me for my reaction.

I smiled, trying not to beam too brightly as my heart fluttered. I had been out on dates with boys before, but I'd never been called someone's girlfriend. And truthfully, until now, there had never been anyone I wanted calling me their girlfriend. "Really?" I almost didn't believe him. Gathering my courage, I took a deep, hopeful breath. "If that's what I am to you, is it too soon to ask you to be my date for the Homecoming dance?"

"No, absolutely not. I would love to take you to Homecoming." He took another bite of his pizza, a big grin on his face as he chewed.

"Wow, really? I honestly hadn't planned to mention it tonight. Now I have a couple weeks to find a dress," I rambled on, wondering why he kept staring at me.

"And I get to know that you'll still want to see me in a few weeks."

"Of course I will. Why would you even doubt that?"

He looked away for a moment, a dark shadow racing across his face. "You never know. Things have a way of changing sometimes. Besides, I haven't had the best luck in the girlfriend department lately."

"I find that hard to believe."

"Let's just say my luck seems to have changed since I got here."

His eyes met mine, and I smiled. From that point, Noah asked me more about my assignment and what else I knew about the town's history. We talked as we finished eating a few more slices of pizza. Once we'd had our fill, Noah helped me clear away the dishes. Then I packed up the leftover pizza and placed it in the refrigerator. As I shut the door and leaned against it, he wiped his hands on the kitchen towel and set it on the counter. "What should we do now?" I asked.

"You tell me."

I thought for a moment, but nothing too exciting came to mind. "There aren't a whole lot of options. We could see what's on TV or go outside and enjoy the stars. It's a pretty clear night." I hoped he didn't find my suggestions too dull or too high-school.

"Sounds good. Either one works for me. What would you prefer?"

"To sit outside. I'm also hoping that Dakota will come home before I go to bed. I always sleep better when he's here. Besides, there isn't much I really like on TV these days. I've never enjoyed all those reality shows." I led the way across the kitchen to the back door and stepped out into the cool night air. Noah flipped the outside light on, and I turned. "No, leave it off. It's easier to see the stars when it's completely dark."

He switched the light off before following me out onto the patio as the back door fell shut with a bang. I rubbed my arms in the cold air, hugging my sweater around my chest. My eyes slowly adjusted to the darkness as I walked to the edge of the patio and sat down. Noah sat so close to me that I could feel the heat from his body.

We gazed out across the yard in silence. The trees loomed, their tall crooked shadows stretching up to the dark sky. A crescent moon peeked out over the branches, and stars speckled like diamonds high above us. I sighed as I admired the night, not even noticing the goose bumps that covered my arms.

"Isn't it beautiful here?" I asked without taking my eyes away from the sky.

"Um-hm," he murmured.

I glanced at him to see him watching me, not the sky, and I laughed. "You're not even looking at the stars."

"I know. I'm looking at something more beautiful—you."

I swallowed nervously, feeling a hot blush race across my cheeks. At least he wouldn't see it in the dark. "Stop. You're embarrassing—"

Before I could finish, Noah leaned over to kiss me. Despite the darkness, my eyelids fell shut as my sense of touch took over.

His lips had barely touched mine when a low, rumbling growl made us both jump. "Damn!" Noah swore, catching his breath. He whipped away from me as he stared across the yard. Dakota's amber eyes and white fangs glowed in the faint moonlight, his head hung low as if stalking his prey. His smoky black fur blended into the shadows behind him.

"Dakota!" I scolded gently. Why was he growling? He had to know that Noah wasn't hurting me. "Be nice," I told him before my thoughts took over. *'What's up with you? You know how important Noah is to me. Please don't ruin this.'*

Dakota sucked in a deep breath, his upper lip lowering over his fangs as he exhaled. He raised his head and approached me, nuzzling my hand with his big wet nose for forgiveness. I ruffled my fingers through his thick fur. "That's better. You're not bleeding anywhere or hurt, are you?" Even though nearly two weeks had passed since he'd come home injured, I still worried when he ventured out into the woods, even if it was only for a day.

As Dakota sat down next to me, I turned my attention back to Noah. "Now I'm the one who's sorry. I hope he didn't scare you."

"I just wasn't expecting him. I didn't even hear him approach. Is he always that quiet?"

"Not always, but he can be. Trust me, he can run through the woods without making a sound. I've seen him do it. I think it's one of those wolf traits he has so that he can sneak up on a deer or rabbit."

Noah shook his head. "He is a wolf. I guess I'll get used to him sooner or later. I'm going to have to if I'm going to date you."

"I hope that's okay."

"It is. After all, you're worth it," Noah assured me with a smile.

As my heart glowed, the wind blew, rustling the tree leaves overhead. I shivered, suddenly missing Noah's strong arms and warm kiss to ward off the chill in the air.

Noah lifted his hand to rub my shoulders. "You're cold. I'll run inside and get our jackets."

I smiled graciously at him. "That would be great. Could

you grab my gray fleece from the hallway closet? It's right around the corner from the kitchen."

"Got it." He dropped his hand away from my shoulder and stood up. "I'll be right back."

I heard him walk across the patio and open the back door, gently easing it shut behind him. As I waited for him to return, I stroked Dakota who responded by nuzzling my neck with his wet nose. "Dakota," I said, laughing as I pushed him away. "That's enough. Your nose is cold."

Suddenly, he whipped his head away to stare at the trees as a twig snapped in the distance like someone or something heavy had stepped on it. I pictured the golden-eyed wolf as I stared into the woods. Dakota jumped up to his feet and stood tall. He growled loudly, the fur on his back standing up as he studied the surrounding forest.

My heart pounded with fear as I wondered what was out there. I watched Dakota, wondering what he would do next. *'Whatever you do, please stay here, Dakota. Don't go back out there and get hurt again,'* I thought.

I soon learned that my efforts to get him to stay by my side were wasted. Beyond the yard deep within the woods, footsteps shuffled through the leaves in a two-beat rhythm. They were quickly overtaken by another breeze that whispered through the leafy branches. Breathing slowly as my heart continued to race, I stared straight ahead into the blackness. A sudden movement caught my eye as the shape of a person darted between two trees. It reflected the dim moonlight for a second before disappearing. Dakota saw it too, and he launched into a run from his standstill. With long fast strides, he charged across the yard and into the trees.

"Dakota!" I called as I scrambled to my feet. I stood right where I was, watching and listening, but only silence and darkness loomed.

The back door opened, and I spun around as Noah appeared with my gray fleece in his hands, his denim jacket already covering his maroon shirt. "Sorry that took so long.

I made a quick visit to your bathroom." He abruptly stopped half-way across the patio when he noticed the fear on my face. Concern swept across his eyes. "Where's Dakota? What happened? I was only gone for a minute."

"There." I turned around and raised my arm to point at the woods. "I saw something, no, I mean someone. Someone was out there."

I didn't hear Noah's footsteps, but I felt him behind me when he stopped. "What are you talking about?"

"I saw a shadow, and it wasn't a moose or a deer or a bear. It was human," I told him, my eyes glued to the dark, sinister woods.

A loud snarl pierced the silence. Another one ripped at it, and the image of the golden-eyed wolf sinking its teeth into Dakota flashed through my mind. The snarls and growls of what could only be two wolves out for each other's blood grew louder in the distance. They continued for a minute, and then a sharp, pain-filled yelp cut through the air like a knife, followed by an eerie silence.

"Dakota!" I screamed, my heart racing with panic. I took off, running for the woods. I had to find him, no matter how far I had to go.

But I didn't make it out of the yard. As I approached the trees, Noah caught up behind me. He wrapped his arms around my chest, trapping me against him as he held me in place.

"No! Let me go!" I cried as I struggled to break free. But I was no match for his strength.

"Laken," he said above my cries. "Stop! I can't let you go out there. It isn't safe."

A lump formed in my throat. I knew it wasn't safe, but it wasn't me I was worried about, it was Dakota. "I don't care! I have to find Dakota. He might need me. He could be hurt!" I squirmed against Noah's vicelike grip, but it was no use. I slowly stopped, realizing he wouldn't let go of me no matter how hard I tried. Trembling, I held back the tears I felt forming in my eyes. "I can't leave him out there," I whispered, lifting my hands to grasp Noah's strong arms that still held me tight.

"Laken, Dakota is strong and he's a fighter. He's going to be okay."

I shook my head in disbelief. "You don't know that." I sniffed, trying to control the urge to cry. *Keep it together. As scared as you are, you don't want Noah to see you come unglued. He just agreed to go to Homecoming with you, but he could easily change his mind if you start acting like a child.* Taking a deep breath, I contained my emotions and spoke in a steady voice. "He's alone out there. You heard them. It was the other wolf. It had to be."

"I know, and that's exactly why you can't go running out there and risk yourself. If it can hurt Dakota, there's no way you, or even I, can defend ourselves against it. Dakota wouldn't want you to put yourself in danger."

I nodded in acknowledgement as I felt his hold loosen around me. Turning in his arms, I leaned my cheek against his denim jacket as I stared across the yard. My jacket lay in a crumpled heap on the patio where he had dropped it before running after me. "What's going on around here?" I asked against his shoulder, feeling safe in his arms, but still terrified of what or who lurked out in the woods.

"I don't know," he whispered. "I don't know."

He rubbed my back, and slowly, I started to relax.

After a few quiet moments, he said, "I think we should go back inside." He stepped back and looked down at me. "Okay?"

I nodded subtly. "Okay."

He released me, extending one arm around my shoulder. We walked side by side to the back door, stopping briefly for him to pick up my jacket. While he did, I turned to look at the woods, but all I saw were the trees and all I heard were the leaves brushing against each other in the cool breeze.

Once inside, Noah dropped his arm away from my shoulder and locked the back door. I stood in the kitchen, not sure what to do next. The lights seemed extremely bright for a few seconds as my eyes adjusted to them. The events from just moments ago resurfaced in my mind. I couldn't forget the human shadow I had seen. But the wolf's yelp was what bothered me the most. I knew I wouldn't be able to sleep until Dakota returned home.

"Hey," Noah said, his voice breaking me out of my thoughts. He sighed as his eyes met mine. "I'm sure Dakota will be okay."

"I hope so," I replied as I wandered over to the table and sank onto a chair. Shaking my head, I stared at the college brochures. The words across the covers blurred as I heard the pain-filled yelp over and over again in my mind.

Noah approached the table and sat down next to me. "Laken, tell me exactly what you saw before Dakota took off."

I shifted my gaze from the brochures to look at Noah. "I don't know. It was really dark. I must have imagined it."

"But you said you saw a person."

"I thought I did, but I must have been mistaken." I looked away from him as I spoke. I knew perfectly well that I hadn't been mistaken. A person had walked right through the woods behind the house. That much I was sure of. But I had no proof. How could I convince Noah of this when it had been almost pitch black? Nothing would make me happier than to truly believe I had imagined it. At least I could try to make Noah believe that. If only I knew the truth, then maybe it would eventually become a distant memory.

"Are you sure?" Something in Noah's voice told me he wasn't convinced that it had been my imagination. The look in his eyes told me that he was worried, and that scared me.

Forcing myself to put up a brave front, I took a deep breath. "I'm sure," I said as convincingly as possible.

My efforts were wasted. Noah rose to his feet, his chair scraping the floor behind him. "I wish I could be. I'm going to check it out. Do you have any flashlights?"

I nodded, knowing that I wouldn't be able to change his

mind. "In the garage. I'll get one for you." I jumped up and walked past him on my way to the door. After retrieving the flashlight I had used to find Ryder a few weeks ago, I returned to the kitchen. I tested the light and it shone brightly. "This should work. Dad must have put new batteries in it." I held it out to him.

Noah took the flashlight from me. "Thanks. I'll be right back." Without another word, he disappeared outside. The last sound I heard was the click of the latch as the door shut before silence took over the kitchen.

The minutes ticked by painfully slowly. The quiet haunted me, and as each second passed, I worried more and more about Dakota. Something strange was going on, something that raised the hair on the back of my neck. Wild wolves didn't roam northern New England in this day and age. What one was doing out there frightened me. But what terrified me even more was the person lurking in the woods. I wanted to pretend I hadn't seen someone tonight, but I knew the truth and I wouldn't forget it easily.

The door handle rattled and my heart nearly skipped a beat until Noah appeared. He snapped off the flashlight as he shut the door. "I didn't see anything. There's no sign of anyone."

My blood ran cold, but I forced myself to appear reassured. "I'm sure it was nothing, then. It was really dark. There's barely a sliver of the moon out tonight and the patio light wasn't even on. It must be all those crazy books I've been reading lately." I tried to make light of the situation, wishing I could believe my own words.

"Let's hope that's all it was," Noah said with a sigh as he set the flashlight on the counter. "Does your dad have a liquor cabinet around here? I could use a drink."

I choked back my surprise. This was a side of Noah I hadn't seen yet. An older, more mature side. I suddenly realized how little I knew about him. In spite of my hesitation, I resolved to go along with him. "Check the cabinet above the refrigerator. There might be something up there."

As Noah headed straight for it, I heard a faint scratching at the door. "Dakota!" I gasped as I raced across the kitchen.

Praying that he was okay, I whipped the door open. Dakota trotted in without missing a beat. His head was up and his stride confident. I scanned the floor for drops of blood, knowing I wouldn't see them against his black fur. Not a single spot of red could be seen on the white tiles.

"Dakota!" I repeated in a half scolding, half relieved tone. "You scared the hell out of me. I told you not to take off!"

I didn't even consider my words as I said them. Noah glanced at me, his eyebrows raised, as he turned from the counter where he was making himself a drink with a Coke and my father's bourbon.

I didn't have a chance to explain how I expected Dakota to understand me. A low growl came from Dakota's throat, and I immediately looked down at him. He had stopped in the center of the kitchen and glared at Noah.

"Hey!" I said sharply as Noah turned around, his eyes locked on Dakota.

"Laken, uh, what's going on with him?" Noah asked as Dakota ignored me and raised his lip, exposing his sharp canine teeth.

"I don't know," I muttered. Marching around to stand between Noah and Dakota, I pointed a finger at Dakota. "You'd better have a good reason for this, Dakota." *'Don't mess this up for me, I mean it.'* Mixed emotions of being pitted between my beloved wolf and the guy who was stealing my heart churned inside me. *'Please,'* I begged silently in a softer tone. *'You know how much Noah means to me.'*

Dakota's growl finally faded. He tossed me a knowing look before whipping around and taking off up the stairs to my bedroom.

I took a deep breath as I turned around to face Noah. "I'm sorry about that. He must be a little on edge from whatever was out there tonight."

Noah's anxious expression relaxed a little as he reached for his glass. "Can't say I blame him. It's been a more eventful night than I expected." He swirled the drink around the ice cubes before sipping it.

A daring thought came to my mind. I knew the perfect way to not only forget the person in the woods but also show Noah I could be mature. "Mind if I have one of those?" I asked, tilting my head in the direction of his drink.

Noah raised his eyebrows, apparently surprised by my request. "You really are trouble. Your parents could come home at any minute."

I glanced at the kitchen clock. "Not likely. It's only eight-thirty. I'll take my chances."

"I thought you said you don't drink."

"I don't. But there's a first for everything, right?"

Noah looked skeptical. "Perhaps, but that doesn't make this the right time for it," he said slowly.

I tipped my head to the side as I narrowed my eyes with a sly smile. "Well, you can either let me try it now while you're here to make sure I'm safe or I could try one while I'm at some wild party where anything could happen."

He took a deep breath. "Fine," he relented. "I'll make you something weak and you can try it. But just one. And I'm only doing this because it will help you sleep and you might need that tonight."

"Yeah, I probably will," I said quietly.

"But not a word to your father. I could get in big trouble for this."

I rolled my eyes. "I think I can keep a secret. My father doesn't know everything about me." There was more truth in that statement than Noah could possibly imagine.

As Noah pulled another glass out of the cabinet, I retreated to the table to wait for my drink. Butterflies danced in my stomach. I couldn't believe I was doing this. I was the good girl. I'd never even thought of stealing a drink from my father's liquor stash before. It was exciting, but also a little scary. *What are you so worried about? It will probably be so weak that you won't even feel it. And it's about time you took a risk. Brooke would be proud if she could see you now.*

Noah finished making my drink and returned the bottle to the cabinet above the refrigerator before joining me at the table. We toasted to better times, joking about someday having a date that didn't get interrupted. I sipped the drink, barely tasting the alcohol. He must have only added a drop of bourbon as I had expected.

We talked for hours, long after finishing our drinks. The alcohol seemed to relax me. Between that and knowing I was doing something I shouldn't, I almost forgot about the person I'd seen in the shadows.

At eleven o'clock, Noah stood to leave. I tried not to let my disappointment show when he gave me a quick kiss before heading out to his car. As I locked the door, the empty house suddenly seemed creepy and images of stalker movies filled my mind. I contemplated running after Noah and asking him to stay until my parents returned. But Dakota was upstairs, so I wasn't really alone. And I didn't want Noah to know I was scared. Only one of us needed to know the truth.

With that thought, I put our empty glasses in the dishwasher and headed up to my room to hide out with Dakota until my parents got home or I fell asleep, whichever came first.

Chapter 18

When I opened my eyes the next morning, bright sunlight filtered into my room through the window. I yawned, stretched, and turned on my side to face away from the window, amazed that I had slept through the night. My eyes closed as I focused on the good parts from last night. Nothing made me happier than Noah's kisses and the fact that I now had a date for the Homecoming dance. Of everything that had happened last night, that's what I wanted to remember the most.

Suddenly, I heard a deep sigh behind me. I flipped over onto my other side to see Dakota sleeping on his big fluffy bed. Memories of his reaction to Noah last night darkened my thoughts. As I frowned, Dakota opened his eyes and lifted his head. He studied me, his expression telling me he wasn't sorry for it. *'Fine, Dakota,'* I thought. *'But you're going to have to get used to him whether you like it or not.'* When he rolled his eyes at me, I whipped over onto my other side and stared at the wall. It bothered me that he didn't like Noah, but there wasn't anything I could do about it.

After a few minutes, I stood and headed down the stairs still wearing my pajamas. The scent of hazelnut coffee creamer filled the kitchen. My parents were in the midst of their Sunday morning coffee and newspaper ritual when I turned the corner from the stairwell. They wore their robes as they perused the black and white pages sprawled out over the table, the edges curled up against their mugs of steaming coffee.

I trudged over to the coffee pot, craving the caffeine to help me wake up. As I pulled a mug out of the cabinet and filled it, my mother looked up from her newspaper. "Good morning, Laken. You're up a little late today. Did you have a nice time with Noah last night?"

I splashed some hazelnut creamer in my coffee before turning to lean against the counter. "Yeah. It was nice. He brought a pizza over. And some raw chicken for Dakota, but Dakota was out late." I purposely left out a lot of details from last night.

If my parents knew half of what had happened, from the person in the woods behind our house to my drinking, they'd never leave me home alone again.

"That was nice of him. What else did the two of you do?" She forgot about the newspaper as she watched me curiously. My father didn't seem nearly as interested in my evening as he continued reading an article, his face angled so that all I could see was his graying beard.

"Just hung out. I asked him to go to Homecoming with me and he said yes." I knew my mother would love to hear that. At least I didn't have to hide everything that had happened last night.

She smiled excitedly. "Oh, that's wonderful, honey. I'll take you shopping for a dress. I hope you don't mind doing that with your mother," she teased, her brown eyes hopeful.

"No, of course not. As long as Brooke can come with us."

"Sure she can. Does she have a date, too?"

"Sort of. She and Ethan made a pact that if she didn't have a date by the end of the week, he would take her. And as far as I know, she didn't get asked by anyone else."

"Oh, they'll make a cute couple. Are the four of you going to go together?"

"I don't know. We really haven't talked about it. It's still a few weeks away." I changed the subject after swallowing a few sips of my coffee. "So, Dad, Noah told me he had to go over to Mrs. Parks's house to rescue her cat."

My father nodded without looking up from his paper. "You got that right. I've been over to her place a half a dozen times this year to get her damn cat out of that tree. It was his turn."

I laughed. "Are you sending him out on all of the silly calls like that?"

"Damn right. He's young. When he gets to be my age and he's the sheriff, then he can call the shots." Suddenly my father lifted his head to look at me. "Why? What did he say about that?"

"Nothing," I assured him. "But I'm glad he told me about it. I have to do a research project on something to do with New England history. When Noah told me about going over to Mrs. Parks's house, it reminded me that her house was part of the Underground Railroad. So now I have a topic for the project."

"That's a great idea," my mother said. "I'll be interested to hear what you learn from it. It's such a shame that she's let her house practically fall apart since her husband died. The town has offered to help her fix it up to preserve it as a historical landmark, but she keeps refusing. How are you planning to do your research?"

"I don't know. I haven't really thought about it since I just came up with the idea last night. I guess mostly online."

My mother wrinkled her eyebrows in thought for a moment. "There's an old library up in Littleton. I mean, it's so old, I bet some of the books have been collecting dust for fifty years now, especially since the dawn of the internet. Most of them were written by people who lived around here. You should check it out. You never know what you might find. I'd be willing to bet you'll find some old memoirs you'd never find online. I have the address of the library with my school papers. Remind me to get it for you later."

"That would be awesome. But first I have to make sure my partner agrees to this topic. It's a group project."

"I can't see how anyone would turn it down."

I nodded. "I hope you're right. I'll be interested to see his reaction when I pitch the idea." I suddenly realized how much time I would be spending with Xander on this project over the next few months. The idea of it was both alluring and frightening. Pushing him out of my thoughts, I asked, "So, Dad, if you've been over to Mrs. Parks's house a lot, do you think you could get her to give me a tour. I'd love to see the hidden compartments where they hid the slaves."

"Not a chance," my father answered quickly, without so much as a thought.

"Too bad. That would be really cool."

As my mother turned her attention back to the newspaper, I reached into the cabinet behind me for a bowl. After pouring some Cheerios from the box sitting out on the counter, I added a healthy dose of milk. Then I carried it with my coffee and a spoon over to the table.

I set my bowl and mug down in the tiny opening between the sprawling newspaper pages and sat down. As I raised a spoonful of cereal to my mouth, my father turned over his paper to reveal the stack of unread college brochures. His gaze lifted from the article he'd been reading, settling on me instead. "Laken, when are you going to go through these brochures and decide which schools you want to apply to?"

I groaned inwardly. *Never,* I thought, but I didn't dare answer my father so truthfully. I looked down at my Cheerios as I crunched on them. My words needed to be chosen carefully. As I looked up and swallowed my cereal, my parents watched me expectantly. "Okay, I've been giving this some thought. The problem is that I don't know what I want to major in. And I don't want to waste money on a school until I know what it is I want to do. So I was hoping that maybe we could reach a compromise." I paused, studying their reactions. My mother appeared to be open to suggestions, but my father huffed with resistance.

"Laken—" he began.

"Wait, Dad, before you say anything, let me explain. What if I enroll at the college down in Plymouth to take some core classes? I could live here and get a part-time job in town. Then later on, when I decide what I want to study, I can transfer those credits to another school and we will have saved money on the room and board for a year or so." I shifted my eyes from him to my mother and back to him.

My mother appeared pleasantly surprised, but my father still objected, although weakly. "It's not about the money, Laken. This is your future. Let your mother and I worry about the money," he said.

My mother placed a calming hand on his forearm. "It's not a terrible idea, Tom."

"Yes, it is. And it's only delaying the inevitable. If she puts it off next year, who's to say she won't continue to put it off?" My father looked back at me. "I never got out of this town, and now I never will. I want something better for you."

"But, Dad, I love this town and I don't want to leave."

A knowing look crossed over my father's expression. "Oh, now I understand. This is about Dakota, isn't it?"

I glanced down at my cereal as I tried to think of how best to answer him. Yes, it had a lot to do with Dakota, but the only way I would convince both my parents to let me stay home next year was if I could prove to them that it was best for me. "Dakota is part of it. I can't take him to college with me. But shouldn't I know what I really want to study before I pick a full-time college?"

My parents exchanged an unspoken look between the two of them. I thought I noticed a brief understanding in their eyes.

Then my father sighed, his expression softening. "Okay.

It's a possibility. Let us think about it for a while. In the meantime, I want you to take all of these brochures up to your room and go through them. I want you to pick at least three schools you're interested in whether you apply to them for next year or the year after next. And don't worry about Dakota. He can stay here with your mom and me. I always figured he would. We'd never turn him out when you leave, and, Laken, eventually you are going to leave here."

Even though my parents hadn't officially agreed to let me stay home next year, I knew I had gotten as much of a concession as I would get today. "All right. I'll get started on it soon."

"Good. Let us know what schools you've decided on by the end of November," my father said. "And I won't forget. So put it on your calendar. November thirtieth."

I nodded. "November thirtieth," I repeated, making a mental note of it.

My father could be reasonable if I met him halfway, so I would have to make sure I didn't miss his deadline.

As my parents turned back to the newspaper, I quietly finished my cereal and coffee, grateful to have a reprieve on my college decision, at least for now.

◌◌◌

Later that afternoon as I sat at my bedroom desk in my black sweat pants and a gray hoodie pouring over my Calculus homework, my phone rang. I dropped my pencil and pushed my book to the side of the desk, grateful for a diversion. I reached for my phone, smiling when I read Noah's name across the screen.

Suddenly, the Calculus problem I had been struggling to solve was completely forgotten. As I swiped the screen, I stared blankly out the window at the trees stretching up to a bright blue sky dotted with puffy white clouds. But I barely noticed the view as Noah's brown eyes and warm smile flashed through my mind. "Hi, Noah," I said.

"Hey. I just wanted to check in and see how you're doing today."

His familiar deep voice sent goose bumps racing down my arms and legs. I couldn't help smiling at my memories of last night, at least the good one of his kiss when he had arrived. "I'm fine, although I'm doing a lot better now that you called."

"Then I'll have to call more often."

"That sounds good to me." I could only imagine the love-struck smile that tugged at my lips.

"Did your parents get home soon after I left?"

"I'm not sure since I went up to bed. They were here when I woke up this morning."

"And you were okay? I mean after I left," Noah said hesitantly, his voice worried.

"Yes, of course. Why wouldn't I have been okay?" I really didn't need him to answer that. The strange wolf and the person sneaking around in the woods last night appeared in my thoughts, but I wasn't about to bring them up. As far as I was concerned, it would be better if we both forgot about them. "Dakota was here."

He laughed softly. "You're right. What am I saying? He's not one to mess with. You were definitely safe. I hope he'll learn to trust me someday."

"He will. Just give him time. He can be leery of strangers."

"Well, hopefully I won't be a stranger to him for long." Noah paused, and just when I was thinking of a way to change the subject, he continued. "Have you thought any more about what you saw?"

"Not really. I'm trying to forget it."

"What about telling your dad? Just to be vigilant."

"No way," I said quickly. "If my dad thinks there was someone out in the woods, he'll put the entire town on lockdown and I probably wouldn't be allowed out of his sight. If it happens again, I'll tell him. I'm just not ready to sound an alarm over something I'm not sure of. It happened so fast that now, looking back, I think it could have been the shadow of a tree blowing in the wind. It was really dark."

"Laken, I know you have your doubts, but I would feel a lot better if you told him." It was almost as if he was pleading with me. Why couldn't he just let it go? I had told him several times that I wasn't sure about what I'd seen.

I sighed, frustrated. I knew that I had really seen a person in the woods last night even though a part of me truly wished that I had been mistaken. Obviously, I wasn't doing a very good job of convincing Noah that it had been my imagination. "I'll think about it, okay? But that's the best I'm going to do right now." As images of the night before flashed through my mind, I twisted a lock of hair around my finger. "I just wish none of this was happening. It's hard to believe that about a month ago, things were pretty boring around here."

It suddenly hit me. Xander and his father moved to town a few weeks ago, right about the time the golden-eyed wolf appeared. Although, for the most part, Xander seemed harmless, I had to admit that his intense stare sometimes scared me. And then there was his reclusive father who locked himself up in their remote house with an alarm system and a driveway gate. Maybe the jewelry making was just a cover story. Did Xander and his father have something to do with the wolf? Could Xander be the person I had seen last night?

That's crazy, I told myself. *You spent an entire day with him last weekend and he was a perfect gentleman. Not to mention how warm and friendly his father was.* Despite my thoughts, I couldn't shake my suspicions. I distinctly remembered him watching me in the school parking lot last week. There was something I didn't trust about him, I just didn't know what it was yet.

"Laken?" Noah's voice broke me out of my thoughts. "Are you still there?"

"Yes, sorry," I said. "I was just thinking about something."

"What's that?"

"It's nothing, really." It was one thing for me to suspect Xander, but I didn't want to plant any suspicions in Noah's mind unless I could prove them. "I was just thinking about how safe I used to feel. We never locked our doors for as long as I can remember, and now everything is different. It's not the way it used to be."

"I'm sure it will all blow over in time," Noah said, but something in his voice told me he didn't believe his own words.

"I hope you're right. But until then, at least I have Dakota."

"Just promise me if you see anything suspicious, anything at all, you'll let me know right away." Grave concern lingered in his voice.

"I will," I promised, a warm glow coming over me as I realized he cared about me.

"Good. Well, I need to run and you probably need to get back to whatever you were doing."

I glanced across my desk at my books. "Calculus homework," I groaned.

"Sounds fun."

"You're welcome to come by and help," I offered.

"No thanks," he replied quickly. "But I'll call you tomorrow, okay?"

"Yes. I like hearing your voice." I also hoped that he would stop by school one afternoon like he'd done last week.

"Me, too. I'll see you soon," he said, leaving me to wonder if he had read my mind.

After a quick good-bye, I hung up the phone and set it down on my desk. I reached for my Calculus book, but I found it extremely hard to resume concentrating. My thoughts bounced from Noah's kisses to my suspicions that Xander had been watching us from the woods. My homework seemed to be worlds away as I stared straight ahead, entranced in my thoughts.

Finally, with a deep sigh, I picked up my pencil and resumed writing what I could only hope were the correct answers to the Calculus problems.

಄಄಄

"Where were you Saturday night?" I fired my burning question at Xander the first chance I got Monday morning which happened to be at my locker before homeroom. I had been in the midst of organizing my books when I sensed him behind me. Without hesitating, I spun around to face him as I glanced around to make sure no one, specifically Marlena or Carrie, was listening. I didn't even want Brooke or Ethan to hear this. I hadn't told them about the person in the woods Saturday night, and I didn't want to.

I stared up at Xander, watching his reaction. The other students milling in the hallway were a blur behind him. He didn't answer immediately, but rather gazed at me curiously, his ice blue eyes meeting my stare.

I was quickly mesmerized by his gaze and handsome features. Somehow he didn't seem as intimidating as I remembered, but that could be because his blue jeans and khaki colored shirt weren't as dark as the black clothes he wore so often.

"Good morning to you, too," he finally said, his voice laced with sarcasm.

"Are you going to answer my question?"

"Not until you tell me why it matters to you."

I sighed deeply, staring at him. He obviously wasn't about to answer me until I explained why I was asking. I folded my arms across my black sweater.

"Fine." I glanced around to make sure no one was listening. "I saw someone in the woods behind my house Saturday night," I stated quietly.

Xander glared at me incredulously. "And you think it was me?"

His reaction made me wonder if asking him point blank had been a good idea. "Well, was it?" I asked slowly, deliberately.

"No, of course not. If you must know, I was out with Marlena Saturday night. Unlike you, she accepted my invitation to the Homecoming dance."

My mood suddenly darkened on two accounts. First off, I knew he was telling the truth. Marlena would never let a guy she was dating out of her sight on a Saturday night. And secondly, jealousy rose up inside me at the thought of Marlena and Xander together.

"Oh," I said. "Okay. I'm sorry. It must have been someone else."

I shook my head and started to turn back to my locker when Xander grabbed my upper arm. I stopped, looking up at him.

"Why would you think I was in the woods behind your house like some kind of psychopath? Do you really think I'd do that?" he asked softly in a hurt voice.

"I don't know. I barely know you."

"But you think I was stalking you? Trust me, Laken, that's not my style. If you don't want to go out with me, I get it. I've moved on. If you want an alibi, just ask Marlena. I'm sure she'd be happy to tell you exactly what we did Saturday night."

"That won't be necessary. But if you must know, sometimes, you—you scare me a little," I admitted reluctantly. I looked up, meeting his blue eyes. "Like when you corner me here at my locker."

He instantly dropped his hand away from my arm. "Were you scared of me when we went hiking?"

"No. That was actually nice. But last week, you acted a little strange after you asked me to the dance."

"And I apologized for that." A faint smile formed on his lips. "Look, there's a lot you don't know right now, but once you do, you're going to understand where I'm coming from."

"Then tell me," I challenged him. "You've been dropping hints like this since you got here. Why can't you just come out with it?"

"Because it's not that easy. You wouldn't believe me, anyway."

"Try me."

"Not so fast. First, tell me what happened Saturday night."

I shrugged, not wanting to talk about it. "It's nothing, really."

"That's not true. You said someone was in the woods behind your house. Were they watching you?"

"I don't know. It was really dark. I saw something move between the trees and I thought it was a person, but it was hard to tell." I glanced away from his stare, aimlessly watching the other students as I suddenly wished he would drop the subject.

"This isn't good," he muttered, looking away from me before his gaze settled on me again. "Listen, Laken. I need you to trust me. I'm glad you told me about this. If it happens again, I need you to tell me right away. Even if it's in the middle of the night, just call my cell phone," he said seriously. "This is really important. Do you promise to tell me if it happens again?"

I knew he wouldn't accept no for an answer. "Sure. But I just hope it never happens again."

"Yeah," he agreed with a deep breath before abruptly changing the subject. "So what are we doing for our History assignment?"

Grateful to talk about something much less frightening, I grinned. "How about the Underground Railroad?"

Xander smiled, pleasantly surprised. "You mean slaves escaping to Canada?"

"That's right. One of the routes went straight through New Hampshire. In fact, a house in town was part of it. I haven't been in it, but I've heard it has a lot of secret hiding places."

"Wow. All I could think of was the Mayflower or the Boston Tea Party. That's a much better idea. I knew there was a reason I picked you for a partner."

"You didn't have a choice, remember? Everyone else had already teamed up with someone."

"I know." He paused, leaning in close. "But I only wanted to work with you," he whispered into my ear.

As he raised his head, my eyes met his again and my breath caught. Tingling shivers raced through me, and I swallowed nervously.

The moment ended abruptly as Xander looked down the hall. I followed his gaze to see what had ripped his attention away from me so quickly. Shiny blonde hair bobbed above the heads of the other students in the distance. Xander backed away from me, his eyes locked on the crowded hallway. "Hey, I've got to run. We'll get started on the project soon. Don't forget what I said earlier." He shot one last quick, almost apologetic smile my way before dashing off into the mob of students.

I sighed with disappointment, watching him until he disappeared into the crowd. With a frown, I turned back to my locker, my mood suddenly as dark as the midnight black sweater I wore.

Chapter 19

Rain moved into the area Tuesday morning and pummeled the region for several days. Heavy, moisture-filled clouds hung in the sky, shielding the blue heavens with their low cover. I trudged to school and home each day in my dark green rain slicker, holding my black umbrella high above me as I ran from the parking lot to school each morning and then back again each afternoon. The steady rain filled dips in the pavement with puddles and saturated the grass. By the time I returned home each day, my shoes and ankles were dripping wet. But the rain didn't bother me one bit. Noah called nightly, lifting my spirits as if the sun had found me through the dense clouds.

The miserable weather also made me feel safer. Hopefully, whoever had been in the woods Saturday night wouldn't return in the pouring rain. And Dakota needed no convincing to stay in and gnaw on raw chicken. He never minded a light misting drizzle, but he only ran outside for quick bathroom breaks at my insistence during monsoon-like downpours.

On Thursday afternoon, I headed to my locker after the last bell rang to get my things before I was to meet Xander at his truck in the parking lot. We had decided to check out the library in Littleton that my mother had told me about.

As I walked down the hall, my phone buzzed in my book bag. I hurried between a few students, bumping into one of them in my rush to get to my locker where I dropped my book bag on the floor and knelt beside it. I reached into it, feeling around blindly for my phone. When I finally pulled it out, I had a text from Xander. *Something came up. I'll meet you at the library at four-thirty.*

I sighed. That figured. Now I would have to drive there by myself instead of riding with him. Perhaps this was a blessing in disguise. I hadn't been too thrilled at the idea of being alone with him for thirty-minutes on our way to Littleton. At least now, I would only have to endure his company at the library while we started our research.

I dropped my phone back into my bag and stood to sort through the books on my locker shelf. Once I had the ones that I needed for the night, I reached for my dark green rain slicker. I slipped it on over my purple V-neck sweater and blue jeans, not bothering to pull my braided hair out from under it. Then I reached for my umbrella before shutting the locker door. As I turned with my book bag strap over one shoulder and my umbrella in my hand, Brooke emerged from the crowded hallway. A navy rain slicker cloaked her shoulders, her shiny red hair brushing against the hood that folded behind her neck.

"Hey, Laken," she said smiling. "Want to grab some pizza in town? I'm so sick of this rain. I just don't feel like going home and being trapped inside one more night."

"I can't. Xander and I are meeting at an old library in Littleton to start working on the research for our History project."

Brooke wrinkled her nose. "I don't even have a topic yet and you're already starting? I wish you would tell me what you guys are doing. You seem a little too excited about it."

"I'll tell you soon enough. But for now, he made me promise I wouldn't tell anyone."

"I still can't believe you ended up with him for your partner. I'm working with Abby and, while she'll do a good job, it won't be nearly as much fun as it would be with a hot guy."

I laughed. Sometimes Brooke's mind seemed to be stuck in the gutter. "At least you won't be distracted."

"Are you admitting that you will be?"

"What?" I gasped. "No, of course not," I lied, trying my hardest to keep a straight face.

Brooke stared at me with a knowing look in her blue eyes. "Good try. You can't fool me. I can tell you have a thing for him."

As I frowned, feeling heat flush my cheeks, a male voice suddenly interrupted us. "A thing for who?" Ethan asked from behind Brooke.

"Xander," Brooke answered quickly, glancing up over her shoulder at Ethan with a bright smile.

Ethan shot her a secret smile and then looked at me, but not before I noticed his brown eyes softening the moment he looked at her. He shrugged. "Where have you been, Brooke? That's old news."

I groaned and rolled my eyes at both of them. "It's not news at all, so can we please stop talking about this?"

"Only if you give me an idea for this stupid History assignment," Brooke pleaded.

Ethan's eyes widened in mock surprise. "You and Abby haven't picked a topic yet? You'd better get a move on it. It's due tomorrow."

"I know. What are you doing your project on? I need help. I'm getting desperate."

"So what's new?" Ethan teased with a warm smile.

She turned and playfully slapped his shoulder. "Hey! Just for that, you're taking me out for pizza before I start on my homework tonight."

"I'm always up for pizza. Laken, are you coming with us?"

"I can't. I'm going up to the Littleton library with Xander. I think I mentioned that earlier, remember?"

"Oh yeah," he said thoughtfully. "But I think he may have left already. I saw him running down the hall a few minutes ago. He looked kind of upset. What was that all about?"

"I have no idea. He sent me a text a few minutes ago saying something came up, so we're meeting at the library instead of carpooling up there."

"Maybe Marlena beckoned," Brooke piped up.

As Ethan and I stared at her, her teasing smile faded. "What? Let's face it, they are an item," she defended.

I sighed. "You're right. And it's none of my business. All I care about is that he shows up at the library on time to help me with our research." I glanced at my watch. If I left the school now, I would get to the library about thirty minutes earlier than Xander. I could use that time to get a head start. "I think I'm going to take off. I'll see you guys tomorrow, okay?"

"Yep," Brooke replied. "But I'm not going to tell you what Abby and I come up with for our History project until you're ready to tell."

"That's only fair." I waved to them with my free hand before turning on my heels and plodding through the crowded hallway to the double doors. Once outside, I paused under the overhang to open my umbrella. Rain poured from the sky, pattering into the puddles that shimmered in the sidewalk dips.

With my umbrella held high over my head, I hurried down the steps and across the parking lot. I tried to dodge the puddles, and yet I still ended up soaking my sneakers. When I reached the Explorer, I tossed my book bag on the front passenger seat and climbed in behind the wheel. I leaned out the door to shake the water off my umbrella, but somehow I managed to spray most of it in the truck and all over my raincoat. Frustrated, I tossed the soaking umbrella in the backseat and yanked the door shut. Rain thundered on the metal roof as I pulled the directions to the library out of my bag. In the dim light, I reviewed them before tucking them into the cup holder between the seats. Then I started the engine, immediately flipping on the headlights and windshield wipers. Once I buckled my seatbelt, I backed away from the curb and drove out of the school parking lot.

The steady rain pelted the windshield as I passed through town. The maple trees scattered between the sidewalk and town buildings were only a blur against the gray sky. Once outside of town, I turned onto a road that twisted up and down through the forest. I carefully navigated each turn, many of them snaking up the mountain with only a metal guard rail separating the road from a steep cliff. In other places, dense branches high above reached across the road, making it seem like night had fallen even though it was barely four o'clock.

By the time I reached Littleton, my hands had grown weary from clutching the steering wheel with a tight grip. The rain had finally slowed, and I was able to relax a little. I passed buildings, storefronts, and a few lonely souls hustling along the sidewalks in their raincoats, some under the cover of umbrellas. The directions took me through town to the end of the business district where I turned onto a side street. I drove by a few Victorian houses set back from the sidewalk behind white picket fences. Then the road curled through more thick endless woods. Just as I began to wonder if I'd taken a wrong turn somewhere along the way, the trees opened up and I saw a cemetery on the right. Directly across from it was a gravel driveway, a faded white picket fence lining both sides.

I slowed immediately, stopping to read the rickety sign at the entrance. Through the misty fog, I barely made out the dull print that read *Littleton Library, Established 1825.* Relief washed over me. *I made it,* I thought as I cut the tight turn onto the gravel.

The Explorer ambled along the short driveway, the tires crunching over the stones. Finding a tiny parking lot at the end, I eased the SUV to a stop and gaped at the ramshackle building in front of me. It was no bigger than a shoebox house on one level. Three steps led up to the front door, and the faded white paint had chipped away from the decaying wood planks. It reminded me of a one-room schoolhouse from the turn of the century. Who knew? Maybe it had been a school long ago. Only one other car faced the back of the parking lot on the other side. If I hadn't seen it, I would have been tempted to turn around without even going in. The windows were dark, showing no signs of life inside. But I had made it this far, at my mother's recommendation no less, so I owed it to myself to at least see if any hidden treasures waited inside.

I shut off the engine and grabbed my book bag from the passenger seat. Easing out of the Explorer, I felt a shiver run up my spine as I stepped out into the cool mist. A crow cawed from across the street, and I jumped, turning to study the cemetery.

A black iron fence surrounded the grassy lot. Gray head-stones, some round at the top and others square, were randomly scattered beyond the fence. Weeds and tall grass grew along the base of the iron fence, and several black crows perched on the railing. An old dead tree rose up next to the front gate, its crooked barren branches snaking their gnarled way up to the gray sky.

I stared at the cemetery, mesmerized by the creepy scene that looked like something right out of a Halloween movie. One of the crows stretched its wings out and fluttered them in the eerie silence, drawing me out of my thoughts.

I finally turned toward the tiny library, forcing myself to walk across the gravel parking lot to the front steps. The wooden planks creaked under my weight as I ascended them to the door. Hesitantly, not sure of what waited on the other side, I turned the knob and pushed the door open. It squeaked in protest, the noise a rude awakening in the quiet. Not wanting to draw attention to myself, I tried to shut it gently, but it continued to creak and groan.

As I entered the library, I found myself facing an elderly woman who sat at an old scratched wooden desk. She rested her elbows on it as she stared at me, her gray eyes blurry behind her thick, black-framed reading glasses. Her wiry silver hair had been swept up into a stern bun. A delicate chain hung down from her glasses beside her wrinkled, sunken face. She wore a white blouse with a ruffled upright collar, a pink cameo hanging from a silver necklace below it. There wasn't another soul in the library. Beyond her station were rows of shelves cluttered with old, musty-smelling books.

"Can I help you?" the woman asked, her voice quiet, yet suspicious.

I smiled faintly, hoping to see her stern expression soften. "I'm here to do some research on a school project for my History class. The topic is the Underground Railroad that ran through New England. Do you have a section on that?"

Her cold stare never faltered. "The books here are organized by date of publication. We have no card catalogue or internet service. Are you sure you're in the right place?"

"Yes," I whispered, unnerved by her stare. I composed myself before speaking up. "My mother is an elementary school teacher in Lincoln. She told me about this library because she thought I might find some books for my project. I'm hoping she's right."

"Very well, then. You may have a look around. But I close up at six o'clock sharp."

I nodded at her and started to venture toward the bookshelves. But I stopped when she spoke again.

"Listen up. This is a library. The quiet rules are strictly enforced, so make sure to turn off your phone and any other gadgets you have while you're here."

I scanned the empty library, rolling my eyes in bewilderment. There was no one here to be bothered by any noise. Yet I simply nodded my head. "Yes, ma'am," I said quietly before wandering off between the bookshelves.

I walked toward the back of the library, glancing at the hundreds of books as I looked for a good place to leave my things. Behind the last bookshelf, I found an old wooden table in the dusty corner. I placed my book bag on the scratched surface and peeled off my raincoat. After I folded it over the back of a wobbly chair, I started browsing the aisles of books, looking for the eighteen hundreds. The Underground Railroad dated from 1800 to 1865, so I would have a big section to work with once I found it.

When I located the aisle marked 1800 to 1850, I started inspecting the books. Some were leather bound, some were hard back, and all of them smelled old and musty. Dust billowed up above each book I pulled out. The covers were generally plain, most of them listing a title and an author on a solid background of dark brown, green, or blue.

For nearly forty-five minutes, I sifted through the books and wondered when they had last been read. I found stories from a lifetime of hardships that I couldn't even begin to imagine. They described frigid winter nights when the only heat in the house came from a fire and food harvests that were picked by hand with the hope that it would be enough to last the long cold winter.

It was nearly five o'clock when I realized that I hadn't found anything on the Underground Railroad. Considering I'd only read through about twenty of the hundreds of books lining the shelves, that wasn't surprising. I also wondered where Xander was. He'd said four-thirty. Where could he be? I hoped he hadn't gotten lost trying to find the library, but he struck me as someone who didn't get lost.

I carefully slid a book of witch trials back between the other dusty books and returned to my things on the table in the back corner. I dug into my book bag to find my phone, realizing I'd forgotten to turn off the ringer since arriving at the library. I quickly switched it to vibrate as I glanced down the aisle to the front desk. A bookshelf blocked my view of the librarian, but I knew she was still there from the occasional footsteps I heard. I sighed, grateful my phone hadn't rung while I'd been browsing the bookshelves. The last thing I wanted was to suffer through a scolding from her, especially since she seemed to expect nothing but trouble from me.

The librarian forgotten, I checked for new text messages and found none. *Where are you?* I wondered, drumming my fingers nervously against the side of my phone. Finally I typed a text message to Xander. *I'm at the library. Are you coming?*

After sending it, I stuffed the phone in the back pocket of my jeans and returned to the aisle I had just left. Instead of resuming my search on the top shelves where I had left off, I kneeled down to browse some of the books at the bottom. I pulled one book out after another, only flipping through them once I had returned the previous book to its slot on the shelf. The fourth one I pulled out was entitled "Memoirs of my Grandmother, A True Hero of the Underground Railroad." I smiled excitedly and set it aside as I continued looking for more on the subject. Since I had found one, maybe there would be more in the same section.

I pulled a few books out at one time, hoping at least one of them contained something about the Underground Railroad. As I reached for the next book along the opening, a black shape suddenly moved in the empty space between the missing books. Two green eyes with slitted pupils stared at me before lunging out toward me with a high-pitched meow. I shrieked as a black cat leaped into my arms for a split second, scratching me as it scrambled down to the floor. I fell backward from my kneeling position, reaching my arms behind myself to catch my balance. My heart pounded as I breathed deeply. It was only a cat, nothing to get too worried about. I watched it scamper off down the aisle and disappear around the corner. *That was fun,* I thought sarcastically. I never expected to be ambushed by a cat in a library, but this was no ordinary library.

As my pulse slowed and I looked down at the stack of books I had piled beside me, I heard the librarian's footsteps round the corner at the end of the aisle. She peered at me accusingly from behind her glasses as she put one finger up to her lips to shush me.

"Sorry," I whispered. "The cat scared me."

With a huff, she turned on her heels to head back to her desk. I rolled my eyes, wondering once again where Xander was. This was supposed to be a team effort. I wasn't about to do all the work only to let him take half the credit for it. Forgetting about the books stacked on the floor, I reached into my back pocket for my phone. As if on cue, it vibrated. *Xander*! I thought. *Finally*! But when I read the screen, my frustration only intensified. It wasn't Xander at all. It was Noah calling. I pushed aside my annoyance with Xander's no-show as a smile tugged at my lips. My heart flip-flopped as it did every time I saw Noah's name light up my phone.

"Hello?" I whispered as I scrambled to my feet and rushed to the back corner table, hoping the nosy, suspicious librarian wouldn't hear me. I leaned against the side wall, facing the cob-webs in the corner.

"Laken?" Concern lurked in Noah's voice. "Is everything okay? Why are you whispering?"

"I'm fine," I assured him, my voice hushed. "I'm at a creepy library up in Littleton and if the librarian hears me talking, I'll probably get kicked out." *Especially after screaming when her cat jumped out at me,* I thought.

"Sounds like fun. What are you doing up there?"

"Research for the History project."

"Oh, right," Noah mused. "Well, listen, I know it's kind of last minute, but do you want to have dinner with me tonight? I could meet you at the pizza shop around six."

I glanced at my watch. It was already five-twenty. Xander was nearly an hour late, and as the seconds ticked by, I grew less hopeful that he would make it at all. If I left the library within the next ten minutes, I could make it back in time to meet Noah. "Sure. That would be nice," I whispered. "I'll be there."

"Great." He paused. "You know, I've been thinking.

This is a small town. I'm the deputy and you're the sheriff's daughter. If people start seeing us out together in public, they're going to talk. Are you sure you're okay with that?"

I laughed softly, hoping the librarian didn't hear me. "Of course. I don't care who sees us. Let them talk. But I have to go now before the librarian hears me." I wanted to ask him if he was okay with it, but I didn't want to keep talking and get in trouble. Instead, I pushed that thought to the back of my mind.

"Okay. See you soon."

A huge grin lingered on my face as I hung up the call. Memories of our kiss in the kitchen Saturday night crept into my mind for a moment as I bumped my phone against my chin. Then I sighed, remembering the pile of books I had left on the aisle floor. I shoved my phone back into my pocket and hurried back to them.

This is just going to have to wait until next time when Xander is here to help, I thought as I kneeled down to return all but one of the books to the shelf. I made a mental note of their location, assuming that there was a pretty good chance they'd be right where I left them the next time I came to the library.

As I thought about coming back here, my frustration with Xander returned. I still couldn't believe that he'd stood me up this afternoon. I had never expected him to blow me off like this, and I really hoped he wouldn't do it again. Until now, I had believed that I could count on him to carry his weight on this project. If he thought I was going to do all of the work, he had another thing coming. A scowl formed on my face as I hurried to the back corner to gather my things, the book of memoirs in my hand.

I reached the table and donned my raincoat, moving my phone from my jeans to the deep side pocket in my coat. Then I hoisted my book bag onto my shoulder and carried the library book to the front to check it out. When I stopped in front of the desk, the librarian was gazing down at a book, one arm outstretched as she stroked the purring black cat lying beside it. The minute the cat saw me, it jumped to its feet with a shrieking meow and leaped off the desk. The old woman sighed with annoyance, not bothering to raise her head as she looked at me over the top of her glasses. She didn't say a word, but rather questioned me silently, her eyebrows raised.

"Yes—um—hi," I stuttered. "I'd like to check out this book." I gingerly placed the book on the desk. "Please."

"We don't do that here," she replied curtly.

"Excuse me?"

"All of the books in this library are authentic antiques. We don't allow them to leave the premises, especially with teenagers."

I sighed with disappointment. "Okay. I'll put it back where I found it." I started to reach for the book, but her hand struck out like lightning to pull it toward her and out of my reach.

"Not so fast, missy. You just leave that with me and I'll take care of it. If you want to read it, you'll have to come back. I'm here every day, seven days a week from nine to six."

I nodded in understanding. Without another word, I turned to leave. I couldn't wait to escape the woman's accusing stare. Never before had I been treated like a disrespectful child. I wondered what my parents would think, and I made a mental note to make sure I told them about her when I got home.

I pulled open the front door and raced out onto the porch only to skid to a stop under the small overhang. It was pouring again. The dark gray sky hid the descending sun and the earlier mist was gone. As the miserable rain pounded the roof and the gravel, I snapped the front of my raincoat together and lifted the hood up over my head, my braid tucked under it.

I cursed as I realized I had left my umbrella in the truck. *Lovely,* I thought, staring out at the pouring rain. I contemplated the mad dash I would have to make to the Explorer.

A lot of good my umbrella does me in the car. I fished my car keys out of my coat pocket and tucked one hand on my book bag to hold it steady. Then I raced down the steps and out into the rain. I ran as fast as I could across the gravel. Yet by the time I reached the Explorer and jumped in the driver's seat, beads of water rolled down my face.

Rain beat against the metal roof as I pulled the door shut. In the tight quarters of the driver's seat, I pushed the dripping hood behind me, feeling the water against the back of my neck. My movements were stiff from the heavy raincoat when I moved my phone from my pocket to the cup holder before starting the truck. The engine was barely audible over the rain. I flipped on the headlights, turned the windshield wipers on high, and started the heat. I couldn't get out of there fast enough, but I resisted flooring the accelerator. Instead, I slowly turned the truck around and guided it down the driveway to the road, my nerves finally fading as soon as I left the ramshackle library and suspicious old lady far behind.

Chapter 20

The windshield wipers pulsed furiously as I crossed through Littleton and then turned onto the road that cut through the mountains and led back to my town. The rain poured steadily, showing no signs of letting up as it streaked down through the headlight beams. I drove slowly, staying under the speed limit in the treacherous conditions. Not a single car passed in the other direction or came up behind me as I covered miles of road up and down steep slopes and around tight hairpin turns.

I had no idea how deep into the mountains I had gone when my phone vibrated against the cup holder. I glanced down at it for a quick moment, but it remained dark. It must have been a text. Whatever it was would have to wait until I got back to town.

As I raised my eyes up to the rain-streaked windshield, a white wolf stood in the middle of the road. Its damp fur reflected in the headlight beams. I screamed, slamming on my brakes to avoid hitting it. It jumped off to the side of the road, escaping an impact with the truck with only seconds to spare. My relief that I hadn't hit it was short-lived. The truck suddenly hydroplaned on the slick pavement as the brakes locked up. The back end fishtailed to the side, sending the Explorer into a spin in the pitch black. I couldn't see anything except the blurred shadows of trees rising up around the truck. My foot locked down on the brake, I clutched the steering wheel in a death grip as the truck veered off the road and down an embankment.

The Explorer slid to a stop, the front end pitching downward on the soft, saturated ground. My heart pounded with fear as tears blurred my vision. My foot seemed to be stuck in place on the brake as I breathed deeply, trying to stop my trembling. I fought to calm my nerves, staring at the windshield wipers moving up and down in unison. The rain thundered against the roof, but I blocked out the noise. All I could think was that the truck had stopped and I was okay. The fact that it hadn't slammed into a tree was a miracle. The headlights shone into the forest, and a huge tree trunk nearly two feet in diameter rose up just inches away from the front grill of the truck.

I'm alive, for now, I told myself. *But I need to get out of here if I want to stay alive. That wolf couldn't have gotten very far in the last few minutes.* I shook my head as the white wolf flashed through my mind. So there were two strange wolves roaming around here, not just one? I couldn't believe it. Where had they come from and why were they here? *Well, one thing's for sure. I won't find any answers sitting here all night.*

With my foot still firmly planted on the brake, I turned the knob on the dashboard to switch the truck into four-wheel drive. As I shifted into reverse, I held my breath, praying that all four tires working together would be enough to get the truck up the steep embankment to the road. *Please work. Please, please, please.*

I eased my foot off the brake and touched down on the accelerator. The Explorer rocked backward and, as I felt it start to move, I punched the gas. But as quickly as the truck moved, it stopped, sinking into the soft earth as I revved the engine. The tires spun aimlessly, and I felt them digging deep into the saturated ground until I finally gave up. I shifted my foot from the accelerator to the brake, realizing that it was hopeless. The ground was too soft to get enough traction, even in four-wheel drive. A feeling of dread washed over me. I was stranded on a deserted mountain road in the middle of a dark rainstorm.

An unnerving chill raced down my spine. I glanced at the doors to make sure they were locked as I remembered the person in the woods behind my house. Could that person be near right now, just waiting for the chance to get to me? *That's ridiculous. I'm miles from home right now. How could anyone know where I am? I haven't seen a single car since I left Littleton,* I thought. *I'll just call Noah and he'll come get me. I'll be fine.* But my thoughts failed to calm the panic that raced through me. I knew better than to rely on a cell phone in these mountains. Coverage was spotty, at best. One minute I could have full service, and the next my call would drop just from going around a tight turn or climbing up a steep hill.

I grabbed my phone as if it was my last hope of surviving this nightmare that was like something out of a horror movie. Only this was real. With a prayer, I swiped the screen to turn it on. The bars in the top corner remained blank. No service.

"Damn!" I swore under my breath as tears welled up in my eyes. I dropped my phone back into the cup holder and leaned my forehead against the top of the steering wheel. Closing my eyes, I listened intently to the humming engine and punishing rain. "I can't believe this is happening," I muttered, desperately wondering what options I had at this point other than getting out of the Explorer and walking. As much as I hesitated to step out into the cold, dark rain, it was really my fear of the strange wolf roaming nearby that kept me from running up to the road. After my encounter with the black wolf at the campground, I assumed that this one wouldn't be receptive to me, either.

But I had to overcome my fear. I knew what I needed to

do, whether or not I was comfortable with it. I turned off the windshield wipers and headlights, sending the woods into complete darkness. When I shut off the engine, the rain pelting the truck seemed even louder. With the keys in one hand, I lifted my hood up over my head. Then, as I shuddered with fear, I opened the door. I had to get up to the road right away to flag down the next car, if there was one.

I twisted to the side and slowly lowered my feet out of the truck, clutching the car door for support as I felt the soggy ground sink beneath my sneakers. The incline was soft and slippery, but I managed to shut the door behind me. Then I turned to look up the hill, my eyes slowly adjusting to the dark. Rain pattered against my slicker, blowing in under the hood at an angle. Water rolled down my face, but I ignored it.

Holding my arms out at my sides for balance, I trudged alongside the Explorer, determined to make it up the hill. I had taken two steps away from the SUV when I heard a growl in front of me. I stopped and looked up. Two yellow eyes glared at me from the top of the embankment. The black wolf's body blended into the shadows behind it.

I stood frozen in place on the muddy slope. As my heart raced, I shivered from both fear and the cold rain. "What do you want from me? You know I won't hurt you," I whispered.

As soon as I spoke, the wolf deepened its growl and bared its teeth. Just like I had suspected the last time, it didn't welcome my attempts to communicate with it. It started heading down the hill, and I instinctively moved backward.

Another growl erupted to my side, and I gasped as I turned in the direction of it. Two more pairs of eyes, one set belonging to the white wolf and the other set belonging to a gray one, were locked in on me. I backed up as the three wolves moved in my direction. I shifted my eyes to each of them, not sure what to do next. I suddenly wished I'd stayed in the truck, but it was too late.

As the wolves stepped closer, their huge paws sinking in the mud, I whipped around and scrambled back to the Explorer. I fumbled with my keys, but my hands shook uncontrollably. As the growling became louder behind me, tears blurred my vision. I spun to face the wolves, pressing my back against the metal door.

"What do you want?" I gasped. "Please, don't hurt me."

The three of them suddenly hushed, their upper lips lowering over their fangs. The rain intensified, but all I noticed was that the wolves had turned their attention to the road behind them. A figure appeared at the top of the ditch. A long trench coat reached the stranger's knees and I made the assumption from the broad shoulders that it was a man. His face was shadowed in the darkness, but I still stared up at him, my jaw dropped open in fright.

"Who are you?" I asked, but he probably couldn't hear me over the rain as he didn't say a word.

In a flash, the wolves sprang at me. I leaped away from the truck and took off running into the woods as fast as I could. Holding my hands out in front of me, I dodged the trees as the wolves snarled behind me. They snapped at my heels as I scrambled to get away, my feet sliding on the slippery wet leaves. I wasn't sure how far I had run before I slammed into a huge tree trunk.

I whirled around, my back to the knotted bark, as the wolves closed in on me. They lingered inches away, their hungry eyes focused on me. I swallowed nervously, my heart pounding. My back pressed against the tree as if I could get farther away from them, but it was hopeless. I was cornered.

'*Please, leave me alone*! *I don't know what you want with me, but I'll do anything if you let me go!*' I begged silently, hoping at least one of the wolves would grant me mercy.

Their growling rumbled again, louder this time, and I heard a rustling in the leaves over the rain. The wolves fell silent at once, and I opened my eyes, curious to know what was happening. They focused on something off to the side, cautiously backing up as if threatened.

Suddenly, a bull moose charged out of the trees, its antlers angled downward at the wolves. They whimpered fearfully as they turned and dispersed into the woods. Then the moose took off up the hill, and I thought I saw the man again for a second before he disappeared.

The moose stopped about twenty feet away from me and raised his head. He snorted noisily, his nostrils ruffling from his breath as he turned to look at me. I watched him as my panic began to subside. As if sensing my helplessness, the moose lumbered down the hill, his hooves sliding in the mud with each step he took. When he reached me, he stopped and stretched his head out to sniff me. His breath whispered across my chin, the soft damp fur on his nostrils brushing against me.

I raised a hand to stroke his wet muzzle. "Thank you," I murmured. "I don't know what would have happened if you hadn't come along when you did."

He nodded subtly, his soft brown eyes meeting mine. Raindrops glistened between his eyelashes and his fur was soaked.

"Stay with me?" I asked. "I need to get back up to the road."

As I headed up the embankment in the rain, the moose walked beside me. He towered above me, his antlers spanning nearly four feet across. And yet he stepped carefully, making sure not to brush me with them.

After we passed the Explorer, the incline grew steeper, the footing more slippery. I almost fell about halfway up and reached out, grabbing the moose for balance. He halted until I had steadied myself, and then we climbed to the top together.

We stopped at the edge of the road and I looked in both directions to see only darkness. The moose stood patiently beside me, his presence calming me, making me feel safe. After a few moments of listening to the pitter-patter of rain, headlights shone in the distance. As they came closer, the moose spun around and disappeared into the woods.

My heart lurched as the headlights eased to a stop in front of me, the rain streaking down in their beams. When they shut off, I instantly recognized the black pick-up truck. I looked up at the windshield to see Xander staring at me. He looked puzzled as his forehead furrowed in confusion. I lifted a hand to wave at him as a single tear of relief rolled down my face.

Whatever the wolves and the stranger wanted with me would have to wait for another day. I was safe for now, or so I hoped.

If you enjoyed reading

Shadows at Sunset

Don't miss

Silence at Midnight

Book 2 of the Sunset Trilogy

Coming in 2016 from
Tonya Royston and Black Opal Books

ACKNOWLEDGMENTS

I'm not sure where to begin with this, so I will start with you. Yes, you, the reader. Thank you for picking this book out of hundreds of thousands to choose from. My hope that readers just like you would find this story someday motivated me over the last two years to finish it. So thank you for your interest and taking the time to read it. I can't tell you how much it means to me!

Now for the people I couldn't have done this without. To my Mom for listening to my ideas day in and day out. Having you as a sounding board was invaluable. Thank you for your support even when all I had to show for this idea were a few handwritten notebooks.

To my husband for sticking by me through thick and thin. This journey has been one filled with ups and downs. I couldn't have done it without you by my side.

To my son, who at the time of publication isn't old enough to read or understand this, thank you for giving us a five-minute scare when you ran off to the stream behind the horse pasture. Your little adventure inspired the beginning action in this story. But I'm grateful that it didn't take until midnight to find you.

To my brother for actually getting the tattoo that I created for Xander. Thank you for bringing one of the images in this story to life and for making the design even better in the end. The fact that you made part of my first novel a permanent fixture in your life means the world to me.

To my sister for your amazing photography. Thank you for taking a fantastic picture that I could use for my website and author page in this book. As camera-shy as I am, you made this one little detail far less painful than it could have been.

To Lauren for reading the first few chapters of this story in rough draft. You were truly amazing to encourage me after suffering through the horrors of my rough draft. Thank you for believing in me even when the early stages of my writing needed so much work.

To Macie for being my first fan and for reading everything I sent you. Your excitement and energy helped me keep going. When others lost interest, you were always there to cheer me on.

To the Figment writers I met along the way, thank you for your feedback and encouragement. I truly enjoyed interacting with all of you. There are too many of you to mention by name, but you know who you are. I'm glad I took a chance on posting a few chapters because I learned a lot about my writing from all of your comments.

To my publisher, Black Opal Books, and the editors, Lauri, Faith and Joyce, thank you for taking a chance on my story and helping me through the editing stages. You showed me some of my weaknesses, and I believe I'm a better writer because of it.

To Jenn Gibson for the beautiful cover designs. Thank you for your hard work and dedication. You really captured the essence of this story and I couldn't be happier with the final covers and bookmarks.

Lastly, to my extended family, coworkers, and friends as well as everyone mentioned above, thank you for putting up with me over the last two years. Thank you for looking at website designs, cover and bookmark artwork, and listening to me ramble on about my writing. I'm sure at times, it seemed endless. But this story would have meant nothing if I had no one to share it with. So thank you for helping me make this dream come true!

AUTHOR'S NOTE

I did a lot of research on the species I used for this story – the wolf. What I learned struck a chord in my heart. There is still a lot of hatred for this species across our country. Some states allow them to be trapped and hunted for sport. I don't understand this, and I never will. There are many organizations working hard to make the world a better place for wolves in the wild. I have found several – Living With Wolves and The Wolf Conservation Center to name a few. These organizations are great resources if you are interested in learning more about wolves and the challenges they are currently facing.

Another part of my research led me to find several sanctuaries around the country that take in wolves and hybrids rescued from captive ownership. These sanctuaries discourage private ownership of these animals. I visited one of them and learned a few things that would definitely make me think twice about trying to own a wolf. For one thing, the sanctuary only allowed volunteers to enter the wolf pens after about one thousand hours of volunteer work. And even then, they didn't guarantee volunteers the opportunity to step into a pen. Apparently, wolves can put a pretty big bruise on your backside. The guide said that these bruises could take months to heal. He also said guests often asked what he would rather have, a wolf or a wolf-hybrid. His answer was a wolf because the hybrids were more unpredictable. In his words, they could never decide if they wanted to be a wolf or a dog on any given day.

I admit that I know nothing about owning a wolf. The only way I would want to own one would be to keep it the way Laken keeps Dakota - by letting him roam free. And let's face it-that probably isn't going to happen. There are also laws regarding ownership of these animals. I don't know the laws, but I can only imagine that complying with them must be very expensive. So if you love wolves, my advice is to do your research, educate yourself, and maybe even find a nearby sanctuary to support.

In closing, now that my first book has been published, I have a new dream. It's not just that readers will enjoy this story, but it's the hope that this story will create awareness for this amazing species. The wolf in this story is truly how I envision a wolf in the wild. Intelligent, loyal, and protective. He captured my imagination, and I hope he captured yours as well!

About the Author

Tonya Royston currently lives in Northern Virginia with her husband, son, two dogs, and two horses. Although she dreamed of writing novels at a young age, she was diverted away from that path years ago and built a successful career as a contracts manager for a defense contractor in the Washington, DC area. She resurrected her dream of writing in 2013 and hasn't stopped since the first words of *The Sunset Trilogy* were unleashed. *Shadows at Sunset* is her first novel.

When she isn't writing, Tonya spends time with her family. She enjoys skiing, horseback riding, and anything else that involves the outdoors.

More information about Tonya and her upcoming endeavors can be found at www.tonyaroyston.com.